B.LUSTIG

First edition.

Paperback ISBN: 978-9-0831367-2-1

Cover Design: Forgetmenot.designs

Editor & Proofread: Mackenzie Letson at Nice Girl, Naughty Edits

Formatting: NRA Publishing

B. LUSTIG

To Kevin,
the love of my life, my best friend, my husband, and my partner
in crime. This one's for you.
I'm sorry it took me so long to realize what you already knew.
You really are my better half.
I will love you until the day I die.

Tot het einde & terug.

AUTHOR'S NOTE

Some of you might experience this one as a wild ride.
But you know what?
Life is a wild ride.
Love is a wild ride.
Life is messy.
Love is messy.
Feelings are messy, and they never do what we want.
Love isn't something you can't control.
No matter how hard you run, no matter how long you hide, it
will catch up with you.
You can't choose love, love chooses *you*.

PROLOGUE

PRESENT DAY

J ULIE'S EYES WIDEN AS she looks at something past me. I'm about to open my mouth to ask what's wrong, when a familiar scent enters my nose.

A potent mix of a citrus, woodsy cologne.

A cologne I couldn't forget, no matter how hard I've tried. Forever imprinted in my soul, even though I've tried to scratch it off with force.

I swallow roughly, while my heart starts to race, afraid of the seconds to come.

"Hey, babe."

My heart literally stops when I turn around, looking into my favorite eyes in the entire world. I could deny it. I could pretend that's not the case, but while his hazel-brown eyes peer down at me, I just can't. I wish it wasn't the truth, but it is. His eyes are still the most mesmerizing thing I've ever seen, with copper swirls dancing around his irises, capable of letting me make stupid decisions and do things I'd never do without him.

In short, I'm still fucked.

Not that I'll tell that to a living soul.

"What the fuck?" I hold his gaze like a warrior, even though I know I won't be able to do so for much longer. You see, Hunter Hansen has that ability over me. A 6'2" frame with a devastating smile. He can make me crumble with one single look. I hoped that if we'd ever stand face to face again, I'd be immune to his energy that effortlessly sucks me into his space. Like an unavoidable vortex, I don't stand a chance.

It took all I had, leaving him on that sidewalk eleven months ago.

Eleven months and ten days.

And yes, I know how fucked up it is that I know precisely how long it's been.

"What's up, Julie?" He averts his gaze from my eyes, giving Julie a nod over my head. Relieved from the intensity, my attention lowers to his lips as he licks them before his eyes snap back to me. His lips curve, noticing where my focus is, sinking his teeth into the soft cushion in response.

"Hey, asshole," I hear Julie reply behind me, with not nearly enough aggravation, as if this is the most normal thing ever.

It's not.

He's supposed to be on the other side of the country, living his jet-set life while we are nothing more than a distant memory. Not crashing my fucking girls' night on the worst day of my life, reminding me I have no clue what I'm doing.

"How are you?" He flashes me his famous boyish grin, dropping his burning eyes to mine. Even though he's twenty-five now and all-man, his shoulders look even broader than the last time I saw him.

"Fine," I say, averting my gaze to settle my thumping heart down.

There is no way I'll be able to keep things distant and acquainted if he keeps looking at me like that. I mean, I'm in a happy relationship; I love Ben.

So, we've hit a bump in the road. Or a mountain, whatever. We will get through it together. But I admitted to myself a long time ago that I have a never-ending weakness for Hunter Hansen, and him staring at me like I'm about to be his dinner makes me forget loving another man real fast.

Who can resist his superpowers?

I'm only human.

"You here to visit your mom?" I bring my drink to my lips, hoping the alcohol will settle the nerves trickling into my stomach. The asshole takes the stool next to me, making himself comfortable, as he turns his body toward my side. I can feel his eyes burning a hole through my skin, making it hard for me to breathe, and I swallow my nerves—hoping, praying, wondering if I can drown the feelings I apparently still have before they come floating to the surface. No such luck.

"Nah, I'm staying."

"You're what?!" I snap my head to his, my eyes as wide as a deer in headlights, my mind going over all the reasons why this is bad news for me. "Why?"

I look at his muscled arms, covered by a red flannel shirt. His sleeves are rolled up, and I resist the urge to run my fingers over the tattoos there, pushing away the need for him to wrap his arms around me. Damn you, Charlotte. Keep it together.

"Because I have unfinished business in this town." He boldly grabs my glass of vodka and lime from my hand, his fingers brushing mine for longer than necessary. An electrifying jolt ripples through my arm at his simple touch. His eyes fill with an amused spark, looking at me from under his signature black snapback.

Jackass.

I watch how he casually wets his lips, then takes a sip of my drink. I should set boundaries, tell him he can't do this anymore. He can't treat me like I'm his for the taking, giving me this flirtatious look and igniting something in my body that I've hidden away with diligent effort. I should slap the drink from his fingers, scolding him for being an arrogant dick. But instead,

I let him, watching his Adam's apple softly bob as he slugs the liquor down his throat.

"You better be talking about your mom, Hunter Hansen." I shoot him a reprimanding look, even though I already know she would be the last reason for him to move back to Braedon. In fact, in reality, he doesn't have anyone left in this town.

"She's the reason I left." He pauses, and I send up a quick prayer. *Please, don't say it. Please, God, don't let him say it.* "You are the reason I'm back."

Fuck.

His hand boldly takes residence on my thigh, bringing back the familiarity I should end right now, while his other hand places my glass back in front of me.

"No, I am not." I turn my head back, closing my eyes for a brief moment and trying to put up an unaffected front. I choose to ignore his hand on my body, and the feeling it's giving me. But the heat that crawls up to my neck tells me I'm failing like a sinking ship.

"I know it took me a while, but I'm back." The sincerity in his voice causes a raging battle between what I feel and what I know as he leans in. As his breath fans my cheek, telling me he's at least two inches too close, my mouth is too chicken to tell him to fuck off.

"Good for you," I manage to snarl instead.

"I want another shot." His voice is all husky and needy, trickling goosebumps down my body. My heart is screaming at his words, knowing I could easily fall back under his spell, but luckily, my mind is controlling my mouth at this moment.

"At what?" I ask, still incapable of looking into his hooded eyes.

"Your heart." Ouch. I waited for this kind of truth for so long, but now all it does is hurt like hell.

"I have a boyfriend." I scoff, finding the nerve to glare at him.

"We both know he doesn't mean shit." He takes another sip of my drink, as if claiming my glass means claiming me. There is a confidence in his eyes that's pissing me off, reminding me of the cocky son of the bitch in the fighting cage.

Ready to play dirty for as long as it takes to come out as the winner.

Refusing to ever lose.

I used to admire it, but right now, it just feels like a threat to my already torn-up heart.

"You don't mean shit," I counter in a lame attempt to insult him, before an arrogant grin washes his face.

"And your pretty eyes tell me you're full of shit."

"Stop flirting with me."

"Never." He winks.

He fucking winks.

He keeps staring at me, like he hasn't eaten in days and I'm his next meal, the corner of his mouth curled up in a small grin. I hold his gaze, hoping he will cower. Hoping I can keep up a strong, determined front, but after a few heated heartbeats, I release a deep sigh.

Right, stupid thought.

"What do you want, Hunter?" I roll my eyes and put my focus on my drink in front of me. Then casually swirl the contents through the glass while faking an indifference I sure as fuck am not feeling, but knowing it's all I've got. It's all I can do to not let him thunder back into my world and fuck up my life some more right now.

"Eight dates. One for every year that I should've made you mine and didn't, and then one extra for the years we'll have in the future."

For a brief moment, my lashes fall and my heart cries. It's like he plants a knife right into my chest with his words, and part of me wants to let it sit there, before I find the strength to straighten the features on my face.

"What? No! I have a boyfriend," I emphasize, throwing him an incredulous look to hide how I'm really feeling.

Can you imagine bringing the world's best fighter home, saying, 'Hey, honey, this is my ex-boyfriend/best friend. I'm going on a date with him?'

Uh, yeah, no.

"Who cares?" Hunter dramatically throws his head back as he drags out the words.

"I do." I pinch my thumb in my chest. "And I bet he does, too."

"I'm not going anywhere, babe." The statement is clear.

It shouldn't mean anything, yet it means everything coming from his mouth. The girl in me is pumping her fist in the air, not even thinking about the consequences. Hunter Hansen being home is the equivalent of trouble. But I'm still a grown woman. Just because he decides he wants to come back home doesn't mean I have to hang out with him. I have my own life now. He decided he didn't want to be a part of it, and I'm going to hold him up to that decision for self-preservation.

"You can't do this. You can't just barge back into my life like that. Expecting everything to be all good." I let out a sigh, pinching the bridge of my nose, hearing Julie snicker next to me. My jaw clenches at the sound of it, and I volley her a death stare with my green eyes.

Thanks for the backup, girlfriend.

"I know, but I'm fucking doing it, anyway."

I should just keep my eyes on my glass, avoiding eye contact at all costs, because one look too many, and I'll be hooked again.

Like a druggie, trying to resist a shot of heroin, free of charge, ready to fuck up your life for a high you know you can't resist. I thought that after what happened last year, I was finally checked into rehab and fully rehabilitated from my Hunter Hansen addiction. But still, my head slowly but surely twists to find his determined gaze filled with regret. Hurt laces his expression while he's holding up this bad boy front. Acting as if everything is well in the world.

It's like looking into a fucking mirror, and I hate how my heart still aches for him.

How I still want him to be happy, more than I want it for myself.

"Eight dates, Charls. Eight dates to convince you to give me another shot. If you still want me to leave after those eight dates, I'll be gone. I promise."

Hearing him call me Charls warms my body in a way no one ever can. It rolls off his tongue so effortlessly, sounding like music to my ears, a tune only allowed from his lips.

I let my thoughts bounce around in my brain like a tennis match, weighing out the pros and cons, even though I already know what the outcome will be. I can see the temptation dragging me under to at least find out if we can somewhat resolve what he threw in the trash.

"No dates." I firmly shake my head. I can't give him that much, because I might as well give him my heart so he can toss it through a shredder.

"Babe," he pleads, but I shake my head firmly.

"That ship has sailed, Hunter. But I'll give you eight days to convince me you're still my friend." I let out my breath, knowing that this is the worst idea ever.

But I can't help myself.

When we first crossed that line all those years ago, I knew one thing. I wanted to keep my friend, more than anything. And when I look past all the heartbreak, I still want that.

I still want my friend.

"Best friend."

"Let's just start with friends, okay?" I glare.

"Fine, but we are calling them dates. And I want eight full days, morning until evening."

Cocky son of a bitch, always has to push his luck.

"Oh God, what the fuck will I tell Ben?" I mutter to no one in particular, throwing my hands up in the air.

"Tell him your best friend is back in town."

"You're not my best friend until you've proven yourself." My head wags as I realize how I don't even fully understand what that means anymore.

Firmly, he trails his arm around my waist while he presses his body against my side. His lips press flush to my ear, his touch making me gasp for air. I close my eyes to not fall apart in his arms when his husky voice rumbles in my ear. Oh, shit.

"Before those eight dates are over, I will have proven to be so much more than your best friend, babe." He places a quick peck on my hair. "I'll see you soon."

Faster than I want, he lets go of my body, and I feel instantly annoyed by the loss of his touch.

Anger grows in my chest, cursing myself at how quickly my senses are sparked alive by him.

"Asshole."

He backs away with a cocky grin on his face, shooting me a wink.

"I am. But I'm your asshole," he agrees, then turns around, walking out of the bar like he owns the goddamn place. I stare at the swaying door with my pulse pounding in my ears until he's out of my sight.

I fill my lungs, trying to control my racing heart. Burying my face in my hands, a grunt erupts from my throat.

Hunter fucking Hansen is back.

I'm in so much shit.

My lips roll to a thin line before I find Julie's judgy look.

Her heart-shaped face rests in her palm, and I detect a hint of amusement in her gaze.

"You could've backed me up there, bitch. You were ready to hire a hitman for him eleven months ago." I frown at my best friend, a little frustrated with her lack of reaction after the infamous ghost of my past came strolling into the bara and ruined my night.

She shrugs. "I still am. But let's be honest, it's not going to change the outcome now that he's back. You two–"

"Don't you dare say it!" I cut her off, not even remotely curious about what was about to roll off her tongue, and I pin her with a stern expression.

Her hands move up in the air, but I catch the parting of her lips quick enough.

"Shut up," I bark before she can say anything.

She just chuckles beside me, bringing her drink to her mouth. "You're so fucked, girl."

"Yeah, no shit."

YEAR ONE

HE WANTS IT ALL.
HE JUST DOESN'T THINK HE CAN HAVE IT.

'Stop flirting with me'

1

HUNTER

I TAKE A SMALL path toward the streaming creek as my heart keeps pounding hard in my chest, my feet never slowing down. The heat radiating off my body only feeds the unease sitting in my stomach after seeing my mother with that pile of money on the table in front of her. My pile of money. The one that was supposed to be my ticket out of this one-horse town. A thought that now makes my chest clench as if it's caught between two closing walls.

But I need it. I need to wallow in the discomfort, before I'll even remotely be able to let it go. I stop in my tracks when I feel the small pebbles of the creek bank underneath my shoes. My head is dying for a breeze, to get a breath of fresh air, but with summer being barely over, it's still seventy-five degrees out.

Still feeling the need to use my already aching muscles in anger, I pick up some rocks from the ground, throwing them into the creek with a roar, one by one. Normally, the burbling of the flowing water calms me down, but right now, it's only a deafening tone. The soundtrack to the desperation that pierces through my heart. I keep going, trying to find a bigger rock every time I've thrown one in, until finally, the fatigue hits me. Placing my palms behind my head, I shut my eyes while sucking air into my heaving lungs, listening to the natural sounds around me.

"You need some help with those bigger boulders?"

My heart just about jumps from my ribcage, and I snap my head toward the unexpected voice, with an aggravated look.

"Jesus Christ, you always sneak up on people like that?"

I look at the girl sitting cross-legged against a tree, with a book on her lap. Her wavy dark blonde hair is slightly highlighted by the sun, making her blue-green eyes stand out even more against her ivory skin.

"I've been sitting here for an hour," she deadpans.

"Right," I say while I run a hand through my sweaty hair, feeling awkward as fuck when I realize she has been witnessing my entire big boy tantrum. "Well, carry on."

I turn around, doing my best to pretend she's not here, but I can't resist glancing at her again, wondering if she's still looking at me. When I rear my neck, I feel disappointed to see her head is back in her book, and she doesn't seem to give a flying fuck that I'm still standing here.

"What are you doing here, anyway?" I turn my frame her way again. My eyes can't help but give her a once-over. Her white sneakers stand out against her tanned legs, which are covered with nothing more than some jeans shorts. Her oversized navy-blue V-neck t-shirt is tucked in at her jeans, giving no indication of her curves, but something tells me they are there even though I can't see them.

She holds up her book with a coy smile, answering my stupid question.

Smooth, Hunt.

"All by yourself in the middle of nowhere?" I curiously take a few steps closer.

"Not really the middle of nowhere, since you came here too." She looks at me with a sassy grin that secretly makes me chuckle inside.

"Aren't you scared some guys might pass by? You know, guys that don't mind taking advantage of pretty little girls?"

She cocks an eyebrow at me in a defiant way, clearly not affected by my question.

"Are you planning on taking advantage of me, tattoo boy?" I see her glancing at the tattoos on my lower arm, and I kinda like the fact that she's checking me out, just like I did with her.

"Please. I can fuck any girl I like just by snapping my fingers." I snap my fingers to prove a point, knowing I'm talking like a douche, but unable to keep my mouth shut. I expect her to shut me down and end this conversation before it fully starts, because my ego blurts out unnecessary bullshit, but she gives me a dim look.

"Not every girl." She shrugs, unimpressed, before dipping her head to keep reading. She doesn't realize she piques my interest even more by appearing unaffected by my presence. I'm used to girls flirting with me. And while lately most girls bore the hell out of me with their lame attempts, I catch myself wishing she will give it a shot.

"Is that a challenge?"

She lifts her head again, looking me straight in the eye with her captivating gaze.

"Does it seem like I'm interested in you?"

"No."

"Then it's not a challenge. And I'm not that little, by the way."

"But you are pretty," I retort as I drop my ass on the ground next to her. The cold grass soothes my heated palms as I run my fingers through it, my eyes trained on her with a side glance.

"You flirting with me now?" She closes her book, holding it in a tight grip.

I can feel her eyes pierce through my soul while I stare into the rolling water. I quickly glance toward her and smile, then turn my head back in front of me.

"I wouldn't dare."

My eyes keep peering into the creek as a flutter enters my stomach, sensing how she is still looking at me.

"You wanna tell me why you're throwing around rocks like you're about to turn green any second?"

When I look at her this time, my gaze stops at her plump pink lips, wondering what they would feel like against mine. Would they feel soft and warm, like a comforting summer night? Or scorching and sizzling, like a drop of water on a hot plate?

She slightly purses them while she raises her eyebrows, waiting for my answer. I avert my eyes and focus on the meadow against my fingertips as I take a deep breath to clear my head.

"I had a fight with my mom," I say, drawing letters on the ground with my index finger to keep my hands busy.

"Must've been a pretty heavy one."

"I've had worse." I shrug, trying to brush it away.

"She the one who did this?" Before I know it, her soft hands are grazing the scratched skin on the side of my neck. A shiver unwillingly runs through my body at the brief physical touch, and my lower abdomen stirs alive, wanting more.

"Yeah, she grabbed my throat," I answer, hoping to distract the growing bulge in my shorts. "She was drunk."

"She do that a lot?"

I turn my head toward her, narrowing my eyes on her vibrant face.

"You ask a lot of questions."

"I pry." She casually shrugs, but I detect her cheeks forming a subtle, yet different kind of hue as her features turn bashful. "I'm shameless about it. Sorry. You don't have to answer if you don't want to. I won't be offended. But I'll still pry."

Her honest answer feels like the breath of fresh air I was longing for, and it immediately puts a smile on my face.

"You're silly."

"Is that good or bad?"

"Definitely good." I chuckle.

"Cool," she says, huffing a laugh.

"How come you ask about the scratches on my neck, but not my black eye?"

The skin below my eye is bruised in a purple and blue palette, a physical mark on my face that is now all for nothing, considering my mother found my stash of money.

She playfully rolls her eyes in a mocking way, then she opens her mouth.

"I know who you are. You're the boy they keep whispering about. Saying you're an illegal cage fighter. I know there are no rules in those fights, but I'm guessing they hardly step foot into the cage with freshly manicured nails." I laugh at her answer, liking the fact that she knows who I am.

"Could've been a girl?"

"True." She nods. "But they look fresh and, somehow, you don't have a 'just fucked' look."

"A 'just fucked' look? What does that look like?" I ask, weighing my chances of her showing me in the near future.

"Like you've just fucked," she says, bored, looking at me like I'm dense.

"You wanna see my 'just fucked' look?" I wink, licking my lips seductively.

"Get over yourself." She glares with a scowl that doesn't match her eyes, and I take the moment to soak in her beautiful face. She's an enigma of contradiction, and fuck me if she doesn't manage to dig a hole into my heart like it's nothing. Her azure blue-green eyes are clouded with sass, yet her stance is made of good girl energy.

"What's your name?"

"Charlotte."

"Pretty. Do people call you Charlie?"

"Only my best friend, but I prefer Charlotte. She is just a lazy little brat who thinks Charlotte is too long."

"Well..." I taunt, while she tilts her head in a daring way. "It is a bit long?"

"Just because you're a cage fighter doesn't mean I'm afraid to slap you." The look on her face is filled with power, and for a second, I actually believe her, thinking this girl would not be afraid to kick my ass. Though, I'm not sure I would mind her doing it, anyway.

"I'm Hunter"—I reach out my hand to her—"but you already knew that."

She grabs my hand and meets my eyes, and I swear to God, it feels like an electrifying pulse runs through my arm before we both let go and fend off our gazes.

"Did you run here, Hunter?"

"Yeah."

"Where do you live?"

"You wanna know where I live now?" I only met her five minutes ago, but I can't help but flirt with the girl, especially because she holds her own without effort. She is not intimidated, and even less impressed. Hell, if anything, she's fucking beating me in my own game without her even knowing it and not putting in an effort doing so.

"I wanna know how far you ran." She keeps a straight face, effortlessly ignoring my beaming smile that is slowly pushing my sour mood to the back of my brain.

"You just want to come over, don't you?"

"Stop putting words in my mouth."

"There's something else I would like to put in your mouth," I mumble, waiting until she smacks me over the head. She doesn't seem like the type of girl who would take bullshit like that from any guy, but it left my mouth before I could push the words back.

Pushing your luck here, Hunt.

When nothing happens, I carefully twist my face toward her and notice her scowling at me once again. It's as terrifying as it is exhilarating, but regardless, it's a welcoming change from the girls who pretend to love anything that leaves my lips.

"Does this shit actually work with girls?"

"Most of the time." I shrug with a big smile.

"Your standards must not be very high."

"I might have to raise them after today."

"You're so full of shit." She chuckles.

It's a sight that melts my heart, and it instantly has me addicted, wanting to put more smiles on her face.

"But I'm entertaining, aren't I?"

"Yeah, you are," she admits.

The corner of her mouth raises in a grin as she gets up, brushing off any dirt that might have stuck on her shorts.

"I need to head home."

"Where do you live?"

"Just to make it clear"—she lifts up a reprimanding finger—"I'm not inviting you over."

"Fine." A little busted, I roll my eyes at her as I push off the ground on my side, helping me to stand.

"Right down the old road. It's the first house when you walk onto the street."

"The one with the huge garden?"

"Yeah."

"I'll walk you," I state as I put my feet in action, not waiting for her response.

"Scared I might get attacked, tattoo boy?"

I casually shrug my shoulders.

"I don't want to risk it." The truth is, she will probably be fine without me, what with it being broad daylight and all, but I don't want this conversation to end.

"So, your mom drinks too much?" she asks, as we walk down the road, side by side. I know she's prying again, but I don't mind it. And that alone is fucking with my head.

"She's an alcoholic. You can say it. I'm used to it." A comforting feeling washes my soul as if we've been doing this our entire life. I don't usually talk about my mother. In general, but certainly not about her addiction. Yet, she manages to get me to blurt out exactly that after five minutes.

"Sorry you have to deal with that. Got any siblings?"

Most of my friends know the situation that is daily life for me, even though I never talk about it, but never have they asked about any of it with the interest she's giving me. I like it.

"My father and my brother died in a car accident four years ago. That's when it got worse."

She gasps, and for a moment there, it sounds like a moan, a sweet, torturous sound, doing crazy shit to my body.

"Fuck, that's what you get for prying," she states awkwardly.

"It's okay." I suck in a deep breath before I exhale loudly, hoping to get rid of the weird feeling in my stomach I can't seem to shake.

"You must really miss them."

"Every day," I admit without hesitation.

"Is that why you fight? Because you're angry at the world?"

Lashes bouncing up and down, her question feels like a hit to the chest. I look at her, tucking my hands into my sweats to make sure I don't wrap my arm around her.

"What makes you think I'm angry?" I ask, ignoring the tingling in my fingers. That small affectionate stroke of my neck gave me a taste of her skin on mine, and it made my body long for more. To feel her tight against my chest, to breathe in her scent and hold her like a sad child grasps onto his teddy bear.

"Are you not?"

"I don't know. Maybe I am." I see fighting as an easy way to get money and a good way to get out some pent-up energy with something I enjoy. Does that mean I'm angry at the world?

"What about you?" I ask, changing the subject. "Any dirty secrets I should know about?"

"Not really. I live with my mom. It's been me and her since I was born. Not sure where my dad is, but I've never felt like I'm missing out. I'm pretty boring, actually."

"You're anything but boring, Charlotte." Without thinking, I remove my hand from my pocket and run it through the soft strands of her hair. They feel as tempting as her lips look. Soft, silky, and meant to be touched. And surprisingly, she doesn't pull away.

"You found me reading against the tree along the creek. Pretty sure that's the definition of boring when you're in high school."

"Yeah, okay, you're boring," I admit with a huge grin.

"Gee, thanks," she says, pulling a face.

"No problem." I gently push my shoulder against hers, putting another smile on her face. We walk a few more yards in silence until we reach her driveway and we both look up at the cozy white home. It doesn't look all that different from my own, but assuming hers isn't overcome with yelling, struggle, and abuse, it looks like a fucking dream to me.

"Thanks for walking me." She stops in front of her house, then gazes up at me.

"Anytime. I'll see you in school."

"Sure."

A grin stretches my cheeks as I try to think of a way to extend my time with her. But she takes the lead by waving me off and moving toward her front steps, so I mimic her as I slowly raise my hand, then trail off.

"Hey, Hunter?" I turn around in anticipation, meeting her kind face, when I hear her sweet voice behind me. "If you ever want to talk, you know, about anything other than your 'just fucked' face, you know where to find me."

A fuzzy feeling warms my chest while pebbles shower the skin on my arms. I'm constantly surrounded by people who want a lot of things from me. Attention, my body, for me to win my next fight. But no one has ever offered to simply talk to me.

"What about my 'before-fucked' face?" I joke with a nudge of my chin, then laugh when she shakes her head, trying to bite back the grin I see lingering on her lips.

"I'm here for any non-fucking related subject."

"I'll see you around, Charlotte," I reply, content knowing I wouldn't let that opportunity go to waste.

2

Charlotte

I WATCH HIM WALK away, his damp shirt still slightly plastered to his muscled back. As if he feels my eyes scanning his body, he turns with a smug look, giving me a devastating wink. The boy is hot, with his broad shoulders and buff arms. He's the bad boy of the school, and even though we've never spoken any more than we did today, I can't deny I've noticed his handsome appearance walking through the halls. I do have eyes, after all. But I didn't expect to feel affected by his energy now that I've experienced it within two feet of my own.

I smile at him with my mouth closed, rolling my eyes, then turn around and walk into my house to shake off the giddy feeling he just fired up.

I find my mama in the kitchen, the faint smell of garlic settled in the air. She looks tired, her face pale and worn out, but she's attempted to cover it up with make-up.

The sad part?

She looks better than she has in the last week. She's dressed in jeans and a sweater, her flowing blonde hair framing her fatigued expression that she hides behind a full smile when she sees me entering the kitchen.

"Hi, Mama, how are you feeling today?" I cuddle into her side as she plants a kiss on my hair, before I break loose and take a seat on the breakfast bar of the kitchen island.

"Good! I feel like myself today." Her eyes are bright blue like they used to be all the time. "I made dinner for you."

"Really?!" I don't remember the last time she cooked for me, simply because life is hard when you are in and out of the hospital most of the time.

"Yeah, your favorite! Five more minutes!" She claps with excitement, and a wide smile takes up residence on my face. It's nice to see my mom like this. Energetic. Happy. Cooking.

If I didn't know she was as white as snow underneath all that make-up, I wouldn't even know she was ill.

"Who was the boy?" she casually asks as she lowers some chicken into the frying pan.

"You spying on me, Mama?" I cock my head, slightly irritated by the fact that she must have been peeking out of the window, but then I catch myself, realizing it's a blessing that she's able to in the first place.

"Just saw you coming home." She flashes me a sweet smile, reminding me I should cherish these conversations. They might get on my nerves right now, but one day, I might not be able to have them anymore, the past being a constant reminder of that.

"Hunter Hansen," I disclose.

"He's cute."

"Oh, please."

"What? He is! And he definitely likes you." A knowing look washes over her face as she glances at me while stirring the oil in the frying pan. A blush appears on her faded cheeks and the corner of her mouth slightly curls. Any normal seventeen-year-old would be dreading a moment like this, discussing boys with their mother, but seeing a smile on her face warms me inside, making me wish there was more to tell.

"He doesn't like me," I argue. "I was reading at the creek, and he just happened to be there and we started talking. He had a rough day. I'm sure he won't even notice me when we're back at school tomorrow."

"I don't know. Looks like love at first sight to me."

"That doesn't exist, Mama." That only happens in fairy tales, and if my childhood taught me anything, it's that fairy tales only happen in books.

She stays quiet, lifting the fried chicken onto two plates, then pours us both a glass of freshly made sweet tea. She takes the seat next to me, making me beam at her in excitement.

"This looks so good, Mama. Thank you." I wait until she settles in her chair before I pick up a piece, tearing off the crispy skin to pop it in my mouth. The herby flavor is everything I remember it to be, and I savor the bite fully before digging in. As I let out a satisfied breath, Mama meets my gaze, matching my expression.

"Don't be so sure, honey. That look in his eyes said he won't be forgetting you anytime soon."

"Hmm, I doubt it," I tell her. But right in that moment, a current of something ripples through my heart, lifting all the hairs on the back of my neck. Because deep down, I'm wondering if maybe she's right.

I'm sitting on the cobblestone wall next to the front door of my high school, reading a book while I wait for Julie to be done with her last class. The September sun is warming my face, while my sunglasses protect my eyes from the blinding light reflecting off the words on the page.

"What are you doing?" a voice booms in my ear, making my heart jump out of my chest, and I slap it with my hand as my book falls to the floor. My gaze meets Hunter's hazel-brown eyes with suspicion, and a weird look of familiarity stares back at me, as if he's been my friend since the first grade.

Hunter grabs my book with a pleased smirk, brushing off any attached dirt against his jeans and handing it back to me.

"Jesus, now who sneaks up on who?" I glare, ripping my book from his grasp.

He ignores my scowl, taking a seat next to me on the wall, his feet dangling as he shows me a wide grin. I can't help but chuckle when I finally glance back at him, opening my book again. Lowering my focus to the words, I use it as a strategy to avoid his gaze and pretend I'm cool as a Colorado winter, but in reality, I'm anything but that. Every nerve on my skin feels like it's waking up from hibernation, moving from the top of my head all the way down to the very tips of my toes. What the hell, Charlotte? It's just a boy.

"Are you going to the bonfire tonight?" Hunter softly pulls the book out of my hands, placing it behind him, before turning his focus back on me. Then he boldly reaches up to grab my sunglasses, placing them in my hair, forcing me to look at him without any barriers. A black Yankees snapback covers his short brown hair, and he lifts it up to put it back on backwards, raising his eyebrows as he waits for my response.

Overwhelmed by the intensity of his gaze, I need a few thumping heartbeats to collect my thoughts.

"Why do you care?" I finally say with slightly narrowed eyes. Hunter Hansen can spend his nights with almost every girl in our class, yet here he is asking what I'm doing with my time? It makes no sense.

"I thought we could hang out?"

"Since when do we hang out?" My eyebrows reach the top of my hairline, wondering if I missed something over the last three years we've been in high school together. He's the rebel, the player who has a side job kicking ass in underground cage fights. It's hard to miss him as he struts through the school with the attitude of a king in the making, but I'm the girl who mostly has her nose in a book.

I'm not surprised he didn't notice me before.

I'm surprised he does now.

"Since you told me you were there if I needed you," he explains, as he starts to draw circles with his fingers on my ripped jeans. His affectionate touch is unexpected, just like it was yesterday when he ran his hand through my hair, but somehow it doesn't make me uncomfortable. It feels good.

"To talk," I deadpan.

"Well, I want to talk to you at the bonfire."

"About what?"

"Does it matter?" His eyes move back up to mine.

"Whatever." I playfully roll my eyes, still curious as to why he has a sudden interest in me.

"I really thought you were a girl of your word." He challenges me with his entire stance, while his eyes are cheerfully holding my gaze.

"You really going there?"

"Come on, humor me," he pleads.

He's hard to resist when he looks at me like that, filled with anticipation, as if he can't do anything without me. I know that's not the truth, but I'm not going to lie, it kinda makes me feel special.

"Do I have to?" I taunt, matching his stance.

"Don't be such a bore."

"Fine. Julie will drag me out, anyway. So, yeah, I'll go." I finally give in, and a beaming smile comes my way as he gets back up.

"Alright, I'll see you there." He gives me a half wave as he's getting ready to walk away.

"Why, though?" I ask, still too curious about the sudden interest in little old me.

A hint of amusement crosses his face, followed by an arrogant smirk that makes it hard for me to keep my stoic gaze.

"I wanna see if you see the difference between my normal face and my 'just fucked' face." He winks as he backs away from me.

"God, I hope not." I gag, sticking my tongue out, suppressing my laugh.

"I'll see you tonight," he replies, then turns around, finally walking away.

"Okay, bye." I chuckle while I open my book again, then press my lips together to hide the bemusement stirring around my organs.

I see the letters forming words, but somehow, I can't stop grinning, looking at the pages without reading a single thing. I never necessarily had an interest in any of the boys at my high school, but yesterday I saw a different side of Hunter Hansen that melted my normally socially detached heart. Talking to him feels natural, like I have the freedom to tell him my biggest secrets and he would keep them safe.

Not that I have any.

I can't resist glancing up, my eyes roaming the parking lot until I meet his gaze again right before he gets into his black truck. He salutes me with another arrogant smirk when he realizes I'm looking at him.

"Since when are you talking to Hunter Hansen?"

I look up next to me, seeing Julie watch Hunter drive away with a deep frown until she places herself in front of me, just like he did two minutes ago.

"I'm not." I do my best to keep a straight face as I close my book and tuck it in my backpack.

"Really? Because that was Hunter Hansen you exchanged a longing look with just now. What? The rude prick didn't even introduce himself properly?"

She shoots me a look, her dirty blonde hair lighting up by the sun, telling me I'm full of shit.

"Shut up," I say, ignoring her brown Bambi eyes that I know are staring me down, while I keep my focus on the movements of my hands.

"What?" I blurt when I finally look up.

"You're a shit liar, Charlie. Always have been."

I suck in a deep breath, not even sure what to say. So he asked if I'm going to the bonfire tonight? It's a public thing, and every senior in town is going to be there.

It's not like he asked me out on a date.

Right?

"We got to talking yesterday. He found me reading at the creek and he walked me home," I confess, trying to be as casual as possible about it.

Her lashes fly up in surprise before her pearly teeth split her face.

"Don't look at me like that. It's not like that."

I get up, ready to go, but she keeps her ass planted where it is. I glare back at her, hoping she will back down, but unfortunately, I'm not so lucky. She decisively crosses her arms in front of her body, silently telling me she's not going anywhere until I tell her everything.

"These are the moments I wish I had my own car," I mumble, wrapping my arms around my body.

"But you don't. So start spilling or start walking, woman!" she squeals with a fake scowl, making me chuckle at her forward approach.

"He asked if we were going to the bonfire tonight."

"We? I'm pretty sure he has no clue who I am, so you mean you."

"Fine," I admit. "Me."

She starts clapping like a seal, as if she just won the lottery, and a growl escapes my throat, slightly annoyed by her excessive behavior.

"Oh my god, Hunter Hansen has the hots for you." She gets up, linking her arm with mine as she starts walking us to her car.

"He really doesn't."

"Ah, you're cute when you're in denial."

"I'm not in denial!" I think.

"Yeah, we'll see about that, girlfriend." She chuckles, and it's filled with mischief.

3

HUNTER

I PARK MY TRUCK in front of the house, taking a deep breath to brace myself for whatever it is I might find as soon as I walk over the threshold. My mother could be all nice, buttering me up, pretending to be the most wonderful mom there is, but those moments are becoming as rare as an eclipse, so I'm not holding my breath. I grab my backpack, climb out of my truck, then make my way toward the front door. All the while, my mood is getting more gloomy with every step I take.

"Hey, Mom," I bellow out of habit when I walk through the door. Something my father always required from us. I still do it in his honor, wanting him to be proud of me even if he's not here to see it. And even if my mom doesn't give a shit if I'm home or not.

When the house stays silent, I let out a deep sigh of relief, hoping I can just chill for a few hours before it's time to head out to the bonfire.

I look into the living room, noticing a heap of hair plastered over the cushions of the couch, with the rest of my mom's limp body draped over the burgundy piece of furniture. My eyes search her face, waiting for a sign of life so I can move on with my day. When she finally snores like a fucking bear, I almost jump out of my skin, but at least I know she's alive. Settling my heart with a deep sigh to relax my lungs, I stroll toward the kitchen to grab a Coke out of the fridge. There is an empty bottle of Ketel One on the counter, and an empty tumbler with barely frozen ice cubes in it, telling me she will be out of it for at least another two hours.

Lucky me.

I reach into one of the cabinets looking for any food, but shockingly, there is nothing more than a box of crackers and some Pop-Tarts. Dragging my feet upstairs and to my room, I flop myself onto the bed, staring at the white ceiling. I grab my hacky sack from the nightstand and start throwing it in the air, my mind wandering off to a set of eyes that remind me of a clear-water lake.

Charlotte.

I never knew her name. We haven't talked once in the last three years, but I did know of her existence. I remember my first day of freshman year; a girl with pigtails walked down the hallway with a denim skirt and a white t-shirt that read: *reading is life*. She was cute, and dorky as fuck, but it was her eyes I'd remembered ever since. They were vibrant and alive, a hard contrast with the grief that was radiating from my own. The blue-green hue that flickered through her gaze was something I'd focus on every time I'd see her around the school premises, like an unspoken promise that there was more to life than just agony. Her gaze always radiated a hope I couldn't find inside myself. She was pure, and I wouldn't dare to taint that. When her eyes met mine yesterday at the creek, I knew right away it was her, even though she ditched her dorkiness over the summer, as if she shed her cocoon like a caterpillar.

Fuck, she's gorgeous.

Still cute with her kind eyes, and just a handful of sass, making me want to know more about her, while I think about ways to get her attention.

Seeking every opportunity to leave the dreadful four walls that are my home, I'm at basically every event possible in this small town, but I know she's not. She rarely pops up at a dance, a bonfire, or whatever other stupid thing the student body comes up with. But I hope she comes tonight. I hope that by breaking the ice the way we did yesterday, I can somehow find a way to keep her around.

With heavy eyes, I rest my hacky sack on my chest, still thinking about Charlotte's pretty face before my thoughts go blank. I must've dozed off, because next thing I know, my mom bursts through the door, and I jolt up with a pounding heart.

Jesus.

"Couldn't hurt you to do some groceries, could ya? You lazy fuck," she yells straight away, making me want to disappear into the mattress.

I'm almost eighteen, and I shouldn't have to put up with this shit anymore, but for some fucked-up reason, I still want to do right by her. Hoping one day she'll realize they died, but I'm still here, feeling just as lonely as she is.

"I could've. But you took all my money, so unless you want me to go stealing some shit, you go." I huff, growing more pissed by the second as she sneers at me. "God knows you can afford it now, or did you spend it all in the liquor store?" I hold her furious gaze with defiance, her brown hair sticking to her head like a bird's nest. She used to be beautiful. A bright smile and twinkling eyes that comforted me after nightmares when I was little. But all that's left are the wrinkles on her face, laced with a despair that tugs on my heart every time I look at her. *'Don't worry, my sweet boy,'* she would say, stroking her palm over my cheek, *'I'll be here until morning arrives. I'll always be here.'*

Up until a few years ago, I believed her. *She would always be there for me.* But now I know that was a lie.

I glance outside, seeing twilight appearing, before I get up, pulling a hoodie out of my closet, and gathering my wallet and keys.

"You watch your tongue with me, boy. In a few months, you'll be eighteen, and you'll be all on your own."

My snort could wake the dead. I'm surprised she even remembered my birthday. But I guess it's convenient, if it means she'll finally get rid of me, right?

I know it's supposed to be a threat, to scare me into complying with everything she says, like she's done in the past. But in reality, my heart pumps faster at the thought of finally claiming my freedom from the hellhole I call life.

"Well, it won't be any different than it is now." I hold my stuff in my hand while I try to move past her, ready to leave her toxic words behind for the rest of night, and still hoping she doesn't drink herself to death while I'm gone. But the look in her eyes becomes frantic, and she roughly pushes my head against the doorpost, making me wince in the process. A sharp pain enters my scalp, as I move to push her off, without hurting her in the process. She's been able to shove me around when I was still fourteen and a lot shorter. But things have changed since then. I can tower above her with my frame, and hurt her without even trying. There were times I had a hard time composing myself, lured in by the temptation to defend myself with force. But still remembering the disappointed look my father would throw my way for fighting my brother over silly shit, I stop myself every time.

Instead, I just take it. Not wanting to hurt my mother.

"Shut up, you little shit." Before I can duck, her palm connects with face. The burning feeling on my cheek has me growling in anger. She makes another attempt to do damage, when I see her fist soaring toward me, but I quickly dart out of the way, creating enough room for myself to trot down the hall, and off down the stairs. I can hear her drunk ass stomping behind me, cursing all kinds of shit that isn't worth repeating or listening to.

When I reach the final step, I give my mother one last glance and let out a deep sigh.

"You're an ungrateful piece of shit, do you know that?" Venom drips from her lips as she tries to not fall from the steps, being drunk as fuck.

"Whatever, Mom." I roll my eyes at her, not even feeling the need to respond anymore, while I open the door and get into my truck. She's yelling shit from the front door, madder than a wet hen as I put the truck in reverse while shaking my head at the embarrassing sight.

I swear, she wasn't always like this. There was a time she would bake cookies with me, help my brother and me with our science projects, or watch movies with us on a Saturday night. But something changed when I was about ten. My mom always liked a glass of wine, drinking one glass with dinner. It wasn't until I noticed her pour a glass of wine with breakfast that I knew something was up. My dad ignored it, brushing it off with a smile every time I'd send him a questioning look.

He shoved it under the rug.

So I did too.

But after the accident, there was no brushing off anything.

Shit got out of control.

And it was no later than a month after the accident when shit got violent as well.

Arriving at the parking lot on the edge of the woods, I park my car, and naturally, I'm the first one here. I lean my head back and close my eyes for a few minutes to take a deep breath. Consciously breathing in and out, I try to push my bad mood away until I startle in my seat from someone knocking on the window.

I turn my head, looking into Jason's wide grin. His ocean-blue eyes are as chipper as always, a big contrast to his light blond cut.

"You wanna sleep the night away? Get out, dickhead," he taunts, then walks into the woods, and I get out of my truck to follow his tracks.

"A little power nap before an all-nighter can't hurt."

"I hope you are well rested, because I've brought this." Without looking back, he holds up a bottle of Havana rum, and I chuckle behind him.

"You're going to get us in trouble, aren't you?"

"Count on it, buddy."

Three hours later, it's eleven-thirty, and almost everyone in the senior class is at the bonfire getting hammered on shitty keg beer. The occasional breeze rustles through the leaves on the trees, cooling down the comfortable temperature of the night. I'm holding my red cup with Coke, casually roaming the open field in the woods, when really, I keep catching myself looking for Charlotte, even after I told myself to stop obsessing at least a dozen times.

Finally, my chest tightens with excitement when I see her walking out of the tree line, her arm linked with her friend's. She's wearing some black shorts, showing off her luscious curves, with a gray hoodie from The University of North Carolina to keep her warm. Gray Converse cover her feet, and I love how cute she looks without making an effort.

"Is she your new flavor, playboy?" I look at Jason on my left, nodding his head toward the two girls, making their way to a group of friends.

"Nah," I reply, knowing she can't be put in that category.

"Yeah? Then why are you standing here gawking from afar?" He jams his elbow in my ribs, erupting a chuckle from me as I crouch forward, grabbing my side.

"Fuck you, asshole."

"You got a thing for book nerds now?"

I huff in response, shooting him a glare, calling him out on his bullshit.

"She's hardly a fucking nerd."

"Yeah, she's definitely a hot nerd," he admits, a smile splitting his face. "You like her, don't you?"

"I do, but it's not like that." Fuck me, I'm so full of shit. It's totally like that, but she's not the girl you fuck and leave.

"Then what's it like?"

It's on the tip of my tongue to tell him she's special. One of those girls you cherish for the rest of your life, because you know they will always be there for you if you play your cards right. I know I can't say that after one conversation, but I can feel it in every fiber of my body. She's one of those gems you can't afford to let go.

She's endgame.

If that's something you want or deserve.

I could just tell him, knowing he'll think I'm nuts, but he would be my wingman, anyway.

But instead, I take the path of least resistance, hoping it's the right one.

"She's my friend."

4

Charlotte

I TAKE THE RED cup from Julie's hand, bringing it to my lips to take a sip, letting the bitter and watery flavor of the beer settle on my tongue.

It's fucking disgusting.

This is my third one, and it still tastes like shit, making me wonder why I'm drinking it at all. We've been hanging out for an hour, and so far, I'm not getting drunk, just more annoyed with all the drunk people around me.

Sometimes I wish I was less boring, that I'd be able to really enjoy all the school stuff going on, but I just can't. With a sick mom, I've learned to look for different things to enjoy. If anything, my mother's illness made me realize life is fucking short. And getting drunk on tepid beer with a bunch of kids doing stupid stuff like Drink Or Blackout just isn't my type of adventure.

It feels like a waste of time.

And time is precious.

"Why are we drinking this crap?" I ask, cocking an eyebrow at Julie, pulling a face as she lets the yellow liquid move down her throat.

"Because we're fresh out of Dom."

Funny girl.

"It's bad."

"It's fucking gross," she agrees with a wince, "but it's all there is, and we need to loosen up."

Her ass shakes from left to right while wiggling her brows up and down.

She looks ridiculous, and I can't help but laugh.

"Seems like you're loose enough."

"Yeah, but you definitely need some more, because fighter boy over there keeps staring at you. So chop-chop, bottoms up with that liquid spunk, because chances are—you're going to need it."

"What?" I quickly follow her gaze, being met by a set of eyes that has my heart jumping in a fight-or-flight way. Shit.

I hadn't spotted him yet, and my nerves were convinced it was for the best. That he really wasn't that interested in me and going with the most likely assumption that he was buried in some chick behind the tree line. It would make so much sense to think I was nothing more than a little blip on the radar for twenty-four hours than to actually believe he wants to spend more time with me.

But our gazes collide, and another wink crushes my senses to pulp.

Maybe not.

My lips lift, an awkward look probably plastered on my face, before moving my attention back to Julie.

"He likes you."

"He really doesn't."

Julie sputters something with her eyes moving to the back of her head as she loops her arm through mine.

"That look he's giving you? That's want, girlfriend. Desire. Maybe even possession. You know that whole *touch-and-die-vibe*."

She drags me toward one of the big logs, taking a seat on it, a leg on each side, and I mirror her stance.

"He doesn't even know me," I cry out incredulously, swirling the beer around in my cup. Touch-and-die-vibe, puh-lease. I might have caught his attention, but it doesn't mean he'll get all homicidal like in some kind of mafia romance novel.

"Well, clearly, he wants to change that."

"Then why is he talking to that cheerleader right now?"

Julie glances over her shoulder, then switches her attention back to me.

"It looks to me like she's talking to him. His eyes are still glued to you." Her eyebrows knit together in an accusing frown.

"That's not the point," I say, brushing it off. "Look, we just talked. He got into a fight with his mom, and I told him I was here if he ever wanted to talk. I'm sure that's all. Besides, I bet he already has his hands full anyway." I keep glancing at the blonde who is now gluing herself to his side. The sight drops a brick in my stomach before I pull myself back and straighten my spine. I don't want to make this a bigger deal than it is. But I still meant what I said. Unlike the act he plays in school, I saw the trouble in his eyes when he mentioned his mom. I know what it's like to not want to be that kid who has issues at home, to be known for just your shitty situation. But it doesn't mean you don't still need someone to talk to. We all need that one friend who just listens and doesn't try to fix it all.

I can be that friend for him. That is... if he wants me to be.

"True," she says. "So what's the plan then?"

My heartbeat stutters when his eyes lock with mine again from across the clearing, trailing a chill down my body that has nothing to do with the descending temperature of the night.

"There is no plan." I twist my focus to my best friend.

"So, what are you going to do when I ditch your ass in a minute? Because he can't keep his eyes off you, and I'm pretty sure he'll save you when he sees I'm basically letting you flounder like a guppy, leaving you on your own."

"Wait, what?!" My eyes widen, hoping I haven't heard her correctly. "You're kidding, right?"

"Hardly, because Jacob just arrived, so I'm going to be exploring some of that fine body real soon. Like—now." She gets up with a beaming smile, my eyes narrowing at her.

"You're a bitch."

"You already know this. How do I look?" She runs a hand through her blonde strands, looking at me in anticipation.

"Like a bitch," I point out, sulking like a little kid. I'm not shy, but leaving me riding solo at a high school event is definitely not in my comfort zone.

"Perfect." She smirks, blowing me a kiss while I roll my eyes in response. "Go have fun, Charlie."

"I hate you," I call out to her back, throwing my foot over the log and next to my other foot when she walks away.

"Yeah, whatever. Call me if you need a ride home." She smirks, turning around, walking backwards. She's bold, way bolder than I am, and her confidence is something I love about her. But right now, it's just an inconvenience. "That is, unless fighter boy already got the honors." She continues as she nods her head in his direction. I follow her gaze, seeing Hunter untangle himself from the bimbo on his side, making clear strides my way.

Oh, boy.

5

HUNTER

I PLACE MYSELF NEXT to her on the log with amusement, registering the rough texture of the wood before bumping my shoulder against hers. She stifles her smile by biting her lip, her gorgeous eyes sparkling at me like the stars in a clear sky.

"Your friend ditched you?"

"I look that desperate, huh?" She grins, running a hand through her dark blonde wavy hair, making me want to do the same. Instead, I keep both my hands wrapped around my red cup, then take a drink of the lukewarm Coke.

"Nah, but I think you'd rather be at home reading."

"Or sitting by my tree at the creek," she murmurs, boldly plucking the cup out of my hand and taking a drink. I turn my head toward her in amusement, watching how she takes a big gulp before I realize what she's saying.

"No beer?" Her eyebrows lift, seemingly pleasantly surprised.

"Nah, the world is hard enough sober. Don't need to fuck with my head anymore."

She examines my face, her green eyes fearless as fuck. It seems like there are a lot of thoughts going through her head, and I expect her to pry again, but instead, she takes another sip of the cup.

"Wait," I say, steering the conversation back again. "Please tell me you don't go there at night by yourself?"

"I would take my dog if I had one. But I don't have one because my mama won't let me."

"You want a dog?"

She nods with a beaming smile that hypnotizes me, and I slightly shake my head to stay focused. "Oh, yeah! A Leonberger or a St. Bernard, you know? Those big fluffy ones?"

"You basically want your own bear?" I tilt a teasing eyebrow.

"Yeah! They are very protective of their owners. I'd love to have one of those fluff balls one day. It would be like having my own bodyguard."

I laugh, enjoying her enthusiasm. "You're serious."

"Dead."

"Well, until you have one, don't go there by yourself in the middle of the night."

"Why not?" Her lashes lower a tad, with a daring expression peeking from underneath.

Damn, she's hot.

"Babe, you're killing me." I look up to the sky in despair, then move my focus back to her bright blue-green eyes. "Give me your phone."

She sends me a glare, not moving a muscle as I hold open my palm.

"Come on," I press, while pulling my red cup back from her grasp to free her hands.

She reaches into the back pocket of her jeans, pulling out her phone and placing it in my hand, her fingers softly brushing my skin. I ignore the somersault in my stomach as we touch while I call myself with her phone.

"When I text you, you better respond. I don't want to wonder where the fuck you are," I grumble, then save her number in my own phone.

"You sound worried," she mocks, an amused look on her face.

"I fucking am." The thought of her being there by herself at night makes me shiver, as this feeling of wanting to protect her forms inside my body.

"Also, real smooth how you just got my number without asking."

"I know, right?" I proudly flash her a face-splitting grin.

"Don't you have a girlfriend?" She plucks the red cup out of my hand once again, taking a sip as if she's been doing it forever. I love this. Her sass settles my nervous system in the most satisfying way.

"I don't do girlfriends. Besides, you're my friend. I'm allowed to be worried about you."

"We're friends now?" she asks incredulously.

Fuck no. Yes. Maybe. It's the only thing I can come up with to make sure she doesn't walk out of my life as quickly as she entered it yesterday.

"I sure as fuck hope so." I pull the cup back from her grasp, looking into her eyes. The moonlight illuminates them in the most hypnotizing way, and suddenly I understand what people mean when they speak about eyes they can get lost in.

Without hesitation, she grabs my chin, forcing my face away so she can look at the scratches on the other side of my neck.

"How did things end with your mom yesterday?" Her touch feels like a warm bath after a long day, and even though I literally just said I want to be her friend, I can't help wanting more. My fingers itch to pull her into my arms, and my eyes land on her kissable lips, making me think about what those soft pillows would feel like against my mouth.

Friends, huh, Hunt? I'm so fucked.

I pull myself together when she lets go of my chin, and a cold breeze instantly snaps me out of my daydream. My hand reaches up to turn my snapback backwards, preventing myself from giving into the temptation to touch her.

"She was out of it when I got home. So I was lucky," I confess.

Her face morphs with a troubled frown, worry dripping from her that melts my stone-cold heart.

"I doubt your mom being 'out of it' can be considered lucky, Hunter." Her tone is serious, and I understand what she's saying, but this is just what it is. I wish I had good memories with my mom after the accident, but I don't. Now the good memories are the ones she's not in.

Like this one.

"It's life, babe. It's okay."

She holds my gaze with urgency, fire flaring in her eyes.

"Say what you want, but it's not okay." The fierceness in her voice makes me smile.

A strand of her hair falls in front of her face, and without hesitation, I bring my hand up to push it behind her ear. My fingers briefly connect with the soft skin of her neck as I take back my hand before holding it open for her.

Now that I have her attention, I don't want to let it slip. I might not deserve everything she has to offer, but I'll be damned to not grasp on for dear life to the scraps she's offering, regardless.

"Wanna get out of here?" I smile, waiting for her to lay her hand on mine.

Something glitters in her eyes as the corner of her mouth rises.

"Go where?"

"Wherever you want." I shrug, meaning every word of it. I'd drive her to the end of the world right now if she asked me.

"Sure." She nods, and my heart stops for just a split second when I feel the heat of her hand as she places it in mine.

6

Charlotte

H E GLANCES AT ME as he pulls into the drive-through of the Burger Shack in town.

"You wanna share a burger?"

"No." I pull a face, looking at him as if he's lost his mind.

"What do you mean, no?" He searches my face while he slightly turns his body, a frown creased on his forehead. "You don't want to eat?"

"I don't want to *share* a burger. I want my own damn burger."

Color me weird, but I feel like when you indulge in the temptation of a greasy burger, you gotta do it right. Not half ass that shit and pretend half a burger is enough for a late-night snack. It's not. If I'm having a burger at ten p.m., I'm having the whole thing.

"You do?" His brows move up to his hairline as his perfectly pink lips curl into an amused grin.

"Am I your friend, Hunter?" My tone is serious, with just a hint of mocking.

I turn to press my back against the door so I can look him in the eye.

"Yeah."

"Then why would you deny me half a burger? Friends don't do that to friends," I sass.

A pent-out breath flies from his lungs with a chuckle before he lifts his snapback, only to put it back on his head. "You're weird."

"Why the fuck is that so weird?" Biting my lip, I hold in my laughter.

"I don't know, most girls want half a burger. Calories and shit." He shrugs, beaming at me as if I'm the most remarkable creature he's ever seen. A look that gets me all tingly in body parts that definitely shouldn't be tingly right now.

"Yeah, well, that's the whole reason I'm in your car, right?" I cock my head a little with defiance as I keep my eyes locked with him. He stares at me, a hint of longing in his eyes that's growing by the second, a hint I inwardly slap away.

Friends. *We are friends.*

"What I will do, Hunter, is give you half of mine if you give me half of yours, preferably one with cheese."

I give him a smile that stretches my face as he just keeps blinking at me, looking awe-struck.

Finally, he grabs his chest. "I think you just took a piece of my heart."

"Oh, shut up." I chuckle, looking away when I notice the car in front of us moving forward. He turns his focus back to the drive-through, placing our order at the first window, even though he keeps glancing at me from the corner of his eye every chance he gets.

Sitting here with this boy feels new, scary, and exciting, yet completely safe and familiar at the same time. I watch him while he pays the cashier, then he's handed the food, placing it in my lap as he drives his truck to one of the empty parking spots, and we start dividing everything up. He places the side of fries between us on the center console for both of us to share, then hands over my double cheeseburger.

"So, why did you ditch your girlfriend?" I take a bite of my burger, lazily leaning the back of my head against the window. I know it's none of my business, but the words roll off my tongue before I can stop them.

"She's not my girlfriend." He sinks his teeth into his burger, keeping his intense brown eyes locked with mine.

"Yet you know exactly who I'm talking about," I mock, taking another bite.

"Told ya, I don't do girlfriends." He shrugs his shoulders.

"Does she know that? Because I wouldn't want any backlash for hanging out with you." My hands reach for a fry, and I put it in my mouth. I know my curiosity might come off as jealousy, but the friendly look in his eyes makes me believe this is a safe zone between the two of us. Besides, with his track record, there's a good possibility I'll get a target on my back just for sitting in his car.

"Psh, if you get backlash from anyone, I'll be kicking their asses myself. Girl or guy." I hold in a moan at his reply, my heart growing just a teeny, tiny bit. "Besides, it's not my problem if she doesn't."

"Right." I smile, reminding myself how arrogant he is.

"What about you?"

"What about me?" I take the last bite of my half of my burger before I hand it over to him, as he does the same with his.

"Why isn't there a guy claiming your time?" he asks while the tips of his fingers sweep against mine when we exchange the food. A soft flutter goes through my stomach, and I sigh deeply with a smile haunting my lips before I reply.

"Probably because you beat 'em to it?"

"Glad I did." He winks, and I completely understand why every girl swoons over him. Hunter looks like trouble, but he flirts like Prince Charming.

"Stop flirting with me." I roll my eyes with a chuckle, silently vowing to myself I won't let him charm his way into my heart like he does with every other girl in our class.

"Fine," he counters as he fakes annoyance.

The level of comfort I feel around him is confusing the hell out of me.

I let my eyes scan his beautiful face, noticing the small scars that subtly add an edge to his expression. His black eye is less visible today, but the cuts on his face still make him look rough on the outside.

We eat the rest of our food in an easy silence before I lie down in the passenger seat, adjusting the back down so I can get comfortable. I reach out my hand to pull his Coke from his grasp, then take a sip. He just smiles, still looking at me in the same position, unbothered by my cheeky behavior.

I'm not sure how I should feel while he keeps staring at me, but as an invisible chord seems to lure our gazes together like magnets, I sink myself deeper into the seat with a satisfying feeling. Like we've created this safe and warm cocoon of our own. Like this is exactly where I'm supposed to be right now.

"My mom has cancer," I blurt.

He winces at my revelation, then blinks a few times, before he lets out a groan and his expression softens.

"Shit, babe. I'm sorry," he replies after a moment of silence between us. I don't blame him. It's the same thing that always happens when I tell people my mom is sick. Because really, how do you respond to that? You barely can, because there is no right response, and anything you say will make the entire conversation awkward.

But not with Hunter.

I can sense how troubled he is at hearing the admission, but it doesn't feel uncomfortable. The air inside the truck doesn't change for the worse like I'd expect. If anything, it feels as if it expands our growing connection, both having moms who can't really take care of us.

"Yeah, since I was eight. Lung cancer."

"That's a long time." His hand reaches out to tuck a strand of my hair behind my ear, looking at me with encouragement to continue, as the soft touch of his skin against mine warms me on the inside.

"I know." I close my eyes, the can of Coke resting on my stomach, as I hold it with both hands. "It's weird, but at this point, I don't think I know any better. You know? I'm so used to her being sick that I can barely remember her not being sick. She's been in and out of remission every few years, and every single time, I hope it sticks. But..." I shrug. "She's pretty sick again now."

"Do you guys have help?" I can detect the worry in his voice, and it unintentionally warms my chest.

"My grandmother tries to help, but she lives out of state, so she's only here every three months. Mrs. Applebaum lets me borrow her car for appointments at the hospital or makes us dinner every once in a while. Other than that, it's just me."

"You've been taking care of your mother all this time?" He lets out a deep sigh, as if he wishes he could take over my burden. No one can take over my burden. And I wouldn't want it any other way. I owe my mother everything; it's why I don't mind taking care of her. She took care of me. Now I take care of her. It's as simple as that.

"It's not like I have a choice."

"That's heavy, babe." His voice is strained, eyes concerned.

"It's okay. I'd rather take care of her than have her six feet under." I give him a smile to make him more at ease, but instead he bites his lip as if he's doing his best to not make a big deal out of it, just like I am.

"I'm sorry, Charls."

"Charls?" I cock my eyebrow.

He lets out a chuckle that lightens the mood, then throws me a playful look.

"As much as I like Charlotte, it's too long for me. And Julie already has Charlie," he clarifies. "I need my own."

"You do realize it's the same number of syllables as Hunter." I smile, pressing my shoulder deeper into the leather seat to keep my focus on him.

He throws back his backrest and gets comfortable, closing his eyes. "More letters don't count."

Instantly, my nose inhales the sweet smell that is his, which slightly overwhelms my senses. A mix of something fresh and woodsy, making me wish I could bury myself in it.

"I'm not sure I'm on board with this. But you'll get a pass. For now."

"Good," he responds, not moving an inch. "So, what is your mom's prognosis?"

"Pff, who knows?" I huff, examining his rugged face once more. His chiseled jaw is completely hairless, and I wonder if he still has a baby face or if he has to shave every few days. He turns his head, silently asking me for more, and I take it as my cue to continue, while getting a little lost in his gaze.

"She's been in remission three times now, but it returned every time. Eight months ago, she had another x-ray where they found another spot on her lung, and they treated her right away. Now she's doing her last chemo and the doctors say it's looking very hopeful. But I don't wanna look too far ahead, you know?" I've gotten excited about my mom fully healing more than once, so this time I'm a bit more vigilant with my hopeful feelings.

He hums in agreement, softly nodding his head. "So you guys don't have a car?"

I shake my head. "It broke down last year. We don't have the funds to replace it. Not yet, anyway. When my mom gets better, I'm sure we will."

"When is her next appointment?"

"Next Thursday at two."

"You can borrow my truck."

"Really?" I look at him with surprise. "Why would you do that? You don't even know me."

"You're a good girl, and you can use all the help you can get, Charls. What else do I need to know?"

An affectionate expression takes over his face, and I've never felt more seen in my life. "I would take you myself, but I have detention the entire week. You can pick me up after?"

"Of course, you have detention," I taunt.

"Gotta keep up my monthly quota," he jokes, igniting a laugh from my chest.

"Thank you, I appreciate it." I beam, a bit stunned by his unexpected offer. He might look like trouble, but this only confirms my first impression of him. He's a force to be reckoned with if you get on his bad side, but deep down, his heart is as gold as the sun.

"Wouldn't your mom mind, though?" The relationship with his mother is all but good and the last thing I want is for him to get into trouble with her.

"Fuck her." His disdain is audible, and for a brief moment, his mood is ripped to shreds, but as quickly as it's there, it's tossed away by another smoldering look.

"Right. Well, thank you. It saves me Uber money," I tell him gratefully.

"Sure," he drawls, as if it's no big deal. A silence forms as we both look out the front window, completely content with just sitting here and keeping each other company.

"I know you don't want to talk about her, but I'm a good listener. I mean, if you ever do, that is. Talk about your mom, I mean," I explain, more clumsily than it sounded in my head. Now that I've had a glimpse of his heart, I want him to have someone to be there for him more than anything. My gut tells me that he has been dealing with life alone for far too long, and I want him to know he's not alone. That I'm here for him.

His head slowly turns toward mine, examining my face with a troubled smile. He reaches out his hand to push back another strand of my silky hair, then cups my cheek. I want to lean into his touch forever.

"I know this sounds weird, since we met yesterday. But there's just something about you. I can't shake it."

I can almost see his heart bleeding right in front of me, making my own hurt for him.

He's keeping up this strong front for the rest of the world, but I see right through the act. See the boy inside of him who's starving for some genuine affection.

"Like what?" I press, covering my hand with the one he has on my face. I can feel the tension rising like a balloon, ready to burst my bubble any second now, but I can't deflect from it either.

He takes a deep breath while his thumb starts to stroke my cheek. There's at least two feet of air separating us, but still, this feels awfully intimate.

"Like the need to keep you close. Forever. Like I can trust you with my life, saving me from the darkness." He looks at me with an intensity that makes me hold my breath, stripping me naked with every second that passes by before he moves his lips again. "Will you be that girl for me, Charls? Will you always be my friend? Friends first?"

I feel my heart fall a little at the word "friend," though that's exactly what I've been telling myself. I want to be his friend; I want to be there for him. I want to be the safe haven he doesn't have.

But then why does it feel like my heart is taking a beating at the same time? Ending us before we even begin? But part of me is also relieved. Relieved because I have a feeling this boy has the ability to hook me with a smile and crush me with a glare. Becoming anything but safe for my heart.

Yeah, friends are exactly what we should be if I want to keep my heart intact.

I swallow hard, then plaster a smile on my face, knowing I want all he can give me. All he has to offer. If he needs me to be his friend, I'll be the best friend he can get.

"I will always be your friend, Hunter. Friends first."

7

HUNTER

I'M SITTING ON THE step of my porch, enjoying the sun warming my skin, even though I feel dead inside. *Numb.* My feet anxiously tap the wood of the steps while I'm swiping through my phone. Basically avoiding my mom until Charlotte arrives to bring my truck back.

"You're nothing but a freeloader."

The winning comment of the day. I would love to say that's the worst she's ever said, but that would be a lie. At this point, I'm surprised she hasn't wished me dead yet.

Fuck knows I have.

The first time she started telling me I was shit, I went to my room feeling exactly that.

Like shit.

Wishing I was the one in that damn car with my dad, and that my brother would've been the one to survive. But then I would realize I'd never want my brother to have to deal with this version of my mother, so I was glad he was spared the experience.

How fucked up is that? Considering your dead brother lucky, because at least he doesn't have to deal with your alcoholic mom?

I grunt at my own thoughts, shaking my head to push my self-pity away by looking at the messages on my phone.

LIZA: LAST NIGHT WAS FUN ;)
HUNTER: IT SURE WAS.
LIZA: WANNA DO IT AGAIN 2NIGHT?
HUNTER: MAYBE

Definitely not if my favorite girl is willing to spend her night with me instead.

LIZA: WORD IS UR HAVING A FIGHT TONIGHT ...
HUNTER: I DO.
LIZA: WANT ME TO BE YOUR PERSONAL CHEER-LEADER?

No.
Fuck no.
I don't take people to my fights other than Jason, but most of the time I go by myself. It's a business transaction for me and nothing more. The last thing I need is some bunny-hopping girl begging for my attention while I'm trying to knock people out.

Though, her question does spark an idea.

The tips of my fingers hover above my screen to reply, when the roaring engine of my truck makes me look up, and excitement across stretches my face. My bad mood disappears when I see that tiny girl parking my big-ass truck in the driveway like a badass. The last few weeks, she's been the only one who can really make me smile; my light in the dark tunnel that is my life. I walk over to my truck, leaning in the open window on the passenger side.

"Hey." She looks gorgeous as ever in her blue jeans and a simple white t-shirt, her blonde strands framing the swell of her breasts.

Her eyes narrow at me as she cocks her head, lips pursing.

"You had another fight?"

I swear, I can't hide anything from this girl. She can read me like a fucking children's book, quickly and without any effort. She notices the smallest change in my mood and it's as terrifying as it is comforting that she knows me this well after just a matter of weeks.

A sweet smile ruffles my lips, hoping she'll drop it while I open the door.

"Hunt." She glares when I reach for the contact and pull the key from the ignition, using it as an excuse to be closer to her. The smell of her flowery shampoo is intoxicating, and I breathe in deeply as I close my eyes. When the key is in my hand, I look up, rest my gaze on her innocent face, resisting the itch to brush my thumb over the soft brown freckles on her cheek.

"I got you something." I open the glove box, pulling out the book I stuffed there yesterday.

Her eyes narrow with a little amusement. "You're deflecting."

"I know." I lift up the book in front of her face, and her jaw drops, her green eyes wide like the most gorgeous marbles you'll ever see.

"Hunt!" She stares at my smirk, then flicks her eyes back to the book and gently takes it from my hands. "You got me the new Aubrey Carrington book?"

The gratitude in her expression melts my heart while pride straightens my shoulder.

"You didn't have to do that," she adds.

"It's no big deal. I saw it when I walked past the bookstore yesterday."

A smile splits her face, her teeth sinking into her lower lip. "Thank you. I love it."

The look she's aiming at me has my pulse galloping and running straight toward the drug that's Charlotte Roux, as I already wonder how I can replicate that smile once more.

"Now..." She tilts her head accusingly. *Shit.* Thought I saved myself out of that one. "Your mom giving you a hard time again?"

"Yeah," I finally admit with a tight voice, letting my head hang above the center console.

"'Bout what?"

I softly snicker, straightening my back to bring up my arms, leaning them against the top of the car.

"About you." A frown forms on her face, and I send her an apologetic look. It was a first, my mom being bothered by whoever I hang out with, but fuck me, it quickly had my anger reach a boiling point and walking out the door. My mother can have an opinion on any other girl she might ever see flash by, but not Charlotte. She can keep Charlotte's name out of her mouth.

"What about me?" Her lips part in shock, though a curious glint bounces through her expression. A grunt of confliction rumbles into the truck. I don't want to hurt her feelings, but I also don't want to lie. Not to her.

"She basically called me an idiot for giving you my truck all the time, when we've been friends for less than a month. Then she started ranting about me being stupid and always hanging around with low-life bimbos." I carefully watch her features, expecting her to freak out on me. But to my surprise, her lips are vigorously pressed to hold back a laugh. Her eyes spark with joy, and I let out my pent-up breath in relief.

"I'm a bimbo now?"

"No." I playfully roll my eyes. "I told her you were anything but a bimbo. That you weren't like that. That you're my friend." My voice lowers with the last sentence, as if I'll be caught in a lie any second now. "Then she was all like, 'I wouldn't know, because I've never met the girl.' And after that, it all went downhill."

Our gazes stay locked while I tug my lip between my teeth, waiting for her to say something. Finally, she lets out a full belly burst of laughter, which is music to my ears.

"Well, she's not wrong about the bimbo part." I press my tongue into my cheek to hide the smile that wants to slip through at her accusation. "She is wrong about *me*, though."

"Yeah, tell me about it," I mutter.

She shakes her head, then leans back, staring at me with her clear lake-colored eyes.

I swear one day I'll drown in them, and I doubt I'll ever come back from that.

"What?" I won't be able to think straight if she keeps looking at me like this. Like she actually sees more than just a rebellious teenager with a fucked-up life.

"You want me to go inside and introduce myself to your mom?"

Wait? What?

"You would do that?"

"Sure." She shrugs. "If it's important to you. Of course I will."

She says it with an ease that would be logical if my mom was the mother she was before my dad died. But she's not. She knows this. She's listened to my dreadful stories almost every night now since the moment we met. But she still sits here with a relaxation I wouldn't expect after knowing what she knows.

"Really?" I ask again, my heart pounding a little from anxiety. If my dad was still alive, I would've been jumping for joy, because Charlotte is the kind of girl you want to bring home.

She's fun.

She's sweet.

She's gorgeous.

She's the whole package, and I know it.

But to my mom, on the other hand?

"Why is that such a weird thing?" I just keep looking at her in awe. "She's your mom. Of course I want to meet her." She gets out, putting her words to action and rounding the car. Clearly being dead serious about this, and I bite my lip, not knowing what to fucking do. Part of me wants to introduce her to my mom, hoping that one day life is different and we can all share a meal together. But then the other part is not even considering it, feeling the primal and utter need to protect Charlotte.

"Charls, I don't know." I grab her wrist before she can make her way toward the front door, and a serene look peers up at me through her thick lashes.

"What do you mean?"

"My mom. She—" I pause, rubbing the back of my neck. "She's not fun to be around right now. I don't want you to feel like you have to do this."

"I don't, silly. I *want* to."

"She's not nice," I offer, hoping to change her mind.

She rolls her eyes, tugging her wrist out of my grip, and starts walking to the front door. She's the sweetest thing I'll ever meet, but she's also a stubborn piece of work when she wants to be. I learned that in the first week when she stole my debit card so she could pay for the ice cream we were getting.

Throwing my hands up in defeat, I jog behind her, making sure I'm the one walking through the door first. Hesitant to open it, I give her a final warning.

"Babe, she's probably drunk. It's not a pretty sight."

"Hunt." Her palm connects with my wrist, her green eyes hitting mine with a level of affection that makes it impossible to say no to her. "I know this. But if introducing myself to her can make your life a bit easier, I will do it. "

She's so fucking adorable.

I can't argue with her, and even if I wanted to, her adamant stance isn't something I can go against anyway.

With a sigh, I open the door, just in time to see my mom saunter from the kitchen to the living room. A bottle of wine in one hand, a glass filled to the rim in the other, with a cigarette dangling between the tips of her fingers. My spine tenses, yet I hoist a smile on my features.

"Hey, Mom, there's someone I'd like you to meet." Her hazy eyes slowly shift to us as a look filled with aversion washes over her face. In that moment, I wish the world could swallow us whole, knowing that whatever comes out of her mouth next won't be pretty. *Hell no* is the first thing that flies through my head, because Charlotte doesn't deserve this, but before I can say anything, my determined little blonde takes a step forward.

"Nice to meet you, Mrs. Hansen. I'm Charlotte." Charls offers her hand with a beaming smile, and I suspiciously wait while my mother eyes her from top to toe. Her brown eyes are bloodshot, and the gray tone of her skin makes her look more dead than alive, yet Charlotte keeps her smile bright.

"So you're the girl fucking him for his car?" she spits, and I notice Charls's face fall, but only a little, her hand still hanging in the air.

"Mom," I seethe.

"Actually, he's just lending me his truck out of the kindness of his heart." Charls chuckles, dropping her hand back beside her body, as if my mother's comment didn't affect her.

"Oh, so you're a freeloader, like he is?" she snarls, stepping a little closer with an ominous look. Without thinking, I step in front of Charlotte, shielding her from any outburst that might occur in the next second, but she lays her hand on my arm, forcing me to look at her with a single glance.

"It's okay." She smiles, then puts her focus back on my mother. I try to detect the bullshit, but before I can find any, she puts on a warrior expression.

"I guess I am, Mrs. Hansen. But he definitely isn't. Thanks to him, I can get my mom to the hospital without the hassle of an Uber or taking the bus." The corner of her mouth curls in a grin that doesn't match her eyes as she keeps talking. "Call me whatever you want, but your son is anything but a freeloader."

I raise my eyebrows in shock, feeling a renewed sense of pride. Ever since it's been just my mom and me, I've felt alone, dealing with my demons and fighting my mom on a daily basis. I don't bring friends home. I avoid my house as much as possible. Jason knows how life changed after the accident, but he doesn't know how awful it really is.

He would never expect that I may need some backup every once in a while.

And to be honest, I never thought I did. But seeing this little spitfire go head to head with my mother, in the most polite way, makes me realize that's exactly what I need.

Someone to back me up every now and then.

"You listen to me, little girl," my mom growls, stepping closer, trying to move around me. "You don't know shit."

"I know your son is doing the best he can, considering you leave him to fend for himself every day," Charlotte says, way more calm and collected than I feel, though I don't miss the accusing tone. I roll back my shoulders, lifting my chin, not sure I know what I did to deserve this girl defending me.

"He's a grown ass man!" My mother's pale features grow flush with each word spitting out of her mouth.

"He's a teenager who needs his parents to take care of him. Who needs his *mother.*"

Oh, damn. This girl says all the things that cut straight through me.

"He's almost eighteen! He should take care of me!"

My insides constrict as I swallow away the lump in my throat that's as dry as the fucking Arizona dessert. I try to keep reminding myself that my mother is sick. She's grieving her husband and her son, and she doesn't really mean all the shit she says.

"Respectfully, but isn't that exactly what he's been doing?" Charlotte retorts.

"Shut your pie hole, you fucking hussy!" My mother takes a threatening step forward, and I throw my arm in front of Charlotte's chest.

"Mom, back off." My jaw ticks, fueled by the rage spreading heat in my stomach. If my mother comes any closer, I won't hesitate to put myself in front of her and protect Charlotte at all costs.

"Don't you tell me to back off, boy!" Her attention snaps to me with a vicious glare. "And you!" She flicks her devilish gleam back to Charlotte, a piercing finger pointed at her. "How dare you come into my house, talking to me like you know it all!"

I feel Charls's hand squeezing my bicep, and I take a deep breath while her presence calms the anger running through my veins.

"I didn't mean any disrespect, ma'am. You're right. I don't know it all. But I know Hunter." Her tone is resolute, swelling my chest. "And that's enough. It was nice meeting you, Mrs. Hansen." Her words combined with the anger surging through me makes it hard to breathe and relax, but I heard them loud and clear. She sticks up for me like I'm hers to stick up for, and even though I'm furious as hell, I've never felt better at the same time. Charlotte moves her gaze up to me while I keep my focus on my mom breathing through her nose like a raging bull.

A very drunk, raging bull.

"Are you coming?" I don't know how she does it, but this girl either has balls of steel or she's a damn good actress.

Without waiting for my answer, she tugs my arm, pulling me over the threshold and into the warmth of the sun again, as I give my mom another disappointed glare.

I wish it was different. I wish she was still the mother who would be excited to meet the friends I brought home. Especially if it's a girl.

But this is just one more reminder of what used to be.

"Bye, Linda!" Charlotte tauntingly beams with a wave, lifting another astonished chuckle, then closes the door behind me. "Come on, let's get out of here."

8

Charlotte

I DRAG HIM BACK to the truck by his arm, then climb into the passenger seat as he rounds to get behind the wheel. He rests his arm on the center console, looking behind him, then puts the truck in reverse. I eye him as he glances at me, his face stoic as fuck, giving me nothing to go on, and I suppress a dreadful moan.

What did you do, Charlotte?

He easily twists the wheel with just the palm of his hand, driving the truck onto the road before he hits the throttle. My heart pounds with a gloomy drum that vibrates through every inch of my body while I wonder what the hell is going on in that head of his.

I close my eyes, instantly regretting every word I said. Leave it up to me to be a complete bitch to his mother. Though I think I was right, I realize it was not my place to say the things I did. This was the first time I met her and while my intention was to hopefully smooth things a bit over for Hunter, I only made it fucking worse. Stabbing the woman with my opinion is a definite way to give her more ammo to shoot at Hunter. I should've just shut up.

We're halfway around town when I finally feel his eyes on me. With a sigh, I hesitantly turn my head toward him with an apologetic expression.

"I can't believe you did that," he says, snapping his head from me to the road.

I run a hand through my hair, then bring my eyes up to his shocked ones, as if the realization of me being a bitch to his mom just hit him.

"I'm so sorry, Hunt," I whine. "I-I just... I should've shut up, but I can't stand how she treats you. I'm so sorry. I didn't mean to be rude, it just blurted out. My mama always tells me to think before I speak, but I still need a little practice."

Maybe a lot, but I just can't help fighting for those I care about. And even if it's only been a few weeks, I care about Hunter. *A lot.*

"What?" His head switches from the road to me the entire time, but I don't miss the chuckle that pushes from his chest. "You think I'm mad at you?"

My brows raise, giving him a tight smile in anticipation.

Of course, I think he's mad at me. The boy lives inside a war zone, and here I am giving him the next battle to fight whenever he walks back through that door, while I go home to my laughing mom. Sick, yes, but still always happy to see me.

"Yeah?" I croak out.

"I'm not mad at you, babe." I can detect the appreciation in his voice, and my pulse slows down a bit, but then it jumps back up, realizing he called me babe.

It's not the first time, as he calls me that a lot, but every time he does, I wish he would whisper it in my ear while his lips explore my neck.

Friends, Charlotte. Friends.

8

He parks his truck in the parking lot of the Burger Shack, then turns his frame toward mine. "No one's ever stuck up for me before."

"Wait, what?" I frown, my throat forming a lump, when I see the sad look on his beautiful face.

He shakes his head, reaching out to grab my hand as his thumb starts stroking the skin on my wrist. His touch is scorching, heating up every nerve inside of me. It's confusing the hell out of me. This boy wants to be my friend, but he keeps giving me affection in the most endearing ways, making it hard for me to not want more.

To not want to feel his hands all over my body.

"No one ever stuck up for me before," he repeats, his gaze completely focused on the point where our bodies connect.

I blink, trying to ignore the burning sensation that is making a fog appear in my head. "W-what do you mean?"

He takes a deep breath, letting his head hang, as if he's ashamed of himself, and I feel my eyes well up. He's amazing. I can see the pureness of his heart, and it's devastating how much he struggles with life.

"After the accident, it was just me, you know?" I nod, even though I have a whole lot of mixed emotions about this piece of information. It's not right. "It was nice to not feel alone just now. To have you by my side, defending me when you really didn't have to. If anything, I should've defended you. She was being a bitch to you." He scoffs, bringing his eyes back up, and when they collide with mine, my heart feels like it's leaving my chest. No child should feel like this. No person should feel unwanted, grieving those he lost by himself. I consider myself lucky. My mother couldn't fully take care of me for the past years, but at least I knew she wanted to.

She wanted me.

67

Pebbles trickle down my spine, realizing there's something else I feel very lucky about when I look into his devastatingly handsome, yet troubled face.

I'm the lucky girl who gets this version of Hunter Hansen.

The one who has feelings.

The one who lost so much.

The one who he doesn't show the world.

The one who seems to be reserved just for me.

My lips show the faintest of a smile as I look into his eyes.

"I'm here, Hunter." I place my hand above his, softly squeezing it. "I'm here. And I will always stick up for you."

His eyes linger on mine, and I can feel the air growing thick as we get lost in each other's gazes. My lips part, taking shallow breaths, and for a moment in time, it feels like the world slows down around us. Like we're sucked into this vortex that's meant for just me and him. The intensity is as exhilarating as it is scaring the shit out of me, and snapping myself out of it, I bite my lip and turn away to break our connection. He clears his throat, placing his hand back on the wheel as if nothing happened.

But I know it did.

He knows it did.

"You wanna go inside or eat in the truck?"

"Truck is fine," I reply, happy he tries to change the mood.

I'm not a car eating person. In fact, I think it's messy and annoying, but I know the Burger Shack always holds at least a dozen people from our high school, and I like having Hunter to myself. I like our little picnics in his truck, where I don't have to worry what anyone thinks of me. Even if the tense moments are becoming more common, not sure what to make out of that, I wouldn't want to trade it for anything in the world.

They're ours.

And I cherish them.

He pulls up to the drive-through and places our regular order without asking. It's an awareness that warms my heart, loving the small things we know about each other that someone else wouldn't know or pay attention to. It tells me he listens to me, even though he could listen to anybody else.

"Double cheeseburger for the pretty girl. Bacon and cheese burger for me."

He hands me my burger, and I grab the one sitting in his lap as he turns his truck back into a lot. I unwrap both our burgers before placing the side of fries in the center console, then give him back his burger.

"So," he starts with a full mouth and a playful glimmer in his gaze, after he tears off a chunk of his burger, "how many drunk mothers have you handled in your life? You looked like a pro back there."

I snicker, chewing my burger, waiting until I swallow, getting ready to open my mouth. But before I can voice anything, his phone starts to ring over the Bluetooth, the sound echoing through the car.

Liza, I read, automatically rolling my eyes.

"Shit," he mutters. "Hold on." He answers the call, keeping his eyes focused on mine. Something he always does. He keeps it short, and his attention is never off me for more than five seconds. The amount of interest he has from girls is insane, and something I knew before we started hanging out. But I didn't expect him to give the feeling they don't matter at all when he's with me. It makes me feel special. "Hey."

"Hey, baby," she purrs through the car, obviously unaware I'm listening too. "You never answered my question."

I cock an eyebrow at him, curious as hell about what question she's talking about.

"What question was that?"

"You want me to come tonight? I would love to see you all sweaty and heated."

I roll my eyes, fake gagging in his direction. A grin stretches his face, as he grabs a fry, and tosses it at me, making it hard for me to not burst out in laughter as I sling it back into his lap. Asshole.

"Nah, that's okay." I know it's petty, but a smug feeling settles inside of me when I hear the clear disinterest in his tone.

"Oh, come on, I really want to come," she whines.

"Sorry, sweetheart, maybe some other time, okay? I gotta go now. See you at school." Before Liza can answer, he ends the call and takes another bite of his burger.

"What's tonight?" I ask as we both hand each other the last half of our burgers to switch. My teeth sink into the meat, welcoming the salty bacon, while my eyes land back on him.

"You'll see." He winks, starting the truck again. He holds the rest of his burger in one hand while the other is holding the wheel, a smirk across his face.

I know that look. He's up to something.

"Hunt."

"Just wait and see, Charls. Do you have a curfew?" He turns his focus and drives onto the main road through town.

"Not really. But I'm never home later than midnight. I don't want Mama to be home alone for too long, you know? The bonfire was an exception."

"You made an exception for me?" A pleased expression is shot my way.

"Can your head grow any bigger?"

"I can grow anything for you."

I push out a laugh, almost choking on my burger, unable to keep a straight face. "Stop flirting with me."

"Fine. I'll make sure you're home by midnight."

I nod in agreement while I finish my burger and watch the road in front of me as we drive through the edge of town to the industrial park. We both silently keep popping fries into our mouths when he stops in front of a big warehouse that looks a bit daunting as twilight is now setting in. A few men are smoking in front of the building while the door is being guarded by a man who reminds me of The Rock. Huge, bald, and intimidating.

"What are we doing here?" I ask, a little wary.

"I'll show you. Come on." He swings his arm back to grab his backpack off the backseat before he exits the truck and waits in front of the hood for me to catch up with him. A little hesitant, I slide out with a deep frown. The temperature is cooling down, and I wrap my arms in front of my body to keep warm. He places his backpack over his left arm, then the other over my shoulder, softly tugging me with him as we make our way toward the entrance.

I settle into his torso, enjoying the comfort of his heat close to mine and his arm protectively around me. He makes me feel safe.

"Please tell me this isn't some party or something?"

"You should know better than to think I'd drag you to a party," he huffs. "I'd rather have you to myself."

"Hunter! Good to see you." The Rock look-alike offers his hand, and Hunter lets go of me to grab it in greeting.

"You too, Jim."

"This your girl?" Jim nudges his chin at me.

"Yeah. This is Charlotte. Brought her for good luck." He shoots me another wink that makes my knees weak while I offer Jim a smile.

"Nice to meet you. Good luck tonight." He opens the door for us, and we're met with a big crowd that I wasn't expecting. The audience is mostly men with an occasional woman strutting around the concrete floor, and in the middle of the big warehouse is an empty fighting cage, with bright lights shining on top of it.

Oh, damn.

"You're fighting tonight?" I ask, following him as he walks around the room. People curiously rear their heads at us, a few of them wishing Hunter good luck as he walks by. It smells stuffy—a combination of cigars, booze, and sweat, and I wrinkle my nose in annoyance. This is where he took me?

"Yeah."

"Well, why did you bring me, when the flavor of the month was dying to go with you?"

He abruptly turns around, smashing me into his hard chest. Steadying me with his hands on my upper arms, I bring my head up to face him.

"Because I wanted *you* to come." His eyes darken, looking at me in a way I can't decipher that causes a shiver to run down my spine, nonetheless. He makes it sound so easy, as if that's all the explanation I need. But I'm not the kind of girl who enjoys watching a fight. Especially when it involves Hunter.

"Yeah, well, I don't want to watch someone kick your ass."

"Pff, no one is kicking *my* ass."

"Hunter!'

"Aah, you don't want to see me get hurt?" he coos in a slightly mocking tone that makes me roll my eyes.

"Only if I'm doing the hurting," I rebuke.

He winces, and his face falls a little before that boyish grin reappears. "Well, that's actually frightening. And kinda hot," he adds.

"Stop flirting with me." I scowl, hiding the smile that's haunting my mouth. His warm hands rub over my upper arms at a soothing pace, making my head spin. "How about I just wait in the truck while I read my book, yeah?" I shoot him hopeful eyes.

"You can do that tomorrow, but nice try, though."

"Hunter, I don't want to see someone punch you in your face!"

"Babe, I've never lost a fight," he explains in a more serious tone, though I can see the appreciation of my worry dancing in his eyes.

"Never?" I frown with disbelief.

"Never."

"Well, what if me being here is jinxing that?" I counter, lowering my eyes to hide the unsettling feeling that forms in my stomach.

"What?" he exclaims. "Are you crazy? No! If anything"—his eyes soften, shaking the cage of butterflies in my stomach—"you'll be my lucky charm, Charls."

9

HUNTER

S HE'S LOOKING AT ME with an uncertain glare that tightens my
heart and strokes my ego at the same time. I like how she's
worried about me, rather than being the girl who wants to hang
on my arm because I have the reputation of being the bad boy
in town.

"Hey." I nudge her chin up, getting a hint of her flowery scent
when she keeps her gaze focused on my chest. "Don't worry,
babe. I'll be fine. I promise."

Her eyebrows crease as she turns her nose up and purses her
lips in a scowl that's supposed to be intimidating.

But really, it's cute as fuck.

"I'm beating the crap out of you if you don't keep that
promise," she spits with a fire in her eyes that makes the muscle
between my legs twitch.

"Beating the already beaten boy? Ouch, that's harsh, Charls,"
I taunt with titled lips, wrapping my arm around her neck and
tucking her into my side. I guide her to the two trailer huts in the
back of the warehouse that serve as a dressing room. As I walk
through the open door of the first one, I'm halted by Charlotte.
With a questioning look, I turn back to her, seeing her lashes
high and frozen at the spot in front of the threshold.

"I'm not coming in." She shakes her head, and my eyes lower to slits.

"Get in here, Charls," I gravel.

"I'm pretty sure 'friends,'" she argues, bringing her fingers up to make air quotes, "don't see each other naked, Hunt."

I take a step, placing myself against her chest. Her gorgeous eyes dilate, and her lips part for just a brief second before she catches herself and snaps them back together in a scowl.

"We can change that?" I tease without hesitation.

"Stop flirting with me." Her automatic reply only makes me laugh, before I rest my hand on her hip with a rougher grip than necessary.

"Have you looked around you? I'm not leaving you out of my sight with all these men around. Just get in there. I'm not getting completely naked. I swear." I grab her arm and pull her in, slamming the door shut behind us. "Unless you want me to."

A frustrated growl rolls from her lips as she takes a seat on the bench placed on the left wall. "Stop flirting with me!"

"Fine." I roll my eyes, a produced smile hitting me in the chest in response. She sighs, as if she's giving up, while I tug my shirt over my head and playfully throw it at her. Her eyes widen slightly, even though she does her best to keep a straight face while she swallows hard, taking in my ripped chest. With a tensed jaw, I try to swallow away the desire building up inside of me. *She can't look at me like that.* It's fucking dangerous.

"Okay. That's my cue. Just tell me when you're done." She brings her knees to her chin as she presses my shirt against her face, then lowers her head until it rests on her knees, and I let out a chuckle.

"You can watch, you know? I don't mind." I won't be able to control the fucking hard-on she gives me with just a flutter of her lashes, but I'm enjoying this too much.

"Shut up, Hunter," she says, her voice muffled by my shirt.

I smother a moan to keep it together before I take off my shoes to get dressed.

"You can look now," I tell her after I've put on my fighting shorts, reaching into my backpack to take out my gloves.

She carefully brings her head back up, while I tug my shirt out of her hands to put it in my bag, along with my other stuff. I quickly wrap my hands, then put on my MMA gloves, before I grab the backpack and nod my head toward the door. "Come on."

A soft blush reddens her cheeks when she lets her eyes roam my body once more, and before I can stop myself, I push my palms beside her head, hovering above her.

She gasps, then rolls her lips in the most torturous way while her gaze is a coaxing mix of fear and craving. A perfect reflection of my own expression, I assume.

"Don't look at me like that, babe."

"I'm not looking at you like anything!" she squeals, even though she doesn't question my comment.

"You are," I croak out, having a hard time keeping it together when I can feel her breath feathering over my lips, tempting me to close the distance. "But you deserve the world and I can't give you that." I don't miss the hint of surprise in her eyes that's gone as quickly as it came, but I choose to ignore it. Straightening my body, I nudge toward the door. "Let's go."

Her shoulders are squared, a bit of defiance creeping in, but without a counter, she gets up and walks out while I hold the door. I quickly follow behind her, linking my fingers through hers to lead her back to the manager of the warehouse. The lights are dimmed, other than the spotlight fixed on the cage, but I still find him pretty easily. Phil's smile cracks through his bubbly face when he spots me swirling through the crowd. "Hunter!"

"Phil, nice to see you." His jet-black curly hair flops in front of his face as I offer him my hand.

"How is it going, kid? Are you going to make me some money tonight?"

"Of course." He lets go as he glances at Charlotte, who's still holding my hand with her stance as tight as her smile, when I spot a shiver trembling from her shoulders. "Can you keep an eye on my girl? I need to grab something from the car." I hand him my backpack and he passes it on to his right-hand man to put it in his office before I untangle my fingers from Charlotte's.

"I'll be right back, okay?"

She glances around us until her reluctant gaze drills into mine, and she nods in agreement.

"Hi, I'm Phil," he says with a short wave as I let her go, then jog outside to get my hoodie from the car. I get back less than twenty seconds later, and Phil is laughing about something she said. The hesitant stance I left her in has completely erased.

"What's so funny?"

"I asked her if she's the reason you've never lost a fight. She told me how she's the only one who can handle you," Phil chirps.

Fuck. That heat of possession hits me right in the gut again.

"Is that so?" I close the distance between us, crowding her space while expecting her to tell me to fuck off with every step I take. When she doesn't, I press my forehead against hers. My breath softly fans her face as I bite my lip, withholding myself from the desire to finally find out what it would feel to kiss her.

Why does she have to make this so hard for me?

"Now, who's flirting with who?" I whisper, looking into her bright eyes, while a voice booms through the speakers behind us.

"Are you ready for the match of the night?" The people around us break out in cheers while my gaze stays fixated on the enigma of a girl in front of me.

My girl.

My *friend*.

Right?

"Hunt?" she says, her voice all husky, sounding like a promise to the desire growing within me.

In response, my hands dig deeper into her hips. "Hmm?"

I want her to want me just as I want her. I want her to tell me *fuck it,'* even though I know I should never let her. I wish I didn't have to choose to give her what she deserves or give in to what I want. And when I see the green in her eyes change to a darker hue, daring me, I hope she takes the choice for me.

"You're up." She pushes me off of her, giving me a wink that makes me gasp for air, then nods to the cage. "You better win, *asshole.*"

Son of a bitch.

I press my lips together, suppressing a smile while I shake my head. She ruins me every time her sass reaches another level, but for her, I'd go to fucking war, no matter how much she destroys me.

"I am an asshole. But I'm *your* asshole," I clarify, backing away from her, then giving her a wink in return. A blush crawls up her cheeks, bringing back her soft side, even though she rolls her eyes, unimpressed. I throw my hoodie her way, and she catches it to her chest before raising her brows in question.

"You're cold." I shrug.

Something flickers in my stomach when whatever sternness was lingering on her face melts like snow before the sun, and I quickly spin on my heel to break our connection. I only have so much willpower. If she keeps giving me sweet smiles like that, I won't be able to keep my hands off her. And it'll be hard to keep saying she's my friend if my lips are glued against hers.

Yeah, I'm so full of shit.

10

Charlotte

I WATCH HIM AS he gets into the cage, wondering if he doesn't have a ritual or whatever it is that fighters do before a fight. I'm not an expert, but him poppin' between those nets without any prep seems a bit cocky, even for him.

"Doesn't he need to, like, warm up or something?" I glance at Phil, still standing next to me. I pull the sleeves of Hunter's gray hoodie over my wrists and bury my neck into it. It smells fresh, yet manly, a hint of him entering my nose that I suck in deeply.

I don't like him bringing me here. Not that I mind seeing him without a shirt, getting all sweaty. But the thought of him getting hurt makes my stomach hurl in anticipation.

"Yeah, but he never does," Phil says.

"He doesn't?"

"Nah, he always gets in and gets out as fast as possible. Trust me, you'll be back in his truck in ten minutes."

"Ten?!" I screech, snapping my gaze up at Phil. "How is that possible? Isn't there like a break between each round?"

"There are no rounds."

"What do you mean?"

He looks at me with a tender expression that makes me feel silly as fuck. "Look, honey, this isn't an organized fight like you see on TV. That referee?" He points at the man in the cage who looks like he comes straight from a biker bar. "He is only there to make sure neither of them dies. There are no rules. There are no rounds. Whoever gets knocked out first loses. It's as simple as that."

I gasp to prevent myself from releasing my burger onto the floor. "Oh, God."

That son of a bitch. He took me to a fight where he's literally risking his life? Suddenly, the chill that ran down my spine seconds again is swept away by a heated fear. This could go to shit real fast. I don't want to watch him get punched until he passes out. *Or worse.*

My face tenses both in worry and anger. "Is that even legal?"

"Of course not." Phil chuckles. "Why do you think he makes so much money when he wins?"

The blood drains from my face, and I don't know if I want to run out the door or run into that cage and kick his ass myself. The other guy is bulky as fuck. He looks like he's the love child of Hercules and Mister T. A frame so chiseled, it's disgusting. Hunter's hot. He's ripped for a teenager. But compared to this man, he also looks really fucking young.

I can't believe Hunter thought this was a good idea.

"Hey, don't worry." Phil nudges his elbow into my side to grab my attention. "He's the best there is. He'll be done before you know it. It never takes him more than five minutes."

I peer up into Phil's brown eyes, beaming at me with amusement. I assume his smile is supposed to be comforting. But instead, it feels like a hand enclosing my heart in a tight grip, while it's trying to break free. I hear him. But I won't believe him until I'm safely back in Hunter's truck.

I turn my head back to the cage when the room turns silent, and the referee asks them if they understand the one and only rule. They both nod their heads before Hunter looks at me once more, giving me a cocky grin.

Arrogant asshole.

I flip him the bird with a glare, ripping a chuckle from him as he gives me another wink. My stomach does a flip for a different reason, but I tuck it as far away as possible, holding my breath as soon as a loud bell starts the fight.

Instantly, my body is showered with pebbles, and I fumble with my fingers, unable to breathe. They start moving around each other, bouncing on their toes, until the other guy moves forward, launching his fists toward Hunter's face. He easily ducks out of the way, and I can feel my heart jump in relief. Hunter counters the move by quickly punching him in the stomach, then the temple.

"Yes!" I call out, along with half of the crowd. The adrenaline rushes through my veins, fueled by both fear and excitement. Baby Hercules waggles a little before he recovers his stance, ready to go again. The look in the guy's eyes is primal, like he's ready to eat Hunter as a midnight snack. He catches Hunter off guard, successfully jabbing him in the nose. His head rears back, and I gasp, bringing my hand up to cover my mouth, while he gets another one the second his head moves forward again. The crowd howls and hoots, cheering it on, while the air around me becomes more loaded with every second.

Letting out a growl in response, Hunter's frame changes, making my eyes wide as a full moon. He seems to grow an inch as the look on his face turns completely feral, and his hazel eyes darken while the muscles in his neck go rigid. He looks like a different man, as if he's shredding his boyish skin, evolving into a warrior.

He's pissed.

As if the first minute was fun for him, but now playtime is over.

As if he's channeling all his anger, ready to kick life's ass.

But I would be lying if I said it doesn't turn me on more than I can hide.

It's both sexy and disturbing at the same time.

Hunter rapidly charges the guy, which effectively deflects the punch coming straight toward his face, but not expecting the next, as Hunter gives him another hook to the temple. His head wobbles, and Hunter takes the opportunity to find his face with his knuckles again.

One.

Two.

Three.

The guy sways on his feet, having a hard time keeping his balance while he keeps receiving punch after punch. Blood is spilling on the cage floor, and I see the guy slowly lose consciousness, making me cringe. My chest slowly drags up and down, each breath in relief, yet trying to push back my nausea.

Finally, Hunter gives him another hook, then slams a punch into his nose, and the guy falls to the floor with an immense thud. Hunter moves to the other side of the cage, panting, taking deep breaths with flaring nostrils. With his hands placed on his sides, we all wait while the referee checks on the other guy. I hold my breath when the big lump of flesh doesn't move, terrified he won't wake up.

I'm glad it's not Hunter, but knowing the circumstances of this fight, I don't want my friend to be a murderer either.

After a few silent moments, the guy stirs, trying to get up, and the air deflates my lungs. Baby Hercules struggles, barely getting on his knees, and the crowd starts to muffle about Hunter claiming victory. When he's not able to fully get back on his feet without falling back down, the referee points at Hunter.

"Winner!" he exclaims, right before the people around me start to cheer. Without waiting another second, Hunter storms out of the cage while someone hands him a towel. He rubs the back of his neck, then he wipes it over his face, walking back to me. His eyes are focused on mine, laced with determination and still showing a gleam of ferociousness, as if I'm the only thing that matters. I now know what Liza meant, saying how she would love to see him all sweaty and heated. His chest glows underneath the dim light, a few sweaty drops rolling down his face as he steps closer to me with big strides. He might be a senior in high school, but at this moment, he looks like anything but that.

He's a force to be reckoned with.

Fuck, it's taking my breath away.

I swallow hard, trying to keep my scowl in place to feign my annoyance as he reaches me.

"I'm going to get his money," Phil mutters beside me, leaving us.

"Hey." Hunter smirks, looking down at me with that same cocky grin, just ten times more intense. The skin under his eyes starts to redden, and my hand reaches up to access his face.

"I hate you."

"What? Why?" he screeches, amused, while my fingers brush the skin on his cheek.

I slam against his hard abs, making him hunch over in response.

"Ouch!"

"One, for dragging me out here without asking me." I prod my finger into his chest. "Two, for not telling me there are *no* rules. And three"—I grab his chin with force so he has to look at me—"for scaring me like that."

He quickly snatches my hand, holding it against his chest as I keep glaring at him, even though I want to wrap him in my arms to make sure he's okay.

I expect some snarky comment, a flirtatious or even mocking look. Instead, his face softens while he brings his hand to the back of my head and presses a lingering kiss on my forehead. The moment his lips land on my skin, I release a satisfied sigh, ignoring the heat that's creeping up my neck.

Damn him for being so damn cute when he wants to be.

He tugs me against his chest while his arms hold me in a tight hug. My cheek is glued to his sweaty skin, and he reeks more manly than ever before, but I embrace it.

Thank fuck, he's okay.

"I'm sorry, babe. Didn't mean to scare you." He strokes my back in a soothing way, and I wrap my arms around his waist, settling deeper into his body. I can hear his heart rapidly beating, and I suck in a relieved breath. We stand like that for a few minutes until Phil comes back with a paper bag. Hunter grabs the bag with one hand while keeping me tucked under his arm with the other.

"It's all there. You've got a new record there, boy. Knocked him out in two minutes and fifteen seconds," Phil says with a big grin on his face. "You better remember me when you go to the AFA."

I feel Hunter chuckle beside me while he brings his lips to my ears, feathering the skin with his hot breath. "Told you, lucky charm." He presses a kiss on my hair, flipping my stomach like a damn bottle throw, then lets go of me to shake Phil's hand. "Thanks, Phil."

"No worries, kid. See you next week?"

A small grunt leaves Hunter's throat before he dips his focus to me, then turns his head back to Phil. "Make that two weeks."

Phil lifts his eyebrows to the ceiling, then brings his attention to me, shooting me a wink. "Bye, darling."

I wave in response as Hunter ushers me out of the building, while people slap his back as we walk by. He looks like a fucking celebrity, but he doesn't stop until we're out the door and into the silence of the night. I suck in the fresh air to calm the adrenaline still rushing through my body.

"What's the AFA?" I ask on our way to the car.

"The American Fighting Association. It's the organization that hosts all the fights you see on the TV. It's where the big money is. You okay?" Hunter stills, a worried look on his face.

My eyes fling up to him, and a sense of sadness washes over me as I clear my throat. Am I okay? I don't know. I guess I am. I'm happy he's not hurt. Not much anyway. But now that the nerves slowly ebb from my body, I'm not sure how I feel. "Why do you fight, Hunt?"

His eyes close for a brief moment, as if the answer is too much to bear. He drags a hand over his face, before it falls beside him, and his lashes fly up with a troubled expression.

"I don't know." Disappointment shimmers in his gaze, probably expecting me to reprimand him for his choice to fight.

I examine his face, seeing the lost boy I saw that day at the creek. A boy who's doing everything he can to stay afloat, even though life keeps making it hard for him. I want to tell him he doesn't have to. That fighting is not the answer to his problems, but I also see how he needs it. When he flipped that switch in the cage, he changed, channeling all his anger and grief. And even though I hate seeing him that heavy and intense, I understand he needs it. It's his outlet, because he can't talk about it.

Because he feels more alone than I could ever imagine.

But you see, that's the whole thing. I don't want him to be alone. I want him to realize that he doesn't have to go to war with a one-man army. I'm here for him.

No matter what.

I sigh, then into his chest, wrapping my arms around his waist again so I can hold him tight.

"Just know that I'm here if you want to talk instead of fight."

11

HUNTER

"*JUST KNOW THAT I'M here if you want to talk instead of fight.*"

It's as if my heart opens the moment the words leave her lips. As if the polluted air that has been surrounding my head since the accident cracks through like the sun bursting through a thick cloud. I can breathe for the first time. Her palms burn on the small of my back while I hold her head close to my body, and I settle my nose against her soft hair.

There's a need that plunges through my chest. I can feel it set roots in my heart with a force that's painful. The need to stay this way forever. The need to make her mine, knowing she deserves better than everything I am. Everything I can give her.

She deserves a prince charming for the rest of her life, and I'm nothing more than the villain. Because truthfully, there is not much that can scare me in this world anymore. I've lost too much to have anything left to be scared of.

But I'm scared for her.

Scared that I will never be able to let her go once I've had her, corrupting her more with every touch, every stroke, and every kiss.

I can't be selfish when it comes to Charlotte.

So, instead, I push every longing thought away as I look up at the stars in the sky with emotions flooding the corners of my eyes. I've been doing this for the past weeks, and once again, I remind myself she's my friend while I rest my chin on her head.

"If I do, it wouldn't be anyone else, Charls."

She untangles herself from my body, looking up at me with her bright eyes. The moonlight reflects in the green swirls even more illuminating than I've ever seen. They keep me hypnotized, the gravity of her pull slanting my vision until I'm locking onto her plump lips. They are slightly curled in the sweetest smile.

"Good. Let's go." She rushes me back to reality when she drags her hand over my stomach, tearing a moan from my throat that I try to muffle as much as I can before she moves herself past me to walk back to my truck.

Torture. Complete and utter fucking torture, but I can't convince myself to walk away from her. I know I should. Eventually. But the primal roar in my heart at just the thought says it all. She holds it in her grasp without even knowing it.

"Wait, hold up." I rapidly snatch her wrist to pull her back. "Can you keep this for me?"

She looks at the paper bag I'm holding up with confusion. "What do you mean?"

"Keep it somewhere safe."

"What? No?" She takes the bag out of my hand, peeking inside, then looks back up to me with a broad gaze. "This is a lot of money. How much is this, anyway?"

"Five grand."

"Five—What the fuck, no, you keep it." She pushes the bag against my stomach, turning around and walking back to my car.

Dammit.

I quickly stalk behind her with big steps before I gently push her against the vehicle. With parted lips, she peers up at me through her lashes, and I realize the mistake I made when I put one hand above her head, caging her in with my torso. The weight of her arousal is throwing me off, giving me a hard time to keep my mind straight. All that is on my mind is filth. My head thinking about how beautiful she would look on the hood of my car.

Naked.

Shut up, Hunt.

With my fingers pressed against her stomach to keep her in place, I give her a serious look.

"Charls, the day we met at the creek, my mom found my money. Twenty grand." God, just the thought of it makes me wanna go back inside and ask Phil for another fight. It was my ticket out of here after graduation. It would give me the opportunity to rent something on the West Coast, doing as many fights as I can until the AFA picks me up. "It was what I had earned in these fights over the last year. She said it was about time I started paying rent. I was saving that for after graduation," I reveal, the desperation etching through my voice. "To get the fuck out of here."

She stays quiet, while a frown forms on her forehead, making the corner of my mouth curl a bit. *She's looks so gorgeous underneath the light of the moon.*

"I really don't like your mother," she mutters with a scowl.

"You and me both, babe," I agree, enjoying every second of her sass. "Please, just hold on to it for me?" I give her a pleading look, lowering my face to hers.

"Okay." She reluctantly takes the bag out of my hand, her cute frown still in place.

"Thank you." I give her a grateful smile, then urge her into the car. "Come on, let's get out of here."

We both climb in before I hit the ignition, the engine vibrating alive beneath us as I maneuver my truck out of the parking lot and onto the road. She quietly stares out of the window while we drive back to town, and after a few minutes, I can't resist brushing my hand through her hair.

"Hey, I'm sorry I freaked you out."

Her head rears toward mine, her gleaming eyes instantly burning through me when I put my hand back on the wheel.

"It's okay. It was only scary until I realized how good you are at it." I throw her a side glance, detecting a bit of pride in her tone. "That was some serious shit. Who taught you how to fight like that?"

"I did. After the accident, I needed a way to get rid of my anger, my energy. I bought myself a punching bag and started hitting that thing every night until I was drained. Then a year ago, some punk-ass kids were challenging me, nagging me, and I knocked out two of the three within three minutes. It was in front of Phil's garage. He came out, asked me if I was interested in fighting for money, and I figured why not?"

"But your mom doesn't know?"

My mom wouldn't know if I was part of a gang right now. She's too wasted every day to register anything.

"She doesn't give a shit about anything I do, so I never bothered to tell her."

The first time I came home with a black eye, I felt kind of proud, thinking she must be able to see me now. She must show me she cares. When she didn't say a word, glancing at my shiner, I knew she really didn't give a shit. That I was as dead to her as she felt inside. It was the day that whatever hope I still had left at things becoming better got tossed out of the window. I had parents and a loving family until I was fourteen, and unfortunately, there wasn't any more in the stars for me.

Charlotte lets out a deep sigh, and she closes her eyes as if it's too hard to hear, while I glance back and forth between her and the road. Her emotions drift through the car, piercing their way through my skin. I feel seen by her. Like I'm in fucking hell and she's holding out her hand, but at the same time, I don't want to take it, simply because I don't want to destroy her.

"I give a shit about you," she states. It's firm. It's clear. And it's filled with promise that envelops my heart like a warm blanket. "From now on, promise me you'll tell me everything? Friends first, remember?"

Two words.

It's only two words, but those two words are more loaded than any other thing that has ever reached my ears. Two words that warm my heart, because I need her as my friend. Two words that carve through my soul because I want her to be so much more than that.

"I promise." I grab her hand, braid our fingers together, and squeeze it.

She gives me a gentle smile, and I hold on to her hand a little longer just because I want to. Looking at the time on the dash, I notice it's almost eleven p.m.

"You want to get some ice cream at that late-night ice cream parlor?"

Her head tilts, her smile spreading to a smirk. "Hunter Hansen, you're a feeder."

"Is that a bad thing?" I glance over at her with a playful grin.

"Oh, hell no, I'm a foodie, so we match perfectly."

Perfectly.

"Right." I release her hand with a deep exhale.

I'm sure as fuck not perfect for her, but I know she's perfect for me.

My eyes move back to the road while we continue our drive in silence until we arrive at the ice cream parlor, and I park my truck in front of it.

"You wanna go in or eat in here?" I fix my attention on her, turning my frame.

"In here. I'll go get it. What do you want?"

"Definitely three scoops." I reach into my door to grab my wallet, tossing it in her lap. "Lemon, raspberry, and clementine vanilla."

A grin splits her face as she takes my wallet out of my hand.

"You're a fruit lover," she states, then holds up the leather folder. "And I'm only agreeing to this because I forgot my bag."

"Oh, yeah, definitely a fruit lover. So many good fruits—peaches, melons." I wink, earning me an eye roll before she gets out of the car, shaking her head with her cheeks high as the sky. I watch her as she marches in, casually brushing her dark blonde hair to the side, then flashes the cashier one of her famous smiles.

I swear to God, I could watch her all day.

I'm used to girls that are high maintenance, always taking an hour to get ready, eating salads instead of burgers, and not wanting to get their hair wet when we go out to the lake.

Charlotte doesn't care about all that shit.

I've popped up on her front lawn more than once, shooting her a text to come take a ride with me, and she takes no longer than a minute, looking sexy as fuck in just a hoodie and some jeans. She is feisty as hell when she needs to be, not willing to let anyone step on her toes, but she's also the most caring and loving person I've ever met. It's not just her mom who she helps in any way she can. It's me, it's the freshman getting lost in the hallway, it's the junior who needs tutoring, and it's the senior getting bullied she spends lunch with if I'm not stealing her away. She has the biggest heart, and I can't deny it's fucking refreshing. And addictive.

The corner of my mouth curls up when she strolls back out with two cups of ice cream, each with a spoon on top. I reach over to open the door for her from the inside.

"Lemon, raspberry, and clementine vanilla for the fruit lover," she quips, lowering herself back in her seat.

"Thanks, babe." I take the cup from her hand, scooping a bite of the lemon ice cream and putting it into my mouth. "What did you get?"

She gives me a playful glint, cocking her eyebrow in that cute way she does.

"What do you think?"

I purse my lips while I think about it as I keep our eyes locked.

"I'm gonna go for," I say, dragging out the words, "cookies and cream, chocolate, and peach for a fresh bite." My eyes narrow a bit while hers widen in surprise. Pride swells my chest when she nods her head, impressed with my answer.

"That's close, Hansen. Damn close."

"What is it?"

"Cookies and cream, chocolate, and orange."

Fuck yeah. "I know you through and through, Charls."

"I guess you do." She chuckles, while the beeping of my phone echoes through the car.

I look up when I notice a message pop up, and I grab it to check who it is, while Charlotte shamelessly glances at the screen, her eyes going wide when she reads the words. *Oh, shit.*

JASON: Yo, birthday boy! Wanna hang at midnight? Celebrate your birthday?

Her gasp echoes through the truck like an unwanted morning gong, and I already know she's going to want to have my head for this.

"What the fuck, Hunter?" she screeches with a big scowl on her face. "You're shitting me, right?"

"What?" I wince, feigning innocence, even though I know where this is going.

"It's your birthday?"

"Well, technically, no. It's tomorrow." I casually take another bite of my ice cream, avoiding her pissed gaze. From the corner of my eye, I see her attention falling to the time on the dashboard for a split second.

"Which is in half an hour!" she yelps, quickly leaning in to slap my arm. But I'm quicker. Before she can hit me, I grab her wrist with a big grin on my face, amused by her blazing expression.

"It's not a big deal." I hold a firm grip on her arm, her pulse throbbing in the palm of my hand.

"It's your birthday! Of course, it's a big deal! How old are you turning?" Another gasp. *Shit.* "Oh, my fucking God!" Green eyes roll to the back of her head, then she swiftly tugs her wrist from my hand, giving her just enough time to softly slap my head.

"You're turning eighteen, aren't you?"

"Ay, what the fuck?" I laugh, ducking to avoid her hand connecting with my face again. I knew she had spunk, but I didn't expect her to go violent on me.

I like it.

"It's not funny! Are you turning eighteen?" She tries to keep her scowl in place, but I see the grin pressing in the corner of her pink lips when she meets my dumbfounded look.

"Calm down, babe."

"Don't tell me to calm down! Are you turning eighteen?" she repeats, reaching out her hand toward my face once more.

"Okay, okay," I confess, putting my hands up in a placating gesture, not being able to keep my laugh inside. "Yes, I'm turning eighteen."

She lets out a disappointed sigh, shaking her head.

"I'm tempted to shove my ice cream in your face, but I like ice cream too much." She holds up her cup, bursting a full laugh from my ribcage.

"Thank God you like ice cream."

"Why didn't you tell me?" The disappointment that's undeniable grinds my molars together. I hate to disappoint her.

"I don't know?" I really don't. Birthday parties are a thing of the past, and with my mother being in the state she is, I prefer it that way. "I haven't celebrated my birthday since the accident, so I don't feel the need to celebrate now. It's just like any other day."

"Except it's not. It's your birthday." Her voice goes quiet, and I let out a moan in frustration.

"I'm sorry, babe. I didn't mean to hurt you."

I give her a concerned look that is returned by an incredulous one from her.

"You didn't hurt me, Hunter. It's just sad that you don't want to celebrate your birthday."

Maybe it is. I guess I'm used to it by now. "Well, stay with me until midnight and it will be the best birthday I've ever had." I brush my hand through her hair while she takes another bite of her ice cream. Her strands feel like silk running through my fingers, stirring all the senses alive that should stay buried for as long as possible.

"Deal," she chirps. "Let's go to my house and hang out on the porch. That way, I can check in on my mom."

"Sounds like a plan."

12

Charlotte

M Y HEART BLEEDS FOR the boy next to me while he drives us back to my house.

It's his eighteenth birthday. The birthday that marks the end of your childhood, the start of your adult life, the one that means you can make your own decisions from now on.

It's what every single teenager waits for. The moment we can stick up our chin and show the world we're all grown up.

Yet, he didn't feel the need to celebrate it.

With an ill mother, I've had to do a lot of things that no kid should. It made me grow up faster and gave me a sense of responsibility that's made me different compared to other kids my age. But while my mother still tried to give me the best childhood she could, always finding moments where I could just be a little kid, there was no such thing for Hunter.

The end of Hunter Hansen's childhood happened the day the car accident killed his brother and father. He lost his entire family and his innocence in one day, and it's killing me to see it.

It's killing me to see and hear him talk like he doesn't matter. That his life doesn't matter, when in reality, he has quickly become one of the most important people in my life.

Hunter pulls up to my driveway, and we both exit the car. It's still warm out for an October night, and I look up to my mother's bedroom window out of habit, sucking in the night air.

"Is your mom up?" He gives me an insecure look that makes me chuckle. He just knocked out a man double his size, but fear flashes in his hazel eyes, thinking about meeting my mother.

"Probably not, but she won't bite if she is." I try to bite back my chuckle, but his cute expression has it slipping from my lips with ease.

"Shut up." He gives me a playful shove as we walk up the porch steps, and I put the key in the front door to open it.

We step inside, the scent of the fresh roses on the hallway side table calming my senses. I love it when my mom buys fresh flowers for the house. It enhances that feeling of home every single time I walk over the threshold. I quietly look around the empty living room as my feet travel toward the kitchen.

"It's kinda scary," Hunters states. When I turn around, he's slowly wandering my way, taking in my entire house.

I've never taken a boy home. I've always felt hesitant because no one was ever important enough, but also because I never really know what state my mother will be in. I'd expected to feel more uncomfortable, bringing Hunter into my house. But seeing him standing there, resting his shoulder against the wall with the moonlight illuminating his features, it just fits. It makes sense.

"What is?" I flick on the kitchen light.

"How our houses are identical from the inside. Just yours actually feels like a home." My skin pebbles at his confession.

I throw my keys on the counter, placing my hands on the cold marble surface.

"You know you'll have that one day, right?" My gaze locks with his as uncertainty washes over his face. Another deep breath makes his chest move slowly, gnawing on my insides.

"I don't know." He shrugs, shaking his head a little. "I'm not sure that's in the cards for me, Charls. I'm not exactly husband material. *Let alone dad material.*"

He can't hide the desire to be called dad one day, because I see it dripping from his expression. He wants it all. He just doesn't think he can have it.

"Just because your mother doesn't give a shit doesn't mean that one day you won't have a family of your own. You can. And you will always be a better parent to your own kids than your mother ever was to you." My face is stern, and his eyes bore into mine, thinking over my words. With a heavy breath, I hold his gaze, thinking for just a second that I can see his eyes glistening with unshed tears.

He's a tough one. He proved that tonight. Hunter Hansen is not easily cracked, but I hate that he's willing to settle with his broken heart, not even trying to mend it a little.

Finally, he drags his hand over his face. "I guess."

I bite my lip in frustration, swallowing the words about his mother that are on the tip of my tongue, because I don't want to ruin his birthday. How dare his mother forget about him. I get that losing a loved one can tear you apart, and I know that even living with that idea is devastating, let alone actually experiencing it. But I hate the woman for forgetting the boy who is still alive.

"You will," I blurt, conjuring a loving smile. "Why don't you go outside, and I'll grab us something to drink?"

"Alright, babe." He disappears through the door that leads to the screened porch, and I watch him take a seat in the lounger before I open the fridge to see what we have.

Glancing through it, I notice a bottle of rum laying on the top shelf, along with some ginger beers.

Perfect.

I pull two tumblers out of the cabinet, filling them with ice to the rim, splashing two fingers of rum in them, then topping them off with some ginger beer. I quickly grab a lime from the fruit basket to cut two wedges and throw them in for garnish.

Now I just need something that can pass as cake.

I peek my head into the storage closet, moving it from top to bottom, looking for anything suitable. An excited squeak leaves me when I notice a bag of Pink Snowballs next to a small package of birthday candles, and I quietly thank my mom for always having birthday candles in the house. Throwing them on the counter, I grab the two tumblers, carrying them onto the porch.

"What's that?" His brows furrow together as he eyes me walking toward him with a big smirk on my face.

"A Dark 'N' Stormy. Duh." I hand him one while putting mine on the table, then turn around to get back inside.

Reluctance showers his features, that polite and well-raised southern boy coming right out as he glances back inside, as if my mother will pop out any second.

"Babe, it's my eighteenth birthday. Not my twenty-first. Plus, I don't like what that does to my head."

It's cute how mannered he acts compared to the bad boy I know, and I twist my frame, pulling a face, calling bullshit.

"I know. And I'm not planning on getting drunk and manhandling you..."

An eyebrow quirks up at me. "You're not? Because if that's the promise, I'll happily get drunk with you."

"Don't flirt!' I bark out in command, a smile sneaking through, still holding out his drink. "One drink, Hunt. Have one drink with me." He stays silent, and I pop a hip. "I know you don't drink much, but you can't bullshit me and tell you've never had a drink in your life."

"Of course I have," he hisses, "but not when your mother is around."

"Relax, she doesn't mind. Sit tight, I got one more thing." I run back inside, putting the candle in the Pink Snowball, before I reach into the drawer for some matches and light it. With my lips tugged up, I walk back outside as I start singing softly.

"Happy birthday to you.
Happy birthday to you.
Happy birthday, dear Hunter.
Happy birthday to you."

With every step, his eyes grow wider, and his lips curl a little more. When I stop in front of him, he's looking at me in complete awe.

My spine shivers under the intensity of his gaze as if he can control my body with just the movement of his thick lashes framing his eyes. He takes in a deep breath with unspoken appreciation, then drags his teeth over his lower lip, shaking his head.

My focus stays on his full lips, causing a flutter in my stomach as I swallow hard to push the feeling aside.

"Come on." I push the Snowball closer to his face. "Make a wish."

"Charls. You didn't have to do that." Maybe not, but the look in his eyes tells me that it's worth doing it anyway. I want him to know that he matters. That he makes a difference in the world. Especially mine.

"No, I know, because you didn't even tell me it was your birthday," I sass, pushing my tongue out. "If it was up to me, I'd be throwing you a party right now. But this is all I can do with thirty minutes' notice."

His expression darkens, and I squeal when he grabs my wrist. He tugs me onto his lap while I hold the Snowball in the air to keep the candle up. Suddenly, his warm breath feathers over my cheeks, and a whiff of his citrusy, woodsy cologne still seeps through the sweat from his fight, teasing my nose, making it hard for me to think. I want to bury myself in his chest, emerging in the safety of his arms, but instead, I keep our eyes locked, not moving an inch.

"This is perfect. You are perfect. Thank you." His eyes move back and forth, drilling into mine, and for a second, I think he's going to kiss me. I want him to. I want to know what his lips feel against mine. If they would be the trigger for an explosion that has been building in my stomach for weeks now. *But I can't.* I dip my chin to the Pink Snowball in my hands.

"Make a wish, birthday boy."

He smiles, breathtaking as always, turning his face toward the candle to blow it out. I pull the candle out, then take a bite with a smug grin.

"Hey! That's mine." His calloused fingers pinch my side, and I squirm on his lap.

"I know, but I couldn't resist. You took too damn long." I let my back fall against the cushion to create some distance between us while I grab my tumbler from the table and take a long sip to calm myself down. My legs are still on his, and he starts to stroke my ankle in gentle rounds. Soft. Torturous. Only making me want more.

I don't want to ruin what we have, and considering Hunter's reputation, that will probably happen if we take this any further. But the aching sensation between my legs tells me I'm not convinced about that decision. Not to mention, the chemistry we clearly have. I've only had one boyfriend in my life, and I was madly in love with him. Lucas lives in the next town and he was a junior when I was still a sophomore. We met at the local carnival, and we were together for a year. We had a lot of fun and he's the guy who took my virginity. In fact, if his parents didn't decide to move to the other side of the country, we'd probably still be together. But even though he was the perfect first boyfriend, and I was heartbroken about him leaving, we didn't have the same chemistry I have with Hunter. Everything with Hunter is... natural and heated at the same time.

We both settle into the lounger, sipping our drinks while we look out into the yard.

"What did you wish for?" I give him a quick glance.

"I'm not gonna tell you."

"What? Why not?" My tone moves up a few inches.

"Because it won't come true if I tell you."

"That's bullshit," I bellow.

"Nah-ah. I'm not telling you shit."

"Oh, come on!" I poke my elbow into his side, breaking out in a hushed laugh, clearly not wanting to wake up my mother.

"What the fuck, Charls? You're really violent today."

"Well, that's what you get when you take me to one of your fights. I get all hyped up, wanting to punch something too." I take another sip with a cocky look, feeling the cold liquid move down my throat.

"You know I can take you, right?" He moves toward me with one of his smoldering expressions crossing his face.

"Stop flirting with me." I roll my eyes, ignoring that same flutter that grows worse every minute of the day.

"Fine," he concedes, not even hiding his glee.

"Tell me what you wished for," I demand again.

"Tell you what. When it comes true, I'll tell you."

"Alright, I can live with that."

"Good." He moves his arm around my neck, tucking me against his side, and automatically, I lay my head against his chest, enjoying the comfort of his body against mine. I could stay like this forever. Spending my nights with him, just hanging out. Talking. Teasing each other. Him flirting with me. Me scolding him for it.

In such a short period of time, he's truly become one of my best friends.

And no matter what, I'd like to keep that.

"What y'all doing?" The door opens with a screech, and my mom steps outside, wearing her bathrobe and some slippers. She looks alright, considering I left her too exhausted to put her nightgown on, even though her face is marked with fatigue. Her skin is pale, her lips a little burst, but nonetheless, she brightens the night with her smile.

Hunter clears his throat, then quickly removes his arm from my body. I straighten my back, throwing my legs in front of me as I feel him tighten with discomfort.

"Hey, Mama." I give her a smile while I glance at Hunter, who's swallowing awkwardly, as if he's getting an unexpected audience with the queen. I like that he apparently feels the need to make a good impression on my mother. "It's Hunter's birthday. I've made us a cocktail to celebrate."

"Evening, Mrs. Roux." Hunter gets up to offer his hand, and she happily takes it before wrapping him in her arms as if she's known him his whole life. Tenderly, I watch it happen in front of me, biting my lip to hold back my grin. I didn't expect my mother to reply any other way, but it still warms my chest.

"Well, happy birthday, Hunter. I hope my daughter has been nice to you?" Her southern drawl is way deeper than mine, bringing out that charm that has its way of drawing people in. I nod in response, refraining myself from rolling my eyes at her, while they let go of each other, and Mama takes a seat in the armchair in front of us.

"She has." Hunter beams, now that she clearly made him feel a bit more at ease. "Even got me a Snowball with a candle, sang me a song and everything."

"Did she now?" Her eyebrows move into her hair as her gaze finds me and a smile splits her face.

"I did." I shrug, then throw Hunter an accusing look. "I would've done more, but I can only do so much when your friend forgets to mention it's his birthday until thirty minutes before midnight."

His shoulders slump with guilt. "I told you, I never celebrate my birthday."

"Why is that, Hunter?" Mama asks while she reaches her hand over the table, silently asking for my drink. I hand it to her, then get up and go back to the kitchen to make another one.

HUNTER

"W HY IS THAT, HUNTER?"
    She's looking at me with the same gorgeous
blue-green eyes as Charlotte, pinning me with the same ability
to melt my defenses in the blink of an eye. While Charlotte's
eyes are filled with joy, love, and excitement, her mama's eyes
come with a sense of comfort that makes me want to open up
to her even though I don't know the woman.

For a second, it reminds me of my mother, looking down
at me while I peer up at her from above my Pokémon duvet,
waiting for a goodnight kiss. But I slam it out of my head as
quickly as it comes.

I watch Charlotte go back inside, then rear my head back to
Elizabeth Roux.

My shoulders jerk, a little lost for words, but she patiently
smiles at me, and I cave, just like I do for her daughter every day.
"After my father and my brother died, we didn't really celebrate
anything anymore." Too busy to get through the day in general.
That first few weeks, I lived off a lot of casseroles and frozen
meals; thank God for the neighbors pitching in. But the more
time progressed, the less they brought, and the more my mother
started buying bottles of vodka, forgetting about groceries altogether. Let alone reminding herself about my birthday.

"I get that." She gracefully brings the glass to her lips, though the fatigue is set on her face. Her head is covered with a soft lilac beanie, and I imagine a voluminous pile of blonde hair sitting underneath it, even though I know the chances are unlikely. "It's hard when life screws you over like that. But take it from someone who doesn't know how many birthdays she's got left..." Her eyes mist over, but she keeps a steady voice, showing an inkling of the strength this woman possesses. It feels bittersweet. I'm grateful that Charlotte has a mother like this, because she deserves nothing less, but it's also a bit gloomy for me, wishing my mother was half as strong as Elizabeth is. "Every single one of them counts, because it means you're still here. You are *still* here and whatever you wanna do or whoever you wanna be, it's never too late." She eyes me with a serious look on her face, as if she wants to make sure I'm listening to her. "Because you're *still* alive. Celebrate your birthday, Hunter. They are important, because *you* are important. At least to my little girl, you are." She brings her glass up to me, a silent cheers in the air while I swallow, trying to process her words. The crickets sing in the night, and I get lost in her mesmerizing eyes. They suck me in like her daughter does, but in a way I haven't experienced in years. With a maternal pride that roars my chest alive. *She makes me feel like I matter.*

"Thank you, ma'am. She means a great deal to me too." I want to be honest with her, even if it's only a little bit.

"Oh, I know." Her wink is taunting, and I raise my eyebrows in surprise. "You've been falling in love with my girl since that first day at the creek, haven't you?"

My tongue darts out as I lick my lips, stunned, then push out a breath. I have no clue how to respond to that while my hand reaches up to rub the back of my neck. *Love.* I don't want to fall in love. Love is messy, and it hurts like hell when people leave. And everyone leaves.

"We're friends, ma'am. She's become my best friend. I have no intentions of messing that up." I lean forward, resting my elbows on my knees, holding my tumbler in a tight grip. It's all I got right now. All I can admit without falling apart, and I can't afford to fall apart. I have to survive long enough to graduate and get out of this one-horse town, chasing dollars in the big cities.

"I know, and you don't have to admit it, boy. You love my daughter. It's written all over your face, and you know it even though you're pushing it away something fierce. One day, you'll wake up and realize your life is worth living. Until then and after, our door is always open for you." She lifts her glass, gulping the entire drink down her throat before putting it back on the table, eyes colliding with mine again.

"How do you know, ma'am?" I don't even know why I ask, because I'm pretty sure I don't want to know the answer.

Her hands rest on her robe, her lips rolling as if she's trying to pick her answer with care.

"Your eyes. You can fool the world, but your eyes radiate the truth."

My head snaps to the side at the screeching of the porch door.

"What did I miss?" Charlotte beams.

"Nothing, just telling Hunter here the importance of birthdays," Elizabeth says.

"See! Even my mom agrees."

"I guess I can't argue with the both of you." I muster a smile, but an unsettling feeling makes my hands tingle. Elizabeth's words frantically fly through my mind, like a bird trapped inside a house, desperate to find the way out. Panicking. I don't know how to feel, but when I glance up at Charlotte, it all disappears. Fear is replaced by comfort, and I roll back my shoulders to relieve the tension in my spine.

"That would be wise, boy." Mrs. Roux gives me a wink, then slowly gets back up. "I'm going back to bed. Two drinks, Charlotte. No more. And no driving, Hunter. You can take the guest room." She lifts her finger in a reprimanding way, something that would be rewarded with an eye roll by any other giving teenager, but for me, it feels like a victory that she cares.

"Yes, ma'am. Goodnight."

"Alright, Mama. Goodnight."

"Goodnight, kids," she muses as she disappears into the house, and Charlotte flops back on the lounger next to me. She casually rests her head on my shoulder, and I bring my arm up to wrap it around her neck, settling her into my side like we did before. The ginger beer lingers, combined with her sweet scent, a potent mix I'd love to nuzzle my head in. The temptation of giving in to my urges grows when her fingers fall to my stomach and the heat of her palm burns through my t-shirt.

"Sorry for my mom bursting through the door. I thought she was sound asleep."

"Don't worry about it, babe." I move my hand up and down her arm, stroking the soft skin that isn't covered up by her t-shirt.

"She likes you. I can see it in her eyes." She looks up with her sparkling eyes, stopping my heart for a second before I put my focus back in front of me, with a sigh that's both content as a little frightened. If these women are as good at reading eyes as they say they are, I'm in deep trouble.

"I like her too, Charls."

14

Charlotte

AFTER HIS BIRTHDAY, HUNTER and I fall into a routine that has me spending more time with him than I ever have with Julie. He picks me up every morning so we can go to school together. We have lunch at the school cafeteria, sometimes with Julie and Jason. But I mostly look forward to the moments he will just stroll into my house like he lives there. The moments where it's just me and him. The moments we hang out and play rock-paper-scissors to decide who will pick out the movie we're watching. The moments he brings over my favorite ice cream or the moments we just drive around town with no destination at all. Our lives are completely synced, and at this point, I can barely remember what life looked like without him.

I know we're supposed to be just friends, and I have no illusions that he goes straight home at night after he leaves my house, but it sure makes it easy to pretend he's mine. But over the last week, I haven't been able to sleep at night, wishing he was there with me. It has to stop. We said friends. We agreed on friends, and I don't want to ruin whatever we have by doing stupid things like giving in to the desire to find out if we could be more.

"Everything with you is easy," he told me the other day. And that's the exact reason I can't make life more complicated for

him than it already is. It's why I need a plan. A perfect plan to get whatever weird idea my heart has out of my head as quickly as possible.

I close my eyes as a shiver lifts the hairs on my neck. I don't have to turn around to know Hunter is standing behind me. I can sense his energy hitting my back, just like it does when I'm cooking and he passes behind me to grab a drink from the fridge. It's a pull too heavy to ignore, but not from my lack of trying.

"Is it true?" Hunter's raw voice booms in my ear, fanning the shell while reaching to the highest shelf of my locker and grabbing the book I need. He rests his hand on top of my locker door, crowding me with his entire 6'2" frame. I can feel the warmth of his body radiate against my spine, lowering my lashes for two seconds to hold back another thrill that's trying to break through the surface of my skin.

"Dylan Dickhead asked you out on a date?"

Meet the perfect plan.

"Jesus, Hunt," I scoff, trying to forget the fact that he's completely in my personal space.

Good luck with that one.

"Yeah, he did." It was the perfect opportunity to follow through with my plan. I was surprised Dylan cornered me after history class yesterday, but after he asked me if Hunter and I were a thing, I quickly reminded myself that Hunter and I are just friends. I love spending every free minute with Hunter, but I'm a senior. Now that Mama is slowly starting to feel better, I should also experience all those silly senior things everyone does. Like going to prom. Cheer on the football team. *Go on dates with handsome guys like Dylan.* He's totally different from Hunter's bad boy exterior, but he's Justin Timberlake cute, and I did have a crush on Justin when I was ten. I figured I have nothing to lose.

"And you said yes?" I can hear the annoyance in his voice while I pretend to rummage in my locker. I can't fully hold back the smug grin that wants to slip out. *He's jealous.* At this point, I'm not even surprised anymore. He's my best friend, but there is always this hint of aggravation in his eyes whenever Julie and I talk about other boys.

"Of course I said yes. Why wouldn't I?"

"Because he's a dickhead?"

"Maybe to you, but not to me," I muse, rolling my eyes, making me wonder if maybe, just maybe, he'll ever admit he's jealous.

"Whatever. Where are you guys going? Dinner and a movie? Some fancy place at the sixth end?" he coos.

Yup, sounds jealous to me.

I conjure a glare to hide the slight amusement that runs through me as I turn to face him. The cut from last night's fight is still bright red and swollen above his brow, but it doesn't distract from his hazel eyes laced with panic. Barely detectable, but I see it. "What's with the tone, Hunter? I don't go and bitch about your dates."

Our faces merely touch, his warm breath on my skin fogging my head, and quickly I turn my focus back on my locker, preventing myself from drowning in his gaze. *Bless my fucking heart.* Will I ever be able to shut down my senses for this boy?

A loud, conceding exhale breezes through my dirty blonde waves until it reaches the nape of my neck, as if he realizes he's being a jackass.

He is.

"You're right. I'm sorry. Maybe we can double," he quietly hums in my ear. His suggestion pulls a snort from my chest.

He must be joking.

"No." There is no chance in hell I'm going on a double date with him and his catch of the fucking week, whatever her name is right now. If I want to torture myself by listening to monkeys talk, I'll just go to the zoo. Besides, I can't have him scaring away my date when he throws his cage fighting in the mix, something he seems to want to point out every time a boy comes within a three-feet radius.

"Why not?" he screeches incredulously.

"Because I want to get to know him and that ain't happening with you around." I stall, refraining myself from picking the last book from the shelf to prevent myself from turning around. I know that if I do that, his smoldering eyes will make me cave quicker than quicksand.

"Oh, please." He huffs.

"I'm serious. You'll throw your dick out any chance you get, wanting to compare."

Shit.

I regret my words as soon as they leave my mouth, knowing he will fully take advantage of it.

Because that's what he does. He might be my friend, but that doesn't mean he'll let any opportunity to flirt with me go unwasted. It's something he does with every girl, yet he seems more up front about it when it comes to me. As if he's staking a claim, without actually claiming anything.

He presses his body against my back, caging me in, while he moves his lips flush with my ears, instantly bringing heat to the nape of my neck. *Damn you, Hunter.*

"I could show you right now that there's no need to compare shit, babe." The vibrations of his husky voice drum all the way through my entire body, and my hands are holding on to the cold steel of my locker to keep me up. But really, I want to give in and lean into his hard chest. I want to give in to his pull, and his constant exploration of our boundaries until I remember how I don't want to spend another night wondering if he could be mine. *No.* I need to stick to my plan. He's my best friend. This is just who he is. His mouth is as big as his ability to flirt. He does it with everyone, joking about almost everything. He might not make an exception for me, confusing the shit out of me, but we do have a special friendship. I'm not putting it on the line. Somehow, that realization snaps me right out of my thoughts with resolve.

"Stop flirting with me," I growl.

"I don't want to." He takes a step back, leaning his shoulder against the locker next to me, as he searches my face for something. I look at him, my face stern, while the craving in his eyes makes me wonder if he's still joking.

But I can't allow myself to dwell on it.

"Fuck *you*. I'm going on a date, so deal with it." I slam my locker closed, then fully face him, waiting for him to dare to say anything else about it.

My green eyes pin him down, and I can feel my heart galloping in my throat as I hold my ground.

"Fine." His serious look disappears as he rolls his eyes with a big smirk, before he throws his arm around my neck, dragging me toward the exit like nothing happened. Our moment is completely gone. As if we don't share and ignore these electrifying moments almost every day. The thought alone makes me giddy and frustrated at the same time. *This boy will be the death of me.*

"I mean it, Hunter. Don't fuck this up for me."

"Never, babe." I look up, noticing him shooting me a wink that makes me push out a deep breath.

He's totally going to fuck this up.

The small sliver of orange and pink still paints the sky when I slide out of Dylan's midnight blue SUV. Brisk air cools my skin as I wait for him to round the car. He's been the perfect gentleman so far. He picked me up at my house, quickly introduced himself to my mother, and held the car door open for me. So far, it's going well.

Casually, he finds my fingers, linking them with his when we walk into the Call's Bowling Alley, then flashes me his teeth. I decide to just roll with it. I'm not the girl who is really affectionate on a first date, but he keeps looking at me like I'm amazing, and to be honest, I like him. I think there's some real possibilities here if I actually open myself up to him. The famous smell of Call's fried chicken wings lingers through the open space as we enter, accompanied by the sound of bowling pins clashing against the floor.

I look into the mirror behind the bar, while we stroll past it over the burgundy red carpet, checking if my black skater dress is still keeping everything in place. He leads us to the desk to inform them of our arrival, and we walk toward the lane reserved for us.

"Are you a good bowler?" Dylan looks at me with his silvery blue eyes, his shaggy blonde hair flopping in front of his forehead in a cute way, his hand still attached to mine.

"Well, like any amateur bowler, that depends on the day. But I seem to do better with a bit of alcohol running through my veins," I joke, letting go of his hand to trade my white Converse for those hideous bowling shoes you have to wear. I threw a strike three times in my life, and it was the night of my sixteenth birthday. My mother had secretly been slipping me some wine after dinner at Rogue Ribs, my favorite restaurant in town, right before we went bowling. I was on a light buzz and turned into a pro-bowler, throwing three strikes, followed by a set of spares. Then my mother slipped me some more wine and Bowling Betty turned into Giddy Greta. Turns out my tolerance for alcohol wasn't very high. *Still isn't.*

"Ah! Well then, it's a good thing I know the bartender."

"You do?" I look up from my shoes, meeting his sparkling eyes with surprise.

"Yeah, that's my brother." He nods his head toward the guy behind the bar, and he gives us a short wave.

"That's your brother?" I cock my eyebrow incredulously, hardly believing it when I look at the black-haired goth who looks nothing like him.

"Yeah. Same dad. Another mother."

"Oh, that makes sense."

"How about I get us something to drink, and you set up the lane?"

"Sure."

"What do you want?" His eyes are beaming at me, his lips forming a grin on his handsome face, and I smile in response.

He's cute.

Cute enough to not be against it if he'd try to kiss me tonight, though the thought alone makes me break out in a sweat.

"Anything with rum is good."

"You got it." He heads over to the bar, and I go to the computer to put in our names. When he gets back, handing me a rum and Coke, and I take a sip to calm my nerves. He's up first, so he grabs one of the balls out of the return and throws it down the lane in a perfect line.

Strike.

I take a few gulps from my drink, incredulously shaking my head, looking at him with wide eyes.

"What?" I blink, unable to hide my shock. "What are you, a pro? You're intimidating me with your bowling skills." I lift my brow to match my flirty tone, and he huffs a laugh in response.

"You can do this." He grabs my drink out of my hands, putting it back up on the table, getting awfully close. I can feel his warm breath over my face while he rubs my upper arms, and I swallow hard before my lips part. "Don't worry, we're just having fun."

"Right." Breaking our connection, I move toward the return to grab a ball. I awkwardly feel the weight of a few of them, making sure I don't pick one that I can hardly carry, and I settle for a nice pink one that perfectly fits my hand. Without looking back, I take a deep breath, then I throw the ball onto the lane in a perfect line, surprising myself. I wait anxiously as it rolls with a modest velocity until the ball crashes into the pins, knocking all of them out.

No shit.

"Yes! I did it!" I turn around, throwing my hands in the air. My eyes collide with Dylan's, who's grinning from ear to ear, clapping his hands, until my eye catches someone approaching behind him.

You have got to be kidding me.

With one of his boyish, yet devastating grins, Hunter walks up behind Dylan.

"Oh yeah, Charls definitely knows how to play with balls." Hunter's gaze quickly finds my glare, hoping he can take a hint, but all I get is a fucking wink.

Asshole.

Dylan rears his head over his shoulder with his brows knitted together until he's met by the smug grin on Hunter's face.

"Hunter," Dylan grates out, barely being able to muster out a curl of his lips.

"What a coincidence!" Hunter beams as if he's completely oblivious to the tension becoming more palpable by the second. "I didn't know the two of you went bowling." A girl with long brown hair moves to his side, and he throws his arm around her shoulder. She gives me a sweet smile that doesn't meet her big blue eyes, and I mirror it with one of my own, because my mother raised me well, then snap my narrowing eyes back to my best friend.

I can't believe he's here.

"Kylie and I were going to play a game ourselves."

"Oh my god! We should totally double!" Kylie claps next to him like a seal.

I put my hands against my sides, shooting daggers as my date moves his head back and forth between Hunter and me in question.

"I'm cool with that, if you are?" He shoots me a questioning look, and I give him a tight smile that I can barely hold up. Of course I'm not fucking cool with that! How the hell am I ever going to stick to my plan if the whole reason I have a plan in the first place makes it his fucking mission to distract me every ten seconds.

"Sure, just give me one second." I strut past him, a fake smile curling the corner of my mouth, pushing Hunter away from Kayleigh—or whatever her name is.

"I'll be right back, sweetheart," he bellows over my head as I push him backwards until we're in the back of the venue.

"What the fuck are you doing here, Hunter?" My blood boils through my veins like lava. I don't even know why I ask, because I know I will get a bullshit answer.

"What? Kylie wanted to go bowling." *Like that.*

"*Kylie* wanted to go bowling." Each word falls from my tongue with more indignation, and I'm really tempted to put my hands around his neck and strangle him. Remind me why he's my friend again?

"Yeah," he dares, enjoying this way too much. "Why? Is there a problem, Charls?"

"You! You are the problem. You're an asshole, and you know it. You're fucking hijacking my date, Hunter. Why? Why can't you just–" I cut off my words, pulling my hair. I wish we were the kind of friends who could go on double dates. And maybe one day we might be, but right now, I need him to back the fuck off so I can actually convince my heart that friends is all we are. I need to find out if I can feel something for anyone else, before my heart crushes in the hands of Hunter Hansen.

"You don't see me crashing your fucking dates," I add.

He moves a little closer, our heads almost touching. He smells fresh, manly, and as intoxicating as ever.

"You can crash my dates anytime, babe. Best friend privilege and all."

My heart skips a beat, feeling him overwhelming me with his energy, hating the effect he has on me. There are moments when we're best friends and nothing more, when we can just lie next to each other and talk, feeling completely comfortable with one another. And then there are moments like this, when he gets in my face, flirting with me and messing with my head. I hate those moments because I can't control them, but I would be a liar if I didn't say I also live for them.

Friends.

I roughly push him away from me, pointing my finger into his chest.

"Don't fuck this up for me, Hunt." A growl escapes my lips, walking back to Kylie and Dylan with a sweet, yet fake as fuck, smile on my face.

One hour of bowling. I can get through one hour of bowling at the double date from hell.

"Never, Charls," I hear him retort behind, and I reply by lifting my hand to flip him off.

Motherfucking asshole.

As much as I need to get over the zoo he manages to ignite in my belly every time I'm the object of his attention, I also love it about him. It's part of his personality, and most of the time, it makes me feel special. That I mean more to him than all those other girls he messes around with. Like he puts me first. But I didn't fully understand how possessive he was going to be until he just crashed my date.

"Okay, who's up?" Hunter rubs his hands together with an excited look on his face, wiggling his eyebrows.

"We can just add you to our game and we can play together," Dylan suggests.

I mumble something in agreement while Hunter and Kylie take the bench opposite me, and she snuggles into his side. My jaw ticks in annoyance, the whole sight making me gag.

This was not what I was expecting when I said yes to going on a date tonight. I wanted to get to know Dylan, see if there is any potential, see if there could be enough to shove whatever feeling I have for Hunter in a box. But my best friend seems determined to keep me single for no fucking reason.

"Alright, Hansen. You're up," Dylan says.

Hunter gets up with a small jump, like the idiot he is, grabbing a ball and throwing it down the lane in a perfect strike.

Thirty minutes later, the boys are having a match of their own, both not willing to lose to the other, while Kylie and I just throw without giving a shit.

I sink my teeth into another chicken nugget, my mouth no longer able to form a placating smile.

I wish I was reading at the creek instead of watching this macho match. They both have 200 points when there is one final round, and I'm ready to go home. Every single round, the date has gotten worse and worse, because those two dickheads seem to think their lives depend on this one game of bowling. I don't even know if it's still a date anymore. The comments between the boys have gotten snarkier the more rounds that've passed. Dylan has barely shown me any attention for the last fifteen minutes, and Kylie keeps playing on her phone.

Yeah, this was exactly what I imagined my night to be.

"Alright, Dylan *Dickhead*. Your turn, so make it count." Hunter gives him another challenging look, shooting me a wink, and I avert my gaze.

I can't even look at him right now. I'm so angry. He's probably going to tell me later how he means well, but the reality is, he took over my date without thinking about how I'd feel about it. He turned it into a pissing match, just like I expected he would.

"Shut up, Hansen. I'll show you something." Dylan lifts the ball to take a small run-up before throwing it down the lane. With the amount of passion he puts into the action, you'd expect them to have some kind of wager and price at the end of the night. If there was a possibility that I could fall for Dylan, it has been shot to hell.

Bored, we all wait patiently until the ball knocks over eight pins.

"Aaah, almost, pretty boy," Hunter mocks, resulting in a glare from Dylan.

He throws again to knock over the last ones, but the ball misses the pins, and moves to the gutter. I look up to the ceiling, knowing exactly how this is going to end, as Dylan takes a seat next to me with a sulking look on his face.

I swear all boys are dicks.

Hunter grabs the blue ball that he's been calling his *"lucky ball,"* before he takes a run-up, throwing the ball in a perfect line down the lane.

I close my eyes, thanking the universe that the night is finally over, because anyone can see he's going to knock them all over. When he does, Hunter lets out a feral roar like he's some kind of neanderthal. Granted, he probably is. I get up to put my Converse back on with a burning desire to get the hell out of here as fast as possible.

"That's how you do it!" Hunter shouts through the entire alley, making me roll my eyes once more.

"Congrats, Hansen," Dylan pushes out of his mouth with gritted teeth, then puts his focus on me while putting his Nikes back on. "You want to go and get some ice cream?"

I take that back; all boys are stupid.

My brows move to my forehead when I shoot him an incredulous look.

"Are you serious?" I don't even attempt to hide my anger.

"I'm guessing that's a no?" Dylan smiles awkwardly, as Hunter watches us carefully from the other bench.

"Yeah, that's a no. Maybe Hunter wants to get some ice cream. He's been getting your attention the entire time. Why stop now?" I tie my shoes roughly, getting up, giving Kylie a polite smile.

"Have a nice evening, Kylie."

I ignore both of the boys, pick up my vest, then stomp off like fire is on my heels.

My anger reaches a peak when Hunter bellows my name behind me, like the little stalker that he seems to be.

"Shut up!" I turn around while my finger moves between both boys. "You're a dick for showing up here, and you are a dick for playing right into his tactics. You were on a date with *me*, but you decided that comparing dicks with Hunter was more important."

Dylan's shoulders slump when he realizes his mistake, an expression of regret washing over his face. "I'm sorry! You're right." He folds his hands together in a pleading gesture. "Let me make it up to you."

"I want ice cream. Hunt, will you take me for ice cream?" Kylie says, her girly voice making me ball my hands into fists, reminding myself to never date anyone from our class ever again.

"No." I shake my head. "Not tonight. I'm out." I spin, stalking toward the door, but not quick enough to not hear Hunter's cold reply while I walk away.

"No, but I'm sure Dylan here can take you."

I suck in the cold night when I walk outside, doing my best to shake my anger off when I start my way home. It's not a long walk, but long enough to regret the fact that I didn't bring a decent jacket. I wrap my arms around my body, doing my best to keep myself warm while marching into the chilly December night with just a vest.

In my defense, I figured I'd be driven home.

"Charls." Hunter's deep voice makes my body shudder from more than just the cold. I keep walking, determined to ignore my best friend for the rest of the night.

"Charls," he repeats with a little more force this time, but it doesn't match my mood. I'm livid and he's the source.

If only he'd have the patience to let me be. Not Hunter. He gets what he wants, when he wants. Myself included. My teeth drag over my lower lip to stop myself from opening my mouth, still hoping he can take my hint of silence and just drop it.

"Charlotte Roux! You're not walking home by yourself, babe. So, you can get in my truck or I'm following you. Up to you."

I raise my hands up in desperation, whipping around, fuming.

He stands there, handsome as ever. A strand of his caramel brown hair refuses to be tamed by product, bouncing on his forehead. Thick lashes frame his intense gaze that's now troubled and filled with regret.

"You were not supposed to be here, Hunter!" I take long strides toward him. "I told you not to fuck it up for me, and what do you do? You *completely* fuck it up for me!"

He runs a hand through his hair, biting his lip. "I'm sorry, okay."

"No, you are not!"

"I am!" he howls. A deep frown creases his forehead as he swallows roughly.

"Cut the crap, Hunter. You got what you wanted. I doubt any guy in this town will date me now."

"I didn't mean to ruin your date."

"Yes, you did! That's the whole fucking point!" Desperation is etched in my voice. "You don't want to date me, but you can't stand me dating anyone else!"

He purses his lips with a guilty grimace, laced with a tiny spark of surprise. Like he's busted, caught with his hand in the cookie jar.

"What the fuck did you think was going to happen if you sabotaged my date?" I add, incredulous.

For just a tiny moment, I think he's going to confess what I want to hear. What really pushed him to drive to Call's tonight. But as quickly as I see it below the surface is as quickly it disappears back into the dark pools of his eyes when his stance changes again.

"Oh, come on. If he can't handle a bit of difficulty from your best friend, he doesn't deserve you, anyway." There is a sharp tone in his voice that raises my anger to rage.

"That is not your decision to make, Hunter!" I exclaim. "You're being ridiculous, and it's fucking unfair. You don't see me telling you who you can or can't date, and trust me, those bimbos won't make it through my list of approval check points either."

His eyebrows pop up, a pleased grin showing on his face. He needs to fucking stop doing that.

"Approval check points?"

Oh, dear Lord, I'm going to kill him. I let out a wail of frustration, showing my teeth as my nostrils flare. This boy is impossible.

"What are you doing, Hunter? We said *friends* first!"

Finally, it seems to hit him. For the first time, he seems to be lost for words. I don't know how long I can keep this up if he's giving me nothing to work with. If he wants to be my friend, he has to be my fucking friend. If he wants to be more.... well, he better fucking tell me.

"Okay, I'm sorry." He scrubs his hand over his face with a pained expression. "I am. I swear. I'm sorry. You're right. I'm an asshole." His chest slowly moves up and down as he keeps staring at me, waiting for me to say something while I take in his words. When I don't, he blinks in innocence, trying to break the tension. "I wouldn't mind you approving my girlfriends, though?"

"Jesus, Hunter!" I can't believe him. "Friends first, remember? *You* started that!"

"*I know!*"

"Well, friends don't do that to friends!"

"I know! I know," he concedes, then quickly reaches out to pull me closer. I let him tug me into his chest, but fold my arms in front of my body to keep myself from wrapping them around his waist while I look up at him. "I'm sorry. You're right. *Friends* first."

"Are we, though?" I ask with uncertainty, not knowing if I want to go down this road, but feeling the need to. "Friends?"

Gold specks swirl through his brown eyes, a glimmer of confusion hitting my heart until he spreads his cheeks in a confident smile. He tightens his grip on my waist, his hands locked on the small of my back. His heat warms me from the cold crisp air, enough to settle the fury.

"Yes, you're my best friend. I'm sorry. I shouldn't have hijacked your date." His hand brushes through my hair, and I swallow, keeping my scowl in place.

"You shouldn't have."

"He was a tool, though, wasn't he?"

"Hunter!" I slap his chest with a reprimanding look as I roll my eyes, trying to muffle the chuckle that wants to escape.

"I'm sorry. Will you forgive me?" He presses his forehead against mine, and I close my eyes at his touch. My mind says no. My heart screams yes.

"You're not out of the doghouse yet. But yeah, I forgive you, *asshole*."

"But I'm your asshole." He smirks when Dylan and Kylie's laughter reaches our ears. We both twist our attention at the entrance and watch them walk toward Dylan's car, arms locked and clearly having fun. I let out an amused laugh, not even pissed about it.

"I guess they're going for ice cream," I say.

"I guess so. Come on, let's go to our spot."

He wraps his arm around my neck, tucking me against his side, guiding us toward his truck. I push out a breath of surrender when I realize he's suggesting exactly what I really want to do right now, showing me that he knows me better than anyone.

I'm still pissed.

I really am.

But there is this nagging feeling in the back of my head telling me that even though this night was a complete and utter disaster, there is only one person I truly want to spend my time with.

15

HUNTER

I TURN MY TRUCK onto the trail that leads to the creek, parking it right at the open spot next to the tree I found her sitting at a few months ago. Ever since that day, this place has been an anchor point for me. A place of hope and safety, reminding me that life can change within the blink of an eye without you realizing.

Good or bad.

I turn off the ignition before resting my hands on my knees, looking at the blonde who seems to occupy the biggest chunk of my life lately. Her light strands illuminate under the moon, highlighting her cheekbones to perfection. I gave her my jacket and the leather pools around her torso, making her look cute as fuck. Gratefully, I pull my lips between my teeth, happy she's in my truck instead of Dylan's.

She is right. I am jealous.

I can't stand to see her with anybody else, even though I know she will never be mine. It was a dick move to suggest going bowling when I picked up Kylie, but the green monster apparently tucked inside my body, lurking under the surface, was really quick to jump up and look for any excuse to see her. Scared as fuck I would find her with his lips on hers. *My turf,* my ego shouted.

"You're quiet," I state.

She slowly turns her head to mine, a slight scowl still on her face, then turns back to the creek in front of her. The sway of her hair lifts a whiff of her rosy shampoo to my nose, and I breathe it in until it settles a warmth in my stomach.

"I'm still mad at you," she whispers.

The words leave her lips, and I can feel a sting in my heart.

"You're an asshole, Hunt," she said.

"I'm sorry, Charls. I don't know what came over me. You deserve the best, and I don't think Dylan is the best for you," I confess, giving her a regretful face, even though it's a partial lie.

I don't regret shit.

The only thing I regret is pissing her off, hurting her, but when I say she deserves the best, I sure as hell don't mean Dylan *Dickhead*. The guy has the same track record with girls as I do. I want her to find someone better than that. Someone who's steady with a bright future. Someone who plans to go to college, buy a nice house, and give her a bunch of kids whenever she's ready.

"It's not up to you, Hunt."

I huff, knowing she's right, but not being able to voice it. Instead, I bite my lip in frustration and stay quiet, staring into the night right past her face, doing everything to avoid eye contact.

"Can you be my friend, Hunt?"

It's a simple question, and it shouldn't be hard to answer, but something tells me there is so much more weight to that question than just those five words. A hidden question that we both avoid asking, knowing we will fuck it up, even though I want to cross that line badly. Why can't I just be her friend? Why does it feel like she has an arrow in my heart? One that's rooted to its core. I could find a fucking chainsaw, but I don't think I'll be physically possible to drill through the lifeline I seem to have with her.

My gaze locks with hers. Her eyes filled with a troubled look, her lips pursed.

"Yes," I reply firmly. "Yes. I can be your friend. I *am* your friend. I'm your *best* friend, and I will always be your best friend."

It should sound like a promise, but it feels like an unspoken prison I just locked myself up in. But prison, gated by her heart, still feels better than not having her at all.

"Then be my *friend*." She emphasizes the last word as I nod, closely looking at how her beautiful face softens as the seconds pass, and we keep looking at each other in silence.

"Come on." I get out of the car, and she does the same. She walks toward the big oak tree she loves to read at, while I grab a few blankets from the trunk, along with an extra hoodie for myself. I lay the blanket on the ground before we both take a seat, resting our backs against the tree, my arm around her shoulder. My nose trails off into her hair, and I can't resist pushing my lips against her scalp. *If only she could be mine.*

We just sit there for a few minutes, staring into the night with the sound of the streaming creek filling the silence. It's not much.

It's just a quiet place with perfect company, but I live for these moments. I live for the moments we just exist next to each other, without a care in the world. Giving me a sense of peace within my fucked-up life.

"Can I ask you something?" Her voice breaks through the night.

"Anything, babe." She doesn't even understand the deepness of that answer. I'd give her my heart, my soul, anything I can give her. It's all hers if she'd ask me.

"Do you tell them you love them?"

"Them?" I drag out the word, not liking where this is going.

"The other girls. Like Kylie."

I huff in response, letting out an amused chuckle. "No."

"No?" Surprise washes over her face when she lifts her chin to face me, and I raise my eyebrows.

"They're just girls I hang out with when you don't have time for me."

"Oh, whatever. Don't pretend you don't fuck them." She wrinkles her nose while the words leave her lips, and I swear I can detect a hint of jealousy in her eyes.

"Sometimes, yeah."

"Sometimes?" She cocks an eyebrow, calling me on my bull-shit, and I let out a laugh.

"A lot of times," I admit, noticing her face fall a little, and I pull her deeper into my side. "But they don't mean shit to me," I add quickly. "They're just girls to pass the time with. It's nothing serious. You know that."

I can feel her sigh ripple through my senses.

"Yeah, I know. They don't, though." She rests her head against my shoulder, her arms wrapped around her knees.

"What do you mean?" I wait for a reply while I play with a silky strand of her hair between my fingers.

"Liza. A few weeks back, she cornered me in the hallway at school. Wanted to clarify that she was your girl, that you *loved* her, and that I needed to fuck off."

"She what?" My head snaps to look at her, the muscles in my neck tightening. "Then what happened?" Liza clearly has a social death wish.

"Told her to fuck off, and then I told her she better be nice to me because I could make her disappear out of your life real quick." She gives me a guilty look, and my anger simmers down as I let out a full belly burst of laughter. I can't believe she said that, but then a big part of me also believes every word. *My girl is feisty as hell.* And I love how she's not afraid to show it if anyone tries to come between us.

"Sorry." She covers her face with her hands, and I peel them off, wanting to see her eyes.

"You're a badass. When was this?"

"Funny enough, the day before, you ditched her for Dana." She chuckles.

"Karma at its finest." I smile as her face goes back to that stern look, her eyebrows furrowed.

"I'm sorry. Here I am, schooling you about how it's not your place to decide what's best for me while I basically threatened your girlfriend, telling her I'd make you break up with her if she didn't play nice with me."

My hand reaches out to cup her cheek as I bite my lip in amusement.

God, I wish I'd been there to witness it. My fingers spread into her neck, the beat of her pulse fluttering against my palm in a tortuous way. The moonlight dances in her green eyes and when her full lips part, it takes everything I have to not close the distance between us.

"Don't be. You were right. You come before all those "*bimbos*," as my mom calls them. In fact, you come before everyone. If they can't handle that, they can fuck off. And Liza is *definitely* not my girlfriend. I don't have girlfriends, you know that."

"Well, your mom is right. She's wrong about almost every other thing, but she's right about those bimbos." She laughs.

I disconnect my hand from her cheek before I wrap my arm around her neck so I can tuck her back against my side.

"She's definitely right about that."

Her body leans against mine as she stares into the creek.

"Sometimes I wonder what the future will bring us. Who will be there, who won't." Her voice is quiet, but I hear her words loud and clear, laced with the fears she's been having for the last decade or so. There are moments when I wish I could trade my mom's life with her mama's. Giving her the health that she needs and giving my mom a reason to keep fighting. I know it's a shitty thing to say about the only living parent I have, and I regret it the second it runs through my mind.

"What's your dream?" she asks, lightness back in her voice.

"To get the fuck out of here." I chuckle, tugging her closer.

She slaps my belly, scowling up at me.

"I'm serious."

"So am I."

"That's not a dream. You can do that anytime."

"Okay, then what's your dream?"

She lets out a deep, content sigh, as if just thinking about it makes her happy for just a moment.

"My dream is to become a writer. A wife. A mom. I want a loving husband who might forget our anniversary, but it doesn't matter because he makes up for it for the rest of the year, making every day special. I want kids. Two. And I want a big porch, where I can write all the stories that are stuck in my head while the kids are in school."

I want that for her.

I take in her words while I feel my mouth turn dry, a tight grip settling around my heart. Most kids would talk about how they want to achieve great things, big things. A glorious career. A big wedding. Money. But not Charlotte Roux. No, she just wants the simple life, as long as it's filled with love. *I wish I could give her that.* I wish I could be more than just her bad boy best friend.

"What?" she screeches when I don't respond.

"Nothing." I shake my head, thinking about the one thing I'd dream of if it were up to me.

"I told you I'm boring."

I look down at her, my eyes dripping with unspoken words. "You are far from boring, babe."

"Come on." She pushes her shoulder against my ribs. "What about you?"

You. My dream is you. "I'll tell you when I find out."

16

Charlotte

H OLDING MAMA'S ARM, I help her down the porch steps while
Hunter parks his truck in the driveway. My belly flutters
when he shoots me a wink in greeting as he rounds the truck
to hold the door open for her. She waggles closer, her frame
looking more fragile with every step. Chemo hit her hard this
time. Last week, she barely came out of bed, her muscles too
weak to hold up her head, and she's only halfway through the
treatment.

Hunter has been here every night. He says it's because he has
nothing better to do, but I know it's because he's keeping an eye
on me. Making sure I'm okay.

I am when he's around.

"Good morning, ma'am." Hunter gives her a formal nod, and
I let out a chuckle at his overly polite behavior while stealing a
glance at his bruised knuckles from his latest fight. I know it's
genuine, but it's also a trait he doesn't bring out for everyone,
and I love that he does so for my mother.

"Morning, Hunter." She lets go of my arm, waving her pale
hand in the air. "I can go in the backseat, it's okay."

"No, ma'am. The best seat we save for the best girl." A boyish
grin splits his face that makes that damn flutter slice through my
stomach again, the twinkle in his eyes not helping matters.

"You heard him, Charlotte. Get in." She attempts to shove me toward the passenger seat, but I plant my feet in the grass, shaking my head.

"He doesn't mean *me*, Mama. I'm pretty sure he means you."

"She's right. This girl wouldn't be here without you, so you automatically triumph over her." Any other girl might have been offended, but for me, it's the opposite. It only swells my heart to epic proportions. I fold my arms in front of my body, nodding my head in agreement while her face moves back and forth between the both of us.

"I'm too tired for this discussion." She shoots us an amused glare, then gets herself into the truck. Hunter gives me a questioning look while we watch her struggle, but I softly shake my head. It's a big effort for her to climb into the damn thing, her lack of energy being as heavy as a ball of chain, but I get into the backseat without helping her, knowing she wants to do it by herself.

Following my lead, Hunter climbs behind the wheel.

"Thank you for taking us, Hunter." Mama pats his hand when we are on our way to the hospital, while I watch the conversation unfold between the both of them from the backseat.

"My pleasure, ma'am."

"Please, call me Liz," she tells him, but he reluctantly shakes his head.

"I don't know, ma'am. My mom might not be doing a superb job at parenting right now, but my dad taught me some common rules, and he would turn around in his grave if I start calling you by your first name after such a short time."

"I think he'd make an exception when he knows you'll be in my daughter's life until the day you die, won't he? Practically makes you family."

Hunter turns his face toward her with a look I can't really decipher, then quickly glances over his shoulder. Pinning brown eyes collide with mine, my pulse a jackhammer for no more than two beats, before he twists his head back.

"Yes, ma'am."

"Good. Then from now on, it's Liz." I can hear the smug tone in Mama's voice, letting us know this is the end of the conversation, and I stifle a laugh.

Mama likes Hunter. She doesn't say a lot about him, and she barely asks. But I can see it in her eyes, in the way she talks to him, and the fact that she treats him like family, no matter what time of day it is. She makes him feel welcome, and it means the world. To him *and* to me.

It takes us no longer than ten minutes before we arrive at the oncology department of the hospital, and I help my mom settle in while Hunter quietly looks around him. The room holds four armchairs, each with an IV stand, even though only one is occupied. He's never gone with us before. Normally, he just drops us off or waits for me back at the house while I take his truck. But this time, he insisted on coming. Said that he wanted to be there for me through the good and the bad. I was thrilled he offered, thinking he'd be a welcoming distraction from all the dreadful faces that roam around the hospital, but taking one glance at his troubled expression makes me wonder if that was a mistake.

"You okay?" I mouth to him when he flicks his gaze up to mine, and he replies with a nod. The silence is taken away when the only woman in the room dramatically clears her throat.

"Morning, Mrs. Parker." My lips curl as I look at the old lady shamelessly eyeing Hunter. She's the epitome of a southern older woman, looking fabulous, her gray hair styled without even a strand out of place, and the same amount of sass still running through her body as when she was sixteen, so I've heard. She's seventy-five, and even though this is the third time she's going through chemo, she refuses to die. She makes these visits a little less depressing.

"Good morning, Charlotte. Is he yours?" An approving look appears, her pearls tugged between her red-painted fingers, while Hunter gives her a wink before I can reply. *Cocky asshole.*

"Something like that," he replies. His discomfort has suddenly evaporated when he saunters toward her with the grace of a fucking prince, then offers his hand.

"Name is Hunter, ma'am. Hunter Hansen. Pleasure."

She jerks his arm a little closer, holding it a tad longer than necessary, as she shamelessly lets her other hand stroke his toned bicep. I can barely cut back a chuckle, watching how he's completely getting manhandled while I help my mother into the chair.

"Fiona Parker. The pleasure is all mine, *Hunter.* You're a bad boy, aren't you?"

"No, ma'am." He shakes his head with a snicker.

"Then why do you have knuckles like they run into a wall on a daily?"

"I fight for some extra cash, ma'am."

Her eyes lower to slits, her eyebrows pulled together. "Why do you need the extra cash?"

Hunter clears his throat, briefly locking his gaze with me before flicking his attention back to Fiona. "To give myself a better life after graduation." He shrugs, his cockiness suddenly leaving the room for a brief moment. "Take care of those who matter." His eyes meet mine for a split second, my heart stuttering.

The air crackles under Fiona's silence, her features changing as if she's trying to form an opinion. "Bless your heart, boy. If that's your attitude, you'll get there. Work hard and stay true to the people you love. Including yourself. You're a good boy."

He awkwardly pushes out a smile. "Thank you, ma'am."

She lets go of his arm, putting her focus on me. "You did good, Charlotte."

"We're just friends," I explain.

"Who told you that *bullshit*?" Fiona blurts, pulling a little gasp from my throat.

"They both did," Mama counters.

"Hey! It's not me!" Hunter scoffs with a playful glint haunting his expression.

"Oh, God. What is it with kids these days? What is it y'all are calling it? Playing hard to get? Let me tell you something, life is too short for that bogus. You gotta grab that girl and kiss her." She raises her arm with a balled fist, roaring the words as she frowns at Hunter. Hunter studies Fiona as if he's weighing out the pros and cons in his head, then he shrugs. "I can do that."

Without hesitation, he aims his frame at me, coming my way with a stroll that lifts his cheeks more with every step he takes. I freeze, my lashes frantically feathering my cheeks until he's almost in front of me, with a dark film falling over his eyes.

"Stop flirting with me!" I yelp.

He presses a smile between his lips, then raises his arms up in a placating way before he flops down in the vacant armchair beside me. "See? It's not me."

"Oh, it's your daughter who's being a pain, Liz," Fiona concludes.

"Hunter, shut your pie hole," I hiss, rolling my eyes.

"Nah, it's really both of them." Mama chuckles while I hand her a magazine, closing my eyes to ignore their ridiculous comments. "But that's okay. They still have time. I'm sure one of them will get their head out of their ass soon enough. Preferably, *before* I die."

"Okay," I wail, with a tone to end the conversation. "Hunt and I are going to see if there are any snacks, so you two can talk about us without giving me the unwanted pleasure of hearing whatever y'all have to say about it."

I grab Hunter's arm, dragging him up before anyone can say anything else, and shove him into the hallway. "You know I'm never going to hear the end of this now, right?"

"Come on, Charls." He swings his arm around my shoulder as we walk down the hall to the cafeteria, that same smug grin still on his face. "You gotta give that woman something to talk about. We could go back and give them even more by showing them our first kiss? I'm down if you're down."

I slap his arm. "Stop flirting with me, jackass."

"Fine," he growls, a chuckle seeping through the deepness of his voice.

When we arrive at the cafeteria, he buys us both some ice cream, even though it's only noon, and we take a seat at one of the tables near the window.

Leaning back against the chair, slightly slouching, I watch Hunter's tongue move out of his mouth over and over again to lick the chocolate off his Magnum. A wave of heat makes me blush, while a tingling feeling forms between my legs, my mind wandering to a place it shouldn't go. Would his tongue feel as good as I imagine it would on my body? Would it feel scorching on my neck? Would it be earth shattering to have him wrap his full lips over my center?

I keep my eyes fixated, unable to look away, slowly taking bites of my orange popsicle. He's looking out of the window, unaware of my mild form of voyeurism, while his tongue keeps twirling around the chocolate. Long intended strokes, switching between just the tip of his tongue to dragging the whole thing over the surface. I swallow hard, parting my lips, and accidentally let out a ragged moan when he sinks his teeth into the chocolate, taking a bite from the top. The sound snaps his head to mine, and his eyebrows move up when he notices the flushed look on my face.

"You okay there?"

Not-fucking-at-all.

"Hmm," I muse, putting my focus back on my popsicle, releasing a groan when I stick my teeth in the cold surface to literally cool myself down.

"You sure?" There's a hunger in his eyes that I know matches mine, and a smirk on his lips that tells me he knows exactly where my dirty head is. *God, I'm so busted.* His tongue darts out as he slowly licks his lips and shoots me a wink. And I automatically reply by rolling my eyes to the back of my head.

Asshole.

"Perfect."

"Okay." His shoulder jerks up, his eyes still filled with an amused glare, and I avert my gaze, lowering to his damaged knuckles.

"Will you ever stop fighting?"

"Why? Scared I'll get hurt?"

"Only your bloated ego." I stick out my tongue.

He sighs, dropping his focus to the table before it snaps back up to me. "Only if I have a good reason to quit."

"Like what?"

He's quiet for a moment before he says, "Like finding something that's more important."

My heart cracks. I hope he finds it. I hope one day, he'll find something he loves to do that doesn't involve him getting hurt.

"What happened with Demi last night?" I ask, trying to change the subject.

He lets out a chuckle while shaking his head. "Not much. She saw me talking to Kayla and apparently wanted my undivided attention. Got pissed, threw a fit, and went home." The words roll off his tongue, as if it was nothing, when really, it was a full on theater show. Very entertaining as well, if I have to believe Julie.

"You know what I don't get?" I lean my elbows on the table, and he nudges his chin in question. "It's common knowledge in this town that you sleep around, trading girls like they're baseball cards, yet they still want your attention. How?" I point my popsicle at him, shooting him an incredulous look. I don't miss the sharp edge of my tone, and I inwardly curse myself for letting my jealousy creep through. But regardless, it's true. I can't even keep up with the number of girls he allegedly sleeps with, yet it doesn't seem to stop any of them from throwing themselves at him whenever they get the chance. I get bored hearing about whatever chick is desperate for his attention this week, yet they keep swarming him like bees to honey.

It makes no sense.

"I don't trade you like a baseball card."

I blink at his answer, not sure what to make of that. "I'm different."

"Yeah." He lets out a sigh before the corner of his mouth curls in a sweet smile, a hint of pain ghosting his hazel eyes. "You are."

"But we're not talking about me. We are *friends.*" An invisible chord forms between us, made out of paper-thin steel. Solid, strong, but still able to snap within the blink of a second. I silently dare him to argue with me. To question our friendship.

"Right." *But he never does.* Instead, he mimics my stance, dropping the intensity that grows between us while he leans his elbows on the surface.

"I don't know, babe. I guess sometimes you have to pray that karma is on your side, and gives you a second chance." He playfully cocks his head with a smug look on his face, and I can't resist reaching over the table, softly slapping his head. "Ouch."

"You're an arrogant asshole." I plop back in my chair. "How you treat those girls shouldn't be giving you good karma, because you let them follow you around, giving them just a sprinkle of fairy dust of attention, even though you know you're not serious with them." I scowl. "It's like a fucking puppy farm."

"True." He leans back, slouching in his chair, licking his lower lip, then takes another bite of his Magnum. "But it's really more like a beehive."

My frown is deep and mocking. "How so?"

"Well, in a beehive, there are a shit ton of workers." He pauses, his expression darkening a bit. "But there's only one queen. The rest of them don't matter."

Pressing my tongue into my cheek, I hear his words. Yet, I'm scared to fully process them. He licks his lips with hooded eyes, then lowers his voice while a lump forms into my throat. "There's one girl I treat like a queen," he continues, his eyes locked on mine, "and I'm pretty sure that's where all my good karma comes from."

Fucking hell.

I narrow my eyes at him, pursing my lips, swallowing away the dryness in my mouth while his haze never deviates.

Like I'm all he sees.

Like I'm the only one who matters.

Fuck, I want to believe him so badly.

He's been sleeping around with a bunch of girls since we became friends, but not once did he give me the feeling I don't matter. I'm the one he puts everything aside for, making sure he can accommodate my every need. It makes me wonder if maybe I'm not crazy. If only I had enough balls to give in to the one need that aches the most.

"Tell me I'm wrong, Charls." The challenge is clear in his squinted gaze.

I shake my head. "You're not wrong, Hunt."

"One of these days, Charls," he says, his voice deep and husky, his words filled with promise, stopping my heart for a beat. "One of these days, I won't be able to hold back anymore."

A breath is stolen from my chest, and I almost drop my popsicle, before forcing myself to get it together.

"Stop flirting with me," I whisper, not being able to say it with as much vigor as I intend to because of the fluttering feeling in my core that wants to jump him.

He doesn't move a fucking muscle. Our eyes stay connected as the tension fills the air between us. I notice his Adam's apple bob when he swallows hard, and unintentionally, I part my lips.

"Fine." He glares before a boyish grin is conjured on his face. "Come on, let's go check on your mom."

The tension disappears in the blink of an eye when we get up, like it does every time we have these moments.

"One day, I won't be able to hold back anymore."

But what if I don't want him to?

HUNTER

I WALK UP CHARLOTTE'S porch steps, catching her sitting on the swinging bench with a thick blanket to keep her warm. Her dirty blonde strands sit on top of her head in a messy bun, pink fluffy slipper boots peeking out from under the wool. She looks adorable. It makes me want to pull her into my arms and cuddle her with my nose buried in her neck. She has her head stuck in her book, even though I know she heard me park my truck in her driveway.

"Babe, it's freezing. Why are you out here?"

Green eyes look up, a smile tugging at the corner of her mouth as she casually lifts her shoulders.

"I like the cold. Why are you not at the winter formal?" The look on her face is both amused and confused, and I can detect the hint of victory in her beaming blue-green eyes.

"I didn't want to go without you," I say, slowly sauntering to the bench with my hands in the pockets of my jeans until I'm right in front of her, towering above her.

"You had a date," she states.

"Yeah, turns out, the only date I want right now is the girl with her nose in a book."

"She probably wasn't happy."

She's right. Molly Kent was not happy when I told her I couldn't go and shoved her onto Jason's dateless little brother. But ever since I went to the hospital with Charls and her mom the other day, I don't really care for school shit any more. Walking the hallways of that hospital reminds me of death. The last time I was there, the doctors had just told my mom that my brother and father didn't make it. I know how fragile Liz is. I see it every single day when I walk over that threshold to help out wherever I can. But seeing Liz in that armchair get a bunch of chemicals pumped into her veins made me realize how close to death she might be. It makes things like winter formal feel stupid and like a waste of time if I can't share it with my girl. I asked her if she wanted to tag along with us, but I wasn't even a little surprised when she told me she'd rather read, keeping an eye on her mom.

Because that's Charlotte; loving and caring to a fault.

"My job of making girls happy is limited to the Roux family. Her last name wasn't Roux."

"Who says I'm not happy?"

"I was talking about your mama. Where is she anyway?"

"Asshole." She flips me off, and I smile in return.

I wave my hand in the air. "Scoot over."

"Nah, you can sit on the floor." When she turns her focus back to her book, I grunt, then push her forward.

"Shut up and make some room."

She lets out a dramatic sigh, faking annoyance, before she moves a bit forward so I can sit in the corner. She settles her back against my side, my arm draped over her stomach.

I like having her close, feeling her body against mine, knowing she's not going anywhere. But at the same time, I'm aware of every move I make, stopping myself from brushing the soft skin on her belly underneath her shirt.

Resisting her becomes harder every day. Every time she flashes me her bright smile, I want to take her face in my hands and kiss her.

"What are you reading?"

"Do you really care?" She twists her head with a dull look, giving me a full glance of her plump lips.

"No, not really." I chuckle, lowering my mouth to her hair. "How is your mom?"

She lets out another sigh, but this one definitely isn't fake. It's filled with worry, and I clench my jaw, hating how troubled she sounds.

"Sleeping. She's been throwing up all morning."

"How much longer?" I ask.

"Two weeks."

"Is there anything we can do?"

A discouraged hum drums all the way from her body to mine as she shakes her head. I can feel the unspoken emotion along with the unshed tears. My hand on her stomach moves up to cup her cheek, and I softly turn her vision back at me.

"You should've called me."

She pulls my hand away, avoiding eye contact, and I rest my hand back on her belly. "Didn't want my mother throwing up on your only tux, Hunt."

I laugh at her attempt to lighten the mood again. Even though it breaks my heart that I can't make life better for her. *Easier.* Wishing I could, somehow.

"I never put it on," I admit, staring into the cracks of wood on the porch. It was hanging on my door when I got home this afternoon, freshly picked up from the dry cleaner. It was my father's tux, and I was excited to wear it, but when I got it off the hanger to change into, something felt wrong. I didn't want to wear a tux that meant so much to me, when there would be a girl on my arm that meant so little. It's when I realized I'd rather spend my night with Charlotte. Making sure she's okay, knowing a seventeen-year-old girl shouldn't have to take care of her mother all by herself. When I do wear my father's tux someday, I want Charlotte on my arm. Even if that means I'm never going to wear it.

"Really?"

"Nah."

"That's a shame. I would've loved seeing you in a tux," she muses, to my surprise.

"Yeah?"

"Mmhmm." Her head falls against my arm.

"Well, maybe I'll put it on one day. Just for you."

"I'm holding you to that one. Don't tell the flavor of the month, though. It'll be awkward." I don't have to see her face to know she's rolling her eyes, and a scoff leaves my lips before I softly press them against her hair once more. The intoxicating smell of her flowery shampoo makes me want to stay there for the rest of the night.

"Any flavor of the month will have to deal with my favorite flavor, anyway."

"Yeah, don't tell them that either," she says, a smile audible in her voice.

"Shut up. Will your mom notice if we get out of here?"

"I wish. We could put up a Fourth of July fireworks show, and she will still be sleeping."

I brush my hand through her hair, knowing I made the right choice by coming here. Cheering up my girl is way more important than some stupid high school dance.

"You hungry, babe?"

"Always."

"Alright, let's grab something to eat."

HUNTER

"**D**AMN, THAT JENSEN GUY got some serious skills. I'd be surprised if he's not drafted soon." Jason takes another bite of his burrito, his eyes set on the TV.

"Are you kidding me? I heard the Knights already have their claws into him. He'll be in the NHL before he graduates from California State." I settle deeper into the velvet blue couch, relaxing my shoulders while rubbing my hand over my stomach. "Damn, I'm stuffed."

Jason glances over his shoulder, then throws a fist into my side that has me grunting. "It shows. When's your next fight? You're getting fat, buddy."

"Shut up, dickhead. You wish you were as ripped as me."

"And dodging fists for some cash? No, thanks." He holds his face with fluttering lashes. "I'm too pretty."

"As pretty as a doorknob." We both rear our heads over the back of the couch with a glare. Jacob stands in the kitchen, an annoying grin spreading his cheeks. Being a college quarterback, his frame is broad and his arrogance through the roof. Pale blue eyes glint at us from above his water bottle as he takes a sip. *He looks like a fucking douchebag.*

"Shut up, Jake." Jason quickly turns with a clenching jaw, not wanting to give his big brother even an ounce of energy. But I can't resist.

I hang my arms over the couch, twisting my body to face him better. "How are you doing, Jake? Sorry, you didn't make the play-offs."

His jaw ticks with a dark expression washing over him, knowing I've hit a nerve. "Shut up, you pathetic fighter boy. I'll talk to you when I'm in the NFL and you're still doing underground fights." Jacob runs a hand through his short blonde hair. It's eerie how much he looks like Jason, even though they are nothing alike.

My chest elevates with a loud laugh, daringly holding his gaze. "If you keep playing like that, you'll be lucky if you can get a janitor job at the Raleigh Rebels."

With a death stare, he runs his tongue along his pearly white teeth.

Jacob Spencer doesn't scare me. He's a bully to his younger brothers, and he was a bully in high school, but he knows I can take him any time of day if he'd give me a chance. He might be a few years older, but that doesn't mean shit.

"You need better friends, *fuckface*," he calls out to Jason.

"I need a better brother," Jason counters.

"Whatever." He screws the cap back onto the bottle, then throws it at our heads. I can easily duck, and it lands in front of the TV.

I shake my head with a taunt. "You're gonna need to put a little more practice in that arm if you ever wanna become a Panther."

"Good idea, Hansen," he says, an ominous expression in his narrowed eyes. "Maybe I'll ask Julie to help me with that tonight."

Jason snaps his head to his brother. "What? You're going to Julie's?"

"What's the matter, baby bro? Jealous?" Jake coos with a look that I want to wipe off his face.

"Don't treat her like shit!" Fire fills Jason's eyes as he points a piercing finger at his brother. His jaw is solid, and I frown at the lack of context I have.

"Find your own girlfriend, fuckface. I'm out." Jake leaves the room with a mock salute, and Jason turns, then rests his elbows on his knees.

"He's dating Julie?"

"More like Julie's dating *him*. I saw him with some exchange student from his class last Tuesday."

I push out a breath. "Of course, you did. Did you tell her?" Jason and Julie are not friends like Charlotte and I are. But I know they have been friendly ever since Charlotte and I started hanging out.

He gives me a bit of a pained expression, conflict bouncing in his eyes. "No. He said it wouldn't happen again."

"Jason." I tilt my head.

"What, man? He's my brother. She's, technically, nothing to me."

"He's an asshole and you're her friend."

"I can't just rat him out like that. It was just one time. He said she was helping him with some kind of paper."

My eyebrows move into my hairline. "And you believe him?"

"I'm not stupid, Hunt." His eyes drop to the floor before they flick back up. "I'll tell her if it happens again. Don't tell Charlotte!"

"You're really gonna do me like that?"

"Come on, man."

I lift my snapback from my head, rubbing a hand over my hair. "I don't know, man. I don't wanna lie to her."

"It's not lying. Just don't *tell* her."

I glance at my best friend, whose frown gets deeper by the second. I'm not sure why he's trying to cover for his dickhead brother, but then I remember I'd probably do the same for Logan if he was still here. I'd kick his ass for cheating, but I wouldn't rat him out either.

"Fine," I growl. "She won't hear it from me. But if she asks, I'm not going to deny it," I add with a little more force. There's no way I'm going to flat out lie to Charlotte.

Her trust means too much to me.

"Thank you." His shoulders relax a bit and the corner of his lip curls in a crooked smile.

"Oh, God." I roll my neck. "What now?"

"Are you and Charlotte making it official yet?"

"We're *friends*," I splutter, even though the word "friend" starts to leave an acid taste in my mouth. For someone who doesn't want to lie to the girl who means the most to him, it sure feels like I'm lying every time I say it.

Jason gives me a dull stare. "You really gonna sit there and tell me you don't want to tap that?"

Before my brain registers my movement, my palm connects with the back of his head. "Don't fucking talk about her like that!"

"Geez." Jason chuckles, rubbing his scalp. "I didn't mean it like that, asshole. There's no disrespect. I'm not my brother."

"You better not."

"All I meant was..." he continues, "did you make a move yet?"

"No." I fix my gaze back on the screen. "And I'm not gonna."

"Why not?" He says it with a level of ridicule, as if it's as weird as a summer storm in December.

My lashes lower a bit as I roll my lips together. *Because making a move could end in disaster.* I need her more than I need to have more of her. It makes perfect sense in my head, but I know it sounds stupid when I speak it out loud.

8

"For what it's worth, I think she feels the same."

I jerk my head, colliding with Jason's blue eyes that hold somewhat of a dare.

I hope she feels the same. I *think* she feels the same. And trust me, there have been numerous moments in the past month when I wanted to say *fuck it* and finally give in to that desperate urge to seal my lips with hers.

But we graduate in two months.

"School is almost over."

"And...." Jason drawls.

"And I'm leaving," I rebuke with a tone that says *duh*.

"I mean? You could stay?"

Stay? I could stay? It's a thought that hadn't even crossed my mind, but as soon as it sparks a little hope in my chest, I fling it away.

"As much as I'd do anything for that girl, I can't stay." Staying would be selfish, because I know I can never give her the future she wants. *She deserves.* "As soon as we graduate, I'm taking my truck and I'm out of here to find whatever fight I can find until I get the AFA's attention. Staying in Braeden isn't an option."

"Why not?" Jason argues. I don't miss the little squint of his eyes that tells me I'm being stupid. But he doesn't get it. He doesn't get that a girl like Charlotte deserves to have it all. My all will never come close to that.

"Because I'll never be good enough for her."

19

Charlotte

T HE SPRING SUN CREEPS onto the wood of the porch, a melody of birds serenading me from my swinging bench. It's awfully hot for an April day, and I welcome the summer with a sweet tea, enjoying the warmth on my skin. With a book in my lap and my body settled deeply into the cushions, I read the next sentence, when I hear the rumble of Hunter's truck as soon as it drives onto my street. I'd recognize that sound anywhere, and every time it tingles a giddy feeling alive. Twenty seconds later, he parks in my driveway like he owns the place, and part of me feels like he does. The last six months, he's been entwined in my life so deeply that I can barely remember what life looked like without him. He's been helping me take care of my mom, driving us to the hospital, hanging out with me when I don't want to leave her alone, helping me study or doing my best to take my mind off everything whenever he gets the chance. Going for burgers and ice cream with him is my favorite thing to do, even though it rivals simply sitting on this porch with him and looking up at the stars.

He's my rock, and I don't know if I'd be able to graduate this year if he wasn't.

I assess how he gets out of his truck, wearing gray sweats that ride low on his hips, and a white t-shirt that hugs his muscled arms.

Fuck, he's getting hotter every day.

He seems to get bigger the more he fights, training his ass off when he's not hanging out with me. The sight of it makes it harder and harder for me to deny I don't want to explore every inch of his body. Because after imagining it in my fantasies for months now, there's nothing I'd want to do more.

A smug grin splits his gorgeous face that doesn't fully reach his eyes as he walks up the porch steps. *Something is up.*

"What are you doing?"

I hold up my book.

"Of course."

"I thought you were going to the creek?" I ask, referring to the conversation we had on the phone this morning. I know the water is still stone cold, but there are always some crazy boys from school that think it's a good time for a swim whenever it's above sixty degrees out.

"I am." He easily lifts my feet, then takes a seat next to me and puts them back on his lap. His hands never let go of my heel, a tight grip burning through my sock.

"But?" I know that look on his face. "You had another fight with your mom?"

"Hmm." He brushes his hand through his hair, avoiding my gaze as he stares at the wood on the porch. I hope he'd fight less with his mom, considering he wasn't home much anymore. But lately, she's been getting into it with him every time their paths cross.

"You wanna talk about it?"

"Maybe later."

"Okay."

I could push him, and he would tell me. He's walked up my porch in this state many times before, but his entire stance right now tells me he just wants to '*be*' instead of talk. We sit there for a few minutes, his hands resting on my legs, while I do my best to read the words in front of me. Which is fucking useless, because I hate seeing him like this, all lost in his own thoughts, looking like he carries the weight of the world on his shoulders. I've been tempted to ask Mama if he could stay with us until we graduate, but ever since Mama's latest chemo hit her like a ton of bricks, I don't want to give her the feeling she's got another kid to take care of, when she can barely take care of her own.

"Come with me?" he finally blurts, and I glance up from my book, then offer him a skeptical look.

"I don't really like parties, you know this." I'm not the type of girl who drinks, nor do I enjoy talking to a bunch of strangers. As much as I hate to admit it, half of the people in my class are strangers to me. It happens when you're too busy taking care of your mother instead of going to social events.

"I know, but I feel like shit, and you're the only one who makes it better." He has a pleading look on his face that pulls a loud exhale from my lungs. I don't take any shit from anyone, having no issues telling people no when I have to... but Hunter Hansen can give me looks that make me forget I even have a spine in my body. "Come with me. We will hang for a few hours, and then we'll get some burgers, just you and me. *Please.*"

I roll my eyes at his low attempt to entice me with food, even though I know I'm going with him, anyway. I don't like him being alone in this state. It makes him act like more of an ass than normal, and I'd prefer his black eyes to not come at all or from the fights he actually gets paid for. Letting him go to the creek by himself right now seems like a disaster waiting to happen.

"Fine," I groan, rolling my neck when my eyes move to the back of my head.

"Thank you." He takes my hand, pressing a kiss on my palm, shooting me a thankful look. Feeling his scorching lips on my body has a shudder running through me, and I lick my lips before I suck in a deep breath to push the flutter back in his cage.

"Ditch me for one of your bimbos, and I will never talk to you again." I lift my finger in the air with a reprimanding tone before he snatches it, pulling me closer. My heart is setting a pace that's as close as a beating drum. Strong, pounding, nerve-wracking. His brown eyes look right through me while I glance at his lips.

"Never, babe."

We arrive at the creek about fifteen minutes later, and I'm relieved when I notice Julie's car on the lot, relaxing the muscles in my back a bit. My eyes roam around the grass, looking for her honey blonde head of hair while there are about thirty people from our class, all dressed in swimming gear, either hanging out around the firepit in the middle, or swimming in the water. I exit the truck, letting my body slide down the side of the vehicle.

"Hey," Hunter booms from the driver's seat, and I turn around to meet his thoughtful gaze. "Tell me when you want to go, okay?"

The look in his eyes tells me he means it, but I'm determined to do my best to be a normal senior today, instead of wanting to go back home and check on Mama.

I nod, slamming the door shut, and he does the same. He pulls a bag with towels out of the trunk, then he wraps his arm around my shoulder, walking us toward some of his friends.

"Charlie!" The familiar voice of my friend reaches my ears before I see her, and I turn around just quick enough to catch her when she launches her body into mine. "You're here! I thought you didn't want to come?" Julie screeches.

She lets go of me, putting her feet back on the ground while I look into her cheerful face. Part of me expected her to be a daredevil wearing a bikini, but it's still hidden by shorts and a thin knitted white top.

"I didn't." I chuckle, briefly locking my eyes with Hunter's.

She frowns, looking over my shoulder.

"Of course." She gives me a wink, wiggling her eyebrows in a playful way. "He's hard to resist, isn't he?"

"Shut up, Julie. He's my friend." *God, I'm starting to hate that word.*

"Ugh, for crying out loud, when are the two of you going to take the plunge, anyway? You're not getting any younger." She rolls her eyes, linking her arm in mine, dragging me to the edge of the water. Flicking my head over my shoulder, I give Hunter an apologetic look while I mouth to him that I'll be right back.

Julie forces us both on our asses, and I take my Converse off to dip my toes in the water. The water is cold as fuck, no surprise there, and I let out a small screech.

"How are people swimming now? It's fucking cold." I glance at the boys, who launch themselves into the water by the rope hanging from a tree.

"They say it's not as bad when you get in." She pulls a face. "I say they're crazy."

I let out a chuckle, and we fall silent, an invisible tension forming between us.

"How are you, girl? Homeboy over there won't let you out of his sight." She playfully bumps her shoulder against mine, as she nods her head toward the boys behind us, and I let out a half chuckle. My fingers play with the grass between my legs while my eyes peer into the water in front of me. We haven't been hanging out in a while because I'm always taking care of my mother, and Hunter claims every other free minute of my time. I know she doesn't hold any grudge about the fact that I'm spending most of my time with Hunter, but I still have this guilty feeling inside of me that nags me now and then.

"I know," I confess. "He's hard to shake."

"Do you want to shake him?" She eyes me, her lips pursed in a smug grin.

"No. No, I don't." I shake my head, throwing snippets of grass into the water, turning my head to glance behind me. Quickly, my eyes lock with Hunter, who's giving me a boyish grin and a wink that makes my heart purr in delight before I turn back around. Heat is flushing my neck, and I let out a sigh, torn about the fact that I feel happy when he's around. *Safe.*

"How are things with Jacob?"

She volleys me a stink eye, seeing right through my path of deviation.

"Never date a college guy, girl." A bitter smile crosses her face. "They are fickle as fuck."

"Not so good then?"

Her entire posture slumps as she fixates on the ground with a vacant stare.

"It's good. In fact, it's great." Bambi brown eyes move back up to me. "When he's actually with me."

"What do you mean?"

A deep, weighted sigh puffs up her chest, the gravity audible enough to pinch my heart a bit. "Jacob and I are great together when he's with me. But when he's not? I have no clue what we are."

"That sucks, Jules."

I can see the unshed tears glimmering in her eyes, but she pushes them away with a tight smile. "I know. I'm gonna talk to him."

Within the blink of an eye, her defeated stance evaporates, and she sits up.

Here we go.

"So..." Julie starts, a judging tone etching through her voice while she throws a pebble into the water. "When are the two of you getting your heads out of your asses?" she asks, repeating the question from earlier.

My eyes widen as I turn toward her, throwing my head back with rolling eyes. "I wish everyone would stop asking that. We are just friends, *Jules*." A scowl that's answered with a look that says I'm full of shit.

"You guys are really persistent with your *'friendship.'*" She brings her hands up, making quotation marks in the air as she emphasizes the word. "Yet, the longing looks say it all."

"What?" I squeal, a little indignant. "We don't share longing looks."

I'm so full of shit.

"Sweetie, you guys share nothing *but* longing looks."

I push out a frustrated breath, glancing over my shoulder again to make sure no one can hear us. "It's complicated, okay?" Maybe if Hunter didn't have such a fucked-up childhood, I would have taken the plunge by now. But I'm scared it won't work out and we won't be able to save our friendship. He'll be left with nothing. *Again.*

"Oh, now you're going with the Facebook status of your relationship?"

"It's not a relationship," I hiss, shooting her a glare. "We're friends. That's it."

"Charlotte Roux, you really wanna lie to my pretty face, and tell me you don't love that boy?" She cocks an eyebrow with a look full of sass.

"Of course I love him." I shrug. It was never about me not loving him. I think I've loved him since the moment I stepped into his truck that night. "He's my best friend. I love you too."

It's one thing to feel more for your best friend than you're supposed to feel. But actually voicing it makes the world go to shit, because before you know it, everything changes. I can't handle change. Not right now. Not when I have no clue if my mom will be around next year. I feel like our friendship is all we've got. And I can't lose that. Neither of us can.

"Don't bullshit me like that. You don't love me enough to want to kiss me. But you love him enough to do a lot more than that. And I sure as fuck know he does."

"What do you mean?" I snap my head toward her.

"Are you kidding me? Girl, that boy is head over heels in love with you."

"No, he's not," I blurt, incredulous, my heart galloping away from me.

"Oh, please. You don't actually believe that, right?"

I blink at her slight scowl, not even knowing what to say, trying to process what she's telling me.

"What makes you think he's in love with me?" I finally whisper, glancing at the boys.

"One, it's written on his face. Two, he doesn't see any other girl than you. Three, he has been flirting with you from day one. Four, he keeps sabotaging your dates. Five—"

"Okay, okay, I get it," I interrupt, trying to shut her up, not wanting to hear any more at this point.

"There is a whole list, really."

"He sees other girls."

"Not anymore." She shakes his head. "Trust me, girls are complaining about it."

"You wanna tell me he hasn't slept with anyone in the last couple of months?" I find that very hard to believe.

"Where would he find the time, Charlie? He's with you *all* the fucking time."

My lips press together, not wanting to believe her. I mean, I know he's with me all the time, but I figured he just meets up with girls whenever he leaves my house. Even if that's at one or two a.m.

"We're just friends," I say again when I have no clue what else to say.

"Even if he is? Do you want to be *just friends*?" The look on her face grows serious. She reminds me of a young Dolly Parton, a real southern belle with the sass to match. She's playful, always looking for fun, but the stern expression in her eyes tells me she's not trying to be funny right now.

I swallow hard, fully aware of the answer to that question.

"Maybe," I admit, pushing out a breath.

"Well, all I know...?" she says as she looks over her shoulder. "It's a *definitely* for him."

20

HUNTER

THIS WAS A MISTAKE.

I take in the people hauling themselves into the creek. Girls squeal when their hair gets wet. Boys holler when they lift into the air by the swinging rope they set up on the big oak on the riverbank, before they crash through the water. A group of guys is trying to light a fire, now that the sun is slowly setting behind the tree line.

But it's all a blur looking at it with my dark mood.

My mother's words still echo through my head like church bells ringing every hour.

"I can't wait until you graduate and get the fuck out of here."

She doesn't mean it was the first thing that snapped into my head. *She's drunk, but she doesn't want you to leave. She'll miss you once you're gone.* But I'm at the point where I need to stop telling myself these lies and accept the fact that my entire family died that night. Including my mother.

I thought coming here was a good idea. That it would push away my thoughts, maybe cheer me up a little, but I was wrong.

It only makes me realize I don't want to be surrounded by people right now.

I just want one.

My eyes keep glancing back at Charlotte. She sits near the creek with Julie, occasionally dipping their toes into the water. She looks relaxed, more relaxed than I've seen her for a while. I don't want to ruin it for her, but at the same time, all I want to do is drag her out of here and hang out in my truck.

I let her be for a while, knowing she hasn't seen Julie in a long time. But at some point, I can't keep up with whatever Jason and the boys are talking about as we hang out on the tailgate of Jason's truck, and before I know it, I jump off.

"Where are you going?" Jason bellows behind me.

"I'll be right back."

I saunter over to check on her, aching to hold her in my arms after the day I had.

Julie's hair sways over her shoulder as we lock eyes. "What's up, Julie?"

"Coming to claim your girl again?" she jokes, wiggling her eyebrows at me as Charlotte twists her body to look up at me too.

"Only if she wants me to." I shrug, my eyes locking with Charlotte's. "Hey."

"Hey."

"You okay?"

"Mmhmm," she muses, giving me a coy smile.

"You wanna go?"

She stays quiet, her eyes moving back and forth over my face, as if she's trying to decipher my mood. I'm praying she can read between the lines, decoding the words I can't say out loud. *Let's get out of here. I just want to be with you. I need you.*

"Nah, we can stay. It's okay."

Fuck.

"You sure?"

"Definitely."

"Alright. You wanna come hang with me for a bit?" I lift my snapback to run a hand through my hair, putting it back on my head backwards. She stays quiet, biting her lip, looking cute as hell, and I do my best to suppress a groan.

Just tell her, man.

"I'm gonna stay here, okay? Hang out with Julie and catch up."

My ribs tighten as a cold breeze rushes through my core. She eyes her friend, and I nod in agreement, even though deep down my heart is saying no.

"Yeah, of course. Just let me know when you wanna leave." I don't wait for her reaction, walking straight back to the rest of the boys. I have no right to be mad, disappointed, or act like an asshole. Still, I can stop the agitated feeling forming inside of me, and I ball my fists. I ended up at Charlotte's doorstep because I needed her when my mom decided to fuck me up in the head. I need her to pick me back up, and tell me I'm not a little shit like my mother keeps mentioning. That I'm useless, or I won't ever get out of this shit town. I know my drunk mother is full of shit, but still, I have this nagging voice in my head that tells me she's right. That I'm doomed to spend my days out here, not getting any further than a shit job in Raleigh. It's feeding my insecurity every time she rants against me.

But Charlotte?

Charlotte makes me forget.

She builds me up, just being with me, existing beside me, comforting me without saying a word. I need her. *Just her.* And I was stupid enough to suggest coming here for no fucking reason. Now I feel this urge to drive my fist into something, proving my mother she's right.

I am a piece of shit.

I push myself up to take a seat on the tailgate of the truck we're standing next to, and I reach my hand out to Jason, standing next to the cooler. The skin on my body feels tight, making it hard for me to breathe as I glance at the two girls again.

"Yo, can you hand me a beer?"

Jason hesitates with a frown, pissing me off even more. "Are you okay?"

"I'm fine," I bark out.

"Sure? Because you usually don't drink."

"I do now." My dark glare silently tells him to fuck off.

There's a stunned flutter of his lashes, challenging me with a single look, but I can't fucking find the fucks to give right now. I need to stop feeling, before I do something that I'll regret.

"We've been friends for years, and all the times you had a drink is countable on one hand. What's going, Hunter?"

"Just give me the damn beer, Jay."

"Alright." He rolls his eyes as he grabs a beer, twisting the cap with a lighter, then hands it to me.

"Thanks."

"You gonna be alright, man?" he asks with a tilt of his head.

I shoot him a fake smile, taking a pull from my beer. The hoppy flavor attacks my taste buds like it did when I drank for the first time, but I ignore it, just chasing the effect of the alcohol.

"Peachy."

There's one thing my mom taught me.

Alcohol is bad.

Showing me all the bad things that come from alcohol made it easy for me not to drink. I'm a bad boy. I'll kick your ass if you

8

challenge me, in and out of the cage. I ditch school if I get the chance, and I'm graduating, but only *barely*.

But you wouldn't ever see me drunk.

Until tonight.

Having zero tolerance, I'm feeling wasted as fuck after six beers and a couple of shots, entertaining everyone with my fast comments.

Everyone except Charlotte.

And Julie, who keeps looking at me like she wants to rip my head off and put it on a stick.

The twilight is setting in, and we're all sitting on big logs around the firepit. I failed to keep up with the conversation for the last, who knows how many minutes, so instead I focus my heavy lashes on the blonde sitting in my lap. She smells so sweet it's disgusting, and every now and then, I squint my eyes, wondering how much of her face is real and how much comes from a bottle.

She's hot.

I think. I'm not sure, because my brain seems to have a hard time figuring out what it needs. She purrs in my ear, burying her nose into my neck.

"You wanna get out of here?" The fake husky voice makes me cringe, but for some fucked-up reason, I keep her on my lap. Having no restraint whatsoever, I glance at Charlotte, who's eying me from the other side of the pit, still sitting with Julie instead of me. After the second beer, I went into full dick mode, barely acknowledging her as I gave my attention to the first girl who came along that wasn't her. At first, I felt guilty, feeling the girl's lips on my neck, while my eyes stayed locked on Charlotte, looking at me with a disappointed glare as I gave her a daring one.

If she wants me, she can claim me.

After the third, I didn't give a shit, and I started making out with Kim in plain sight, for everyone to see. Is her name Kim? Or is it Jen?

It's something short.

"Yeah, sure. Let's go," I reply.

My hands on her hips guide her up, before I do the same, needing a second to hold my balance, then I wave at Charlotte. Because apparently, I have a death wish.

She stares at me, unimpressed, a dull look plastered on her face.

"Come on, let's go, Charls," I bark.

It's funny, because there's this very loud, yet distant voice in my head that's yelling something like: *abort mission* and *don't fucking do it.* But it's not as loud as the voice that's telling me to live up to my reputation, since that's all I got left anyway.

Charlotte shoots Julie a confused look, who shrugs her shoulders in response. Then she gets up as I do my best to make sure the world stops spinning by taking deep breaths.

Charlotte walks past me, without giving me a second glance, stalking toward the truck with a scowl on her face. Wrapping my arm around Jen's neck, or Kim's, who knows, I tug her along with me, following Charlotte. Her hips do that swish swash thing you see in movies, her gorgeous waves bouncing with every step forward. Her anger is shown in every flick of her hips, and I bite my lip to suppress a moan.

When she reaches the tailgate, she turns around, holding her hand up. I like seeing Charlotte all riled up, making demands. She plants her hands on her sides.

"Keys." Her bark is loud, vibrating all the way to my toes. But then her luminous green eyes widen, a shocked expression cutting through my heart when she shakes her head, pointing at the girl under my arm. "Hold up. She's not coming."

Clearly unaware of the little vixen I just released with my dickish moves, the girl under my arm seems to think this is a good time to open her mouth.

"Excuse me, *bitch*. *You* are not coming." She takes a threatening step forward, and instinctively, I tug her back as Charlotte folds her arms in front of her body with an amused scowl on her face. Her eyes are shooting daggers, and the sweet girl I know is completely replaced by the sassy girl tucked inside of her. She doesn't let her out often, but when she does?

Fuck me, it steals my breath away.

"You better not be planning on fucking her in the back of your truck while I drive your drunk ass home."

I bite my lip at her words, her gaze fixated on mine.

What was my plan anyway?

Find a spot with this girl and fuck her until I'm sober? A year ago, it would sound like the perfect plan. But the fucking problem is... there's only one girl I want. And it's the thunderstorm standing in front of me. It's the reason I haven't slept with anyone in months, knowing they could never live up to the fantasy I have in my head.

"You've got some nerve, Hansen." The tone in her voice is low and menacing, telling me I need to be careful, but the damn alcohol inside me doesn't get the memo.

Just shut up, Hunter. "You can't tell me who I can or can't fuck. I'm fucking Jen tonight," I slur.

"Kim," I hear a voice clarify beside me.

Dammit, I knew it was Kim.

"Kim," I recover.

Charlotte stalks forward, pointing her finger against my chest, ignoring Kim beside me. I want to snatch her wrist and shut her up with my mouth crashing against hers. But her fury has me rooted, like a fucking bunny hoping the wolf won't rip out its neck.

You're a fucking pussy, Hunt.

"I *never* tell you who you can or can't fuck! Don't you dare pull that shit on me! I don't care who you fuck! I *never* cared who you fuck! But I do care about you dragging me out here, and then expecting me to leave with you and your flavor of the month." Her voice grows louder with every sentence she pushes out, showing her teeth as if she's about to bite my head off. *She might.*

I'd let her, because she's right.

Drunk Hunter doesn't agree, though.

Drunk Hunter thinks he can afford to be an asshole.

Drunk Hunter is a dumbass.

"Well, that was clearly a mistake, anyway," I sneer, lowering my head closer to her face, my fury matching hers. "I should've left you sitting on your damn porch." Our eyes stay locked, like two magnets unable to resist the pull. Kim and anyone else completely forgotten.

"I would've, if you didn't show up at my doorstep."

Without a second thought, I press my hand into her stomach, pushing her against the cold metal of my truck, caging her in as my breath starts to fan her face. I hear Kim mutter some shit behind me while my intoxicated body tries to stay focused on the girl I call my best friend.

"You want me to stop coming over?" I growl.

"I do if you're going to keep acting like an asshole!"

"I wouldn't be an asshole if I actually would've seen you tonight!" I roar, making her wince before the fiery look on her face turns into wildfire. I might be drunk, but I don't miss the silence that has formed around us, and I realize we've caught everyone's attention.

I'm totally fucking this up.

"How the fuck dare you?! You do *not* get to act like a baby, when for once my world doesn't revolve around you!" Her shouts are as feral as her eyes, yet she's still gorgeous as an angel. Her words expand the rock in my stomach, but before I can tell her she's right, she pushes me off her, slapping my face.

What in the actual fuck?

The feeling of her palm connecting with the skin on my cheek burns the intoxication right out of my body, leaving nothing more than the anger that's been the root of my energy the entire day. I roughly grab her wrist, pulling her flush against my body, my hand moving up to grip her chin, forcing her to face me as I glare down at her in a dominating way. My chest is heaving as I look into her fearless eyes.

"You know slapping me doesn't impress me anymore."

Her eyes slightly widen, putting her scowl back in place while I squeeze her chin out of frustration.

"You don't come to me for pity," she grates out. Time seems to stop around me as I take a deep breath to calm myself down, trying to find the right words rather than swing her over my shoulder and throw her into my truck.

"You're right," I rumble against her face, with a menacing tone, her eyes fluttering when my breath fans her face, "I don't. I come to you for support, because I fucking need you when everything else is going *shit.*"

"And I'm here," she howls, for everyone to hear. "What fucking more do you want, Hunter?" The ache in her eyes sobers me right up, but instead of pushing my asshole behavior to the background, all that it does is expand the fear I'm sensing.

She can't walk away too. I won't let her.

"*You*! I haven't seen you all night, even though you're here for *me!*"

"I can't do this." She frantically shakes her head. "I can't be at your beck and call, if all you do is take! A relationship is a two-way street, Hunter!"

"Shut up," I bark, increasing my grip on her face, unable to let her go.

I can't.

She slaps my hand away, trying to push me off her, but I keep a hold of her wrist, while her other hand tries to slap me again.

"Let go of me, asshole."

I wish I could. I wish I could set her free and walk away.

"Hunt," a deep voice growls beside me, and I find Jason glaring at me. "Let her go."

I grind my teeth, letting go of her wrist. She rubs the hurt skin on her arm, shooting me another glare while Jason approaches us, holding up his hand with a disappointed look on his face.

"Keys." Wanting to avoid a fight with both my friends, I reach into my back pocket, slamming my keys into his palm.

"Get in. Both of you," he orders as he climbs behind the wheel.

I glance at Charlotte, following his move until her fury-filled eyes snap toward me, shooting me deep in the chest.

"I'm calling shotgun. You can climb in the back, or the tailgate, for all I care, but don't you *dare* come near me." She pokes her finger into my chest, then rounds the truck to get into the passenger seat, and I bring my hand up, pinching the bridge of my nose while closing my eyes.

What the fuck are you doing, Hunter?

"Err, Hunter?" Kim's voice rings somewhere around me like a loud and screeching alarm when you want to sleep in. She's still here? *Fuck's sake.*

"What?" I twist my torso to look at the blonde I was planning to take home.

"We can go to my place? My parents aren't home until midnight."

Charlotte's door slams shut, and I wince. "Yeah, not gonna happen, sweetheart."

I went to Charlotte today, hoping spending my time with her would make this day at least somewhat better. Instead, I fucked it up even worse, hurting the one girl who is always on my side.

"Hansen, get your ass in," Jason barks at my back after he opens the window.

Rubbing a hand over my face, I look in front of me, locking eyes with Julie. I expect her to shoot me a glare, to be angry with me for fighting with Charlotte. God knows I deserve it all. But she sends me a sympathetic look as she purses her lips and shrugs her shoulders. I shake my head at her. The last thing I need is people feeling sorry for me. This is my own doing.

Spinning on the spot, strutting back to my car, I climb into the backseat.

Jason hits the throttle without waiting for me to have my seat-belt on, and I get pressed back against the seat. The suspenseful energy is filling the truck with tension, their anger feeling heavy on my chest, and I do my best to keep my focus on the road. My head feels fuzzy, and I take deep breaths, trying to get it together while my eyes stay focused on the girl in front of me. Her stance is rigid, ready to lash out at me if I dare to talk to her again.

I shouldn't talk to her.

But there is a lot of shit I shouldn't do, and the amount of alcohol still running through my veins doesn't seem to shut me up.

"Babe, I'm sorry."

"Don't fucking *'babe'* me," she growls, her tone dripping with adversity, keeping her gaze focused on the road in front of her.

"Okay." I bring my hands up in surrender, staring at the back of her neck through my lashes. "*Charlotte.* I'm sorry."

She snaps her body toward me, sending me a look that comes straight from the devil. Her eyes are greener than normal, glowing in the dark, and the stern look on her face makes me either want to hold her until she relaxes again, or hide in a corner, hoping she'll forgive me as time passes.

I swallow hard at the sight of it while she points her finger at me, her feral voice bringing goosebumps over my body.

"Next time you want to drink, you better leave me at home, because let me tell you something, *Hansen.* I'm not taking your shit. I'm your friend, and the minute you're going to start treating me like one of those bimbos—I'm outta here."

"*Best* friend," I whisper boldly, keeping my eyes locked with hers.

"That wasn't best friend behavior, asshole."

"I know. I'm sorry."

"Save it. You can tell me *that* when you're sober." She straightens her body again, as if she can't fathom to look at me anymore, and a sharp pain goes through my heart.

This is the exact reason why I can never cross that line with her. I'm doomed to hurt her. Maybe not all the time, maybe not at first. But in the long run, I'm not the guy you marry, living in a house with a picket white fence. I'm the bad boy from your youth, the one you tell your friends about when you're pissed at your husband.

"Will you forgive me?" I whisper, barely audibly, even though I notice Jason locking his gaze with me in the rearview mirror.

She lets out a frustrated sigh, running her hand through her silky hair.

"Ask me that tomorrow, Hunter," she breathes out, the fatigue noticeable in her voice.

Tomorrow.

Right.

21

Charlotte

M Y EARS REGISTER MY bedroom door opening before a heavy weight on the mattress makes me shift in the bed. I wrap my blankets over my shoulder, tugging myself deeper into the warmth of the sheets, then turn my head, expecting Mama's face there to tell me good morning. But a set of hazel-brown eyes peer down at me, regret in his gaze and fatigue on his face with his snapback on backwards.

"What the fuck, Hunt! What are you doing in my room?" I screech, my eyes widening in horror. He's been relentlessly crossing every line in the last few weeks, but appearing in my bedroom at the crack of dawn is a new one.

"Your mom let me in." He sits with his back against my headboard, his legs spread out in front of him, as if he's been doing this his entire life, with his signature smirk gently breaking through the surface of his handsome face.

Asshole.

"My mom le—What time is it?" I glance at the clock on my nightstand.

"Six a.m.," he answers casually.

"Oh shit, she couldn't sleep. Is she in pain?" I turn around so I can look up at him while keeping my body safely wrapped in my sheets. If my mom answered the door at six a.m., that must mean she's feeling like fucking crap, and probably has been hurling over the toilet the entire night. Thank fuck this was her last week of treatment.

"Yeah, think so," he admits with a troubled look before it softens. "Don't worry, I made her a cup of tea."

My scowl drops in favor of a tiny smile. "You did?"

He hums in agreement as the corner of his mouth curls in victory, knowing he scored some points with that.

"That's sweet." I suck in a deep breath through my nose, closing my eyes, ready to go back to sleep.

"Are you going back to sleep?"

"Hmm, yeah." I might be conceding to Hunter lying next to me, but I'm not going to entertain him at six in the morning. He was a dick last night, and even though I know he's here to make up, I'm not going to give it to him that quick.

"No, get up!"

I open one eye with a frown on my face.

"Why?" He's definitely not in the position to burst through my door and make commands. The little shithead took me to the creek when I didn't even want to go, and then he was planning on fucking one of his bimbos in the back of his truck while I was waiting? *Yeah, wrong girl, Hansen.*

"I got you a puppy."

"Really?" I quip with excitement, my lashes jumping up with hope.

"No," he deadpans.

"Fuck you."

"I wanna show you something," he says, softly.

"You have a phone. Just send me a photo." I glare, pursing my lips a little to keep myself from ending that sentence with *"asshole."*

"Get up," he groans with force this time.

I know he wants to push me out of the bed, but knows he's going to fuck up more if he does. I like being in this position, making him hold back in his dominant ways.

"It's Saturday," I state matter-of-factly.

"Exactly. A whole day to fill." He shoots me an excited look, giving me a slight push, and I keep my eyes locked with his, a scowl in place.

"I hate you, asshole."

His expression darkens a bit, that little spark of desire attacking my stomach. "There's a fine line between love and hate, babe."

"Stop flirting with me."

"Fine, but only if you get out of bed."

"Funny," I mock, "here I thought you preferred your girls in bed."

His gaze finds mine, blinking frantically while lust forms in his eyes, his chest moving up and down slowly, and I realize the mistake I just made. He stays quiet, licking his lips before he drags his teeth over them, looking frustrated as fuck.

"Don't tempt me." His glare is confusing. A torturous mix of annoyance, desire, and hope, and when his gaze drops to my lips, I remind myself of what happened last night.

Do I want to stay mad at him? *One hundred percent.*

Am I also curious about how he plans to make up to me? *Abso-fucking-lutely.*

I let out a growl, turning my body away from him, not able to look him in the eye any longer. "Ugh, whatever."

"Don't *ugh* me either. I'll wait downstairs." I feel the mattress shift, as he gets back on his feet, and I turn my head again, watching him towering above me, making him look even bigger than he already is. He grabs the back of my neck, then lowers his lips to my forehead. The warmth of his skin on mine has me lowering my eyes, catching my breath.

"Just trust me, okay?" He tilts my head to force my gaze to meet his. "*Please.*"

"Okay." I nod.

"If you're not down in ten minutes, I'm coming to get you."

"What?" I yelp, tugging the sheets up to my chin. "What if I'm naked?"

An evil grin appears on his face, and gone is his humble posture.

"Hmm, let's make it five."

"Stop flirting with me!"

He rolls his eyes, walking out of my room.

"Get dressed, Charls."

"What should I wear?" I call out to the hallway.

"Something that can get wet!"

"You better not be taking me to the creek for a swim!"

His head peeks back in, that boyish smirk way too cheerful for my mood.

"I'm the first to admit I'm stupid fifty percent of the time, but I'm not *that* stupid."

"You could've fooled me."

"I can fool anyone *but* you, Charls," he says before he disappears again, and I shake my head.

I'm not so sure about that.

Thirty minutes later, I'm sitting in the passenger seat of his truck, though not wholeheartedly. He was smart enough to get me a tea to-go, and a donut, making it easier for me to be slightly nicer to him, even though he's still number one on my shit list. I rest my head against the window, my eyelids still heavy, tempting me to close my eyes again as I watch the streets pass by.

I was so mad when I got home last night. I ignored the dozen texts he sent me, too raging with fire to type anything back that I wouldn't regret later. That was, until Jason sent me a quick message, and my rage turned into pain.

"He said something about his mom being right," it said.

And I realized exactly why he turned into a two-faced douchebag as soon as he decided drinking a beer was a good idea. I was fully planning to go to bed angry with a newfound determination to make him crawl back into my good graces. But when I remembered him telling me he got into another fight with his mother, my heart fucked my plan right over. Instead, I fell asleep with tears lingering in the corners of my eyes, wishing I could fix everything for him.

My sympathy doesn't excuse his behavior, though. Just because he's hurting, it doesn't give him the right to treat me like shit. Best friend or not.

We reach the end of town, and he drives his truck toward the mountains, making me wonder where we're going. He scans my profile, knowing I'm dying to ask, but instead I keep my jaw tight.

"Look, Charls..." He finally pushes out a breath, breaking our silence. "I'm sorry about last night, okay?" I keep my gaze focused on the road in front of me, taking a calculated bite of my donut. "I was a dick, and I should've brought you home."

"You should've never taken me there in the first place," I snarl.

"I wanted you there."

"Clearly, you wanted to fuck *Jen* more." I look into his guilty eyes.

"Kim," he jokes, and I pluck a piece of my donut to throw it at his head.

"Whatever, asshole."

"I did want you there, but you were with Julie the entire time, and Kim just... distracted me." His admission is sad, and even though it reaches my heart, it also snaps my anger back in place.

"So, it's my fault?" I sure as fuck hope he will choose his next words wisely, or I'll bitch slap the hell out of him. *Again*.

"No," he says with a firm shake of his head, then hits the brakes with more force than I anticipated, parking the truck on the side of the road. The sudden stop has me bouncing back and forth in my seat. My hair flops in front of my head, and I shoot him an incredulous look he chooses to ignore.

"It's not your fault. Nothing is ever your fault. I'm an asshole most of the time. You're my best friend, and the *best* thing I have in my life. Frankly, you're the only good thing I have in my life."

"That's not true," I whisper.

"It is," he chides. "It's fine. I know it, and I'm happy I have at least you. My mom was being a fucking bitch again. I take comfort in having you around. After those moments, I *need* to have you around. I know it's not fair to you, and trust me when I say, I'm trying to work on it. But yesterday, I needed you. When you weren't there, I did what I always did before I had you—distract myself with *chicks*." He emphasizes the word, and I turn up my nose. "Because that's what I do. That's what I've been doing for the last few years. No, it's definitely not your fault. It's my fault for being a weak fuck, not just asking for your attention when I need it, but instead burying myself into the girls who don't mean shit to me, when really, I should've just hung out with you and Julie." He drags his hand over his face, and I notice the desperation in his features.

I can literally feel my heart crack in my chest.

"Yeah, you should've," I agree, unable to hold on to my grudge. "But I get it. Just don't do it again. I'm always here for you, but if you need me, be with me. Don't tag me along like some accessory."

8

He lets out a relieved breath, relaxing his shoulders into his seat. Then, he rests his head back before that smug grin returns to his face.

"Hell, you're one hot accessory, though."

This boy.

"Stop flirting with me." I jokingly scowl, but also reach out my hand to him. He grabs it without hesitation, linking it with mine, then presses a kiss on it.

"We cool?"

I'm not sure, to be honest, because even though I can feel the anger simmer out of my bones, it hurts to question if he will ever be okay.

I nod with a coy smile. "Yeah, we cool."

"Thank fuck." He lets go of my hand, pulling the truck back onto the road, and I take another bite of my donut. The air in the vehicle feels lighter, instantly lifting up my mood.

"Where are you taking me, anyway?"

"You'll see." He throws me a wink that makes a deep sigh escape my lungs, a burning desire forming between my legs.

Fuck.

22

HUNTER

I TURN MY TRUCK into an open space between two trees as I turn off the engine and look at my best friend next to me. "Are you ready?"

She glances around, her eyes roaming the area that's in the middle of the woods without any sign of life in plain sight.

"Hunt?" she says carefully.

"Yeah?" I hold the door open, waiting for her.

"Is this where you're going to kill me?" She blinks.

"Kill you? Babe, I can't live without you," I cry out incredulously.

Letting out a chuckle, we both exit the truck while I reach in the back to get out my backpack. I hang it on my shoulder while she's waiting for me on the only path there is. When I reach her, I wrap my arm around her neck, tugging her along as I press a kiss to her hair, glad she somewhat forgave me for my asshole behavior from last night. I couldn't sleep. I was as drunk as a fiddler, yet I couldn't sleep, wondering if I lost her forever. Finally, I fell asleep around midnight and luckily woke up five hours later with a newfound determination to fix the damage I'd done.

"Nah, this is not where I'm going to kill you," I begin.

"Oh, thank God," she jokes, dramatically gripping her heart.

"This is where I'm going to kidnap you, and keep you for the next thirty years as my personal toy."

She stops in her tracks, our bodies disconnecting, and I turn around to look at the scowl on her face that makes my laugh echo through the woods. A bird rustles through the leaves of the noise as I lock my gaze with her jaw that fell to the ground.

"That's not even flirting anymore," she states, her hands firmly planted at her sides, though I can see the excitement in her eyes.

"So, now you *do* want me to flirt with you?"

"I didn't say that." She purses her lips with a busted look on her face before I turn around to keep walking with a smug grin on my own.

"You didn't have to."

"You're an asshole, Hunter." Her footsteps stomp behind me.

"But I'm *your* asshole, Charls."

I wasn't joking when I said I'm not sure how long I can resist this thing I feel for her. The feeling that makes me want to tear her apart and make her scream out my name. She's my best friend, but I'm not sure how long that will be enough for me. For both of us. Last night was a dead giveaway. Since the moment we started spending our days together, I loved getting that sparkle of jealousy from her. It filled my chest with pride and made me feel wanted. But last night was a whole different ball game. Last night was a desperate attempt to get her attention, and I hurt her in the process.

The more days that pass, the harder it becomes for me to let go.

And while at first, I could still keep my hands to myself, I catch myself physically reaching out to her more and more. Wanting to keep her as close as possible at all times.

We keep walking for about five minutes while she's huffing and puffing behind me, the occasional swear word leaving her lips.

"Are we there yet?"

I look up at the steep few yards we have to climb, and I reach my hand out to her.

"Almost." I give her a wink, laying her hand on mine, and I help her up the small hill until we reach the top. She sucks in a deep breath when she notices her surroundings, a look of awe forming on her face.

I bite my lip in satisfaction, pleased to see the exact reaction I was going for.

"Wow," she whispers, the corner of her lips curling into an amazed smile as she looks up at me. I mimic her expression when she pushes her body against mine in a side hug, and I wrap my arm around her. "This is gorgeous, Hunter."

"I know. My dad used to take us here," I explain while we look over at the waterfall in front of us that leads into a clear blue quarry. A line of trees hides this special place from the outside world, only traceable if you know where it is or you spot it from above. The water is deep in the middle, but the edge we are standing on gradually slopes down, making it the perfect spot to go for a swim. "My brother and I would go diving, while my mom and dad would keep an eye on us from the edge."

Her arms tighten around me, as if she's grateful I took her here.

"How has this still not been discovered by a bunch of touristy people?"

"Apparently, it's been some kind of secret in my dad's family. Wanting to keep it for themselves, my father didn't even let us take any friends when we were younger. It was the reserved spot for a family day."

She gazes up at me, and my eyes focus on her plump lips, looking perfect as ever.

"Well, I feel honored. Thank you for sharing it with me."

I bite my lip, resisting the urge to press them against hers, going for the second best option by planting a lingering kiss on her forehead.

"Who else would I share it with, babe? Come on, let's go swimming."

Grabbing the blanket out of the backpack, I watch how she takes off her Converse, then dips her toes in the cold water. Her eyes pop out of her head, her teeth pressed against each other.

"It's cold?" I chuckle, setting up everything I packed this morning.

She raises her fingers, pressing her thumb and index finger slightly together.

"Just a little."

Her feet slowly move toward me, and I plant my ass on the gray plaid blanket that I put over the pebble stones, tapping on the free spot next to me.

"Come, sit. We can wait a bit for the sun to get a little warmer."

She lies down, then closes her eyes while the morning sun warms our faces. It's another warm day for this time of year, and it won't take long before we'll be fried out here in the sun, but I don't care. All I care about is having her for myself all day, within the privacy of this special place.

"You're not going back to sleep, are you?" I softly poke her side.

She peeks one eye open, then closes it again.

"That's what you get when you, one"—she lifts her finger up in the air—"make me tired as fuck during the night by fighting with me."

"I—" I interrupt, ready to go into defense mode.

But she brings her other finger up with a shushing sound, making me press my lips together.

"And, two"—another finger lifts in the air, and I eye it amusingly—"wake me up at the crack of dawn. Who does that? Also, were you allowed to drive just now?"

"What? Of course, why?"

She pops onto one elbow, facing me while her head rests on her hand.

"Because I'm pretty sure you went back to the creek last night and had a few more drinks. Maybe even got laid. Anyway, chances are, you're still drunk." She rolls her eyes, and I push out a gasping breath. I know she's joking, but I'm taking this moment to push her buttons some more, anyway.

"One," I say, lifting my finger, just like she did, "I went straight home *after* we dropped you off." She cocks an eyebrow in disbelief. "Two. I didn't fuck anyone last night, but you already know that since we fought about it for ten minutes. And three, I'd never drink and drive."

"Good," she says with a satisfied look on her face, a smile curling the corner of her mouth.

I lie back, looking up at the sky, my hands folded on my stomach.

"You know, Charls. If it was anyone else, I'd think you might be a bit jealous."

"Right. You mean, just like how you sabotage every date I go on," she counters, and I slightly turn my head to look at her, met by an amused glare.

"Yeah, exactly like that," I admit, turning my gaze back to the sky. "I'm man enough to admit that."

She lets out a mocking huff. "That you fuck up all my dates, or that you're jealous?"

Her words reach my ear, and I pop onto my elbow, mimicking her stance while my free hand reaches out to cup her cheek, instantly making her face fall a little when I touch her. Her skin feels like velvet in my palm, and I want to move it lower to explore the rest of her body.

"I'm jealous," I concede. "I'm jealous, Charls. And yes. I'm not afraid to admit that." Her lips part, and I know she can feel the tension rising between us while I wait for her to say something.

"Why?" she whispers, her voice laced with desperation, though I'm not sure what kind. Is it desperate to be more? Or is it the hope to let things stay as they are?

"Because you're the most incredible person I've ever met. You're sweet, you're fun, you're easy to be around, and you're hot as fuck," I tell her, pulling a chuckle from her, "but most of all, you're my best friend. And even though I know it's not fair to demand your attention all the time, I can't help myself from feeling like I don't want to share *you*. Because I don't. I want you all for myself, because when I'm with you, *I* feel like myself."

"Is that why you took me to this quarry in the middle of nowhere?" she asks playfully, doing her best to remove the tension that is thick and demanding between us.

"Yes." I laugh. "That's exactly why I took you here. And I also have some making up to do after last night."

"You do."

My tone turns serious again. "I'm really sorry about last night, babe. I was hurt, and I don't think when I'm pissed. I never meant to hurt you, though." I give her a pleading look, hoping we can move past this again, and just be *us*.

Hunter and Charlotte.

Best friends.

Always.

A long, emotional exhale fans my face, her green eyes squinting just a little.

"I want to stay mad at you so bad," she confesses.

"So why aren't you? God knows I deserve it."

"No, that's the problem, Hunt." She spreads her fingers over my jaw, keeping me in place with a strong grip. Her touch burns through my skin, singing my groin alive. All I want to do is slide her on top of me and kiss her like she's never been kissed. But the sharpness of her gaze demands my attention.

"You *don't* deserve it," she points out, with a bladed tongue, "you don't deserve any of the crap you've been thrown at in life. But neither do I. We shouldn't take it out on each other. *Ever.*" Her hypnotizing eyes glitter with frustration, the heated feeling of her palm still fogging my mind. "You can't take it out on me. We have to be better than that. *You* have to be better than that. We have to stick together. Do you understand?"

I'm not sure how and why she walked into my life. Sometimes I wonder if my dad sent her to me. Or maybe Logan, since he always loved torturing me. Most times I realize I'm just fucking lucky that she sees something in me that I can't find. I keep waiting for the other shoe to drop, convinced one day life will break us apart. But right now, I'm just so fucking grateful I have her on my team. Even when I don't deserve it.

"Do you understand?" she repeats, commanding.

"Yeah, babe. I hear you." I pull her close, linking our foreheads as one.

"Promise me." Her breath feathers my lips, but I still don't give in. I don't silence her with the desire I've had for so long, because I don't want to betray her trust. I don't want her to think I'm not listening. I hear her, and I would promise her the world if I could. "I promise. You're right. If I could turn it all around, I would." I let go of her, a trembling feeling ignited in my core when she studies my face with a ghost of a smile.

"I know. It's okay."

I let out a relieved sigh, still noticing the fatigue on her face, feeling a bit guilty about the fact that she didn't get a lot of sleep last night because of me.

"You lay back, take a nap. I'll make sure there are no bears to come chase us out of the woods."

"Hunter." She flicks her chest up, leaning on her elbows. "There are bears here?"

"Don't worry. I've got bear spray."

"Right, that really helps my nerves," she says outrageously, and I push her body back against the pebble stones with a laugh.

"Just take a nap. We've got all day."

8

She fought me on the nap thing for another ten minutes, claiming she was fine, until finally she shut up and closed her eyes. It didn't take long until I noticed her breaths becoming slower and steadier, drifting off into a slumber.

Like the obsessed son of a bitch I am, I watched her for long minutes, taking in every inch of her features before I started playing with my phone, wondering what my life would look like without her in it. The thought alone makes me wanna hurl up my breakfast. Even if I can't have her all, when it comes to Charlotte, I will always want anything she'll give me.

When an hour later, the morning sun burns on our skin, she stirs awake, letting out a deep yawn. A groan escapes her lips, and I drop my phone to my side, turning my head to face her as she slowly opens her eyes.

"Morning, sleeping beauty." I rest my head on my arm.

"I fell asleep," she states, moving up on her elbows, as if I didn't already know. Her cheeks are a bit puffy, that cute 'just woken up' expression in her illuminated eyes.

She's fucking perfect.

"Yeah," I blurt, a clear *duh* tone in my voice.

"The sun is burning." She covers her eyes with her hands, squinting against the rays of sunshine.

"Yeah, I thought about putting some sunscreen on for you, but I'm not sure you'd appreciate my hands on your body while you're unconscious." An evil grin washes over my face and her head twists toward mine.

"Your flirting is getting darker by the hour." She sits up, her blonde hair swishing over her shoulder as she studies me.

"Told you, babe. One of these days."

"Shut up, asshole." Getting up, she peers down at me, a beaming smile on her pretty face. "Let's go swimming."

We take off our clothes, exposing her skimpy bikini that has me groaning inside when she slowly walks toward the water, dipping in her toes like she did earlier. My eyes give in to a full once-over, taking in the swell of her hips, moving smoothly to the curve of her ass. It's perky, fitting just right in her yellow bottoms, and my hands ache to be trapped between the fabric and her skin. Her back tenses as she sucks in the muscles of her core, clearly not impressed by the water temperature. I throw my pants off, revealing my swimming shorts before I follow behind her.

"Fuck me, it's cold." She looks over her shoulder with gritted teeth and a terrified expression.

God, she's cute.

I shake my head as I close the distance, then lower myself to scoop her up in my arms. Without a second thought, she wraps her arms around my neck, and I bite my lip to push back the sense of how good she feels against my body. Cradling her, I stroll the final steps until the water submerges my legs.

"What the fuck are you doing, Hunt?" she screeches, panic etching through her voice, but there's a hint of joy lingering in her eyes. "No, put me down. No! No! Put me down!" She tightens her grip on my body, pressing herself against my chest as she tries to climb higher when the water reaches her butt.

I let out a laugh while she keeps screaming at me, making this all the more fun.

"Put me down! No, Hunt! I will never talk to you again! Put me down!"

"Whatever you want, babe." As the words leave my lips, her eyes widen, realizing what I'm doing when I let her go, dropping my arms beside my body.

"NO! You asshole! I hate you! Pick me back up!" She clings to me, wrapping her legs around my waist, leaning backwards to look at me with an angry scowl. Her center presses against my aching dick while I playfully look at her, my hands resting on her hips. I catalog every inch where her body is connected with mine, taking note of how perfectly she fits in my hands. Her thighs press harshly against my hips, her fingers locked behind my neck to keep herself up, but the rest of her body stills when our gazes collide.

"I hate you," she says, faintly, our faces nearly touching.

"No." I smirk, dragging my lip between my teeth. "But you probably will after this."

Without giving her any chance to respond, I lower my body, taking her with me until we're completely under the water. When the cold water envelops us, I let go of her before I resurface, throwing my wet hair back with a grin splitting my face. She comes back up huffing and puffing, her dark blonde hair completely plastered over her cheeks like a drowning kitten, and her angry eyes find mine.

I can't help but laugh when I see the fire-filled look on her face as she splashes water my way.

"You asshole!" The amount of water that hits me in the face becomes more and more, her movements more frantic with every splash. Finally, I leap forward, her squeal loud and echoing through the open clearing. Diving underwater, I reappear right in front of her. My body is screaming for her touch, and I softly grab her side to tug her toward me. She grows quiet, her fury quickly replaced by anticipation.

"It's not that cold, is it?" I whisper, placing my forehead against hers, while I wrap her legs around my waist under the water, cupping her hips. I can't resist moving them farther, until my palms are settled on the curves of her ass. Our lips are almost touching, and I'm waiting for her to pull back any second now.

She shakes her head, swallowing hard. "No, it's not. But you're still an asshole."

For a second, I think she's going to kiss me when her eyes move to my lips, and she leans in. But she moves past my face, resting her chin on my shoulder, her lips grazing the skin on my neck.

"I know, babe." I brush her long hair aside, then place a kiss on the crook of her neck to match. Goosebumps trickle down her skin, willing me to believe that it's the result of my touch, even though it could easily be the cold water. We stay like that for a few beats, surrounded by nothing more than the sound of falling water into the quarry, while we are completely content in each other's arms.

Just existing.

Together.

"Tell me something about your dad," she finally says, resting her cheek on my shoulder while I keep holding her in my arms. I move my head to look at her, our lips so close to brushing, a sweet smile on her face. I bite my lip to not dive in, moving my head back to look out at the water in front of me while I think of something to share.

"He was an athlete," I start.

"Really?"

"Mmhmm," I say, nodding while I walk us back through the water to the less deep part. "He was a Hurricane."

"What?" Admiration ebbs through her tone, pride filling my chest. "A North Carolina Hurricane?"

"Yeah. He retired from being a pro when I was about eight. Started training the kids. He was great with kids. Not just Logan and me, but every single kid he met. All the boys at the club looked up to him, which made me even more proud he was my dad, you know?"

"Did you play hockey?"

"I did." I move us back to the edge, then plant my ass on the pebbles underwater, the water still wrapped around my waist, while she straddles me. "Logan and I were really talented. We became midget minors a year before we were eligible. We dreamed about being hockey-playing brothers, always getting a two-for-one deal. We wanted to win the Stanley Cup, *together.*" My face falls, and I swallow, having a hard time thinking back to those carefree moments at the stadium when it was just my father, my brother, and me. He was hard on us, always pushing us to do better, but also always making sure we had fun. We'd play tag at the rink after our training, and he'd win every single time, even though Logan and I got better every year. Those are the moments I miss the most, hearing our laughter echoing through the rink while the cold air numbed my face.

Young, wild, and free.

Not a care in the world other than becoming a part of the NHL as soon as possible.

"But then they died," she says with a cracking voice as she moves her head back to face me. Her gorgeous green eyes find mine, and I expect to find pity there, but instead they're filled with love. *Affection.* They are beaming at me with hope, because that's what she's been giving me for the last year.

Hope for a better future.

"But then they died."

A troubled sigh flutters over her lips, and before I realize what she's doing, her hands cup my face, and her pink lips land on mine. Stunned by the move, I freeze for a moment, until I snap out of it and wrap my arms tight around her waist. It's heated, soft, filled with tenderness, and even better than I imagined it could be. It feels surreal, like utter bliss, everything I need but don't deserve. She sets my entire soul on fire, sealing my fate as if it wasn't already set in stone. But it's the form of intimacy that's making my heart race. Our kiss lacks lust; feeling our lips locked together is comforting, loving, the boost of confidence I craved after opening up to her.

Finally, she breaks our connection, way too soon for my liking, pressing her forehead against mine as I wait for her to say something. Her eyes move back and forth while our lips continue to brush against each other.

"I'm here, Hunter Hansen. Always," she says breathlessly.

"I know, Charlotte Roux. I know."

The corner of her lip rises. "Best friends *first.*"

I nod in agreement, and she gets off me, standing up in the water.

"Friends *first*. Although," I admit, standing up next to her, "you're making this really hard for me to not flirt with you if you're going to keep planting your lips on mine."

She gives me a small push with a playful glare.

"Shut up, asshole."

23

HUNTER

I STOP IN FRONT of Charls's house, and the corner of my mouth lifts, watching her on the swinging bench. It's her favorite place in the whole world. She loves our spot at the creek, and she likes hanging out with me in the truck, just doing nothing. But I know she's the happiest when she's sitting on her swinging bench, reading a book.

She gets up, and my breath catches in my throat when I notice the sliver of skin separating her white tank top from her jeans. I already know I'm going to find an excuse to run my hand over her bare stomach today, my mind not even fighting the aching in my fingers anymore.

She crosses the front lawn before she climbs into my truck.

"Hey, babe." I smile from under my sunglasses, her sweet flowery scent instantly lingering around me, elevating my good mood to epic proportions.

"Hey." She returns my smile, buckling up, and I put the truck in reverse to maneuver it back onto the road.

After that day at the quarry, the lines have blurred. She still shuts me up when I flirt with her, but there's desire reaching her eyes instead of a scowl. She doesn't correct me when I call her "my girl," and there's not even a reprimand when I touch her without any real reason. She's basically giving me a fucking hall pass and I'm taking full advantage of it. Any chance I get to wrap my arms around her, stroke her cheek, or even plant a kiss on her hair? I take it.

My soul has been throbbing impatiently, waiting for a do-over of that kiss. It's been three weeks, but I can't fucking stop thinking about it. I've just been too much of a chicken to give it another shot. What if it was just a *friendly* kiss, nothing more? A loud voice is thundering like a hurricane, telling me that's bullshit. She wants me to kiss her again. I can see in that taunting sparkle of her gaze that haunts me at night.

But I haven't built up the nerve. *Not yet.*

"I just need to go home real quick. Have a brief shower, and get some clothes, alright?"

She turns her head to meet mine. "Yeah, sure. You've been in the gym all day?"

Her eyes slowly drag up and down my torso, my body still damp from the workout I just had, and I notice how she swallows hard, licking her lips. Her body language could be totally innocent, but fuck me—it's playing tricks with my dick at the most inconvenient of times. Subtly, I try to adjust it in my pants, glad I'm wearing sunglasses so she doesn't see the discomfort that has to be written all over my face.

"Yeah, been training with that ex-marine. He's been teaching me some real good shit."

"That's good! When's the next fight? Tomorrow?"

"Yeah, are you coming with?" My eyes plead.

"Of course." She grabs my arm, squeezing a little. "I wouldn't miss it."

The last few months she's come to almost every fight, and it creates a newfound energy as soon as I walk into the spotlight of the cage. The knowledge that she's waiting outside for me has changed the game. The goal. The future. As more time passes, I come to the sheer conclusion I want her there for every fight. I want her to be the first thing I see coming out of the cage with or without pay-per-view cameras on my face.

I still want to get the hell out of this one-horse town as fast as possible, starting over and making new memories.

But I want to do it with Charlotte.

I said we could never be more than friends, knowing I'll never be good enough for her. But every day I get more selfish about it, shifting the lines.

What if I *can* make it work?

What if I can have *her?*

The thought has crossed my mind daily.

I take the moment to turn my palm up, grabbing her hand so I can link her fingers with mine. Without looking at her response, I hold her hand as we drive toward my house in silence. My thumb gives in to the temptation, stroking her skin, searing the softness of her palm into my membrane.

Every chance I get.

"My mom is home," I explain when I park my car, letting go of her hand.

"So?" I love how casual she sounds. "We've met. She's a bitch. Let's go." Before I can stop her, she slides out of my truck with a faint smirk on her kissable lips.

"Are you coming?" She doesn't wait for my reply, sauntering toward the front door while I exit my truck and follow behind her with a smug grin lifting my cheeks.

Since the first day Charlotte met my mother, she hasn't been impressed one bit. She also holds her own like a pro, barely replying to my mother's snarky comments. If my clear weakness wasn't already a dead giveaway of how I felt about this girl, the smart-ass yet polite comments she throws at my mother truly convinced me I hit gold when she walked into my life. *I'm definitely keeping her.*

I follow her up the front porch, before I open the door. A cautious glance has me scanning the living room. *Please let her be gone, please let her be gone.*

"Ma?"

Her messy head pops above the couch, her face turning into a scowl when she notices Charlotte standing behind me.

"You brought that witch with you again?" Bloodshot eyes look feral.

"Don't fucking call her that!" I protectively wrap my arm around Charlotte's neck to tug her with me as I make my way upstairs. Away from the mother figure with more gin in her veins than blood at this point.

"Hey, Linda," Charlotte drags out with a dull look on her face, offering her a short wave.

Little sassball.

"Where the fuck you going? There better not be any fucking in this house! I'm not gonna be taking care of your kid when you knock up that little witch!"

My mom's frantic shouts have my molars grinding together by the time we reach the top of the stairs, but Charlotte beats me to it.

"Don't worry, Linda! We only *fuck* in his truck."

I laugh, then grab her face in my hands, planting a kiss on her forehead.

"You're the best," I muse, beaming, softly pushing her into my room.

My mom shouts some other shit, but I slam the door shut, blocking her from my ears.

"Is she coming to graduation next week?"

Graduation. I can't believe I'm graduating. It's bittersweet, knowing it marks so many endings. At the beginning of the school year, I wasn't even sure I was graduating, but it turns out study dates with Charls have been a great motivation for that cap and gown.

"Pff," I huff, "probably not. She'll have a date with her bottle."

There used to be a time not so long ago when those words would feel like a parasite. But lately, they haven't been cutting as deep. I'll be leaving soon anyway.

Charlotte turns around, shooting me a troubled look. "I'm sorry, Hunt."

"It's okay. I'm used to it." I ruffle her hair with a smile, just something to keep my hand busy.

"It's not *o-kay.*" She pushes off of me with a scowl, looking adorable as hell.

"I'm gonna go take a quick shower, you chill, okay? Five minutes."

"Sure."

She flops on my bed, and I hold still for a second, blinking, noticing how good she looks there. Her slight tan sticks out on the dark blue sheets, bringing out the colors of her eyes. I'd wanna spread her wide, my dick agreeing with me once more.

Baby steps, Hunt. I'm getting more confident about the possibility of claiming her as mine, but jumping her in my childhood bedroom with my spitting-mad mom downstairs might tip the scale the other way around. Spinning on my heels, I bite my lip, trying to calm myself as I close the bathroom door behind me.

I quickly undress before turning on the shower and placing myself under the warm water stream. The fatigue hits me, relaxing every muscle in my body except for the one between my legs. The one that's still thinking about the girl lying on my bed.

My girl.

My hard shaft is bobbing against my stomach, and without a second thought, I place my hand over my dick while I rest my arm on the cold tiles, my forehead pressed against the wall.

I softly start stroking my shaft, imagining it's Charlotte's hand that's moving over my body. I swallow hard when the sensational feeling grows, pretending it's now Charlotte's luscious lips, playing with my balls as I keep moving into her mouth. My jerks quickly speed up, fueled with my fantasy displayed on my bed in the other room, until a growl forms in the back of my throat, and my release splatters all over the white tiles while I bring both my hands up to the wall, trying to catch my breath.

"Fucking hell," I mutter, feeling flushed.

My lungs inhale and exhale at a ragged pace until, finally, I feel my dick relaxing. I give myself another minute to crawl back to reality, pushing away the desire to crawl on top of the blonde of my dreams instead.

Breathe, Hunt, breathe.

Knowing I'm already taking too long, I briefly wash my body, then turn off the water. I dry off, putting on my jeans that were lying on the bathroom floor. Running a hand through my wet hair, I glance into the mirror, then I open the bathroom door just in time to watch Charlotte come out of my closet. I swear, sometimes I wonder if this girl is sent out here to torture me. Roaming her long legs until I reach the hem of my dark gray hoodie, I feel my dick springing to life again. She stops in her tracks, swallowing hard, as she fixates on my bare chest. In a torturous pace, she lowers her gaze, bits of my skin burning up as her vision roams down inch by inch. Chest heaving, I focus on her, mirroring the lust I spot in her eyes.

"What?" She finally clears her throat, rapidly averting her gaze, though her flushed cheeks show her awareness of the damage already done.

"You're wearing my hoodie."

Her eyebrows move up in surprise. "Oh, I thought you wouldn't mind?"

"Not at all." I might jump her in the next ten seconds, but I sure as fuck don't mind. I walk past her, into the closet, grabbing a dark green shirt off the shelf, then tug it over my head. When I walk back out, she's leaning against the doorpost of the closet, eying me with suspicion.

"Are you fucking with me?"

I groan at her choice of words, then shake my head. "Definitely not."

But trust me, babe, I wish I was.

"Then what?" she screeches while I slowly close the distance between us, staring into her green eyes.

"Nothing." I lean in, resting one arm against the doorpost above her head, bringing my lips barely an inch from hers. "Looks damn good on you."

"Stop flirting with me," she says, even though I can hear a hitch in her voice.

"Can't." I shake my head, pushing her back into my room. "You look too hot."

She lets out a frustrated groan, flopping back onto the bed, clearly trying to create some distance between us.

"Are you ready?"

"Not sure. Can't we just stay here?"

"You basically put me in a headlock to go!"

Yeah, stupid Hunter.

"I take it back. Let's just stay here and watch a movie." Netflix and chill, probably a dumb suggestion.

"Hunt, it's the last bonfire before graduation. Half of our class will be off to college soon."

"You can't stand half our class."

"I know, but I already missed so much." My heart tenses at her gooey eyes.

"You can't look at me like that."

"Like what?

"Like that!" I gesture at her. "With those puppy eyes."

She snorts. "I'm not looking at you with puppy eyes!"

"You are! You're looking all cute and adorable, not to mention fucking hot in my hoodie."

"Hunter!"

"What?" I scoff, feeling bold. "Can't say you're hot, Charls? Because you look very hot," I tease. "Extremely *hot*. In fact, can I help you out of my hoodie? You look a little flushed. Wouldn't want you overheated and all." It's a joke. It's always a joke, but really, it's anything but.

Her soft cheeks turn a rosy pink, her lashes fluttering as she throws a pillow at my head.

"Stop! *Please.*" Her plea does very different things to my still very much active groin, and a loud growl rumbles through the room.

"Fine." I look around the room for my wallet, spotting it on my dresser before I put it in my pocket. "Ready. Let's go."

After we go through the drive-through of the Burger Shack, I take us to the edge of the woods, where the boys have set up the final bonfire as seniors. It's the last Saturday before graduation, and I had to convince Charlotte for days to come with me.

A decision I now wholeheartedly regret, because having her curled up against my chest, watching a movie, sounds so much more appealing than making small talk with people I'll never see again after next week.

I point my finger at the tree line in front of us when I notice Julie getting out of the car with Jacob. "Julie's here. What does she see in that guy?" He has that same arrogant grin on his face, strolling around like he's better than us just because he's a sophomore in college. I swear, I have no clue how he and Jason are even related.

I catch Charlotte's frown from the corner of my eye. "You don't like him?"

"I'd like him better if he showed up as roadkill one day."

"Why? He's Jason's brother. How bad can he be?"

"You do not want the answer to that question."

"That bad?" Her head tilts at me with wide eyes.

"We're hoping Jacob is adopted," I deadpan. Biting my tongue, I temper my possessive streak, the one that wants to growl and tell her to never come within a ten-foot radius of Jacob Spencer. "Just do me a favor? Stay away from him. He's bad news."

"He's dating my best friend. How do you expect me to do that?" Her lashes flutter with a little bit of incredulity, her plump lips parted, just enough for me to imagine what they would look like wrapped around my.... *Fuuuuck, Hunt.* Shut up.

I rub a hand over my face, a groan vibrating against my palm. "I know. Just... tell Julie to be careful. Please?"

I tentatively hold her gaze, our eyes locked, as if she's trying to look for answers in my features. Finally, she nods, then offers me a sweet smile, melting my possessive heart within a second.

"I'm gonna hang out with her for a bit, okay?"

"Sure. Come find me after?"

She nods in response, then exits the truck, jogging toward her friend. My eyes trail her movement as she launches herself at Julie. I let out a chuckle as I lock my truck and make my way to Jason and the rest of the boys, giving them all fist bumps in greeting.

"Where's your girl?" Jason asks, a smug grin on his face.

"Hanging out with your brother's girlfriend."

My eye catches the shift in his jaw as a feral expression hits me. "Don't even go there."

"I gather you haven't told her."

"I told her to be careful. She told me she was a big girl."

"Ouch." My brows knit together.

"Hey, I tried, man." Jason throws up his hand, but he can't hide his disappointment. It's set in his tight smile and the quick glance thrown Julie's way.

"She'll figure it out. She's smart." It's a fucking lie, because she's been hanging out with Jacob for weeks and is still not fed up with him. In my book, that's the equivalent of sticking a red flag to his forehead and choosing to pretend it's not there.

"Let's hope so. Anyway..." Jason's smirk gives away the subject he wants to address, and my eyes roll to the back of my head hard enough to fall to the floor like marbles.

"Everything good with you and your girl?" His dirty blonde eyebrows flick up and down.

"She's not my girl, man." The lie makes it hard to hold back the grin tuggin' the corners of my lips.

"Yet, you know exactly who I'm talking about. Besides, you didn't correct me just two minutes ago. Just admit it. She's your girl."

"Shut up." I chuckle.

Jason takes a pull from his beer, eyeing me from above the bottle.

"What?"

"You know, I took bets at the beginning of the year. Saying she'd be your first girlfriend by the end of the semester."

"Well, I sure as fuck hope you didn't put a lot of money on that."

"I didn't, thank fuck." He looks up to the sky with a look of gratitude, then turns his gaze back to mine. "But I still think it's true, though." He pushes me a little farther toward the tree line, out of earshot of anyone else, lowering his voice. "When are you finally going to make it official?"

My chest burns up at those words, feeling busted as fuck. Jason isn't the type to gaslight me into anything. I know he likes Charlotte, and it's no secret he's been suspicious of our relationship from the beginning, but hearing him encourage me to go for it... to officially make her mine? It does weird shit to my organs.

"I don't know, man," I say, simply because I'm not sure what to say. Denying it would be a lie. But I also don't want to tell him anything if I'm not a hundred percent sure Charlotte and I are on the same page.

"Look, I have no clue what she sees in your dumb ass, and I think you should thank God on your knees for the fact that she forgave you after what you pulled at the last bonfire, but fuck me. Stop torturing yourself, man." His hand drops forcefully on my shoulder with a firm grip. "You *love* her."

The word *love* has me snapping my head toward him with a deep frown. Like... do I care about her? More than anything in the world. Is she special? I'm sure heaven has a special corner for people like her. But love? That doesn't exist in my vocabulary.

"I don't *love* anyone. Love is bullshit. Yeah, she's my friend. And I care for her. And I'm not gonna deny that I want to throw her against the wall and fuck her like she's mine. But I'm not sure I can't do that. Not without risking what we have, and that's what matters most."

He folds his arms in front of his body, giving me a blank look as I hold his gaze. A lump forms in the back of my throat, as if I just poisoned myself, and I do my best to push it away.

"But what if you could be more?"

It's a simple question, one I've been asking myself for a while now. It sounds as easy as two plus two, but in my head? The outcome is never four.

"I need to figure out shit with her first, so I'd appreciate it if you drop it until then," I say, my tone final. I won't risk my friendship with Charlotte just to see how she would feel underneath me. It's not worth it. No matter how badly I want it. If we're doing this, I need to be confident I won't lose her in the end. I need to make sure we're both ready.

"Alright, man." Jason slams his hand on my back in a friendly way, and we walk back, dropping the conversation like I asked, talking about sports for the rest of the night.

When the twilight kicks in, I'm still hanging out with them while Charlotte is talking to Julie. Jason never brings it up again, but for some reason, his words keep lingering in the back of my head.

What if you could be more?

I glance at Charlotte, on the other side of the fire, her dark blonde hair shining from the reflection of the flames. As if she can feel my eyes on her body, she turns around, locking her eyes with mine, shooting me that gorgeous smile that is the first thing I think of when I wake up.

The corner of my mouth curls up in a pleased smile as she starts to walk toward me, keeping her eyes focused on mine. There is a longing in her eyes that I haven't seen before, and I suck in a deep breath as she reaches us.

"Hey boys," she says, and they all greet her in union. "Can I borrow him for a while?"

"Sure," they all bellow with a suggestive tone, making me chuckle a little behind my ginger beer.

She reaches out a hand, and I quickly take it, linking our fingers as she leads me toward one of the logs around the fire. I squat to take a seat on it, my legs folded out in front of me, before I guide her onto my lap, resting my hand on her hip.

"Are you having fun?" she asks, glancing at me over her shoulder.

"Yeah. You?"

"Hmm, I am now," she muses in a way that makes my insides swirl. An eyebrow cocks up, wondering if she's flirting with *me* now.

"Why is that?" I clear my throat, sounding husky as fuck as she turns her face to look at me again.

"Well, we're graduating in a week. Mama is doing alright, it's summer, and I'm spending the night with both of my best friends. That's a win in my book."

"It definitely is." Having her on my lap is a win too, but let's not push too hard right now.

We sit like this for about half an hour, until the night has fully set in, and most of the people have already left, yet I'm not planning to leave, feeling completely content with her close to my body. I close my eyes, every now and then resting my lips on her back, that's covered by the fabric of my hoodie, wishing it was her bare skin.

As if she can read my mind, she finally moves the piece of clothing over her head, and I let out a small groan at the sudden torture fest that's about to occur.

"What are you doing?"

"The flames are hot."

I suck in a sharp breath, my jaw ticking when the safe boundary formed by the piece of clothing is now completely lifted, exposing the soft skin of her shoulder, as she's wearing nothing more than a tank top. Even though I know I should resist, my mouth keeps brushing her soft skin, wanting more with every touch, while a different question gets louder in my head with every passing minute. *What if we're ready to be more?*

24

Charlotte

F OR THE PAST THIRTY minutes, I've been hyperaware of Hunter's calloused palms on my hips, his fingers grazing my skin every now and then. Each time our skin connects, I sink deeper into his embrace, unable to resist his touch. My go-to is to scold him for it, telling him to stop flirting with me, but I don't this time. The boundaries we've set are becoming hard to see, and I can't find it in myself to care.

I don't know why I kissed him that day at the quarry. It's like something pulled me in, and before I knew it, my lips were on his, and all I knew was that it felt right. It felt right in that moment. It felt right with *him*. And not that I was surprised... it always feels right with Hunter.

I could still feel his kiss on my lips days after, and I've been dying to feel them all over again. For him to lose control and gather the nerve to do the thing I want more than anything, but haven't found enough courage to do again myself.

Letting out a content sigh, I stare into the dancing flames, when I feel his breath fan the skin on my shoulder, causing my body to drum to a tune I've never felt before. It's humming all the nerves beneath my skin alive, scorching, electrifying, and vibrating with enough force to drill deep into my core. I'm assuming it's unintended, him having no clue that he's close to making me combust into flames any second now by feeling his mouth so close to my skin.

I assumed wrong.

It isn't until he presses a lingering kiss on the same spot, that I realize he knows exactly what he's doing. With my skin blistering under his soft lips, I turn my head, immediately meeting his hypnotizing eyes that are clearly longing for more. The moonlight dances in his gaze like sparks of mischief, and the corner of his mouth raises in that boyish grin. The one that melts any restraint I have for him every single fucking time, while my breath stutters as his hand spreads out over my stomach. The heat of his palm has butterflies swarming to his touch like a magnet, and I drag my lower lip between my teeth to hold back the shudder that's trying to break through. His thumb gently rubs tiny circles below my shirt, each more calculated than the last. You can't see anything from the outside because it's only his thumb that disappears under my shirt, but the feeling burns me on the inside like an eternal flame.

"You look gorgeous all flushed, babe. I like it." His open mouth lands on the nape of my neck. *Hot damn.*

I suck in a breath, doing my best not to close my eyes and really give in to his touch.

"Stop flirting with me." My hoarse voice lacks strength, and it doesn't surprise me that when I let my eyes fall to his, he raises his eyebrow.

"Do you really want me to, though?" He swirls his arm around my waist in a controlling way, tugging me closer against his chest, his other hand brushing away my hair to plant a kiss in the crook of my neck. This time, he makes me gasp for air and, unwillingly, I close my eyes. He opens his mouth, then starts to nibble my skin. I have to hold back a moan.

"Do you need me to stop flirting with you, Charls?" He rustles against my neck in between kisses.

Yes.

No.

Yes.

Fuck no.

My mouth stays shut with a hum, not sure about what I want and what I need. My eyes glance around us, hoping no one will notice Hunter's successful attempt to cross the line more blatantly, but also not giving a flying fuck if they do.

"What are you doing, Hunter?" My face turns toward him, even though I know I shouldn't.

I've put him in the best friend box, because it's safe. Because we agreed on that from day one, but here he is clearly breaking that rule, and I can't deny he isn't the one who haunts my fantasies when I'm alone. I can't deny that I want this.

I want *him*.

"Taking advantage of the fact that we are both drunk and won't overthink it."

I furrow my brows in an incredulous look, trying to ignore the intense feeling of his hand still caressing my stomach.

"I had one drink, and you had a ginger beer."

"Hmm, in that case—I'm just winging it." His counter is murmured against my shoulder, making my stomach flip with anticipation, before he grabs my hand and lifts us both to our feet.

"Let's go." Without waiting for my response, he drags me behind him, making me glance back to see if anyone notices, as we make our way to his truck. An exhilarating feeling grows inside me, although I haven't figured out yet if it's excitement or straight up fucking fear, knowing that whatever we have, it could be changing in mere seconds.

When we reach his tailgate, he yanks me in front of him, twisting me on the spot to face him. There has always been a hint of craving in his eyes whenever he would throw me another flirty line like the playboy he is, but now there is a craving in his eyes that he's never shown before. A savage lust that is set to devour me, making me want to throw out every reason I can find to not give into this pull. He roughly slams me against the cold metal of his truck as he presses his hands beside my head, caging me in.

Bad boy Hunter as my best friend is fun, adventurous, and playful, always the one putting a smile on my face, but bad boy Hunter, ready to shred my clothes to pieces, is making me gasp for air. He leans his forehead against mine, while his panting breath fans my face.

"I will stop if you tell me to, but fuck—I'm really hoping you won't." His nose brushes against mine, our lips closer than they're supposed to be. I only have to move an inch to close the space between us, and press my lips against his once more.

But *really* kiss him this time.

Kiss him like there is no tomorrow.

Kiss him like he's mine.

"We're best friends, Hunt," I state, even though I'm dying to let my tongue dart out and give in to the longing that is slowly crushing the restraints inside me.

"I will always be your best friend." He moves one hand in my hair, fisting it, keeping my head in place. "But right now, I want to be *so* much more."

He doesn't wait for my reply, and somehow, I knew he wouldn't. He is not a gentleman; he isn't the boy who needs reassurance. He acts first and thinks later. Something I school him about on a regular basis, but in this yearning moment of internal desire, I'm *so* glad for that trait.

He runs his tongue along my lower lip, and my lips part in response. Finally, he pushes his tongue against mine and all boundaries we have set vanish into thin air in that same second. My hand grabs his neck, demanding him to deepen the kiss as he explores the inside of my mouth, slow and lingering. Massaging every inch he can find, I enjoy the tingling feeling that starts to form between my thighs as he keeps kissing me in the most sexy and affectionate, yet demanding, way. I never once doubted he would be a good kisser, but feeling his body against mine, with his tongue rubbing against mine sensually, makes me realize that's an understatement.

Fuck, he's a great kisser.

He feels like the sun on a cloudy day, his touch magical and capable of pulling me out of whatever numb state I was in before this. He never stops, steady, gentle, as if he wants to relish this moment for as long as possible. Each move, each tilt of his head, each time our tongues find each other again, it all gets tattooed on my membrane, wondering if he's setting a standard no one can ever surpass.

After a while, he moves his head back, leaving me disappointed, because I sure as fuck am still craving more.

His thumb moves up and down my cheek as he bites his lip. "Let's go to *our* place."

I nod in agreement, making a big smirk appear on his face. He grabs my hand, walking me back to the passenger side as he opens the door, and I place my foot on the step to climb inside. I drop my ass on the seat like I've done numerous times, then I look back at him. It feels different. Everything feels different.

He puts his feet on the steps, pulling his body up in one move, hovering his face in front of mine. "Remind me to get you drunk more often."

A wink is volleyed my way and, simultaneously, my mouth curls into a smile, relieved that even though the boundaries have blurred, we can also still be us.

"Stop flirting with me."

"Fine." He chuckles, then presses another kiss on my lips. He moves back down, slamming the door shut before he rounds the truck, and gets behind the wheel, then takes off as if nothing happened. As if we're driving around like we didn't just share the best kiss of my life.

But after feeling his body so close to mine, I hate the space that is now between us, like an awkward, invisible sibling that is forced to tag along. It has my fear and insecurity growing with each mile that passes, giving me way too much space to think of all the reasons why this isn't a good idea. As if he can feel my thoughts, he reaches out his hand, grabbing my neck, softly pulling it to make me scooch closer to him. I slide right next to him and settle into the side of his chest, instantly feeling better from the warmth of his body. He wraps his arm around my shoulder, keeping me in a tight grip against him while he plants an affectionate kiss on my hair. It's weird how in the last five minutes we crossed a line we were never meant to cross, but somehow it feels as comfortable as ever.

We drive to our spot in silence, and for a minute, I nestle my head closer against him, closing my eyes. A contentedness settles in my veins, and even though my thoughts are still laced with a hint of fear, I'm fully aware that there's no turning back now. There's no turning back from this. I know he'll leave his mark on me, like a wound that will never quite heal, forever embedded in my life.

Five minutes later, he parks his truck next to our tree and shuts off the engine. I glance up at him, looking into his hazel eyes that are staring me down. He cups my cheek, narrowing his eyes, placing a soft kiss on my lips.

I sigh, knowing he ruined me with a single kiss.

"What's on your mind, babe?"

"What if we ruin it?" I know the question is useless because the outcome will stay the same. We're on this bridge and we're getting to the other side, no matter what. But I need him to tell me we'll be okay. We won't lose what we have. I want him in every way possible, but I *need* him to stay my best friend.

I can't risk that.
I'm not *willing* to risk that.
He smiles, brushing my lips with his thumb.
"It's us. We won't."

25

HUNTER

"WHAT IF WE RUIN it?"

A gradient of desire and insecurity peers back at me. The question is loaded, I know that. I can't make any promises, because there's a good chance I'll fuck it up. But looking into the eyes that are the fuel of my existence, I know I will do anything to keep what we have right now.

I press another kiss on her lips, sealing my reply with a sliver of hope while silently praying I'm right. That we won't screw this up.

"Wait here, I'll be right back."

Leaving the door open, I head to the tailgate, spreading out the blanket I have in the back of the truck, while throwing a second one in reach, then head back to Charlotte. Another smile splits my face when I look at her, grabbing her legs to wrap them around my waist as I pull her closer and press my lips to hers. Fuck, I've been waiting to wrap her around my body for so long. *To kiss her like this.* A shiver runs through my body when her hands land on my neck, parting my lips to deepen the kiss. It feels like I've been waiting for years instead of months, and even though I can't wait to rip her clothes off, I also want to enjoy this moment. Take it nice and slow, and drink her in until she's screaming my name, like she's done in my dreams.

I lift her out of the car, cupping her peachy ass, slowly walking us to the tailgate to drop her onto it, our lips never parting.

"Fuck, babe." My jeans are growing tighter, while my hands are migrating up the soft skin underneath her shirt as I trail kisses up and down her neck. She lets out a soft moan as her breath caresses my ear, feeding into my hunger. Scraping my teeth over her cheek, I move back to the corner of her mouth, pushing up the hem of her shirt so I can cup her breast. The swell fits perfectly in my palm, and I push her bra down to rub a thumb over her puckered nipple.

"Tell me to stop, Charls. Tell me you don't want this, and we'll go back to what we are." For a split second, fear threatens to drag me under, wondering if she'll tell me exactly what I don't want to hear. But it's all gone when she grabs my chin, her darkening eyes narrowing in on me.

"I want you." Her tone is husky, begging me for more, and I lose all doubt when she roughly presses her mouth against mine.

I pull her shirt over her head, unclasping her black lace bra and taking her nipple into my mouth while massaging the other. She cries out, throwing her head back as her hands run through my hair, her nails scratching my scalp in a scorching way. Breaking our connection, I step back, moving my shirt over my head, taking in every inch of her. She's looking at me with a hungry gaze that makes me lick my lips while I stare at the perfect curves of her breasts.

"I've been waiting for this since the first day we met." I huff, closing the distance again until I crash my mouth against hers. Our kisses become more frantic, and her fingers undo my jeans, pushing them down while I do the same with hers. I roughly push her back to the floor of the tailgate, dragging the fabric down her legs, and throwing the jeans to the ground. As I bite my lip, my thumb brushes over her dampened thong, making me gasp for air when I push the fabric aside and her wetness becomes fully exposed.

"Fucking hell." Our eyes link, her green ones trained to mine from under her lashes, a seductive spark shining back at me. The light of the moon illuminates her dark blonde waves, and she looks like a fucking dream. Like a siren, hypnotizing with just the humming of her breath, the glistening of her pussy taunting me like a forbidden fruit.

I press my nose between her legs, breathing her in like she's my life support. The sultry scent is mixed with a sweetness that will forever be settled in my senses, kicking in a possessive streak. She's mine. My index finger trails along the edge of the lace until I reach her core and I push the tip of my finger into the soft flesh of her walls.

"Goddamn." I pull my lip between my teeth. "*This* is mine." My finger pushes deeper, sinking into the warmth of her slick pussy, and it finalizes my fate. My destiny.

I will fuck this up, but the outcome will stay the same. Charlotte Roux is mine. But what's even more terrifying... is that I'm hers. I can feel it settling inside me like a lifetime scar. She's planted herself at the very core of my being, and whatever happens, whatever she will choose, she will own me in every way possible.

"Move back," I order, tapping her thigh.

She lifts up onto her elbows, crawling backwards, her eyes still locked with mine.

I climb up the tailgate, placing my chest over her legs, softly pushing them to the side to give me full access. She reaches out her hands for me, but I push them away, placing a kiss on each thigh as I take off her thong.

"What are you doing?" Her tone is weak, her eyes bright with passion.

"Cherishing you with my tongue, baby." I tauntingly run the tip of my tongue over her folds. "Has someone ever touched you like this?"

"No." It's pushed out with a breath, a pleading moan following right behind it.

"Good." I dive my hands into her thighs, pressing her deep into the metal of my truck. "Because this is *mine*." A soft kiss lands on her opening, and she whimpers at the touch, the sound lifting the hairs on the back of my neck. "Do you hear me, Charls? I'm the only one who can kiss you here." My tongue briefly flicks over her sensitive nub. "The only one who's allowed to eat you like you're the oasis in the Arizona desert. Do you hear me?"

I dig my fingers deeper into her skin, and her gaze finds mine again.

"Do you hear me, babe?"

She nods. "It's yours."

It sure as fuck is.

"Holy shit!" she cries when my mouth covers her core. I stroke my tongue through her center, then take each lip between my own, gently sucking and nipping. Her saltiness combined with her soft moans turns me on even more as I bury my tongue inside of her while my thumb circles her clit. Her legs squirm underneath me, trying to break free, but my arms keep them firmly in place. She tastes like heaven, causing my mind to fog into a state that literally elevates my soul. A sharp sense of pride curls my lips when a few drops of moisture dripping from her entrance, firing up my craving to have her explode against my face.

"Hunter, I can't," she screeches desperately, yet with a clear longing in her voice.

"Sssh," I blow against her flesh, taking her bundle of nerves into my mouth, flicking the button that ignites her. She starts to pant, arching her back to give me better access as her nails dig into my shoulders, and I push a finger inside of her. The tightness of her walls tells me she's close as I continue to thrust.

"Oh my god. Hunt!"

"Let go, baby," I growl. My tongue draws circles around her most sensitive spot and soon I feel her quads tense as her pussy lifts up an inch closer to my face. Her fingers move into my hair, and she possessively holds my face still as she starts to grind her core against my mouth in the way she pleases.

"That's it. Take what you want."

"Oh, fuck. Hunter! Hunter, I–" Her breath catches in her throat, and she cries out her release while I relish her cream on my tongue. I suck it up, wanting to imprint her taste on my memory. I wait until the twitch of her hips grows slower and slower before I start to suck her clean, lapping around her folds, careful to avoid her throbbing clit as she relaxes at every new touch.

"Are you good, baby?"

An agreeing murmur reaches my ear, and I laugh, giving her gleaming pussy one more kiss before I push my boxers down. Grabbing a condom out of my jeans, I then climb on top of her.

"Hey, beautiful," I whisper when our faces are aligned.

"Hey, handsome." She lets out a giggle, resting her hands on my neck while I take the second blanket and throw it over my back to keep us warm, then press an affectionate kiss on her lips.

"I want you, Hunter Hansen," she breathes against my lips, a lust in her eyes that makes her even more desirable. Without waiting any longer, I roll the condom over my head, aligning the tip of my shaft with her center before I slowly push in, stretching her wide. Her lips part more the farther I get, as she throws her head back. Her tight walls enclose me in a way I have never felt before, making me wonder why I've waited all these months. She feels better than I've ever felt, like she's made for me in every way. My forehead rests on her shoulder, catching my breath, and I start thrusting inside her. Slow and scorching moves that pull out until the very last inch, right before I push myself completely back in. A shudder tracks down my shoulders, and my eyes shut as I'm starting to ride a wave of pure ecstasy.

"Hunter." She throws her head back.

"You like that, babe?" My hand goes to her hair, fisting it in a dominating way, feeling the desperate need to own her. To show her all the devotion I have for her while I'm buried inside of her.

"Yes, keep going," she pleads.

I do as she says as I grind my hips against her body. Hooking my arm behind her knee, I press my cock even deeper, my balls slapping against the cheeks of her ass with every move. Her eyes roll to the back of her head, and I bite my lip in concentration, examining her pretty face. I keep looking at her to make sure I'm not hurting her until she locks her gaze with mine, swallowing hard as she gives me desperate pleas.

"More." *Fuck.*

I throw my head back, pumping inside of her even harder while my thumb rubs her clit with the same pace, making her moan louder with every thrust.

She feels incredible.

I've fantasized about this moment, but feeling her is better than I could've ever imagined. Like we've been working toward this moment for ages, finally being able to lose ourselves to each other in oblivion. Like she's my light at the end of the tunnel. The reason I kept going for so long. It doesn't take long before I can subtly feel the tightness of her walls around me increasing, squeezing me tight.

Her hands grab the blanket underneath her, holding on with a whitening grip as she bucks her hips, until I tip her over the edge, making her explode. The clenching of her pussy quickly milks me for all I'm worth. With a feral roar, I pump a few more times, feeling my shaft go numb at the sensation of emptying myself inside of her. I've never felt pleasure this intense.

"Fucking hell," I mutter against her neck, pressing my entire weight on top of her as my body goes limp. She wraps her arms around my back, placing a trail of kisses on my neck while I'm still inside of her.

"That. Was. Amazing," she says between kisses. "I could stay like this forever."

I softly nibble her ear, and she lets out a giggle.

"Hunt," she reprimands.

"Now that I've had a taste, I don't think I can go without anymore."

The tips of her fingers move up and down over my spine, making a shiver run through my body.

"I don't think you have to," she whispers, her mouth flush with my ear.

I move my body up just slightly so I can look into her eyes.

"Yeah?" I smile.

She nods, a silent understanding forming between us before pulling my neck to bring my lips to hers. Our mouths collide again, this time lacking urgency, but still filled with a form of affection that means so much more.

"How do you like my *just-fucked face*, babe?"

"Fucking handsome, you arrogant asshole." She laughs, and I snicker in response.

Her hand moves up, brushing the skin on my chin with her thumb, her eyes sparking with lust once again.

"I want more, Hunter." She presses a gentle kiss on the corner of my mouth, her tongue darting out in a playful way. "Give me more. *I want it all.*"

I close my eyes, biting my lip, feeling the hunger growing between my legs once more, my cock eager, knowing I will never get enough of her.

"You're gonna kill me, Charls."

"As long as we die happy together, we will always be fine, right?" There is a pledge in her eyes that I can't resist, a thirst I need to take away, even though I know it will probably never dry up. I don't miss the unspoken words between the lines, my chest expanding with the hope of her being there until I take my last breath.

"With you, I will always be fine." She smiles at my reply before my mouth clashes against hers, ready to do it all over again.

26

Charlotte

I WAKE UP FEELING the safest I've ever felt in my life. The warmth of Hunter's body glues us together, while his sleeping breath softly fans the back of my neck with his nose buried in my hair. His hand is plastered around my waist, and I let out a satisfied sigh.

Last night was—*perfect*.

It was as if a volcano erupted, bursting out all the feelings that we'd kept tucked inside for way too long. It wasn't just the best sex I'd ever had, not that I have a whole lot to compare, but it was a connection that was long overdue. When he drove me home, his hand linked with mine as if it had never been different, and I knew I didn't want the night to end. There was a feeling creeping inside of me, wondering how long our bliss would stay, and I wanted to stretch the moment out for as long as possible.

I feel his lips brush my neck as he murmurs against my skin, digging my head farther into my pillow to wallow in the feeling.

"Morning, babe."

"Morning." The fluttering in my stomach is almost unbearable. He tugs me closer against his chest as he leaves a trail of kisses moving from my shoulder to my neck.

"Do you know how long I've been waiting to do this?"

"Stop flirting with me." I chuckle out of habit.

"I'm not. I mean it. I've been wanting to taste you since the first time I saw you."

I spin in his arms to face him, our noses touching as I press a kiss on his soft lips.

I would be a liar if I didn't admit I felt the same.

We'd been doing our best to stay best friends for so long, denying the depth of our feelings, when really, we'd both been longing for more.

More touches.

More kisses.

Holy hell, definitely more kisses.

"I could get used to this," he says, while I look into his mesmerizing eyes.

"Me too."

My hand reaches up to run across the stubble on his chin, before I lean in once more, craving another kiss, as if I'm trying to make up for the time lost.

"What do we do now?" I whisper.

"What we always do." He shrugs, tucking a strand of hair behind my ear, making it sound so simple. "Just with lots of sex."

I let out a laugh, rolling my eyes at his comment. "I'm serious, Hunt."

An ominous feeling is waiting to take over, as if a thundercloud will destroy my perfect summer day. I want to find a gust of positivity, convincing myself it's just my fear talking, but I can't completely shake it either.

"So am I, babe. It's still us. You're still my best friend. Nothing has to change. Other than the fact that now I'm going to kiss you whenever the fuck I want."

"Well, *something* has to change." I furrow my brows, teasing.

"Yeah? What's that?" He places a soft kiss on the corner of my mouth while his hand migrates down to my legs, getting awfully close to the area I want him to be.

8

"No more bimbos."

He throws his head back in laughter.

"Why would I want another girl if I got you, Charls?" His hand strokes my cheek. "I haven't been with anyone else in six months."

"Really?" I guess Julie was right. I can't deny my heart jumps like a jackhammer with excitement.

"It wasn't as important as spending time with you." My throat swells up. "No more bimbos, Charls."

"You swear?" Emotion is swirling in my eyes, but I put in my best effort to hold it back from falling over my lashes.

"I swear." He leans in, licking the seam of my lips, demanding me to open up, and I let out a deep groan in agony. He was gentle and soft with me when we got home, doing our best to keep quiet for my mama, even though I knew she was knocked out from her latest treatment, but I'm not sure if she's still sleeping, and I don't want to get caught with Hunter between my legs.

Though I'm ready to arch my back, asking him for more when his hands brush the inside of my thighs.

"Not here." I huff, frustrating myself.

"You wanna get breakfast, or wanna *be* breakfast?" That same boyish grin appears on his face that awakens my already addicted pussy, and I playfully slap his chest.

"Hunt. My mom is home," I hiss.

"So?"

"I'm not sure if I'm ready for that."

"What? You mean, telling her we had sex?"

I nod my head while giving him a pleading look. He huffs in amusement.

"Babe, she already knows. I ran into her when I went to the bathroom."

My brows raise in shock.

"Are you kidding me?"

"Nah," he deadpans as I look at him incredulously.

"What did she say?"

"You want her literal words?" His arms tug me closer against his chest, peering at me while the corner of his mouth lifts a little.

"Yeah."

"She said, and I quote: *'Took you long enough, Hunter.'* And then she went back to bed."

"And then she went back to bed?" I repeat.

An amused feeling enters my body when I think of my mom's reaction, knowing once again that I have the best mama in the world. I didn't expect her to be against it, but I expected her to tell me to be careful and not risk our friendship. You know, just give me some kind of warning, like any other mother would do. But the fact that she called Hunter out like that tells me I can't keep secrets from that woman, no matter what state she's in.

"Mmhmm," he muses, pressing another kiss on my lips.

Now knowing Mama knows Hunter is here, I feel no restraint as I cup his head, softly darting out my tongue against his mouth, making him groan against my lips.

He softly nibbles my lip, then he moves to my ear, his lips brushing my cheek in a scorching way.

"If you don't want me to fuck you with your mama drinking her morning coffee downstairs, you better stop right now, Charls. Because there's no holding me back if we cross that line. I've been holding back for too long." His voice is husky, and needy, filled with a promise that makes it impossible for me to say no.

"I want you to fuck me." Without wasting another second, he crashes his mouth against mine, and I wrap my leg around his waist. Pressing my center against his morning wood, I let out a whimpering moan.

His hands grab my hips, as he digs his fingers into my flesh in a way that makes me want more, thinking about all the ways I would let him dominate me. All the ways I want him to destroy me. He rolls me onto my back as he climbs on top of me, his lips devouring my neck while I feel the longing grow between my legs.

I want to pull his head back, to press my mouth against his, when the deafening sound of his phone snaps us out of the moment.

"Nooo," I screech as I throw my head against the pillow. He lets out a growl, landing his forehead against my neck, his teeth softly scratching my skin in frustration. I close my eyes at the burning feeling when he ends it with a kiss and gets off of me, rolling himself to the other side of the bed.

I look up to the ceiling, unsatisfied, praying this won't take long.

"Yeah," he rumbles into the phone, resting his back against the headboard, then reaching out his arm to tug me toward him. "Yeah, this is Hunter."

I roll on my side, placing myself against him, while he wraps his arm around my back and starts to stroke my skin. I close my eyes for a second, enjoying the relaxed feeling of the steady moves of his fingers going over my body, a shiver running down my spine.

"Are you serious?" There's excitement in his voice.

I snap my head up to him, examining his features. There is a stern look on his face, while his eyes are beaming, until the corners of his lip raise in a big smile.

"Yeah, yeah. Sure. When? Yeah, of course. Alright. Thank you. Yes. Okay. Bye."

Annoyed by only half the conversation, I give him a confused look.

"What was that?"

"That was someone from the AFA."

Realizing what he's saying, I move up so I can see his face some more, cocking my head.

"Okay," I drag out.

A mixed feeling enters my body while I keep staring at him in anticipation. I want him to get every chance to have a better life, but I can't help seeing that thundercloud moving above our heads, thinking that same chance might actually take him away from me.

"They want to sign me." My heart falls as the words fly from his mouth, while I raise the corner of my mouth to give him a smile. I do my best to put on a cheerful face, even though it feels like someone just jabbed a knife in my gut. Killing me slowly as I'm bleeding on the inside.

I launch myself at him, wrapping my arms around his neck.

"That's amazing! Congratulations!"

His arms circle my waist in a tight grip as he digs his face into my hair.

"This is what we've been waiting for!" I lean back to find his gleaming eyes.

"I know!" I agree, even though I have no clue what *this* means. "You deserve it!"

"They need me to come to LA next week, to get the papers sorted and stuff."

He's leaving. For the last few months, I knew this point was coming someday, knowing his talent would take him places. But he didn't have any plans after graduation, and I was going to community college to be close with my mom, so I figured we'd still have time. But now... right at the point when we're finally owning up to our feelings, they are taking him away from me.

I swallow hard, shifting a little on the bed, and he notices my distress, even though I still have a smile on my face.

"Hey, what's wrong, babe?" He cups my cheek, his eyes narrowing.

"Nothing," I lie, shaking my head. Whatever feelings I'm having right now, it's not fair to voice them to him, knowing it will make him doubtful about leaving. "I'm happy for you!"

But he sees right through my lies, a thoughtful expression coming my way as he lowers his head to lock our gazes. "I'll be back, Charls. It's just for a few days to sort the papers, and then I'll be back for the summer. There are no fights until August."

I nod, doing my best to push away my gloomy mood. "I know! It will be great. You're going to kill it." I press a kiss on his lips in hopes of burying my feelings, yet he doesn't fall for it.

"Look at me." He breaks our kiss, then grabs my hips, lifting me onto his lap to straddle him. "Come with me."

The look he's giving me reminds me of that day at the creek. A lost boy, praying life will get better one day. His eyes are begging me, and I really want to say yes. There is nothing I want more right now than to start a new life with Hunter by my side. Exploring the world together. My heart is expanding at the knowledge that he wants me to be part of his future. Of this new adventure he's going to start.

But I know I can't. I know this isn't my adventure to go on.

My life has been on hold since I was eight, and I don't mind.

I can't be selfish. Not while Mama is doing her best to stay alive.

She gave me life, now I have to help her keep hers.

I softly shake my head, my eyes welling up.

"My mama, Hunter. I can't," I explain, making his face fall. "If it was just me, I would. I would go anywhere you want me to, but it's not just me. It's been me and her for so long. I can't give up on her."

He lets out a troubled breath, pressing his forehead against mine. The air between us grows thick, making it hard to breathe as we hold still for a moment. Something about this moment feels final. It feels like goodbye, but I'm too scared to speak about my fears.

"I know," he muses. "You don't have to explain. You're an amazing person, Charlotte Roux."

"You're going to kill it in LA," I whisper against his lips.

He tucks my head against his chest, wrapping me in a tight hug, and I feel as if he's holding on for dear life. I know I am.

"We will make it work, babe. I promise." His lips brush my hair, and he gives me a kiss on the top of my head.

"I know we will." I push the words out with confidence, even though it feels like a lie. We can't make these promises, because neither of us really knows if we can keep them. But I still treat it as my buoy in the middle of the ocean.

My heart is weeping, holding on to a little rope of hope, praying that he's right. That we will make it work, no matter what happens.

27

Charlotte

M Y EYES WELL UP when Hunter gets on the stage to take his diploma. His signature smirk shines bright, and I convinced him to trade his snapback for the burgundy cap that came with his gown. He seeks me out, and my heart jumps in my throat when he throws me a wink.

I'm so fucking proud of him. I'm going to miss him like crazy when he moves to LA after the summer, but I'm so proud he's going with his diploma in his pocket. He graduated even though his entire high school career was overshadowed by neglect while trying to survive his mother's addiction.

I'm sad for Hunter that she isn't here, but when I glance over my shoulder, I see my own mama on her feet, clapping like the proud mother he never had. The strap of her yellow sundress slips off her shoulder, but she's looking better than she had in weeks, getting more color in her cheeks every day. It's the final thing that closes my throat and pushes my tears over the edge.

They roll down with joy as I watch Hunter walk down the steps, locking his gaze with mine. Worry chisels his features sharp and tense, a silent question in his eyes. I quickly shake my head with a smile, and his expression softens, but not until he roughly pushes down my lane, stomping on a few feet along the way.

"This is not your aisle, Mr. Hansen. This is for the graduates from M to R," I joke, right before he pulls me into his arms. Strong, calloused palms fall onto the small of my back as he studies my face with his hazel-brown eyes that stand out even more against his gown.

"What are they gonna do? Expel me?" I snicker at his joke while he wipes away the moisture on my cheeks with a piece of his gown. "What's wrong?"

"Nothing." I look up, my hands resting on his arms. "I'm just so fucking proud of you. You graduated."

His eyes snap shut for a brief moment, a loud exhale flaring his nostrils as he relaxes underneath my touch.

His forehead falls against mine. "*We*. We graduated."

"I know."

His lips move closer, his hands trailing up until they rest in my neck. With his thumbs on my jaw, he tilts my head, his face hovering above mine.

"Do you know how amazing you are?"

"Stop flirting with me."

His grin slips through. "Never, babe. *Never.*"

With a side-eye, I can feel the kids in our class zooming in on us, and I slip my hands up to lock them behind his neck.

"Everybody is watching," I whisper against his lips.

"Good. I want everyone to know you're mine."

"Didn't you already tell everyone in our class they couldn't date me?"

A guilty smirk splits his face. "I did."

"In that case, I'm pretty sure they already know."

"Oh, they know." His breath heats my lips. "But now I want to show them."

He crushes his lips against mine, pressing deep, with an urgency that has me savoring the moment. I breathe in his cologne, knowing I'll never get enough of the woodsy scent. His tongue pushes inside of me, slowly caressing my own, and I let out a moan. I wish we had more than just a few months, but at the same time, I'm happy I still have the entire summer to do this. To claim him as mine and kiss him whenever I feel like it.

I completely submerge in his energy, melting against his body while the world around me seems to fade away. His kiss becomes more frantic, more demanding, but then suddenly a jerk of his shoulder breaks his lips from mine.

"Glad to see you two are finally done with your bullshit." Jason smirks, his hand firmly planted on Hunter's shoulder from the row behind mine. "But you're holding up the line."

Both our gazes snap to the stage, and I lock eyes with the principal. The old man holds the microphone in front of his lips, one eyebrow cocked to his hairline in a reprimanding look.

"Charlotte Roux?" His voice echoes through the sound box on the stage, an entertained smile cracking through. "You still want your diploma?"

I hide my smile behind my palm, then nod.

"I think you're up, babe," Hunter whispers in my ear, then places another kiss on my neck before I let go of him. I lock eyes with my mother on the way to the stage, and another tear slips down my cheeks. My mother is here, Hunter and I finally took the plunge, and I'm about to graduate. *I'm so fucking lucky.*

I step onto the stage with pride, shake the principal's hand, and move my tassel to the other side with a grin that reaches my ears. Hollers of my name are shouted by Hunter, Jason, Julie, and my mother, expanding the laughter from my throat before I run down the steps, ready to fly back into Hunter's arms.

I launch myself at him, and he catches me with ease, his sculpted arms tightening around my waist. "We did it, Charls."

"We did it."

"I couldn't have done it without you."

"Not true, Hunter Hansen. You can do anything you want."

He lowers me to my feet, dipping his chin. "Right now, I want to kiss you."

His lips find mine, until Jason booms in his ear. "Pay attention, dickhead. I'm next."

"I'd rather look at her than you, idiot," Hunter grunts before we both hoot out a laugh.

We watch our entire class take their diplomas, then cheer with the rest of our classmates as we toss our caps in the air.

"Whooo! It's summer!" Julie throws her arms around Hunter and I, a bright smile lifting her cheeks.

"Can't fucking wait!" Jason joins us, wrapping his arms around us all.

"Get the fuck off me. I can't fucking breathe," Hunter teases.

"If you can't breathe, it's because this blondie took away your ability to function." Jason bops my nose with his index finger, a taunting expression glinting in his deep blue eyes.

"Yeah, Hunter becomes a fucking smitten little kitten when you're around," Julie pitches in.

"Smitten kitten?" Hunter and I echo with a matching incredulous look before we all bark out a full laugh. I glance around my friends, each of them vibrating with the same feeling that's been growing inside of me in the last week. I haven't felt this happy in so long. It's officially summer, and I think it matches well with the phase I'm walking through.

Warm, comfortable, and ready for our next adventures. After this, we will all split up and go our separate ways, but I'm deciding here and now... I'm never saying goodbye to these people. I refuse to. I will do everything in my power to keep them in my life, no matter what challenges I still have to face.

Including Hunter.

My gaze crashes with Hunter's, his hazel eyes sparkling against mine, our planned separation suddenly feeling less daunting than before. We're gonna make this work. We still have the entire summer to figure it out, and I know we will find a way.

His smile mirrors mine, our vision blurring out everything around us again, until he snaps his head down, reaching for his phone in his pocket.

He reads the screen, and I see his face fall a little before he flicks his attention back up, then glances around the three of us. "Sorry, I need to take this."

"I'm so happy for you and Hunter!" Julie squeezes my arm, but I'm fixating on Hunter's back, trying to catch parts of his conversation.

"Yeah, me too." My tone is flat, my heart picking up its pace. I hold my smile, but inside, a voice in my head is screaming. My gut roars with a sinister feeling, tensing my muscles.

"Are you okay, Charlie?" Julie lowers her head to force me to look at her, but I move past her, lasering in on my best friend. Hunter's posture becomes more defeated with every second, the tightness of his shoulders showing his disagreement about something.

"I'm not sure." I shake my head.

I know this feeling. I've felt it numerous times before, and the last time was when I woke up with Hunter lying next to me.

"Okay, yes. I'll see you then," I hear Hunter say, before he finally turns back. His eyes snap to mine with the sharpness of a butcher knife, my heart dropping to the floor. With a guilty expression, he takes a few steps to stand in front of me.

"That was the AFA." *Don't say it.* "They need me to fly to LA tonight."

My eyes mist over, a lump the size of a fucking bowling ball building in my throat.

"For how long?" I manage to croak out, but one look in his troubled gaze already gives me a clear answer.

"For the rest of the summer."

And I feel my heart break a little.

"I'm just going to tell them that I need a couple more weeks." Hunter's standing on my front lawn, lifting his snapback from his head to run a hand through his hair.

I don't want to have this conversation. Period. I knew it was inevitable, and the thought alone was chipping away at my heart. But I had convinced myself that we had at least the rest of the summer to figure it all out. That we still had time to make memories and come up with a solution that would work. I was silently praying that my mother was feeling a lot better at the end of the summer and I could go with him. I secretly had been applying to a few universities, with the intent to have options, if by the end of the summer we'd still want a future together.

But the minute he got that phone call, I knew everything I planned was vanishing in front of my eyes. There was no avoiding it. There was no way around it. Our burning flame was bright and short-lived, and I know that the distance will ruin whatever more we wanted to build beyond our deep friendship. It's too soon to make a definite decision when we really just admitted our feelings five days ago.

We need more time. Time we don't have.

Sitting on the steps of my front porch, the sun burns down on me with a heat that's scorching. The warm wood that's connected with my ass has me glued, unable to move as I look into his warm eyes. Pain is etching through them, as if his heart is being torn in two, and I do my best to keep my emotions in place, knowing I will make him doubt his decision if I shed even a single tear.

I can't ask him to stay. It's not fair. So, instead, I push out the words that feel like razor blades moving down my gullet.

"It was one night, Hunter. We shouldn't put it all on the line for one night. Not now that you're going to be halfway across the country half the time."

"It wasn't one night! It was more than that, and you know it!"

"You have to go. This is what you've been working for."

"What if I've been working for you?" His voice is strained.

"Hunt." He can't. I can't let him do this.

He brings his fist to his lips, closing his eyes. My tongue presses against my cheek to hold in the water that's pooling behind my own.

"What if I don't want to do this without you?"

"No. I'm not going to let you do this. You're going."

He shakes his head, pressing his lips together. "I just got you."

"You'll always have me. Nothing is going to change that."

"You know what I mean."

Of course I know what he means. My heart is yelling at me, demanding to stop digging the hole I'm about to fall into. But asking him to stay would be selfish. Giving him a reason to put it all on the line would make him regret it all in the end. I have to have faith that we will find our way. This is not a forever goodbye.

"I think you should focus on fighting right now. That's your future."

"What does that mean?" His shrug lacks energy, gutting me.

I suck in a breath of fresh air that stretches my neck with a determined smile, hoping I can at least fool him if I can't fool myself. "It means that we'll go back to being best friends."

"Best friends?" Frustrated, he turns his back to me, looking up at the sky.

"It's the only option, Hunt," I continue. "You can't have any distractions. You can't be worried about me when you're in California and I'm still here in North Carolina. At least until my mama gets better. And then we'll see. Maybe I can go to college in California. You can take me to Disney."

He turns his head back to me, looking at me with his piercing gaze. It feels like he's grown in the last week. He's no longer the boy I met that day at the creek. He's all man, ready to take control of his life.

"Is this what you want?"

No.

"That's all we can have right now."

He studies my face while regret gets stamped on my chest, harder and heavier. But I can't back out. I have to trust it will all work out at some point.

"You know you're part of my future, right?"

I smile at his words, my heart feeling betrayed by my own actions. "Best friends forever, right?"

He nods, then his arm reaches out to pull me from the steps as he tucks me into his side.

"Best friends forever," he confirms, pressing a kiss on my hair.

The corner of my mouth rises in a small smile, and I press my cheek against his chest, wrapping my arms around his waist.

"I'm proud of you, Hunt. Claim your place, win that debut fight, show those fuckers you are there to take over, and who knows? Maybe you can ask them if you can fly back home for a few days in a couple of weeks? Or maybe Julie and I can visit when you're all settled in. It'll be fun."

"I'd like that." His lips land on my hair once more. "Though I'm not sure I won't kiss you if I get you alone, Charls." He chuckles, and I quickly slap his chest in response, with a grin splitting my face.

"Stop flirting with me."

We've been friends since the first day we met, having a comfort between us that makes being friends the easy part of our relationship.

We can do that from whatever place we are in the world...
Right?

28

HUNTER

I STARE OUT OF the floor-to-ceiling windows of the big house in the Hollywood Hills they gave me to stay in. It's bigger than any house I've ever seen from the inside, and it's hard to realize this is where I'm going to be living for the unforeseeable future. A year ago, I'd be pumped at the opportunity, but now it's all overshadowed by the girl I wanted to share it with.

"Man, this is fucking sick," Jason bellows from behind me, slapping me on the back. "Did you see? It has five bathrooms!" A tight smile curls my mouth when my eyes lock with his beaming face.

"It's insane, really." It really is. Here I am, an eighteen-year-old boy on track to be the next best thing in MMA. When I got that phone call from the AFA, I was ecstatic to fly toward freedom. But it was with a heavy heart. Looking into Charlotte's blue-green eyes as I walked toward the gate yesterday was the hardest thing I'd ever had to do, and I wasn't prepared for it. Ever since it was just my mother and me, I'd been waiting for the moment I could spread my wings, leaving everything in Braedon behind without as much as a second glance. But last year changed that for me. Now I'm leaving the one thing behind I want to keep more than anything.

With a pain in my chest, I pull my phone out of my pocket, dialing Charlotte's number before putting the phone to my ear. My heart starts to race, looking over the Hills as the dial tone sounds, loud and ominous. Something in her voice yesterday felt final, and I know I have to let her go. I know it's not fair to ask her to leave her life in North Carolina and just come with me. But now everything feels different. From the moment I landed in LA, calling her felt like torture, as if something erased the easiness between us, even though I'm dying to hear her voice.

"Took you long enough, Hansen." I can hear her smile through the phone, and instantly I'm smiling.

"Sorry, babe. Things are hectic here."

"Yeah? Bet they're all gushing over the new prodigy? Got any groupies yet?"

I rub the back of my neck, thinking about the welcoming party last night.

"Just some people who are dying to meet the new fighter we signed," Gina Partridge from the AFA told us. She's my new manager, and wastes no time getting the ball rolling in whatever they got planned for me. Jason and I thought it was going to be a small gathering after the flight, have some drinks, that kinda thing.

Instead, we walked into a big pool party, where everyone cheered us on as we entered the room. Everyone wanted to shake our hands. We got offered drinks as soon as our glasses were empty, and within ten minutes, girls dying to get our attention surrounded us. It was a huge contrast with the small-town life in Braeden, and it did stroke my ego in more ways than I anticipated. We had a grand night, feeling like big shots at an LA party, but my mind kept wandering off to Charlotte with every girl who tried to glue herself to my side.

"Yeah, it was fun. They threw us a big LA party. I don't even remember all the hands I shook."

"That's good. Did you ask them if you could fly back in a few weeks?"

"Yeah, I did," I start, rubbing my hand over my cheek. "Fuck, Charls. I can't."

She stays quiet for a few seconds, the silence speaking loud and clear. "You can't, or you don't want to?"

"I want to! Of course I fucking want to. But they got me an entire team to work with. A trainer, a coach, food specialist, even set me up with some kind of media chick. They're putting me on a tight schedule for the rest of the summer. Starting tomorrow. They even agreed to take Jason on as my PR-guy. Giving him a contract as the one controlling my social media while he still goes to Stanford."

"Oh," she says quietly, the sound cutting like a knife right into my aorta. "That's great, Hunt."

You know how you can feel when people are happy for you, and when they are just bullshitting you? That's the thing with Charlotte. I know she isn't bullshitting me. She's thrilled for me, supporting me to the core, but I can feel the hurt that I know is going through her body. She'd never voice it, refusing to be the one to hold me back, but after the last week, I know pieces are getting scraped off her kind heart.

Because that's how I feel. That's how my heart grows more black and cold inside my chest. With complete and utter agony that's felt within every molecule of my being.

"I'm sorry, Charls," I offer, closing my eyes to imagine her gorgeous face. "I'm so sorry. I really thought we could at least have a few more days."

"Hunter Hansen." The tone in her voice is reprimanding, and I can imagine the slight frown on her forehead that makes me chuckle every time. "Don't you dare apologize for following your dreams. This is what you're supposed to do, and I want you to go and grab it. Show the world you're the world's best fighter, ready to kick anyone's ass who tells you otherwise. Don't you worry about me. I'm still me. We're still us, right? We can visit each other. And I'll cheer you on, screaming at the TV. Besides, you need to gain some fans so you can include those pay-per-views in your contract. Make sure you bring in the big money."

I chuckle. "As soon as I bring in the big money, I'm flying you out here."

"You fucking better."

"I will."

"Hey, Hunt?" I hum in response. "Just have fun. Enjoy it all." I hear what she's saying between the lines, but I don't want to hear it. The thought of continuing on without her tears me up inside. "*Please?*" she adds.

"Okay," I concede, but only because I don't want to make her feel worse than she's already feeling. Than I'm already feeling. I let out a deep sigh, knowing I'll miss her more than anything, but she's right. I need to focus.

"Best friends forever, right?"

Nodding at her words, I stare at my faint reflection in the window. "Yeah. Best friends forever."

"Good. Stop sulking then," she says, a finality in her tone.

I let out a chuckle, walking back to the couch, flopping myself onto it.

"Fine." Rubbing my face, we stay quiet for a few beats, enjoying the silence that forms between us. "I'm going to miss you, Charlotte Roux."

"I'll miss you too, Hunt. You gonna call me every night?"

"Hey, shithead! Gina is here. She needs you to sign the contracts." Jason's voice blasts through the room, rippling a chuckle from Charls.

"Tell Jason he better take good care of you, or I'm coming for him."

"Who are you talking to?" Jason jumps over the back of the couch, dropping his ass next to me. His blond hair is longer than usual, a lost strand springing free in front of his frown.

"Charlotte. She says you better take care of me, or she's coming for you."

"Oh, don't worry, girl. I'll make sure he's taken care of. Does that include orgasms?" he screams at the phone as he wiggles his eyebrows up and down. I throw my fist at his chest.

"Ouch!" he yelps.

"Shut up, asshole," I growl, listening to Charlotte's laughter in my ear, relieved she doesn't take his words seriously.

"He's going to be a total player, isn't he?" Charlotte asks.

"Yeah, he is." I smile, softly shaking my head, hearing a set of heels tapping on the marble floor and into the living area. Turning my head, I look up at Gina, the epitome of a businesswoman wearing a black pantsuit. "I gotta go, babe. And yeah, I will call you every night."

"Okay. Bye, Hunt."

"Bye, babe."

"Who was that?" Gina takes a seat on the loveseat in front of us, giving me a mocking look with her coffee-brown eyes and red painted lips. "High school sweetheart?"

"His best friend," Jason answers, as I give him a glare, telling him to shut up.

"Well, she'll be soon forgotten once you've got a taste of these Californian girls who will be begging you to take them home." She gives me a wink, getting the contracts out of her briefcase, and placing them on the glass coffee table, then she shoves one of them in front of Jason.

"I'm here to fight," I counter with a scowl. "Not to get pussy."

Gina looks up with surprise, her gaze moving back and forth between Jason and me, as she offers me a sweet smile and hands me a pen.

"Of course."

Leaning forward, I rip it out of her hand, rolling my eyes as I slowly shake my head, before I go over the contract in front of me, ready to sign up for my new life.

A few minutes later, all signatures are where they belong, and Gina flicks her gaze between Jason and me.

"So, how do you like the house?" Dark eyes scan us expectantly, and Jason and I share a look.

"It's great. A little big for just the two of us, but I'm not complaining." Jason shrugs as we nod in union.

"It is a little big," she drawls, cocking her neck a little, "but that's because you'll be sharing it."

Fuck no. "What? With who? You better not be throwing in some chick for publicity."

"Relax, geez." Palm up, Gina's eyes grow wide. "I see that whoever she is, she's still got your panties in a twist. Don't worry, *fighter boy*. It's a guy."

I release my pent-up breath, avoiding Jason's glare pinning me down. He's been asking what the deal is with Charlotte and I, now that I'm on the other side of the country, but I've been avoiding the conversation as much as I can because I don't fucking know.

We're not together.

We're friends.

But she's still running through my mind like we're more than that, and right now I'm not ready to let that go. *Not yet.*

"Who is he?" I try to keep my tone flat.

"The LA Knights latest purchase; Jared James Jensen."

YEAR TWO

YEAR TWO

THIS IS EXACTLY WHAT OUR FRIENDSHIP HAS ALWAYS BEEN.
CONFUSING AS FUCK.

*'When have I have ever been okay
with that?'*

29

HUNTER

I T ALL FEELS WRONG.

    I look into the mirror, biting my lip while I stare at my flushed face, not completely recognizing myself. They hooked me up with new gear, and even my hands are wrapped into better bands than I've ever fought with before.

I expected to feel a rush of adrenaline from hearing the crowd outside the door, getting amped up because of the fight before me. But really, I feel numb.

This isn't how I envisioned it. When I got the call that the AFA wanted me, I always pictured Charlotte with me. Cheering me on for my first fight. Hugging me and calling me a showoff when I win. But instead, the empty dressing room feels more daunting than the cage I'm about to step into.

With a deep sigh, I lock gazes with my reflection.

Focus on the goal, Hunt.

Make it big, then do whatever you want.

A year ago, that sentence would end there: make it big.

Now, I want to make it big to have choices. To buy myself time, even though I have no clue how much time I need.

I take my phone from the table, needing to hear her voice.

"How are you feeling?" I smile when Charlotte answers after the first ring, making me think back on all the fights she's been to with me at the warehouse. Those days seem like forever ago, when really, it's only been a couple of weeks.

"Pumped." *It's a lie.* But I know that my survival mode kicks in as soon as I'm gated with nothing more than my opponent to go up against.

"You better beat his ass."

"I wanna beat your ass." *Fuck, I miss her.*

"Stop flirting with me."

"Fine." I roll my eyes with a smile, enjoying the fact that she sticks to our routines. I've been enjoying the last two weeks, trying to get used to LA life, but I still need her. I still need our phone calls to keep me grounded, reminding me where I'm from.

"How is Liz?" Her mother has been doing good, and I'm keeping my fingers crossed, hoping she'll be able to stay without Charlotte for a few days so I can see her.

"Good! We went to the bookstore today. Bought a new romance book."

"You mean word porn?" I tease.

"For your information, *asshole*"—I can hear the smile in her voice—"it's a historical romance."

"No sex?"

"Nope." Her 'p' pops, reminding me of her luscious lips, and I simultaneously lick my own.

"Boring."

"Asshole mode on, *check*."

A smile creeps around my mouth. "I'm your asshole, though." Her sigh is loaded, filled with unspoken words neither of us is brave enough to release into the world.

"Are you watching?" I ask, changing the subject.

"Of course." She huffs. "Just... don't drag it out too long."

"Why, babe?" I mock.

"You know why." I can almost hear the scowl on her face that I saw every Friday night when she was waiting outside the cage for me.

"I wanna hear you say it."

"You *really* are an asshole."

"Say it, or I will go those three rounds, stretching it for as long as possible, knowing you are going bat-shit crazy on the couch."

"Fuck you," she spits, and I bark out a laugh.

"Say it."

"I don't want to watch you fight longer than necessary," she finally admits, and I grin at my reflection in the mirror, knowing those are the only words I need before I go out there.

"I miss you."

"I miss you too," she whispers, though I can hear the hesitation in her voice that's trying to keep this strictly friends between us.

"Second round, babe. Beginning of the second round."

"You have to make a show out of it, don't you?" I can practically hear her eyes roll.

"It's my first fight, babe. Gotta make an impression, right?"

"Just get out of there unscathed."

Her concern lifts the tension from my muscles, like taking off my jacket and telling me I'm ready. "Always, babe."

"Promise?" she asks softly, the tone of her voice making a flutter grow in my stomach, and I drag a hand over my face. *Fuck, I wish she was here.*

"Promise."

30

Charlotte

I WALK INTO JULIE'S yard, finding her on the screen porch while sipping a sweet tea and reading a magazine after she sent me a text telling me to get the fuck out of the house.

Her literal words.

At first, I protested heavily, but when she compared me to a mix of a hermit and a cat lady, I felt obligated to show her I'm not any of those things.

When I look at how I've spent the last ten weeks, she's kinda right, though.

It's funny how fast the days pass by when you do nothing significant. Other than taking care of my mother, and hanging out with Julie and Jacob, who I now know is indeed the asshole Hunter paints him to be, I've been reading the entire summer. I actually think Mrs. Dennis from the local library is feeling sorry for me, because every time I walk in, she keeps eyeing me with this sympathetic look on her face. I re-read all the classics in the first month of summer, and now I've been reading some romance books, trying to fill my days, while other kids are preparing for college.

Me? I'm just out here missing my best friend.

After his first fight, the media exploded around him. Suddenly, everyone wants a piece of him, a few girls *literally*, if I can believe the tabloids. But with more media attention also comes more obligation, and lately, our daily calls have changed to weekly calls. Now I haven't spoken to him in ten days.

I'm happy for him, and so fucking proud. But it doesn't stop my heart from leaking drops of blood every day I wake up and don't hear from him.

"Hey, girl." Julie looks up as I walk through the door and take a seat next to her on the wooden armchair, throwing my feet on the table in front of us, mimicking her stance.

"Hey! Sweet tea?" Her flip-flop covered feet fall to the floor, leaning forward to grab the can filled with sweet tea as she pours me a glass, topping it off with a fresh lemon wedge.

"Thanks." I grab the glass, taking a sip of the cold drink as I close my eyes and lay my head back, looking up at the ceiling.

"What were you doing yesterday?" *Here we go.* Turning my head toward her, I blink at her in innocence, giving her my sweetest smile. "Dear Lord, Charlie. You really gotta balance it out a bit more. You hardly get off your front porch."

"I get off my front porch!"

She cocks her head, shooting me a look that tells me I'm full of shit, and I roll my eyes at her. I mean, I still need groceries and all that stuff?

"Only because either your mama has a hospital appointment, or I force you to. It's not healthy. At least when Hunter was still around, you'd go out and shit."

Right. "Yeah, well, he isn't."

Hearing the disappointment in my voice, she gives me a questioning look, turning her back to the side of the chair so she can face me.

"You haven't heard from him?"

"We talk." I shrug, trying to act casual about it, when really, it's tightening my stomach. "Like once a week. But the conversations keep getting shorter, because he's always at some party, or training, or that Gina woman needs him for something."

"You miss him, don't you?" I keep my green eyes trained on the ceiling to keep my tears at bay, knowing they are there just waiting to burst out.

"Like crazy," I confess, pushing out a breath. "It's weird, because I want him to succeed. I want him to be the best fighter there is, so it's not like I want him to come back, but I feel like he's slipping away. We spent so much time together last year that I have a hard time filling my days without him. No offense." I give her a tight smile, and she responds with a big grin.

"None taken. I have no intention of competing with Hunter. I'd pick that fine body over you any time of day," she jokes. "But yeah, I get you. You've been inseparable throughout senior year, and now he's on the other side of the country, living a different life."

"Yeah. The more time passes, the less we seem to talk."

I'm not stupid. I knew our friendship would change the second he got on that plane.

If this whole twist of fate isn't a sign to tell us that we aren't anything more than friends, I don't know what is.

And I just need to accept that, I guess?

But being friends is a lot harder when we're both on the other side of the country, living completely different lives.

"Why don't you visit him?"

I snap my head toward Julie. "I don't know?"

Probably because I'm a scared little girl, not very keen on setting myself up for rejection? I wasn't the popular girl in high school, barely fitting in, but it wasn't awful. I was too busy to worry about anything other than schoolwork anyway. But going to LA? It feels like throwing me in the creek before I learned how to swim.

Spending time with Hunter there will be different, and I'm not sure it's a good difference. He might be my friend, but I'm pretty sure he knows how to swim in the great ocean that's called California.

What if he doesn't want to keep me afloat while I'm there?
She rolls her eyes, shaking her head.

"There's no reason not to? I mean, not anymore. Your mama has been doing pretty good all summer. I'm sure she won't mind if you go to LA for a couple of days. You still have two weeks before classes start."

How she's putting it, it seems like a simple thing to do, and yeah, I've thought about it. But I don't dare to voice it to Hunter, not sure how he'd react.

"Whatever insecure thoughts are running through your mind right now, stop it." She scowls, and I purse my lips with guilt dripping from my chin. "He's gonna wanna see you, too. You know this. Just book a ticket, and go see him for the weekend."

"I don't know, Julie. What if he doesn't want me there? What if he's busy all weekend?"

"Then you spend time with Jason. We sure as fuck know he's not doing anything other than playing Hunter's wingman," she mutters, with a frustrated glint drifting around her brown eyes. "Either way, just go. Before you know it, classes will start, and you'll have no time to visit anymore."

I keep staring at her, as I'm letting her words run through my hesitant mind while my heart jumps for joy at the idea.

"Stop thinking about it, Charlie. In fact, we're putting you on a plane tomorrow."

She grabs her phone off the table and starts tapping the screen like a madwoman.

"What are you doing? I have to ask Hunter first!"

"No, you don't. Delta has a flight tomorrow at noon. I say perfect."

"Julie."

"What?" She gives me a daring look, bringing up a finger. "You have two options. Either you let go of him, stop sulking, and start living your life, like he is. Or you find out if the two of you are still the same and go to LA. Your call, Charlie." She presses her lips together in a thin line, doing her best to keep a straight face, trying to let me decide what I'm going to do. But I can see the fire in her eyes, challenging me to back out.

If she puts it like that.

"Fine," I huff. "Book it."

31

Charlotte

I WAS PETRIFIED.

I was petrified to tell him I was coming, and I'm petrified now, walking out of LAX airport, waiting to see his gorgeous face. It's ridiculous because I've spent my entire senior year with him, but my heart keeps pounding in my chest, stopping for a second when my eyes finally lock with his.

He looks the same, yet totally different. His arms have buffed up even more, stretching his tattoos in a breathtaking way, peeking out from under his black t-shirt. The California sun has given him a tan that makes his hazel eyes pop from under his backwards snapback with an intensity that heats my core within a split second.

Why does he have to be so fucking hot?

I swallow hard, wondering how he's going to react. Rapidly blinking, I wait until a ghost of a smile expands to a full, devastating smirk, and I take that as my cue to drop my shit and run toward him, launching myself against his body.

I wrap my legs around his waist, holding my arms tight around his shoulders as I bury my nose in his neck, breathing in his woodsy cologne. His nose snuggles in my hair, his scorching lips finding the skin on my neck to plant a lingering kiss on the spot underneath my ear.

"God, I missed you, babe," he breathes, his mouth flush with my ear.

His arms are locked around my body, and he tightens his grip, tugging me even closer as I lean back to cup his face.

"I missed you too," I confess, my eyes moving back and forth, looking into his deep hazel-brown ones. My lips part, feeling the need to cover his mouth with mine, even though I'm not sure if I'm still allowed to do that. When I notice his gaze moving to my lips, he fists my hair, bringing me closer to his face, that same hunger appearing in his eyes that I've been seeing for so long, yet now feels like a distant memory.

"I know we agreed on *friends*, but I'm not sure I can let you fly back to North Carolina in a few days without having one more memory of your lips on mine." His voice sounds husky, and I bite my lip as a longing feeling boils inside of me.

"I think you can have one freebie."

"Yeah?" A boyish grin appears on his face, and I brush my nose against his, softly nodding as he crushes his lips against mine.

The touch of his lips covering mine feels overwhelming and satisfying at the same time. *God, I missed kissing him.* His hands rub my hips as we stay connected, and I do my best to not let my tongue dart out, knowing I won't stop if we cross that threshold again.

"Ahem." I register Jason demonstratively clearing his throat behind us. "How about we take this to the house and the two of you can suck face there?"

"Hi, Jason," I quip with a giggle when I break our connection, pressing my forehead into Hunter's shoulder. He lets go of my legs, softly putting me back on the ground, then brings me back against his chest, pressing a lingering kiss on my forehead.

He feels like home, and all I want to do is cuddle up against him and watch a movie. I look up as he dips his chin, feeling happy as fuck that he's standing in front of me again.

"Maybe that was a bit too friendly," he jokes, causing a chuckle to leave my lips.

"Yeah, maybe."

"Come on, let's go." Jason gets my bag while Hunter throws an arm over my shoulder, escorting me back to a black Escalade.

"*This* your car?" I stop on the pavement, his arm falling from my body as I stare at the enormous car in front of me.

"Pretty sweet, huh?" Jason chimes in, throwing my bag in the backseat as he holds the door open for me. With my mouth agape, I take in the extravagant vehicle, then twist my head toward Hunter.

"It's not mine," he explains. "It's just a car the AFA provided for us to use. I'm not rich, Charls. I *promise*." His gaze is filled with pain, confusing me a little.

"Yet!" Jason bellows as he climbs behind the wheel, and Hunter gives me a small push to urge me into the car.

I get in, smelling the fresh leather as I look around inside, realizing how different his life must really be right now.

Hunter gets in on the passenger side, then glances over his shoulder. "You good?"

"Yeah." I nod. "I'm good."

I think.

I rest my head against the window, taking in the streets of LA as we drive to their house. Palm trees stand tall in the sunlight, just like in the movies, and the number of Chihuahuas prancing down the streets makes it clear we're no longer in Braeden, North Carolina. But it isn't until we reach the house they live in that it's perfectly clear how much of a difference there is.

Jason drives to a brown gate, opening it with a code, before he moves forward to park the car in front of a modern white house. The house has tinted windows that are floor-to-ceiling high, surrounded by perfectly white concrete walls, and you don't have to be a genius to understand this is a multi-million-dollar home.

I'm gawking, blinking in awe, as Hunter opens the door for me, giving me a measured look while waiting for my reaction.

"*This* is your house?" My eyes are as wide as saucers, and my hand reaches out to pinch Hunter on his arm.

"Ouch! What was that for?" He rubs the area with a slight scowl.

"Just wanted to make sure I'm not dreaming." I slide out of the car, looking at the big house in front of me with narrowed eyes, while the sun burns on my back.

This is the kind of house you see in those reality shows everyone likes to watch. Spacious, luxurious, and nothing I'd ever see from the inside if Hunter and Jason weren't my friends.

"Pinch yourself, then!" he bellows, giving me a light push.

"No fun." I shrug, sauntering to the front door until I wait for him to open it.

He walks in first, followed by Jason carrying my bag, and I saunter behind him, looking up at the high ceiling, before my gaze lands on the glass stairs. The floor is a brown marble, making it look rich as fuck, while the black steel finishes make it anything but stately.

"Who owns this house?" I blurt as I keep walking farther before my sight settles in on the backyard. Particularly, the infinity pool that almost stretches the width of the entire yard.

"Sweet Lord, I know you told me you had a pool, but I didn't expect it to be this big?" My jaw drops to the floor, and I give Hunter an incredulous look, then turn toward Jason, who's look-ing at me with his arms folded in front of his body, a pleased look on his face.

"Not bad, huh?" Hunter says as his phone starts to ring, and he pulls it out of his pocket, glancing at the screen. "I gotta take this. Jay, can you show Charls her room?"

"You mean your room?" Jason's remark has me frozen on the spot.

The blood seems to leave Hunter's face, my heart cramping with an increased tempo.

We didn't discuss where I would be sleeping, and now the awkward look he's throwing me doesn't help to put me at ease.

"My *own* room, Jason," I reply with a tight smile. Hunter presses his lips together with what I think is disappointment, but it's gone when he nods before he leaves us. Jason studies my face, ignoring the last five seconds. With a sympathetic smile sliding on his cheeks, he walks toward me, giving me a slight push in the opposite direction. "Come on, Roux. This way."

"Jason, this house is—I don't even know what it is? This is like a dream."

"I know, it's like we woke up in MTV cribs or something."

"Oh my god, it really is." I follow him to the guest bedroom, and I jump onto the perfectly made king-size bed, shaking my head. Everything has a soft cream color, from the duvet to the curtain and the fluffy floor.

"This is your guestroom?"

"Yeah, on your left is Hunter's room. The asshole claimed the biggest." Jason points a thumb to his right. "Jensen sleeps down the hall."

"Jensen?"

Jason's eyebrows glue together, raking a hand through his light blonde hair. "He didn't tell you about Jensen?"

I shake my head, my shoulders instantly tightening, wondering if that's some chick that moved in with him.

"He plays for the LA Knights."

"A hockey player?" My neck stretches with a tiny smile, wondering if that brings up bad or good memories for Hunter.

"Yeah, you'll meet him later tonight, but he still had practice." Jason's leaning against the doorway, his arms crossed in front of his body. "You settle in for a while, get some rest. We've got a party tonight."

"A party?" I give him an unimpressed look. The last thing I want to do right now is go to some party. I'd much rather spend some time with them, just hanging out. Catching up. Hearing all the silly stories I'm sure they have after living here for the entire summer.

"Don't worry, I'm sure Hunt won't leave your side for a minute." He throws me a wink that I'm guessing should be reassuring, but instead it feels like someone just punched me in the gut.

A party.

Yay.

I'm staring out of the window at the Hollywood Hills, the Hollywood sign clearly visible if I stretch my neck to the right.

I can't believe I'm here.

I'm not really a glamor kind of girl. I don't do parties, and I rarely dress up, but I've seen the movies, and I'd be lying if I said I didn't dream of seeing the Hollywood Hills at least once in my life.

And here I am.

"Not a bad view, huh?" I turn around as Hunter walks into the room.

He's wearing dark jeans, with a navy dress shirt, looking clean and fresh. His sleeves are rolled up, showing off the chiseled curves of his tattooed arms, while his boyish grin peeks out from under his snapback.

He takes my breath away.

"Not bad at all." I turn back around, putting my gaze in front of me as he stands next to me. It's weird; it feels like something is standing between us. Like an invisible wall of questions and thoughts keeps us from being fully...well...*us.*

"It's not mine, Charls."

I furrow my brows, glancing at him in confusion. "What do you mean?"

"This. It's not mine. It looks nice, and right now, it seems like I've made it big time. But it's not mine. If anything, it's just a piece of candy that they're dangling in front of my face. They barely paid me for that first fight. Until I win some actual fights, this is just pretend." He waves his hand through the air with a look on his face I can't quite explain. He's supposed to be happy. He's supposed to finally feel like he's getting somewhere, but I still see the darkness threatening to pull him under.

It's as black as that day he found me reading at the creek, and it tightens my throat because this is not the Hunter I'd gotten so used to seeing before graduation.

That Hunter was lighter. *Happier.*

When I realize what he's saying, I cock my head, my eyes slightly annoyed.

"Hunter Hansen, don't you dare be ashamed of what you've accomplished."

"But that's just it!" he counters. "I haven't accomplished anything yet."

"No, but those people at the AFA know you'll be the best there is. Don't pretend you don't deserve this. You do. You worked damn hard for this." I give him a slight push, trying to make him laugh, poking to see if the boy who left me is still somewhere inside of him.

"I guess."

"Well, I *know*." I grab his arm, giving it a squeeze. "Don't be that little boy your mama wants you to be. She doesn't matter. *Nobody* matters." *Not even me.* "Only you. And you're doing damn good."

His face falls as he turns his body toward me, his hand reaching up to cup my face. "God, I've missed you."

I can see the slight movement of his head, as if he's doubting whether to kiss me, and I feel that same flutter in my gut that I've been feeling for a long time.

"I'm here now."

He shakes his head, like he's trying to snap himself out of whatever thoughts are running through his mind, before he lets go of my face.

"Taking you to a party tonight."

"Yeah, I heard." I pull a face that makes him roll his eyes.

"It'll be fun."

"Hunt, I'm not the party girl," I start, followed with a sigh that vibrates my body from head to toe. "You know this. Can't we just watch a movie?"

"You know these parties are nothing like the shit in high school?" He cocks a brow as I keep a straight face, unimpressed at his attempt to convince me.

"You found me reading at the creek."

"Come on, Charls. You're only in LA for two days. You can't go back to Julie, telling her you didn't go to a party, right?"

"I think she'd understand," I deadpan.

"Shut up, don't be a bore. We're going." His voice holds a finality that makes me repeat his words with a mocking tone, like a five-year-old, and his gaze darkens. He takes a step closer, getting in my personal space the way I'm used to. The way I've been yearning for the entire summer. I glare up at him, daring him with my eyes, as his narrowed ones move back and forth.

"Don't tempt me to shut you up in the only way I know is effective."

God, I want him to. But I know we can't cross that bridge anymore. Not if I want to keep my heart intact.

"Stop flirting with me." I swallow hard, doing my best to keep his gaze like a warrior, resisting the urge in the tips of my fingers to rip his clothes from his body.

"Get dressed, babe." He winks, making my heart melt on the spot. "We're leaving in an hour."

He walks out, closing the door behind him, and I let the air slip from my lungs.

I need to make sure I don't touch any alcohol tonight, because I'm not sure if he's going to keep pushing my buttons like that. I want to be pissed at him, remind him we agreed on friends. But as I look up to the ceiling, thinking about what to tell him to make sure we don't move past that threshold again, I realize there is no way.

Because this is exactly what our friendship has always been.

Confusing as fuck.

32

HUNTER

IT'S TEN P.M. WHEN we walk into the VIP area of Le Chic, the newest club in town. It's weird how easily doors open now that I'm the newest addition of AFA fighters. Ever since we've arrived, Jason and I don't have to wait in any queue, even though we're not twenty-one yet, and tonight is no exception.

I wait for Charlotte as she follows us, placing my hand on the small of her back, guiding her up onto the balcony that oversees the entire club. It's everything you'd imagine when you think about LA and a new club. The furniture is a luxurious black leather, with crystal elements that make it look fancy and expensive. A huge ass chandelier is hanging in the middle of the club, illuminating the floor with a disco light that's hooked up with a massive ornament.

I look at Charlotte, who has been gawking at everything she sees the entire day, and now is not any different. She's wearing a little black dress, with some black motorcycle booties that make her the rebel I know she can be. She doesn't fit in with the rest of the girls in the club, in their designer dresses and high heels, but she looks gorgeous. If anything, it makes me like her even more. Her dark blonde wavy hair falls perfectly over her shoulders, and I softly tug it to get her attention.

"What are you drinking, babe?"

"Water."

My eyes widen, shooting her an incredulous look.

"What?"

"You're at a club in LA, even though you're too young, and you're gonna drink water?"

"Since when do you drink?"

I can't unseen the disapproval in her eyes. "Just a *little* more since I moved here. No biggie."

Her candy pink lips purse with a deep frown. "Do you remember what happened the last time you got drunk when I was around?"

How the fuck can I forget? It took me a week to believe she actually forgave me. Though watching her green eyes flare up a bit has me wondering if that's really the case.

I push a strand of her silky hair behind her ear, bringing my lips close to her neck so I have an excuse to breathe in her sweet scent. "I'm not saying get drunk. I'm saying have a drink. Relax."

The sigh that follows is deep, and I narrow my eyes at her, wondering what is going on in that pretty little head of hers.

"Maybe later, okay?" she offers, and I shrug my shoulders, then continue ordering her water. It takes a minute for the server to come back with our drinks, and we all stand next to each other, roaming the club from the balcony.

"So, this is what you two have been up to this entire summer?" Charlotte looks up at me with a smile, though I can see the disappointment in her eyes.

Fucking hell. I was trying to avoid this look by taking her to a club instead of hanging out with her back at the house. There's nothing more I want right now than to pull her on my lap, with her settling her head in the crook of my neck, watching some stupid movie. But the thought of having her in my arms only makes me want more, and I know that will confuse everything for her. Hell, it will confuse everything for *me*. We're not togeth-

er. We're friends. We made that very clear when I left. The more we keep pushing those boundaries, the more our friendship will be destroyed. I just know it. So, I took the safe route and brought her to a party instead. That way, I won't be tempted to touch her every chance I get.

"Pretty much," I admit with a shrug as the server hands us our drinks.

The three of us take a seat on the leather couch, with Charlotte sitting in the middle, as Jason and I have both our arms spread out over the back.

"Have you ever been to California, Charlotte?" Jason takes a sip from his drink, offering her a questioning look.

She shakes her head, giving a quick glance my way.

"Do you like it so far?"

"It's different," she responds with an unimpressed look.

I cock my head a little, looking at her while my hand softly strokes her hair. I can feel the cloud of uncertainty she's floating on and it's tugging on my heart more than I want.

"You okay?" I ask.

She brings her attention back to me, sucking in a deep breath, plastering a big smile on her face. "Yeah, I'm great!"

I'm not buying that.

"You sure?" I squint my gaze, placing my hand on the back of her neck, giving it a light squeeze.

"Positive. Now tell me all about your LA life." Her head moves back and forth between Jason and me with a beaming smile. I shoot her a look, telling her silently I know she's full of shit, before I lean forward, resting my elbows on my knees, then nudge my chin at Jason.

"Jay is better at storytelling than I am."

Jason mimics my stance, rubbing his hands together like he's been waiting for this moment the entire day, and I roll my eyes with a chuckle as I take another sip of my drink.

An hour later, Jason has listed all the girls he slept with in the past two months while my head gets foggy as fuck and I feel hammered. *So maybe one drink became a little more.* I figured it would help keep me occupied from getting into Charlotte's space, but that's backfiring. The more I drink, the more confident I feel around Charlotte, and I can't help touching her while we are still sitting on the couch, listening to Jason's excessive stories.

A brush of her hair there.

A touch of her knee here.

A stroke of her arm.

If I can find an opening, I'm taking it, even though the brief touches are becoming scorching, fueling the need to drag her to the bathroom and kiss her until she sees stars.

"Wait, so you didn't realize they both offered themselves to you? Together?" She blinks at Jason with an amused grin on her face.

"No! I thought I was working both of them, figuring one of them would end up in my bed, eventually. Little did I know my dream would come true." He brings his hands together in a thankful gesture, looking up at the sky.

"They gave you your first threesome?" She chuckles.

"It was marvelous!" he groans with excitement, dramatically throwing his back against the couch.

She laughs at his theatrics, and I marvel at her smile, soaking it up like it's the sun on a cold winter day. She grounds me. Panic already surges through me, thinking she'll leave again in a couple of days, and I rest my palm on her neck, just to remind myself she's real. She's here.

Her eyes slowly find mine, piercing and breathtaking. It's like the air grows thicker as she studies my face, while my thumb brushes up and down her skin. Automatically, my gaze drops to her lips, tempting me to lean in and take them as mine. But a loaded exhale flies over her mouth, curling in a strained smile.

"Well, on that note. I think I need to use the bathroom." She gets up, breaking our connection and walking toward the stairs. I watch her every move until she's out of sight, and Jason gives me a rough push, followed by a fist on my leg.

"What the fuck, man?" I growl when I see an athletically built guy walking up the same stairs, his eyes following Charlotte before turning his head with a wide grin.

"Don't even think about it, Jensen!" Our third roommate strolls toward us, then reaches out his hand to both of us.

"She yours?"

"She sure ain't yours," I counter, taking another sip of my drink. He flops his 6'1" bulky frame on the couch on my left. His dark hair is longer on the front, dancing a little around his forehead before his cheeks curl.

"That doesn't answer my question."

"It's his best friend," Jason answers for me, and I shoot him a death glare, because that's not the full explanation I want Jensen to pick up on. Charlotte might not be mine, but there's no way in hell I'm going to let Jensen near her. Or any guy, for that matter.

"Oh, shit." He tilts his head in disappointment. "That's your girl? *The* girl? The one you left at home?"

"That would be her," Jason mutters under his breath. "She's not *his*, though. Something Hunter seems to have forgotten for the last hour."

"Shame." Jensen smirks. "She's fucking hot."

"Shut the fuck up and stay away from her!" I snap.

"What are you doing?" Jason yelps with wide eyes, throwing his hands up in frustration. The disapproval is dripping from his tongue, and I don't even bother to seek out his glare. Instead, I close my eyes.

"What are you talking about?"

"Charlotte!"

"What about her?" I'm not sure why I'm acting all coy, but at this point, it's all I got.

I twist my head at his annoyed face, narrowing his eyes on me. "She's your *best friend*. You're not together, and she's leaving in two days. Stop touching the damn girl!"

Rolling my eyes, a guilty feeling trickles down my skin, and I quickly take a sip of my drink to ignore it. "What are you talking about? I'm not doing shit."

"Oh, no?" He scowls, then flutters his eyes at me, placing his hand on my knee, then strokes the back of my neck in a mocking way and finally slapping me over the head. "This is *not* what best friends do. You keep touching her like she's yours. She's not."

"Whatever. What do you care, anyway?"

"Because you're confusing her! In two days, she's gonna get on that plane and fly back to North Carolina. If you're going to keep acting like you two are together, you'll break her heart all over again. She doesn't deserve that. Stop confusing yourself and stop confusing *her*," he blurts with annoyance, narrows his eyes on me.

I hate how fucking right he is, but the biggest issue is I don't know how to stop it. I don't know how to rein in my impulses when it comes to Charlotte, and the longer I hold Jason's stern expression, the more I feel like this was all one big mistake.

I should've never let her fly out here, because I knew it was going to be torture for both of us.

"That is ..." Jensen chimes in, "unless she is more than your friend."

With a bucketload of guilt, I flick my gaze to Jason as a knowing look appears on his face, challenging me to tell them otherwise, and I hold his gaze as I swallow hard. *Fuck.* It hurts, but I'll give her what she asked for.

"No, she's my friend. Nothing more. She made that perfectly clear," I answer resolutely, remembering the day I flew out here.

"It was one night, Hunter. We shouldn't put it all on the line for one night. It means that we'll go back to being best friends. It's the only option."

"Then fucking treat her like that," Jason barks, deep blue eyes flashing with a little anger.

I nod in agreement, knowing he's right, as I grab my glass from the table, pouring the rest of the contents down my throat, then I snap my hand at the security guy with an approved look. She wants it like this, and I'm the bastard who will give her what she wants.

He gives me a nod, before he does the same to the security guy down the stairs and a few girls move up the stairs a few seconds later.

"Now *that's* what I'm talking about," Jensen cheers beside me, and I rest my back into the couch, letting my eyes roam over a brunette who's fluttering her lashes at me. She looks a few years older than I am, a gold dress hugging her curves. She's hot. Not Charlotte gorgeous, but hot enough to make a point. And by the relentless thumping of my heart that's telling me I'm making a mistake, a point definitely needs to be made. For Charlotte. And for me. We're *friends.*

"Hunt, are you sure you want to do this?" Jason scolds.

"What? You thought I was bluffing." I swallow the bile back into my stomach, keeping a straight face. He's the one who said I should treat her as my friend and nothing more. The only way to get that message across is to do it drastically.

"Your funeral, man." He rubs a hand over his face, frustration washing his expression, clearly not happy with the decision I made.

I give him a comforting smile as my attention is stolen by the girl taking a seat on my lap. Her face is caked in make-up, probably making her prettier than she really is, and her boobs seem to barely fit in her metallic dress, but my dick doesn't care when she slowly grinds her ass on my lap following the beat of the music. I quickly glance at Jensen, who's giving me a thumbs up, then lay my head back and close my eyes, enjoying the friction going on between my pants. My heart is yelling at me to stop, knowing this is not the girl I want on my lap tonight, but my mind wins the battle.

My mind knows the girl I want is no longer an option.

My mind knows the girl I want will be on a plane back to North Carolina by the end of tomorrow.

I can't put my focus on Charlotte, because life gave us both a different set of cards to play with.

I need to cut Charlotte loose, because she deserves more than what I can offer. Even if it means breaking her heart in the process.

33

Charlotte

WALKING INTO THE BATHROOM, I'm reminded once more that I'm no longer in North Carolina as I look at the gold metallic walls, with another chandelier hanging in the center of the room. The area is spacious, like you need to have some bathroom etiquette just to be allowed to touch the faucets, yet there are only four stalls, all occupied.

I wait patiently for a stall to open, glancing at myself in front of the mirror, hoping I still look somewhat presentable, even though I know I definitely don't look like your typical LA girl. My green eyes are staring back at me with a sad look on my face, and I shake my head, trying to get rid of it.

As much as I love hearing all the shit Hunter and Jason have been up to, it also feels like he's slipping further away from me the more they tell me. He seems to blend into this world really easily, and I'm not even surprised, because he's that type of guy.

That type of guy who mesmerizes people with his boyish grin, captivates you with his charming words, and has enough confidence to persuade you to follow his lead. LA might have brought him here, but he'll be king of the city soon enough.

I can already see it.

I know he didn't mind looking out for me in high school, always giving me the feeling I was more important than anything.

But this jet-set life is a whole different game. I noticed the girls ready to throw themselves at their feet when we entered the room, scowling at me like they wanted to rip me apart.

"Suck it up, Charlotte," I mumble to myself, taking a deep breath, as one of the stalls opens and a tall girl walks out of it like she's a princess. Her rose pink dress perfectly hugs her hips, and her long brown hair is styled with wavy curls bouncing around her head. I quickly glance at her perfect face as she grabs a lip gloss out of her small designer purse and red-oes her lips.

Not wanting to keep staring at her, I offer her a coy smile, turning around to do my business.

"Wait," she yelps, making me turn around to face her. "You're that girl who walked in with Hunter Hansen, aren't you?" She gives me a friendly smile that doesn't match her eyes, and I raise my eyebrows at her.

I shouldn't be thrown off by his newfound celebrity status, but I am. It's weird that the boy I used to spend my entire day with is now some kind of public property. That I have to share him with the world. But I guess this is our new reality. The reality where it's not just the girls of my class who want him, but any girl out there. The reality where my best friend... isn't just mine anymore.

"Yeah, that's me." I fold my arms in front of my body in a defiant stance, knowing exactly what's about to happen. I've seen enough movies with mean girls and her energy reeks of Regina George meets Blair Waldorf, as if she invented the character herself.

"What are you?" She waves her lip gloss over my body in a condescending way. "His girlfriend? High school sweetheart?"

I huff in response, letting out a sarcastic chuckle and throwing her a scowl, though the accuracy of her assumption also cuts in my heart. "I'm his best friend."

I want to lie and tell her we're more than that, but I made him promise we were friends. Lying about being his girlfriend is not something a friend would do.

"Aaaaaaah, now I get it." She turns back around to face the mirror with an evil smile on her face, and I narrow my eyes at her.

"What the hell is that supposed to mean?"

"Nothing." She shrugs, her back still my way while her eyes stare at me in the mirror. "I just assumed you were his girlfriend since they've let no girls up, yet they have for the last few weeks. Figured he needs to keep up the non-cheating boyfriend appearance, but since you're just his best friend"—she turns around, her brown hair spreading out in the air—"I guess there's no harm in making a play on that sexy fighter then." She gives me a wink.

"Actually, we're just catching up. I'm pretty sure he's not available for hook-ups tonight." I glare. "Maybe you'll have better luck next week."

Her eyes narrow at me as she takes a step closer, getting into my personal space, towering above me with her high heels.

"Don't think you're special, sweetheart. I bet a bunch of girls got up there as soon as you walked off the VIP deck. You're just his *friend*. You won't give him pussy tonight. But I will." My face falls when she purses her lips in amusement, then walks out the door while I feel the oxygen evaporating from my lungs.

Blinking rapidly at my reflection in the mirror, I grab the cold marble of the sink with both hands, trying to hold myself up, as I feel a tight grip enclosing around my chest. I close my eyes, taking deep breaths, trying to get my thoughts back on track.

She's right.

But he's never put any girl before our friendship, and I'm sure he won't start now.

He's single, and free to do whatever he wants, but he won't be hooking up with anyone tonight. Not when I'm here to see him. He wouldn't do that to me.

I get into the stall to pee, then wash my hands, getting ready to get back out there. Giving myself a once-over with a few deep breaths, I try to gather my confidence, like I did back in high school.

When I'm walking back up the stairs, I feel much better, deciding I will let nothing ruin my night. I'm in LA with my best friend, who I haven't seen in forever, and I'm going to enjoy the limited time we have together.

With a smile splitting my face, I reach the bottom of the stairs and instantly my face falls at the sight in front of me. Jason has his arms wrapped around two girls, while some girl is giving Hunter a lap dance, and some guy that wasn't here when I left ogles me with a red head tucked under his arm.

Oh my fucking god. That asshole!

A lump forms in the back of my throat while my heart races and a stone settles in my stomach. Breathing in through my nose, I notice the girl from the bathroom standing against the railing of the balcony talking to her friend. She quickly sees me, shooting me an evil smile that makes me clench my jaw, and I raise my chin, refusing to show her my discomfort.

For a few moments, I stand there, my feet frozen to the floor, not knowing what to do. The humid air mixed with alcohol makes my stomach somersault in agony while I wait for my fight-or-flight to kick in.

I want to get up there and slap the smirk he aims at the girl in his lap right off his face. I want to drag her off and kick him in the nuts, because the bastard should've known better than this. I don't care if he's the fucking king of the jungle or the newest fuckboy in LA, but this is just a fucked-up move.

I watch him with a heaving chest as he takes a sip of his tumbler filled with an amber liquid. The memory of Kim on his lap a few months back flashes in front of my eyes, only fueling my anger. *I knew this was a bad idea.*

Glancing between Hunter and Jason, I think about what the hell I'm going to do, until Jason notices me, and a busted look appears on his face. I offer him a questioning look, and he gives me a sympathetic one back, pushing the girl from his lap while he tries to get Hunter's attention. When he's too wrapped up in his new girl to notice, I shake my head with a humorous laugh before I turn around, storming back down the stairs in a cloud of anger.

I know, technically, I have no right to be angry, even though it feels like he stabbed me in the back, piercing right through my heart until it pops out on the other side of my body.

I get it.

He's single.

He doesn't owe me shit.

But I've never been okay with third wheeling while he's hooking up with some girl, and that hasn't changed. I came here to visit him, to see my best friend, and to spend time with him. Not to watch him getting dry humped by some bimbo. Feeling angry as fuck, I strut out of the crowded club until I reach the pavement outside, and I look around, wondering what the fuck I'm going to do. Frustrated, I grab my phone out of my boot, dialing the one person who can help me.

"What's up, girl? Are you calling me to tell me you're at some fancy LA party?" Julie's voice booms through the phone, and any other time, it would make a smile appear on my face. Right now, I just wave some air onto my flushed skin, trying to hold back the emotions growing thicker than my rage.

"I'm taking the red-eye home, and I need you to tell me that's a good idea." My voice cracks, and I close my eyes to push back the tears forming behind my gaze.

"Whoa! What happened? What's going on? Where's Hunter?"

"Getting dry humped by some girl in this fancy club we're at." *I can barely believe my own words.*

"That dickhead," she growls. "Where's Jason?"

"Next to him with his hands on *two* girls."

"Oh, they are really living the life, aren't they?" The tone in her voice is mocking, and I know she's trying to cheer me up, but I'm not having it. I just want to leave to get my ass back to the East Coast, where I belong.

"I want to leave, Julie." I fill up my lungs with the fresh air of the night, then tentatively blow it back out. "I want to leave, and I don't even know how. My stuff is at their house, which, by the way, is fucking huge, and it has an infinity pool and everything. Oh, and you can even see the Hollywood sign looking out of the window. The Hollywood sign, Jules," I ramble, a few frustrated tears slipping down my cheeks. "It's ridiculous. We're not even twenty-one, but no one batted an eye when we arrived at this club. It's grand, and it's glamorous, but it's not *fucking* me, and I want to leave. But now I don't even know where they live, so I can't get a cab to get my stuff, and I don't know what to fucking do!" I pinch the bridge of my nose.

"Okay, first. Breathe."

I suck a deep breath, doing what she says.

"Good. Now breathe out." Deliberately, I exhale, repeating the move as I hear Jason's voice calling out my name behind me.

"Charlotte, where are you going?" Ocean blue eyes impale me with worry.

"Home."

"Is that Jason?" Julie asks through the phone.

"Yeah."

"Good. Tell him to take you home. If you really want to leave, then leave, girl. No point in torturing yourself."

"Alright, I'll call you later." I hang up the phone, looking into Jason's friendly face, shimmering down my anger a bit, even though I'm angry at both of them.

"You can't go home." He gives me a serious look, his hands rubbing my arms, trying to comfort me.

Before I can respond, Hunter comes bursting out of the club, a bewildered look on his face. Without waiting for any response, he pushes Jason to the side, grabbing the back of my neck in a possessive way that almost makes my heart stop.

"What are you doing? Where are you going?"

Oh, fuck no. Trying to keep it together and hold my ground, I put a scowl on my face and look up. His hazel eyes swirl with darkness, fueled by alcohol, I'm sure.

"Home."

"The hell you are," he growls.

He glances left and right down the street, noticing the curious faces pointed at us, then grabs my arm, pulling me a few yards away.

"What? You don't want your new friends to see what an ass-hole you are?" I snicker with anything but humor.

"Shut up, Charls." He spins me, pushing my back against a wall in an alley, out of sight. "Why are you mad?" His eyes shoot daggers at me as I give him a stern look, noticing Jason standing at a distance behind him with his arms crossed in front of my chest. I'm not scared of Hunter. I know he will never hurt me, but knowing Jason, I also know his scowl is probably for his friend instead of for me, and it's giving me that extra spark to keep my rage blazing.

"Because I came here to spend time with you! Not to watch you hooking up with some girl!"

"What do you want from me, *Charlotte*?" He slams his palms against the wall beside my head, caging me in, getting into my space like he has many times before when he didn't get his way. But this time, it's different. This time, it's filled with frustration, fueled by an angry energy that's overwhelming. "You said friends. And now, here you are, pissed because I'm getting attention from some girl? Are you jealous? Is that it?"

My hands ball to fists, refraining myself from slapping his face to the other side of the city. *The audacity of this fucking guy.*

"You clearly drink more," I tell him as calmly as possible.

"What the fuck is that supposed to mean?"

"It means as soon as you start drinking, you change into a righteous ass," I shout at his face, my fury taking over, not willing to be treated like some insignificant girl.

I'm a good girl, I know that. I might not be bold and seductive like those chicks inside that club. But I'm a good person, and there is no chance in hell I will ever let any guy treat me like shit. Not even Hunter fucking Hansen.

"Oh, you're so full of shit. Just tell me you're jealous, and I'll ditch that girl to fuck you tonight."

No.

No.

Just *fucking* no.

My jaw drops to the floor, and my ears feel like they are turning red hearing the shit he's actually saying to me right now. "Fuck you tonight?" I repeat his words with a tone that's deep, growling, and ominous. "Because that's what I am to you? Just a *fuck*?" I hustle him off me, strutting past him, trying to create space between us and not kick him between the knees. How dare this son of a bitch talk to me like that.

I can't take more than three steps until he grabs my arm, but I can only be a good girl for so long, and I spin on my feet, connecting my palm with his cheek. "Stay the fuck away from me! Don't you dare talk to me like that! Like I'm one of your skanks. I'm not. And you better damn remember that, *asshole*!"

"Then tell me what the deal is! We were having a good night until you stormed out of the club!" he shouts in my face, throwing his snapback over his head as if it's keeping him from punching something.

"*We* were having a good time until *you* decided it was a good idea to invite some girls to the party."

"They were already there," he pipes up, trying to be a smartass.

I pull my hair with a huff, my emotions getting the best of me. Shaking my head, I bite my lip to prevent the waterworks from exploding.

"What is wrong with you? I fly across the country to see you, and here you are, trying to hook up with some girl? When have I ever been okay with being present for that? When?" I shout, my voice cracking more with every syllable, while the hurt inside of me grows like an evil tumor.

His gaze stays trained with mine, his rage slowly getting replaced by something that looks like regret.

"Never," he finally mutters, taking a step closer to erase the distance between us.

I take a step back, and his face falls at my move, pain washing his features. My eyes peer up into his, softly shaking my head as I give him a disappointed look. This was a mistake. We can't keep doing this any longer. I can't do this any longer. I know I said friends, but I owe it to him to tell him the truth, and to see if we could work, no matter how bad it might end.

I can't be scared to lose and love him at the same time.

I need to choose.

We keep staring at each other; the tension forming a thick wall between us.

I'm dying to break it down, to let it all out, knowing I have to, but it seems to grow higher and higher, and before it's growing above my head, I suck in a deep breath.

Before I chicken out, I open my mouth, giving him the words I've been scared to share for so long.

"I love you, Hunter." His eyebrows move up in shock, and a glint of hope shines in his eyes before they narrow, pushing it out as quickly as it appears. My heart falls, but there's no way back. I scrape out every ounce of bravery I can find in my body, finishing what I started, even though I already know I'll fly back home tonight with only half a heart. "I think I've loved you for a long time now. So yeah, you're right. I am jealous. I'm jealous because I have to go home again tomorrow, when all I want to do is stay here with you. I love you, and I think you love me too. I need you as my best friend. *But I want more.*"

His chest slowly moves up and down as he takes deep breaths, staying quiet as he processes my words. Jason keeps eying us, giving me a proud look that makes a tear escape from the corner of my eye.

Moments pass, feeling like forever, when finally I know he will not give it to me. He will not push back his fear for me. My lips part while it feels like my heart is crashing to the pavement in a thousand pieces, leaving nothing more inside my body than an empty feeling.

"C-Charls, f-fuck," he stammers with a terrified look on his face.

"Don't." I shake my head, offering him a small smile while I wipe the tears away with the back of my hand. "It's okay. You don't have to say it. Best friends, right? That's what we are. That's all we've ever been."

He doesn't answer, instead he swallows hard as I see his gaze wandering off, his thoughts taking over, the strong man being replaced by the young boy I met at the creek that day. Looking lost in his life, having no clue what to do.

"Hunter," I bellow, trying to snap him out of his thoughts. His eyes lock with mine, desperation washing his face, and I close the distance between us, placing my hand over his heart as I look up at him, knowing he's close to losing his shit. "It's for the best."

Finally, he nods, his stern look still piercing through me as I do my best to stay strong. You know how sometimes in life you reach a turning point? The end of the road, and all you can do is go left or right, hoping you'll choose the right path? This is it. I know that no matter what happens after today, whatever Hunter and I have, this moment will change it. It can either destroy us, or it can build us as high as a skyscraper, but looking into his troubled gaze, I know it's not my decision anymore.

I confessed.

I can't force him to do the same.

"I'm leaving." Not waiting for his reaction, I look past him at Jason. "Can you take me home?"

Jason nods, and I look up one last time, cupping his cheek. His silence is slowly killing me inside. Yet I pretend to be fine.

"Goodbye, Hunt." Giving him one last smile, I break our connection. He moans, a sound that aches all the way through my bones, and I sense his hand going over my stomach as I walk toward Jason. With fire and Jason on my heels, I trot down the street, resisting the urge to look back.

"Are you okay, Charlotte?" Jason asks, trying to keep up with me.

"Not even a little bit," I confess without hesitation. "But I will be."

34

HUNTER

I ABSENTMINDEDLY SWIRL MY feet through the cold water of the pool, staring into the ripples of the surface. The sun burns on my bare chest, but not as much as it's frying my pounding brain. It feels like a knife is jammed into my skull every time I angle my neck a little differently, but I welcome it. I fucking deserve all the torment I can get.

All the times my mother told me I was a worthless piece of shit, and yesterday, I finally proved her right. *I fucked up so bad*.

"You think that if you sit there long enough, the sun will melt your sins away?"

I glance up, wincing when a jolt of pain runs through my scalp.

"The sun ain't that powerful." I rear my head back in front, my gaze colliding with the Hollywood sign as Jensen lowers his body into the pool.

"Ah, shit, that's cold."

"Pussy," I mutter.

The asshole splashes water my way, a shit-eating grin on his face before he completely submerges into the pool. Two seconds later, he jumps back up like a fucking dolphin, glistening in the sun, before swinging his dark hair back.

His smile remains, but it lowers when he studies my stance. "She'll come around, man."

I snort, a humorless laugh echoing over the water. "She won't. Not this time." I saw it in her eyes. The sheer disappointment. Regret. She told me she loved me, and I couldn't say it back. But it's not even that. I think we could've overcome that. No, it's me deliberately hurting her because I freaked out. *Again.*

"Yeah, okay. Thanks, Jules." Jason walks out on bare feet, his phone to his ear, and I look up at him when he stands beside me. His navy shirt matches his eyes that are squinting at me with a scowl that hasn't left since last night.

"Charlotte got home safe."

I swallow, fixing my gaze back in front of me.

"Do you wanna talk about it?" He sits down beside me, his lower legs sinking into the water while Jensen flips his attention back and forth between the two of us.

"About what?" What's the fucking point? She's not coming back, and I can't fucking blame her.

"About the fact that you pushed the one person away who was willing to put up with your sorry ass?"

I groan, then snap him a glare that comes straight from hell. "I don't fucking deserve her, J." Nobody does. But certainly not me.

He huffs. "You got that right."

"Fuck you!"

"No, fuck you! You don't want to own up to what you feel for her? Fine! Whatever rocks your boat, buddy. But you didn't have to hurt her like that. Before all this bullshit, you once told me that she was your friend. That your friendship with her was the most important thing in your life."

"It is!" I yell, ready to punch in his fucking face. Our friendship is the most important thing I have, and I still managed to fuck it up.

"Then fucking be her friend! Don't treat her like a groupie! She deserves more than that."

I shake my head, whispering, "She deserves the world." I lift my misted gaze up at Jason. "But I can't give her that."

"Why not?" Jensen throws me a bored expression, running a hand through his wet hair.

Because girls like her don't end up with guys like me?

"She lives in North Carolina, and now I live here. She wants a family with a white picket fence and a dog. Look at me." I spread my arms. "That's not me. I can't give her what she wants. I need to let her go. It's not fair to her."

"That's fucking bullshit," Jason mumbles, and I close my eyes, ignoring him.

"So pursuing"—Jensen waves his hand in front of my face—"whatever it is that is going on between you two isn't an option."

"No."

"Okay..." Jensen drawls. "So if you can't give her what she wants, how about you just give her what she *needs* instead?"

A deep frown creases on my forehead, painfully straining the muscles. "What do you mean?"

Jensen shrugs. "I don't know her, but by the looks of it, J-man here is on your girl's team more than yours." *No shit.* "So clearly, you did fuck up bad..."

"Are you going to keep pointing out the obvious, Dumbledore?" I already have a fucking headache the equivalent of hitting a brick wall. I don't need these two to get all cryptic about shit I already know.

"Just be her fucking friend, Hunt," Jason chimes in, rolling his eyes. "It shouldn't be so fucking hard, since that's what you've been doing for a year."

"She's not gonna talk to me, J!" It's easier for him to say. I called her ten times today, yet he's the one telling me she got home safe. She doesn't really want to talk to me.

"Not today, no, *asshole*." Jensen snickers, then splashes more water in my face. "But you didn't get your ass in a LA mansion pool because you're quitter, right?"

My eyes narrow, colliding with the daring expression in his.

"Win her back," he dares.

"How?"

A playboy smirk forms on his lips. "One day at a time."

35

HUNTER

HUNTER: I fucked up.
HUNTER: I'm sorry.
HUNTER: Can you forgive me?
HUNTER: I'm an asshole.

HUNTER: Please talk to me.
HUNTER: I'm sorry, Charls.
HUNTER: Will you ever talk to me again?

HUNTER: I'm not giving up.
HUNTER: We're best friends, Charls.
HUNTER: Please don't give up on me.

HUNTER: Come on, Charls. It's been two weeks.
HUNTER: Talk to me.
HUNTER: You can't ignore me forever.

HUNTER: Heard you're going to UNC.
HUNTER: Congrats.
HUNTER: I know you're going to kill it.
HUNTER: I miss you.

36

Charlotte

I WALK UP THE porch, a deep sigh erupting from my entire body when I spot the pink peonies on the doorstep. They are set up in a big vase I know isn't my mother's, so it has to come from the flower store as a whole. With my keys in one hand, and the groceries in the other, I look for the card, even though I already know who they are from.

The front of the card is white, embedded with gold letters in a cursive font that says *"sorry,"* and rolling my eyes, I flick it open.

If I could turn back time, I would be sitting on your porch right now.

Goddamnit. The asshole is going bigger and better every day, and it's annoying me as much as it's tugging on my heart to text him back. I lift the white vase, setting it next to the other five that came in the last five days.

"More flowers from Hunter?" Mama steps onto the porch with a cup of tea in her hand. Her blonde hair is growing longer every day, but she keeps it in a red headband so she can grow it out of this awkward length.

"Yup."

"He's persistent." She glances at me from over her mug.

"That he is." He's also a first-class asshole, a relentless player, and a distant memory. Okay, the last one is a lie, but I'm hoping that the more times I tell it to myself, the sooner it will become true.

"How long are you gonna keep this up?" I don't miss the hint of judgment in her tone.

"Probably forever." I challenge her with a slight scowl, but she counters it with a bored expression. "You think I should forgive him."

"I think you miss him and he misses you."

"Whose fault is that?" I snarl.

"His." She nods, not an ounce of doubt in her green eyes. "And if you're a hundred percent sure that your relationship with him isn't salvageable, by all means keep ignoring him, and eventually, he'll give up. But if there's a part of you that still wants him to be part of your life... stop torturing yourself."

A lump the size of a marble forms in the back of my throat, aching.

"He really hurt me, Mama."

"I know, and if you can't forgive him, I understand. But if you can? Well, you and I both know life is too short for regrets." With that, she leaves me alone with my thoughts as she strolls back inside, the porch door slamming behind her with a loud thud.

Fucking hell.

Damn you, Mama.

37

HUNTER

CHARLOTTE: THANK YOU FOR the book.

With one hand holding up the towel around my hips, I almost let my phone slip out of the other. My heart feels like a jackhammer trying to break free with excitement curling my lips. Finally, she's sending some kind of sign of life after four weeks of radio silence. I had to ask Jason to ask Julie if Charlotte was fucking okay. *"Tell Hunter to fuck off"* was Julie's response, which made it clear I was still in the doghouse. I figured changing my tactic to gifts might help. Thank fuck it did.

HUNTER: What book?

I wait for the dots to appear, my heart in my throat when she's taking longer than ten seconds to reply. With each second that passes, I regret my joke as I anxiously wait.

CHARLOTTE: That Kamasutra book you sent me?

What the fuck.

CHARLOTTE: That wasn't yours?
CHARLOTTE: My bad, must've been Brad then.

HUNTER: Who the fuck is Brad?
CHARLOTTE: The guy I went on a date with yesterday.

Oh, hell no. Vigorously, I hit the dial button, the tone sounding annoyingly in my ear, but it's no surprise that it quickly goes to voicemail.

HUNTER: Pick up the phone, Charls.
CHARLOTTE: I'm not sure you have earned that privilege yet.

Goddamnit.

HUNTER: Are you trying to give me a heart attack?
CHARLOTTE: Maybe. Is it working?
HUNTER: Charls.
HUNTER: Please stop torturing me.
CHARLOTTE: I don't think I'm ready to let you off the hook just yet.

Bullshit. The fact that she's texting me back shows she's giving me an inch. I just need to gently take it, make sure I don't spook her so I can take the rest of her.

HUNTER: Then I'll wait.

Five seconds later, my phone vibrates in my hand, her name flashing across the screen, and I answer it with my face split in half. Some smart-ass flirt sits on the tip of my tongue, but there's still a *CAUTION* sign hanging above my head, so I settle for "Hey."

"*Then I'll wait?* What is this, some reverse psychology?"

Confused, yet amused, I shake my head. "What are you talking about?"

"The Hunter I know is a deaf son of a bitch and would have been harassing me the moment I texted you back."

"Technically, I have been harassing you for a month now."

"That you have."

We fall into a loaded silence, and I assess my face in the mirror. The corners of my cheeks gently lower, frowning at my reflection.

"I'm so sorry, babe," I tell her, eventually.

I hear a gust of breath slipping into my ear, my heart ready to jump out of my chest.

"I know," she says.

"I fucked up."

"You did."

"I'm sorry."

"You already said that." There's less ice in her tone with each sentence, relaxing my shoulders.

"I mean it."

The line goes silent again, and I anxiously wait for her to say something. Anything.

"I hate you," she whispers.

"No, you don't." I know this girl better than anything, and as much as I deserve it, she doesn't hate me. She's not capable of hating anyone.

"You're an asshole," she repeats, as if I don't already know.

My brown eyes dilate, gold specks growing as I stare back in the mirror. "I'm *your* asshole."

I hope she can read between the lines, even though I don't even fully know what it says.

"I need you to be my friend, Hunter." Leave it up to this girl to rip out my heart and cradle it as it weeps in her arms. Her words kill me inside.

"I am your friend."
"Then act like it!" *Okay, I deserved that.*
"I will. Just... just don't ghost me, okay?"
"Don't give me a reason to ghost you."
I nod, catching my own grin rising in the mirror. "I won't."

38

Charlotte

M Y EYES BOUNCE OVER the screen, picking up with a tiny smile when I realize it's pretty early for him to call, considering it's not even eight a.m. on a Tuesday.

"Are you okay?" I stroll over the UNC campus, my head buried in my faux fur hood to protect my face from the crisp January air.

"No." Hunter's resolute tone blasts over the line.

Yeah, I figured. I wish I could tell you that Hunter and I picked up where we left off, albeit from different coasts. But it turns out that our friendship worked better when we were in the same state. We talk, but not as much and never this early in the morning. More like every other weekend to catch up, and even those phone calls are becoming more awkward lately. It's just hard to discuss your life when you're living so differently. I avoid talking about campus life, because I'm convinced he doesn't want to hear about the friends I'm making, or the guys I date just to expand my horizon further than the man who stole my heart and flew to LA. Just like I know he holds back on sharing about his life outside of his training schedule.

"What's wrong?"

"How's your mom doing?" Deflecting. Okay, something must really be bothering him. I could steamroll him and tell him to hang up unless he wants to be honest, but I'm in a good mood, so I'll give him a few moments to work up the nerve for whatever reason he's calling.

"Really good. She told me she's taking Pilates classes, and she made some friends." It's a relief that Mama is doing so well. She sounds more like herself every month, and it's allowed me to enjoy college more than I expected. After I went home for Christmas and saw with my own eyes that she was shining like never before, I even gave myself permission to go to a New Year's Eve party with Julie.

"That's really good, Charls. I'm sorry I wasn't home for Christmas."

"Pff, don't be silly." I have to admit, I was a bit disappointed when the AFA decided he got a fight in Russia on Christmas Eve, but it is what it is. It's not like he has a reason to come to Braeden, after all. His mother probably drank her way through Christmas. "How is your mother?"

"Still drunk," he replies with a cynical yet exhausted tone. His frustration is palpable, even though there's a thousand miles between us, and it's coming at me in waves, pulling the air from my lungs. He sounds like he's been running around the city all night and still can't get rid of whatever nagging feeling has settled inside of him.

"Hunt," I start with a hint of reprimand, "did you sleep last night?"

"Hardly." There's no joy to be found in his chuckle, the starting shot of something brewing inside of me that doesn't feel good.

"What's going on?"

The gust of his exhaling breath is loud, followed by a deep groan. "I just hate this LA bullshit."

That doesn't sound good.

"What are you talking about?"

8

The silence that follows is pregnant with something dark and heavy, reminding me of one of those scenes in horror movies when the demon is about to pop up.

"They want me to start dating Laurie Simpson."

Oh, hey, *devil baby*.

"What? Who?"

"Gina. My publicist. *The AFA.*" He pushes out each word with more dread, but it doesn't even come close to the meteorite-sized brick that just landed in my stomach while my feet come to a halt in shock.

"And what?" I snap. "You missed the fine print of your contract that states that they can dictate who you date?"

"Sorta."

"Sorta?!" My own high-pitched tone has me glancing around me in embarrassment, a few students giving me a deep frown. I put my feet back in motion, then lower my voice. "Hunter, that's ridiculous! Why do they care who you date?"

"They want to expand the brand. Get rid of the reputation that only criminals and thugs are fighters."

"And getting their youngest and best fighter linked with America's supermodel slash sweetheart is the way to do it?" His deafening lack of words is reply enough. "Hunter, you can't be serious?! Do you even *want* to date her?"

You could hear the crickets sing over the line if there were any, and my heart thunders when nothing fucking happens. Not a groan, not a growl, and sure as fuck no syllable to pronounce the word 'no' that I'm waiting for.

"Oh my god. You do?"

"No!" he quickly replies, then it's followed with the groan that's at least ten seconds too late. "I don't know, Charls. They said it could get me more sponsor deals. That usually pays more than my fights. Her dad is one of the biggest realtors in the state, and he's taken an interest in the AFA. It's why they wanna link her to a fighter."

"Right. Money." I fail to hide my disappointment.

"Charls, please. It's not real. It doesn't mean anything."

It's what my heart wants to hear, but my mind is scolding me like a librarian eyeing me from above her glasses. It's not fair. We are *friends*. I have no right to tell him who he can and can't date.

I roll my shoulders, then lift my chin as I do my best to keep a steady voice.

"No, you're right. You should. It's good for publicity. For your brand."

"Yeah?" He sounds as unsure as I feel, but I push through. I don't want to, and my heart wants to knock me over the head, but I already told him how I felt. I didn't work out.

"Yeah, of course! Besides, it could be good for us, you know? To keep some boundaries for when we date other people."

"Are you dating someone, Charls?" he growls.

"No!" I rebuke. "I'm not! But I mean, eventually we will, right?"

A loud and deep grunt rumbles in my ear, and I imagine him rubbing a hand over his head, like he always does when he's frustrated. "I don't like this."

That makes two of us.

"It's okay, Hunt. It's all good. We're all good." The lump in my throat is proof that it's a blatant lie, but I choose to ignore that.

"Are we really, Charls? Because I can't lose you."

"We are," my voice cracks a little, and I curl my lips up to force a smile on my tensed cheeks. "Just promise me one thing?"

"Anything."

"Promise you'll tell me when it gets real. Promise we'll still share the big things with each other. I know our relationship

8

changed"—a loud sigh flies from his lips—"but promise me we'll never become strangers."

"It's never getting real. It's just for the brand."

"Just promise." I wait, raking my teeth over my lip, with my eyebrows knitted together. I need him to tell me this doesn't change things any more than they already are.

"I promise," he says.

But even though it's what I wanted to hear, fear grips my throat, telling me it's nothing more than an illusion.

39

HUNTER

"**I** GOT YOU SOME seats in the family section tomorrow."
Jensen drops his ass next to me on the couch, shoveling
an omelet into his mouth while holding the plate below his
chin. His black-and-white Knights t-shirt hugs his bulky biceps,
matching my own. But his shoulders are built like a fucking
cargo ship, being every bit the hockey player he is.

"Thanks, man."

"Are you bringing the girlfriend?"

"That would require me to have one."

"Fine, *fake* girlfriend."

"Laurie is not my girlfriend. Fake or not. We're just hanging
out."

He cocks an eyebrow, as if he wants to say, *who are you lying
to?*

"What? She's not!"

He shrugs, fixating back on his food. "I don't know, man. Does
she know that?"

"What do you mean?"

"She's been here a lot the last couple of weeks. Didn't know
Netflix and chill was also required when you agreed to this
whole theater."

"We're just getting to know each other."

"Hmm," he muses, then pins me with dark blue eyes. "Did you kiss her?"

"*No.*" My molars grind together at half the lie, then I confess. "But she kissed me."

He chews, disapproval dripping from his face.

"Don't you start as well." It's bad enough to have Jason up in my game the entire time, telling me what an idiot I am for agreeing to this publicity thing in the first place.

"She's into you, Hunt." He rears his head back to the TV. "You might not be willing to commit, but she sure as hell is."

Laurie and I did click. I have to admit that. I didn't expect it, but if you look past the whole girly shit, she's cool. Our first "date" went smoother than expected, and she wasn't awful to hang out with. Definitely better than the girls in high school. Well, except for one.

"Do you like her?" Jensen drops his empty plate on the coffee table, propping his heels on top of it.

"Yeah, sure."

"Hmm, convincing." He pins me with a taunting smirk, then grabs my knee in a painful grip. "Word of advice? You have to let one of them go, or you'll lose them both."

"What are you talking about?" I scoff, becoming really good at pretending.

"You know what I'm talking about."

I know. I just wish I wasn't.

40

Charlotte

"I'M SORRY, BUT I don't think I can get used to this." Julie throws the tabloid on the counter, and I don't even have to look down behind my glass to know what it will show.

"It's not real, Jules. It's just pretend."

She hangs her upper body over the marble counter, skepticism written all over her expression. "Yeah, you keep telling me that."

I glance down at her, taking a big gulp of my sweet tea. "What, Jules?"

"Nothing." She lifts her torso until she's standing straight again, her blonde hair falling over her sunflower tank top.

I tilt my head a little with a dull look to call her out on her bullshit. I know when she's got something to say, and in this case? I'll be lucky if she keeps it shorter than a Shakespearean play.

"It's just that..." she starts, dropping her gaze to the photo of Hunter and Laurie on the cover, then flips it back, her brown eyes radiating with reluctance, "have you talked to Hunter lately?"

"Yeah, we talk every week."

"I mean, about Laurie." No, definitely not about that. I keep up a non-affected front, but I've been successfully avoiding talking to Hunter about his new *girlfriend*, fake or not. I don't trust myself to stay in the best friend role if I have to pretend it doesn't hurt. It does. Kills me inside, but if I tell him that, I risk blurring the lines again.

"We don't have to talk about Laurie, because it's not real." *I hope.*

"Are you sure about that?" *No.*

"Positive."

"Charlie, I—"

"I know what you're about to say, okay?" I cut her off, turning around to grab her a glass from the cabinet, then filling it with the pitcher of sweet tea in front of me. "I'm not blind. I see the photos just as much as you do, but he promised he'd tell me the important things. If his fake relationship turned serious, he would've told me."

I shove her glass forward, locking eyes with her. Her features soften, her tongue darting out to lick her lower lips as she assesses my attempt at holding a stoic expression. The fact that she doesn't argue with me tells me I'm failing miserably.

"I just don't want you to get hurt again."

I push the oxygen from my lungs, mustering a smile. "I know." *That makes two of us.*

41

HUNTER

"I T'S TIME TO GET out there, Hunter." My trainer pins me down with an impatient glare.

"Not fucking yet!"

Hearing the dial tone in my ear, I wait, squatted against the wall in the locker room until it's already time to get into the cage. *Come on, pick up, pick up.* When it goes to voicemail for the third time, I clench my jaw in frustration before sending her a text.

HUNTER: Where you at, Charls?

CHARLS: I'm in the shower.

HUNTER: Way to get me all riled up.

CHARLS: Stop flirting with me. Have a good fight.

HUNTER: No wait! I need to hear your voice.

My heart relaxes a little when she finally calls me back, the sound of water clashing against the tiles in the background.

"What round?" she asks.

"Are you watching?" I don't expect her to. I never expected her to, but knowing that she's watching me, always lit a fire to my ass. I like pretending she's with me, just like she was for most of my fights in high school.

"Of course. Why do you think I'm having a shower *now*?"

"So you can put visuals in my head that spark me alive?"

"Stop flirting with me, Hunt." She sings out the words, putting a smile on my face.

"Fine." I bite my lip, thinking about water cascading all over Charlotte's naked body. Streaming down her curves, glistening her skin with temptation. Her wet hair...

"Hunter?" her call out cuts my daydream short, and I blink at the ceiling to pull myself back.

Fucking hell.

"Yeah?"

"You better win."

"I always win."

"Cocky asshole."

"I'm your asshole."

She sighs, loud enough to be audible over the noise of the shower. It's one I can feel in my bones, aching, because I can see the black cloud moving in from a mile away.

"Not anymore, Hunt." *There it is.*

"Hunt, what are you doing? Come on, you need to move. *Now.*" Jason catches my attention when he waltzes in the dressing room with big strides. Impatience pinches his face, and I get to my feet, grunting.

"I have to go."

"Go get 'em."

"Promise you'll watch?"

"I promise." I can hear her smile, igniting one of my own, before we end the call. I hand Jason my phone for safekeeping.

"Charlotte?" He hands me a bottle of water, and I take a small sip out of it.

"Yeah."

"You guys still talking?"

"Now and then." Definitely not as much as I'd want us to be. We both do our best, but we seem to have a hard time catching each other at the right time. And when we do? The conversations are different, more strained. Like there isn't just a giant elephant in the room; no, there's a whole fucking herd.

"You cool with that?"

My gaze locks with his as I go over his words.

Am I cool with that?

No.

But I can't seem to fix it. As easy as our relationship was back home, is as difficult as our relationship is now that we have a thousand miles between us, and neither of us knows what to do about it. We try to stay connected, but I can't help but feel like we're growing apart.

"Hansen, it's *fucking* time!" Gina pops her head in the door with a glare that speaks as loud as her telling me she'll rip my balls off if I don't walk out there within the next five minutes before she disappears again and we hear her heels tap away down the hallway.

"Nothing I can do about it." I shrug, getting up and walking past him, out of the room. "Showtime."

42

Charlotte

J ULIE BURSTS THROUGH THE door, slamming the door shut with
a loud bang, making me jolt a bit as I look up from my desk.
"Dear Lord, Jules. I'm trying to study."

"Well, you can stop trying, because once you've heard what
I heard, your head will process *nothing*." She bounces onto her
bed, and I look up at her with a furrowed brow.

"Have you seen the news?"

I frown at her definition of news, pretty sure she hasn't been
watching CNN in the last hour. "US Today is not news, Julie. It's
gossip."

"Yeah, well, the latest gossip is that Hunter is *moving in* with
Laurie."

My face falls, even though I do my best to keep it straight as I
feel my heart pounding out of my chest.

"Are you shitting me?"

She shakes her head, her eyes staying completely focused
on mine for several moments, probably wondering why I'm not
freaking out yet.

Truth is, I am.

There's a weird sensation that brings every nerve in my body
alive, but in a way that makes me want to go to bed and sleep

it off, hoping it's not there anymore when I wake up. Like some kind of stomach bug.

I slowly get up, walking toward my bed beside her, dropping my back on it as I stare up at the ceiling, hypnotized by the string of lights we hung up.

"Show me." I reach out my hand for her phone.

She places it in my hand while I keep my gaze on the ceiling, swallowing hard, trying to find the courage to look at whatever shitty article will ruin the rest of my day. Or week. *Or maybe even fucking year.* Bringing the phone up, my eyes look at the screen to see a picture of Hunter walking hand in hand with the most popular model in LA. They've been dating for months now, so I should be used to it right now. But still, bile rises in the back of my throat as I soak up the discomfort that it's giving me. Hunter is looking as good as always, his tattooed arms even more chiseled, his torso covered by a white t-shirt. A black snapback sits on his head, as if he's been trying to stay incognito, but his boyish smirk gives his identity away. Laurie looks great, as always, in a dress that hugs all her curves, sparkling enough for a night of clubbing even though it's broad daylight. It doesn't escape me that she's everything I'm not. One of the most famous realtors in LA is standing next to them, as it looks like they enter a house that is listed for sale as said in the article. I keep scrolling down, torturing myself with every new picture that appears, until the last one feels like a knife cutting through my chest. I watch Hunter's mouth covering hers, forming a pit in my stomach, making it almost impossible to not hurl up my lunch.

I knew this day would come.

I saw it coming from the moment he told me he was going to date her to please the AFA.

She's gorgeous, successful. A carbon copy of the girls he used to fool around with in high school.

But I'd expected the fucker to tell me.

Instead, I find out through US Today.

I know this last year we didn't touch base as much as we used to. In fact, lately, we only catch up every month or so, and our conversations are getting shorter and more superficial as the time passes by. ·

It's mostly me, I guess? With every fight he wins, his Instagram account grows by thousands within days, and by the time word got out about him and Laurie, he hit one million followers. We are living different lives.

He became a millionaire real quick, living that same lifestyle when he wasn't in the gym. He posts pictures on yachts, exclusive trips, launch parties, and he's always with her. His life is filled with glamor and champagne, whereas mine is filled with instant noodles and cheap beer.

I became more hesitant about sharing my simple college life. So, I get it. We're not as close as we used to be, and both of us are to blame for that. But I still expect him to share the shit that matters? Moving in with the girl you claimed not to be serious with is a big fucking deal in my book.

I breathe loudly, my anger taking over my nausea as I grab my phone from my desk, getting comfortable on the bed, yet feeling like a knife is going through my heart.

"What are you doing?" Julie's eyes flash with panic, widening when she watches how I put the phone to my ear.

"What do you think? Telling him he's a fucking asshole."

"Charlie! You can't do that!" she hisses. "He's not *your* boyfriend."

"I know, Julie." I scowl, throwing my pillow at her in frustration. "I'm his *best* friend, right? As his best friend, I expect *him* to tell me he's moving in with someone. Not some fucking trashy magazine."

"Technically, I told you."

"Shut up." I listen to the dial tone, getting more pissed the longer it takes for him to answer. I'm about two seconds away from throwing my phone across the room, when finally, his voice sounds.

"Hey, Charls." His oblivious tone only builds the rage inside of me.

"Hey, *Hunt.*" I glare into the room. "What's going on?" My voice is ominous, and I know he can hear it when he lets out a deep sigh.

"You found out."

"It's kinda hard not to find out when it's all over the damn internet, Hunter."

"I'm sorry. I was gonna tell you."

"When, Hunter? Your last fight was last week. Don't tell me you weren't planning on moving in with her then."

He stays quiet, and I close my eyes, shaking my head in frustration. When I open my eyes, Julie's sitting in front of me. She's giving me a sympathetic look, offering me a sweet smile as her chest moves up and down slowly, silently telling me to breathe.

"What do you want me to say, Charls?"

"Well, that's the thing, Hunt. I wanted you to say anything. Because I thought that's what friends do. We share the important shit with each other." And it hits me. This is the end. *This is it.* That final push that's been lurking in the shadows. I can feel my heart crumbling inside my chest, making my voice strained and unsteady. "But we haven't shared shit in the last year."

"What are you saying?"

I close my eyes once more, feeling them well up while the fatigue in my body takes over. I'm so tired of trying to keep our friendship what it was. But while he's in California, living the best life I might wish for him, I'm here. Trying to get a degree, staying close to home to make sure I can be home within a few hours if I need to. He's exploring the world, fighting. I can't go any farther than The University of North Carolina, because even that two-hour drive back home seems like forever, in case my mama might need me again.

"I'm saying we should stop pretending. We are not friends. Not anymore." Tears start to stream down my cheeks, but I know it's true. We might have been great together, but the distance made us grow apart, and living different lives killed us. We knew it from the moment I landed in LA last summer, but we refused to believe it.

We believed we could make it work. Or at least, I truly did.

But at some point, you have to acknowledge defeat and just accept that you can't.

"I wish you the best, Hunter. I hope you get the life that you deserve. Because you deserve it all. But we have to let go."

"Charls." His voice tells me he knows I'm right, and with that thought, I say goodbye once more.

"Don't call me anymore, Hunt." Before he can say anything else, I hang up the phone with a heavy heart, before I slide my body to the floor, breaking down. Burying my face in my hands, I sob, feeling Julie's arms wrap around me. The pain is threatening to pull me under, pouring out of me like the Hoover Dam just broke, the hole getting bigger when I notice my phone next to my knee, relentlessly buzzing over the linoleum floor.

Hunter.

I close my eyes, tears flowing heavily, because I know I can't pick up that phone again.

"Sssh, it's okay, girl. I got you." Julie strokes my hair, cradling me as I let it all out.

The frustration of last year. How badly we tried to make it work, to stay friends, to stay connected, but no matter what we did, we both knew we were slipping away with no clue how to hold on. It takes me a few minutes to calm down, and I reach for my phone, seeing twenty missed calls from Hunter.

"You think I made the right choice?"

"Hard to say, girl," she answers honestly, brushing my hair out of my face. "But I think it was necessary."

I nod in agreement, looking at my phone.

"He's gonna keep calling."

"Yeah, he is." She lets out a sad chuckle. "You want to answer it?"

"No." I shake my head, wiping tears away with the back of my hand. "I don't."

Answering that phone will give him the chance to lure me back in, and I need to break loose from Hunter Hansen, preferably before it tears me apart.

If it hasn't already.

YEAR THREE

NOT GOING TO LIE, IT HURTS.

'Time really flies by.'

43

HUNTER

"**Y**OU THINK BARRINGTON WILL make him first driver?" I nudge my chin toward the Formula One race on the TV, then take a sip of my beer. It tastes bitter, a good combination with the nagging feeling that has permanently settled inside of me, like a leech on my back in a spot I can't quite reach.

I've been drinking more. It seems to be the only way to get through the endless parties Laurie's dragging me to, the only cure to get out of my own head for a few hours.

"Oh, yeah, for sure," Jason replies. "He's ending in front of his teammate for three races now. Mark my words, he's the newest champion. He'll break records."

I nod in agreement, then twist my head at the sound of the front door getting slammed shut with enough force to knock it out.

"Look, baby, I get that you're doing your job and all, but trust me when I tell you that you've got nothing to worry about," Jensen grunts, rolling his eyes as he strolls into the living room. "So, what?" he continues. "You're just here to make my life miserable? No calling you *baby*. Got it. Anything else you want to bitch about, *Miss Stafford*? Great. Bye." His sports bag falls to the floor with a loud thud as he rounds the couch, then lets his phone clatter to the glass coffee table and drops his body beside me.

"Your little PR girl is still giving you the cold shoulder?" I smirk.

"More like determined to set my ass on fire." He pulls my beer from my hands, pouring the last of it down his throat.

"That was mine," I deadpan.

"*Was* is the right description."

"Why does she hate you so much?" Jason's amusement is audible, though he stays fixed on the race.

"She must be a fucking alien."

I snort with humor. "What, because she can resist the almighty Jared James Jensen? Son of a politician? Hockey rebel?"

My sarcasm earns me a death glare that only makes me chuckle. "Don't you have somewhere to be? You don't even fucking live here anymore."

That results in a similar glare from me. "Shut up."

"Oh, trouble in paradise?"

"More like he's living in hell and coming to paradise every chance he gets. AKA, our house," Jason chimes in as his phone starts to vibrate from where I put it down beside my thigh.

Julie.

"Fuck you, J." I throw a pillow at his head as he gets up, then glance at his phone clutched in his hand. "You still talk to Julie?" A pang of jealousy snaps through me, knowing that the line to Charlotte is shorter for Jason than it is for me, now that she's cut me out of her life completely. I don't blame her. But I sure as fuck miss her. I wish we could at least talk every now and then, just so I can hear her voice and make sure she's okay. But her unanswered phone calls made her wishes clear.

Blonde eyebrows form a frown. "Of course, I still talk to Julie. She's my friend."

"She's your brother's girlfriend," Jensen informs flatly, as if we're not aware, and I snicker at his wit.

"So?" Jason cocks an eyebrow.

"So? Why is she calling you?"

"Probably because my brother is being a dick to her." With that, he strolls away to take the call.

"God, you two are so whipped by the girls from your past," Jensen mutters, kicking off his sneakers before propping them on the table.

"I have a girlfriend," I argue.

"One you're avoiding half of the time."

"I'm not!"

"Then why are you on our couch four nights a week?" He blinks with a fake smile and a challenging look.

"Because..." I lift my snapback to run a hand through my hair. "I like her. She's sweet. Fun. *Hot*. But she's fucking high-maintenance, man. She changes outfits three times a day, spends half the day making selfies, and she's always squealing about some superficial shit with her girlfriends. I moved in with *her*, but most of the time, it feels like I'm living with a fucking sorority. It doesn't help matters that she doesn't know what real life is like, and has never had to struggle for anything."

"Sounds like a fucking dream! Can I come?"

My elbow lands on his side. "I'm serious!"

"So am I?" Confusion washes his face. "Look, man. This is what you wanted. Just accept it. If I learned anything from growing up with my parents, sometimes it's better to just accept it."

I study his expression, trying to read between the lines of the sudden gloom in his voice. "Got experience with that?"

"Too much to tell." He shakes his head, then conjures his cheeks into a wide grin. "But if you need me to escort some of Laurie's friends out of your apartment, just let me know?"

I laugh, rolling my eyes. "I'll keep that in mind."

Charlotte

"O H, CHARLIE, I'M SOOO glad you came to UNC with me. I don't know what I would have done without you." Julie hooks her arm in mine as we strut over campus, both having a cup of ice cream in our hand.

Hunter tried to call me a few times every single day for a week, then he called me once every week, but after that, he stopped. Not going to lie, it hurts when I see another picture of him and Laurie on the internet, but I do my best to avoid it, and distract myself by trying to get new connections inside the campus.

I'm in college, for crying out loud. More than enough people to keep me entertained.

"I know. I'm really glad I did. I'm pretty sure I'd feel miserable being stuck in Braedon community college with everyone from our class going off to the big schools."

"Right! And imagine all the parties you would've missed. Still can't believe I got you out of your books as many times as I did." She chuckles.

"Neither can I." I laugh.

The first time Julie dragged me to one of the frat parties, I wanted to hide and run, thinking it would be the same disaster as it was in LA. But it seems like college parties are more my thing. I actually really enjoyed myself, and it felt refreshing being in a new environment. Though I still enjoy a quiet night with a book at the dorm, I go out with Julie every other week now.

We take a seat on one of the benches in front of the campus, savoring the sun warming our faces as we keep eating our ice cream. The sweetness of my cookies and cream is alternated by the fresh taste of my orange scoop, reminding me of Hunter because, apparently, I like to torture myself every now and then.

"Can't believe we're sophomores. Time really flies by." I place my spoon between my teeth, dragging it out as the ice cream drops on my tongue. "How are things with Jacob?"

Her sigh speaks volumes. "It definitely would be better if we'd be going to the same school."

"So, still shit, huh?"

"Not really. We just don't see each other a whole lot, and it fucks with my head."

"You mean, the rumors about him and other girls?"

She gives me a reluctant look, doing something to me, because I'm used to Julie being confident and perky. "Jason says I have nothing to worry about."

Hearing Jason's name lifts my eyebrows, but then I nod, hiding the urge to ask if she knows how Hunter's doing. I shouldn't care. *I don't care.* "I'm sure Jason would tell you if his brother was cheating on you. They are not exactly friendly."

"But they are still brothers," Julie rebukes.

"Jason hates Jacob, Jules." I give her a reassuring look, then pull my phone out of my bag, noticing a missed call. "Oh, Mama called me."

"Oh, how's she been? She's really doing good, right?"

"Yeah, she's thinking about taking a part-time job in Bett's Bookshop."

Dialing her number, I place the phone against my ear while I wait until she answers.

"That would be cool. You two used to hang out there all the time," Julie reminisces with a sweet smile curling her pink lips, and I mimic it, thinking about all the Saturday mornings my mother and I would snoop through the shelves.

"Hey, sweetheart." Mama's soft voice graces my ear, warming my heart but making my face fall when I notice the tone in her voice. My good mood is whipped out of the air as if lightning strikes me, a bad feeling folding around my heart.

"Hey, Mama. You okay?"

"No. I'm not."

"What's wrong?" I keep staring in front of me, seeing from the corner of my eye how Julie is throwing me a questioning look.

"I went to the doctor's today. They found another lump."

Desperation washes over my body, paralyzing me from head to toe. Not even knowing how to respond to that. Wondering when this nightmare will be over. *If* this nightmare will ever be over.

"How bad?" My voice breaks.

She stays quiet as I hear her push out a breath. "It's bad."

Swallowing hard, I turn my gaze to Julie, feeling my heart pounding against my ribcage, still staring at me in anticipation while I know there is only one option for me. As much as there is a feeling inside of me, dying to be selfish for once, I can't. I can never live with myself if I do. Without hesitation, I take a deep breath, knowing I'll have to prepare myself for another round of hospital visits.

It's gonna be okay.

We've done this multiple times before, and we can do it again.

"I'm coming home, Mama."

YEAR FOUR

THIS IS WHERE SHE BELONGS AND IT PINCHES MY HEART,
BECAUSE IT'S THE FLIP CONTRAST OF WHERE I BELONG

'We're not friends.'

45

HUNTER

I PARK IN FRONT of the local pub, getting out of the truck, followed by Jason, as we glance around at the old, decayed building. It seems like yesterday when we were sixteen, desperate to flash our fake IDs for a drink. Never worked, though. I blame Jason's blonde hair, blue-eyed baby face.

"Feels weird to be back here, man." Jason lifts his black LA Knights snapback, scratching his head, giving me a flustered look. We haven't been home since we moved to LA, always being busy with something.

Or at least that's what we told ourselves.

That we needed to set priorities. Jason had exams to study for. I couldn't leave because of my gym schedule. But after Jason's parents got divorced two years ago, they both moved to a different part of the state, and he had no more reason to come back to Braedon, North Carolina.

My mom didn't give a shit if I visited, as long as she got her damn check in the mail every month, and all our old friends are in college in another state or have moved on from our small hometown. Not to mention, the only reason I still had to come back to the East Coast cut me out of her life.

"I wonder if Joe still works here?" A chuckle leaves my lips, walking toward the entrance of the bar.

"Man, that guy really was relentless."

"Only because you looked like a fourteen-year-old Backstreet Boy."

Jason gives me a playful shove. "You think *your* bad boy looks fooled good old Joe?"

"Pff, of course they did!"

"The man could practically smell your immaturity."

I open my mouth to counter with something smart-ass, but my attention is caught by a voice on my left.

"Hey! You're Hunter Hansen, aren't you?" A bulky guy is sitting on his bike, getting ready to leave. The man looks rugged, with his long beard and wrinkles framing his eyes, but his beaming smile makes my mouth curl up in a friendly grin.

"Yeah, that's me." He offers me his hand, shaking it firmly as he slams his other hand on my back in a kind gesture.

"Great fight the other night! Next one is for the championship belt, right?"

"That's the plan." I smile awkwardly, glancing at Jason patiently waiting on the side. I'm used to the attention by now, having lived in LA long enough to know there's always someone who wants something. But I didn't expect anyone back home to be asking for autographs, considering the people in Braeden aren't that easily impressed in general. Especially since most of them have known me since I was just a kid.

"Hey, man. Do you mind taking a picture with me? My grandson is a real big fan." He holds up his phone before I nod and hand it to Jason.

"No problem." I stand next to the guy as he wraps his arm around my shoulder, and we both smile at the camera, giving Jason the opportunity to snap a few pictures.

"Thanks a lot, man! Have a great evening." He gives me another friendly tap on the shoulder while we wave him off and resume our walk to the entrance.

"Well, you definitely are not Hunter Hansen, the *troublemaker*, anymore." Jason opens the door of the bar, walking in. The smell of booze and smoke hit me in the face when I follow behind him.

"Nah, I still am. The only difference is that I get paid for it now," I joke, roaming the area.

The wood floor creaks under our feet as we make our way to the bar, ready to take a seat on one of the empty barstools, when Jason pulls my shoulder, holding me back.

"Well, shit." Glancing at him, I notice his wide eyes staring at something in front of him, and I turn my head to follow his gaze, right until my heart literally stops beating.

Standing like a beacon in front of me, I blink, wondering if I'm imagining shit while she places a drink on one of the tables. Her dark blonde hair looks shiny as always, hanging in waves down her back while her bright eyes seem to light up the room. Green, with blue swirls in the middle that trap your soul if you stare into them too long.

Charlotte.

"What the—" I blurt, my jaw dropping to the floor. Mesmerized, I watch her every move, fighting the desperate ache tingling in my fingers to wrap her in my arms and convince myself she's real. That she's standing in the same room as I am, and she's not some kind of mirage.

She reaches out her hand to grab the twenty-dollar bill from the patron's hand, shooting him a wink that makes a gymnast out of my stomach when he tells her she can keep the change. She's wearing a black t-shirt, with tight black jeans, bringing out every curve of her matured figure, and I shake my head at the thought that wanders off to the memories of her skin under my palms.

My heart starts to gallop when she strolls toward us, looking at the work wallet in her hand, before she snaps her head up, giving us a friendly smile like she would greet any other customer. For just a split second, time freezes, just long enough to capture her gorgeous expression and print it onto my membrane for a later moment. But sooner than I want, the blood drains from her cheeks while mine lift into a grin.

"Oh, shit." Her platter drops from her hands, in shock, her eyes bulging out of their sockets, and I reach down to pick it up for her.

She blinks at me like I'm the devil himself when I take another step forward, handing her the platter.

"Hey, Charls."

"Hunter." She swallows hard, taking it from my hand, then glances at Jason, giving him a tight smile. *She looks beautiful.* Healthy, happy. Like this is where she belongs, and it pinches my heart, because it's the flip contrast of where I belong. But it makes no sense, considering Braeden is two hours away from Chapel Hill, too long for a side job in the local bar.

"What are you doing here? I thought you were at UNC?" I take another step closer, feeling my hands twitching to touch her.

"Yeah, well, a lot has happened." She offers me a smile that's etched with fatigue and doesn't reach her eyes before she rolls them to the back of her head, and I purse my lips at the sight of it.

We used to share our entire life with each other, and now I don't even know why she's back in her hometown. When she cut me out, I was pissed. It felt like she was abandoning me when things got hard, confused, like everyone else. It wasn't until later that I realized she was right, and how we're trying too hard to keep something that we'd never get back. At least not while we're on different coasts. But it didn't change the fact that I felt something was missing. And standing in front of her, I wonder if she's still the thing I've been missing all this time.

"Are you working all night?" I bite my lip, knowing it's a dumb idea to go down this road, but I can't help myself. Now that she's here, walking back into my life like a fucking hurricane from the past... I want—no, I *need*—to talk to her.

She shakes her head with fire sparking in her gaze. "I'm not doing this with you."

"Doing what, Charls?" I step into her space, pinning her down with my lips pursed in annoyance. There's no way in hell I'll walk out here tonight without having a normal conversation with her. Whatever the fuck normal is for us nowadays.

"This." She waves her finger in the small space between our torsos. "You and me. We're not friends. Don't pretend like we are."

She turns, but I catch her arm as my thumb brushes her skin in soft strokes. Her eyes drop down to where we connect, parting her lips before she flicks her haze back up at me.

Those blue-green eyes will be haunting me tonight.

"We could," I argue.

"That would require for you to know what a friendship is."

"Shut—" I swallow the word, treading carefully. Goddamn, the girl is already testing my patience and it's both annoying as it is exhilarating. "I know we didn't end things well, but have a drink with me. Catch up. I want to know how you've been. How you've *really* been." I give her a pleading look while my eyes move back and forth, looking for an answer. She glances at Jason behind me, and I press my lips together, praying she'll say yes.

Her eyes radiate conflict, igniting hope in my chest.

"Come on, Charls," I coax. "I'm an asshole, you already know that. But aren't you at least a little tempted to have a drink together?"

"I'm tempted to hit you over the head." *Liar.*

"You can do that." I shrug, then flash her a cocky grin. "*After* we have a couple of drinks."

Her eyes narrow, her puckered lips pinched, as if she's trying to hold back the smile that's lingering in the corners.

"I'm only agreeing to this because I was planning to stay back for a drink anyway," she says, then presses her finger against my chest with a reprimanding look. "But no flirting."

Another lie, but regardless, I bring my hands up in a placating gesture, chuckling. "Fine."

"Cool. Don't bother me, though. I still have to work." She gives me another death glare as she walks off to the next table, and I can't help staring at her peach ass walking away from me.

"Was her ass always that sexy?" I mumble to no one in particular.

"Nah, it's definitely grown." Jason's arms are folded in front of his body, a look filled with approval plastered on his face.

"Stop looking at my girl." Slapping him on the chest, I break his gaze, and walk toward the bar, suddenly feeling a lot lighter than I have in a long time.

"She ain't your girl," he reprimands.

We both take a seat on the stools as he gives me a mocking look filled with judgement, and my eyes roll to the back of my fucking head, praying he's not going to make a big deal out of this.

"You know what I mean," I huff.

"Oh, I know what you mean. It's these moments when I wonder if *you* know what you mean."

"What are you blabbering about, shithead?"

Jason chuckles with an amused grin that I want to smack off his face, before he shakes his head, signaling the bartender. "Never mind."

I can't help but glance behind me, looking for Charlotte, watching how she's charming her way around the room with her beaming smile.

"I guess it's a blessing in disguise that old witch broke her leg, ain't it?" He places my beer in front of me with a knowing wink, and we clink our bottles together while I give him a wide grin.

"Cheers to that old witch." I'll never fucking admit whatever Jason's got in his head at seeing me and Charls together again, but I'm sure as hell thanking my mother for giving me a reason to be here tonight.

8

"Not gonna lie. I'm confused." I turn my head when I hear her sweet voice next to me, my face instantly lightening up. "What are the two of you doing here?"

Her hands are planted on her sides, her beautiful features stern, fixed in half a glare.

She's clearly not welcoming me with open arms, but it's way more than I'd expected from her after she froze me out for over a year.

"My mom broke her leg," I explain. "Couldn't let her starve. Set up some help for her. We're heading back to LA tomorrow."

"I'm sure the old witch could cast a spell or two if she got really hungry," she mutters, getting on the stool next to me, a mix of disdain and annoyance on her face. Not sure if it's aimed at me or my mother, but feeling her energy so close to me makes me not give a shit either way.

"Funny, that's exactly what I said," Jason pitches in, bringing up his glass to her.

"How are you, Jason?"

"Good to see you, Charlotte."

"You too." Her co-worker places a Moscow Mule in front of her, and she mimics his move, then brings her glass to her plump lips, taking a sip. I watch how she licks her lips, swallowing the contents down her slender neck, feeling my dick stir alive.

Fuck.

"What about you?" I start, with a huskier voice than I intended.

"What about me?"

"What are you doing working in the local bar?"

Her eyes peer at me as she takes another sip, like the answer to that question falls heavy on her heart. Without thinking, I place my hand on her knee in encouragement, waiting for her. I can feel our connection sparking back to life when I touch her, making a shiver run down my spine as the hairs on the back of my neck stand up. *Fuck, fuck.* Doing my best to ignore the feeling, I keep looking at her with anticipation. Her little flinch tells me she feels it too, but her chin stays high, her features sporting a look of steel.

"Halfway through sophomore year, Mama found another lump." Her exhale tightens my chest. "It was bad. I moved back home, and I've been going to community college ever since."

Pressing my lips tightly together, I watch her face as the words leave her lips.

Regret has my head wobbling on my neck, feeling like even more of an asshole than I already am. I hate that she went through that again.

Without me.

"Babe," I start.

"Don't." She brings up her hand. "I don't need any pity. It's fine. She's doing better now. At first, they only gave her a few more months, but she was eligible for an experimental trial at Duke University, and that's really been working. I'm only working at the bar one night a week. Just to get out of the house for anything other than groceries, hospital visits, or classes. Life is pretty boring in Braedon now that everyone has gone off to college." Her lips are lifted, yet strained, and she brings her glass to her lips once more. It reminds me of my eighteenth birthday, that Pink Snowball and her lips on a tumbler in celebration of me. She wormed her way under my skin that night, and I've never been able to fully get her out.

"How do you do that?"

"Do what?" she asks, the heat in her eyes simmering down a notch, claiming a little victory in my chest.

"Always see the positive in everything."

"It's not like I have any choice, Hunt. I can't just cry in a corner. These are the cards life dealt. Gotta play the game."

I shake my head in awe. "You're something else."

"You already knew that." She gives me a taunting wink that makes my heart jump, and I let out a laugh before my gaze settles on her.

"Are you flirting with me, Charlotte Roux?"

"I wouldn't dare, Hansen," she counters, though her cheeks pinken.

She would. If not because she wants to, for the simple reason of trying to get a rise out of me, but the danger is? It only makes me want more. Desperate to relive the memories of our past, even if it's only for a brief moment. Turning around, I scan the rest of the bar, looking for an empty booth. When my eyes land on one, the corner of my mouth rises as I slowly twist my gaze back to her.

"Let's have a seat, get some privacy." I expect her to give me some kind of snarky comment, and for a few beats, that's exactly what I see laced around her irises. Defiance. Reluctance. But her nostrils flare when she pushes out the air from her lungs and it all disappears with it. She nods, sliding off the stool as she starts making her way to the empty booth, and I follow her tracks.

"Hunt." Jason demands my attention, and our gazes collide. His sharp jaw is locked, a pleading expression in his eyes. "We're leaving tomorrow."

"I know."

"You're going to regret it."

Frowning, I give him an incredulous look, because even though he had a front-row seat for my entire history with this girl, and I know where he's coming from, he's also fucking wrong. "I'll regret nothing regarding this girl, man."

With a shrug, he fixes his gaze back in front of him, downing the last of his beer.

"Your funeral."

46

Charlotte

S LIDING INTO THE BOOTH, I watch him intently, assessing his
face like I want to make sure it's engraved in my memory,
though we all know I couldn't forget about him even if I wanted
to. God fucking knows I've tried.

He narrows his eyes on me as he moves closer, our hips
touching as we sit in the middle of the booth, and I take a sip
of my drink to avoid staring at his lips. I still have the tolerance
of a sixteen-year-old who's allowed a sip of her mother's wine,
but right now, it's giving me the confident buzz I need to be able
to hold my ground against the man who once had my heart.

It's strange how sitting here with him, after all this time, feels
both awkward and comfortable, the same familiarity we used
to have from day one still wrapping around us. Jason gives me
a quick glance, and I raise my eyebrows at him in question,
hoping he can silently tell me what the deal is, but he shrugs his
shoulders with a shake of his head, as if he's just as confused as
I am.

I take a deep breath, deciding to just go with whatever happens, determined to face this blast from the past that life threw
in my face. Not that I'm complaining.

"So..." Smooth as ever, his arm slips over the back of the booth
behind my head. "You look good, Charls."

I wish my heart didn't do a backflip because of the way his nickname for me vibrates over his lips, but goddamnit, it fucking does. "Thanks."

"How have you been?" His gaze turns serious, as if he's set to find any lies that might roll off my tongue, not willing to take any bullshit answer I might feed him.

"I'm good." It's an honest answer. I really am good.

Do I wish I was still at UNC with Julie? Of course!

Do I sometimes wish life was a little more exciting? Definitely!

But my mom is slowly getting better, hopefully indefinitely this time. My grades are good, so chances are I'll be graduating next summer, and though my life might not be the most exciting one—I'm satisfied with it.

"Are you?" He studies my face with skepticism.

The corner of my mouth curls in a coy smile as I place my hand on his knee. His gaze glances to my hand, swallowing hard as his gaze locks with mine again, a craving glittering in his eyes. *Oops.*

"I wouldn't lie to you. I'm really good, Hunt."

Finally, the features on his face soften, taking a sip of his drink as his tongue darts out to lick the contents from his lips. He's still sexy as fuck.

"Are you single?" He's looking at me like a hungry tiger, and I curse my fucking vagina for purring alive. This is not the time to wake up, girlfriend. Especially not with Hunter Hansen. You can't dine and dash with him; he's bound to take everything you own, including body, mind, and soul. *I fucking know this.*

My lashes lower in a tiny scold. "I said no flirting."

And of course, this only sparks the asshole to throw me that boyish smirk he's mastered so fucking well. "This isn't flirting. This is me showing an interest in an old friend. So, are you?" He inches closer, close enough for me to breathe in his woodsy, citrus scent that instantly sends my mind into overdrive.

"Yes," I confess. "But you ain't."

I give him a knowing look, and he lets out a full belly laugh, his leg rubbing against mine in the movement, sending an annoying jolt of excitement through my stomach.

"Are you keeping tabs on me, babe?"

"Pff," I huff, taking another sip of my drink. "It's hard *not* to when you're all over the news."

Something dark flashes in his hazel eyes. "I'll never get used to that."

"I can imagine." We fall silent, staring at each other, the lust slowly simmering down, reminding me of the friendship we used to have. He's definitely gotten older; the features in his face have matured in the most handsome way while his bulky arms make him even more attractive than he was before. Like the dark prince any girl wants to be protected by. For the outside world, that's exactly what he is.

A dark prince.

A rebel fighting his way through life.

But I still see him.

I still see the boy looking for a deeper meaning in life, looking to be loved, yet being scared as fuck when it comes his way. Thinking he doesn't deserve the happily ever after that he so desperately wants. I want to scold him, give him a hard time for hurting me, but I find it impossible to not look past the hard exterior he shows the world. Sometimes I feel like I'm the only one who can find the door that leads past it, and I still can't resist peeking in, even though I should run for the fucking hills if I want to keep my heart intact.

"Are *you* happy, Hunter?" I cock my head at him, my hand reaching out to his neck, brushing the bruises that have formed from his last fight. I shouldn't. But I want more than anything to feel him under my palm, ignoring the fact that he's not mine to touch. He snaps his head my way when our skin connects, his eyes wide as his lips part. The air changes to something palpable, consuming and addictive at the same time. Briefly, his eyes shut, as if he's soaking up the heat radiating from my fingers, before he opens them with a pain that I've never been able to take away, but damn me if I didn't try. Doing my very best to show him that he matters. That his feelings matter. Because they matter to me.

"I guess," he says.

"You're a shit liar, Hunten Hansen." I pull back my hand, grabbing my glass from the table, swirling my ice cubes. "You always have been."

"Only with you." A small chuckle leaves his lips, and I smile. Realizing how much I've missed this. *Us.* How is it possible that after more than a year of silence, he can walk in and it still feels the same? Like our souls click when they shouldn't fit at all.

"To be honest, Charls?" His hand plays with a strand of my hair, his gaze darkening. "I don't know if I'm happy. From the outside, it seems like I have it all. I'm one fight removed from that championship belt. I have more money than I can spend in a lifetime. I live in a fucking villa in the Hills. What's there to complain about? But when you ask me if I remember the last time I was happy, it has nothing to do with anything back in Cali."

"Okay," I drawl, a little scared to follow up on his gloomy confession, bringing my glass to my lips again. "When was the last time you were happy?"

"The quarry."

I choke on my drink, incredulously coughing with wide eyes until my head slowly turns his way. *You've got to be shitting me.*

"The quarry?"

His eyes are serious as hell, but that boyish grin slowly enters the surface of his features, and a shiver runs up and down my spine when his hand strokes the nape of my neck. My eyes move to the back of my head at the scorching movements, and I take a deep breath, trying to keep it together. *This is bad.*

"It's true, Charls. When I think of the word happy, that day pops into my head. *Our day.*" He moves closer, leaning in, and I can feel his breath fanning the skin underneath my ear. His hand massages my neck, and I close my eyes while a longing feeling builds between my legs. *This is bad.* But then why does it feel so good at the same time?

"What part?" I turn my head toward him until our lips are almost touching, and I stare into his mesmerizing eyes. He will always be my forever sin, and right now, I just want to let go over everything I *have* to do. Everything I'm *supposed* to do and just give in to this everlasting pull.

"The part where I finally got a taste of your sweet lips."

"Oh, yeah?" I try to fake indifference, but who am I kidding?

"Yeah," he croaks out, his tone gravelly and needy, while he softly squeezes my neck in a possessive way. "The soft touch of your plump lips against mine."

Oh, I'm in so much trouble.

His hand moves to my mouth, and he drags his thumb over my upper lip, then pulls it down, making them part in anticipation. He lifts his snapback to put it back on backwards, and I let out a deep sigh, the move making me feel like I'm back in high school.

"You still remember?" I want to close the distance between us, but part of me is holding myself back, telling me I shouldn't. That I can't cross that bridge again tonight, because we'll be hurting each other by the time morning falls.

"I do. I can never forget." He nods, his nose skimming mine. "But I need a reminder."

Before I can respond, his lips crash onto mine, my hand latching out to grab his shirt in a tight grip, and in that exact moment, it hits me. It hits me when his tongue darts out, pressing against mine in an unstoppable hunger. It is as if in that moment a door opens in my head, and he barges in. Making me realize he is meant to be mine.

That he is destined to be mine.

It isn't the first time we've kissed, and it probably won't be the last time tonight, but for me, there is only one clear vision and it's labeled *Hunter Hansen*. Everyone that came before him doesn't mean shit. Anyone that will come after him won't mean shit.

He's my weakness, my everlasting craving, my never-ending addiction. The world around us seems to blur, the two of us spiraling down a rabbit hole I don't think we will ever really come out of as his hands start to move all over my body. He presses me hard against the booth, and deeper into the leather while his hand snakes under my shirt, our mouths never disconnecting.

"I can't stop, babe." He huffs between kisses, making me nod in agreement.

"Me neither."

"I want you."

Cupping his face with my hands, I push his face back, looking into his eyes.

"Then take me."

The corner of his mouth moves up in a cocky grin that makes me swoon every single time before he slides out of the booth, his arm circling my waist as he drags me behind him.

"Wait," I call out, my hands propped on his chest, a shocking realization popping into my head. "You have a girlfriend." My eyes widen in horror, thinking about how he's about to cheat with me while his girl is waiting for him in California.

"Charls," he says, his stance calm and composed, as if he doesn't have a care in the world, holding out his hand. "We broke up two weeks ago."

"You did?" I blurt, incredulously.

He lowers his head, grabbing my chin to look me in the eye.

"I don't lie to you. Ever. You know that."

I blink in response, thinking back to all the moments he could've made life easier by lying but didn't, knowing deep down inside, he's a lot of things, but a liar has never been one of them. My mind is telling me this is a terrible choice, that I should call it a night, and wish him well until we meet again. But you know what the thing about the mind is? It's never as loud as the heart, screaming in your ear with a damn megaphone.

I glance at his hand, then look up at him, our gazes locking as the tension rises more and more between us.

"Are you coming?"

Shaking my head at my own stupidity, I place my hand in his as he lifts me off my feet.

Of course I fucking am.

"Sssh, Hunt! I don't want a run-in with the Wicked Witch of the East!" I hiss, laughing, when he tries to undo my shirt as we burst through the door.

"It's past midnight; she's sleeping. Or passed out from the booze. Either option works, really," he jokes. I try to run up the stairs, getting out of his grasp and into the safety of his room. But his hand reaches out, slamming me back against his chest as he fists my hair. I keep telling myself this is a bad idea, that if we want to relive the past, *this* sure as fuck isn't the part we should focus on. But every moment his hands land on my body, those thoughts get extinguished as easily as blowing out a match.

"I'm not sure I can make it all the way up, babe." He leans in, leaving a trail of kisses along my neck that lower my lashes.

"If you would just stop touching me for five seconds, we could."

"Hmm, can't. You taste too good."

I roughly push him off, letting out an excited screech when I look into his indignant face, before I run up the stairs while he chases me. When I burst through his bedroom door, I stop in the doorway, glancing around the room in a bit of shock. Nothing has changed in the last three years since he left.

"It's like you never left," I whisper. It's eerie, but at the same time comforting, knowing that some things haven't changed.

Rough hands push me forward, and I hear the door slam behind me, before his chiseled arms circle my waist from behind. With one hand, he moves my hair from my neck, a hot breath tracing the valley of my skin.

"When I look at you, I wish I didn't," he says, groggy, every word drilling into my core. Not getting any time to process what he's saying, he spins me, his lips covering mine, and I bring my legs up, wrapping them around his waist as he carries me to the bed.

We both land on the bed with a thud, never breaking contact, as if I'm drowning and he's the oxygen I've been lacking. My hands reach for the hem of his shirt, dragging it over his head. Licking my lips, I hold back, enjoying the sight of his bare chest while the tips of my fingers stroke his hard six-pack. An extra set of tattoos is carved into his skin, and I gasp, tracing the lines.

"Fuck me," I mutter, not understanding how much his body had changed until this very moment.

"That's the plan."

When he pulls my hands above my head, I arch my back, wanting to feel him between my legs. He roughly pulls my shirt over my head, then pushes my jeans down until I'm lying in nothing but my lingerie, feeling completely exposed but not giving a fuck right now. Thank God I put on a matching set this morning.

He's looking at me like he will tear me apart, and I want nothing more. I arch my back to unclasp my bra before throwing it across the room.

"Still the prettiest thing I've ever seen." He drags a finger from my ankle all the way up to my thighs, and I let out a moan, biting my lip as the sensation makes my body shiver. My thong is growing wetter by the second, and I swallow hard when he finally moves his finger up and down the damp fabric.

"You want me, babe?" If you'd asked me this morning, my answer would be: *not in a million years*. But now? There's nothing I want more. In fact, I'm pretty sure my brain will not function properly until I get the release that was named and claimed by Hunter Hansen from the moment he put his lips on mine.

I frantically nod, having a hard time finding my words while my senses force me to let out a desperate cry. Before I can answer, he rips my thong off my body, spreading my legs wide as he crawls toward my center.

"Good girl." *Oh, someone mop me off the floor.*

His tongue darts out, licking through my center, and I cry out in pleasure as he kisses my pussy like he kisses my mouth in a dozen contradictions. Sweet, but eager. Gently, but determined. Slowly, but surely. So fucking surely. He eats me like he hasn't eaten for days, but still manages to savor like I'm his fucking oasis.

This blissful fog clogs my brain, my vision blurring with each moan that rumbles through my lips. I've only slept with Hunter a handful of time, but suddenly I remember why no one could live to up to it.

"Shh," he says, brushing his lips against my folds, shutting my eyes. "You don't want to wake up the Wicked Witch of the East." Just as the words leave his lips, he sucks my clit, and I let out a desperate screech that makes him laugh in response. Not wanting to wake up his mother, I press my hands over my mouth, muffling my own grumbles as he keeps working his way around my aching clit. His moves are filled with intent, knowing exactly what he's doing when he softly caresses the area around my sensitive nub with the tip of his tongue. *Oh my fucking GOD.*

Nearly touching, combined with long sucks and long strokes, moving all the way up, until he comes back down, pushing his tongue inside of me, licking my tightening walls.

A finger enters my body, stretching me wide in a taunting way, his lips covering my throbbing clit when I feel my orgasm building inside of me, making me bite my finger to make sure I don't cry out in pleasure. His free hand reaches out, pulling me up, so that I'm leaning on my elbows. Cupping my breast, he keeps going at a scorching pace as I throw my head back, enjoying the ride. But when I flip my gaze back, his eyes are staring at me with a predatory look, like this chase to my high is as important to him as it is to me. They pin me down with his tongue between my legs, wordlessly ordering me to release in the most intense way.

My body takes over, climbing the summit as fast as I can. His fingers move into my mouth, and I suck hard, groaning, while he does the same on my clit. Finally, he covers my mouth with his hand as he flicks my clit at a quick pace, and he pushes me over the edge, shattering me from the inside. I let out a faint scream, muffled by his hand, while I ride out my wave of pleasure as my legs shake until the moment passes.

My body goes limp, and I look up at the ceiling, panting as I hear him take off his pants, putting on a condom when he moves his body over mine. His lips hover above my face with an arrogant smirk.

"Missed me?"

"Shut up, asshole," I mutter, crushing my lips against his. His tongue dances with mine, and I can taste my own saltiness on his lips, turning me on even more.

"I want you, Hunter," I huff, pushing my nails into his bare ass, demanding him to take the plunge.

"God, you're so sexy." He rests his face in my neck, leaving a trail of kisses on the crook before his tip aligns with my center. Without waiting another second, I push him inside of me, crying out a delicious moan when I feel him stretching me.

"Fuck," he mumbles against my skin when I feel his teeth sink into my neck. My hands hold his head locked against me as he starts to thrust, and a flood of emotion washes over my body. The warmth of him melts any wall that stood between us, and I can feel my body and mind perfectly aligning as they open up to him in every way possible. Like a kaleidoscope, my body alights now that it's glued against his, and I know I'm absolutely and utterly fucked.

My eyes well up when my own question runs through my head like an omen, asking me when the last time *I* was happy. He keeps pushing against my walls at a blistering pace, while I close my eyes, scared to voice what I knew since the moment I saw him standing in front of me today. Knowing that if I admit it, I'm gone. Forever caught in his grasp, with no way out. Yet I know there is no denying it.

Because for once, my mind and my heart are exactly on the same page, knowing there is only one answer to that question.

Now.

Today.

Hunter Hansen makes me happier than anything else in this world, even if it's just for five minutes, giving him the ability to break me with *every* single word, *every* single move, yet I would take the risk *every* single time.

He grunts above me, his hand fisting my hair, demanding, when he locks his eyes with mine, giving me a possessive look that reminds me of the alpha male he shows in the cage. His jaw clenches and his face tightens, showing me he's close to his release.

"Deeper," I cry, my eyes never deviating from his, pressing my nails into his arms.

His hips push his shaft even deeper, grinding along my clit just the way I like it. It doesn't take long before I can feel my walls tightening once more, and he lets out a growl, pushing a bruising kiss against my lips. Then he presses his forehead against mine as he picks up the pace, bringing us both closer with every second.

"Fuck, Charlotte. I'm coming." I let out a moan in encourage-ment, pushing his ass closer against my body until finally his face goes rigid, and my walls squeeze his dick in the best way. He lets out a feral cry, and I do the same when he drops himself onto my body. The fatigue relaxes his muscles as I enjoy his weight on top of me.

My hands move to his back, brushing his spine with my nails, while I can feel his breath on my neck.

"Fuck, babe," he murmurs against my skin, making me let out a sex-drunk chuckle.

"I know." The corner of my mouth moves up in a content smile, before my face falls just a little, wondering how long we will be able to stay like this.

47

HUNTER

I BRUSH HER HAIR out of the way, exposing her pretty face as her cheek rests on my chest. I watch her closely, a warm feeling in my gut when I feel her torso slowly move up and down at a steady pace while my hand is draped on her back.

Never in a million years did I expect to wake up like this when I walked into the bar last night. When her dark blonde hair crossed my vision, it felt like I got struck by lightning. Frozen in one place, yet completely electrified.

Now she's here.

In my arms.

I wanna say it's weird. Strange even, to grasp the feeling she thunders alive in my core, because I haven't felt it in so long. I desperately want to hold on to it. *To her.* But I already know I'm gonna have to let her go again.

I press a kiss to her forehead, while my hands gently brush her back, and she slowly stirs awake, letting out a soft moan that breezes all my senses alive.

"Morning, babe," I whisper against her hair.

She gives me a sweet smile, her eyes barely open as her gaze scans around the room. "I can't believe after all these years we had sex in your bedroom. It's still exactly the same."

I chuckle, knowing teenage Hunter is fist-bumping me right now.

Holding her in my arms, I glance around the room that looks a lifetime away from the life I'm living right now. Everything back in LA is luxurious, spacious, and grand, representing the life I've made for myself, while this tiny teenage bedroom reminds me exactly where I came from. I don't miss a thing from this house, but lying here with Charlotte makes me realize this still feels like home.

When I left, a few years ago, I literally threw some clothes in a weekend bag, tossed an old family picture in there that reminds me of better times, and left. Jumped on that plane and never looked back. As soon as I started making money, I bought this house, and sent my mother a check every month, making sure she always had a roof over her head and food on the table. Or liquor, whatever she prefers.

But I never felt the need to come back to Braedon after Charlotte went to UNC and ended our friendship, simply because I didn't have a reason to.

"Feels like a teenage dream." *A wet dream I'd like to relive over and over again.*

"You think your mother is gonna freak out on me?"

"Do you care?" I smirk, brushing my lips against her forehead.

"Nah, not really."

"I'm sorry I didn't go to see *your* mama," I offer, staring out of the window, looking out at the big oak tree I used to climb out of.

"That's okay. She's actually away for the weekend with a friend."

"Really?" I ask, surprised. "She's really doing good then?"

"Yeah." She nods, glancing up at me. "I don't want to get too excited, you know? But yeah, she's feeling great. She glows more every week, and she's almost done with the treatment, so hopefully, she'll be in remission after that, but the prognosis seems really positive."

"That's great, Charls. I'm so happy for you both." I stroke her arm affectionately. "You gonna get that dog now then?"

"Ha!" A spark of joy travels across her face. "Can't believe you remember that."

"I remember." Sometimes I remember so much, I wish I didn't, but I don't tell her that.

The look on her face falls a little, as her eyes soften. She bites her lip, like my words cut her heart deeply, then she shakes her head before another smile appears.

"No, I don't want another thing to take care of. Not yet. When Mama is better, I want to explore the world a bit. Maybe travel after graduation. See what else is out there, you know?" She moves her body up, resting her head against my shoulder. "I could even visit you sometime." The tone of her voice is careful, as if she's not sure if I want her to, and I hate how she picks her words like that.

"Yeah?" I brush her cheek with the backs of my fingers, peering into her eyes that are filled with insecurity as they keep looking at me in question. "That would be great, Charls."

She sucks in a sharp breath, bracing herself for whatever words are about to come out of her mouth, and I shoot her an encouraging smile.

"You know I still love you, right?" she confesses, stuttering my heart. Staying quiet, I swallow hard, as my eyes just keep blinking. My mouth turns dry, and I ball my hands into fists, not knowing what to say.

She means a lot to me. Maybe even the world. But I vowed to myself a long time ago that I don't do *love*. I don't want the heartbreak that is bound to happen when you give your heart to someone else. It's the reason I asked for her friendship all those years ago, making sure she wouldn't leave and take my heart with her.

I didn't expect her to do it anyway.

I can see the panic hit her body, making her let out a troubled chuckle, putting a smile on her face that doesn't match her eyes.

"Sorry, I didn't mean to make you uncomfortable. I shouldn't have said anything."

"No, don't." I grab her hand. "It's fine. It's just—you know I'm not capable of love."

"That's a lie, Hunt," she whispers with pity.

"Maybe." I shrug. "But I can't give you what you deserve."

She gives me a coy smile, nodding, before getting out of bed to collect her clothes.

"It's okay, Hunt. I get it."

"Are you mad at me?" I throw the covers off my body, getting up to close the distance between us, not willing to let her run out the door if we're not cool. I need everything to be settled between us, because I don't think I can go another year without her. I will never be able to give her what she wants, but I hope that we at least broke down enough bricks between us that we can be friends again.

"No." Her tone is harsh, yet I can see by the look in her eyes that she means it. "Why would I be mad?" she asks, pulling her jeans over her legs, then grabs her shirt from the ground, throwing it over her head. "It is what it is, Hunter. Your life is there. My life is here. I know you don't want to say those words." She shrugs, muttering with a mocking expression. "Even though it's only eight letters."

Nodding in agreement, I grab her hand, dipping my head as my other hand takes a hold of her chin.

"Can we keep this, though?"

"What's that?" The tension in the room rapidly rises, now that we are face to face once more, and the memory of last night is still fresh in our heads like a forbidden dream.

"This. You and me. I don't want to go back to LA and not talk to you like we have for the last year. I want to know what's going on with you. I want to know how your mama is doing, and I want to get a picture when you finally get that dog."

She tries to give me a cautious look, though I can see the smile she's trying to hold in. "I don't know, Hunt. The last time, that didn't really work out well." Then she dramatically rolls her eyes. "You practically neglected me."

"I neglected you?" I huff indignantly, a smile on my face as I jokingly push her back and grab my sweatpants from the floor while she gathers the rest of her stuff. "You weren't exactly blowing up my phone either."

"I was in college. There were too many boys demanding my attention."

Her words make me take a long stride toward her, crowding her space, as I narrow my eyes at her.

"We both know there's only one boy who can really demand your attention."

"Stop flirting with me."

"Maybe." My eyes move back and forth over her face, clenching my jaw to resist myself from covering her lips with mine again, but I want nothing more.

To devour her.

To corrupt her like only I can.

To flirt with her until she's sick of me.

She swallows hard, and I tell myself she's feeling the same struggle, before I take a step back to get dressed, and I hear her let out a soft breath of relief. Quietly, I get my shirt off the floor while she waits for me, resting her back against the door, eying my every move.

"What?" I nod my chin toward her with an arrogant smirk.

"You're an asshole." She purses her lips, but doesn't seem pissed. No, she's enjoying this just as much as I am. Loving the banter we throw at each other like we used to every day for a year. "But yeah, we can keep *this*."

She pushes off the door, sauntering toward me, then stops in front of me, her face more serious than before, silently demanding me to really listen to her.

"But you have to put as much effort into it as I do. Both of us. If we're gonna be friends again, we really need to *be* friends. You gotta share the important stuff with me, even if it involves some kind of fucking bimbo." She dramatically rolls her eyes, and I lick my lips, amused. "I don't want to read no shit on TMZ before you tell me. That includes whenever you get back together with Laurie."

"That's not happening anytime soon." Considering I told her she's a superficial little girl, who has a better relationship with her phone than with her boyfriend—AKA *me*—I doubt she'll be trying to catch my attention when I get back to LA.

Charls's eyebrow cocks in a dare. "You said that before."

"I called her superficial," I counter.

"Ouch." She winces, then I catch the smug smile. "Not your smartest move, Hansen."

"I know."

"Well, it doesn't matter. Laurie, or whatever other supermodel that might pop into your life. You have to tell me about it. I can't be your friend if I'm in the dark all the time."

"What are you suggesting?" I tilt my head at her.

"Every other Friday, we call and catch up."

Less than I was aiming for, but I'll take anything she'll give me. "Can I call you on fight night?"

Surprise washes over her face. "You'd rather start your fight night with me than your girlfriend?"

"She is not my girlfriend," I rebuke like a smartass. "But yes, I want to call you before I get into that cage. It's a ritual. I can't do it with anyone else but you. Bad luck and all."

"You're one fight removed from being the welterweight champion. You clearly can do without a little luck."

I grab her chin, my fingers possessively spreading over her cheek as I bring my lips close to hers. "I can do without it. But I don't *want* to."

Her reply is barely audible. "Okay."

"So I can call you?" I let go of her face and a ghost of a smile lands in the corner of her pouty lips.

"Is your favorite ice cream flavor clementine vanilla?"

"Right." I chuckle at her defiant stance, adoring how cute she looks as she pulls a face at me. "Okay, babe. Every other Friday."

She offers me her hand, and I incredulously shake my head at her silliness before I take it, shaking it in agreement.

"Deal," she quips, a pleased smile on her face.

"Deal."

YEAR FIVE

I STILL SEE MYSELF STANDING ON THAT SIDEWALK AND
HIM TELLING ME HE DOESN'T SAY THOSE WORDS

'Well, do you?'

48

Charlotte

PICKING UP A BOTTLE of scotch to put it back on the glass shelf behind the bar, I hear my phone ring. I glance at the screen, and a smile appears on my face as I pick it up.

"You ready, champion?"

"I'm not there yet," Hunter huffs through the phone.

I can hear the tension in his body, etching through his voice while I imagine him standing in front of the mirror, looking at his reflection as he tries to get his head in the right space.

"Yet. You will be in an hour." I grab a bottle of tequila from the shelf, pouring myself a shot, figuring I deserve one to calm my nerves on fight night. Even though we weren't talking for a while, I never missed a fight, always keeping my gaze locked with the screen until he would finally release the tension in my body by knocking out his opponent.

But today is a whole different level.

My nerves have been rolling through my stomach the entire day, knowing this is his most important fight so far. The final fight to take that belt home and claim that champion title.

"You don't know that."

"Yeah, I do, Hunter. You've been working for this for ages. You got this. The only question is, how long are you going to make him believe he can actually beat you?" I bring the glass to my lips, throwing the contents down my throat, making a sour face as I put a lemon wedge in my mouth.

"Wouldn't you like to know?" He chuckles, and I can hear the tension slowly shimmering away as he slips into that flirtatious mood he'll probably never get rid of.

I smile, loving how I'm still able to loosen him up, the tequila making its way down my body in a scorching way.

"Oh, come on. You're not really going to make me suffer like that, are you?"

"Why not?"

"Because one, we agreed to be friends again. Meaning you don't give me a heart attack every chance you get. And two, because I know you're dying to tell me, anyway."

"Am I now?" He laughs.

"Come on, we both know you're calling me because you fight better if we keep our rituals alive. You said so yourself."

He stays quiet, the corner of my mouth rising in a wide grin, knowing I've got him there. Though he never admitted it, I heard the rumors that were going on while he was still fighting in high school. Phil once told me that he was even better ever since he brought me along, calling me his lucky charm to everyone who wanted to hear it. One day, I couldn't be there because my mother had a terrible week, and he dragged it for fifteen minutes, putting everyone on edge since everyone expected him to knock the guy out in the first five minutes.

"First round."

"Oh," I cheer out. "You're not even going to pretend?"

"Hell no, that belt is mine, Charls." His confidence crawls back into his voice.

"Damn right, it is."

"Are you ready, baby?" I hear a woman's voice in the background, wiping the grin right off my face.

"Who's that?" I frown.

"Laurie." He says her name as if it's nothing. As if it's the most normal thing in the world, but to me, it feels like another punch in the gut. I know I predicted it, but maybe deep inside I was hoping I was wrong. But hearing her purring voice coming over the line reminds me once more that we are just friends.

Nothing more.

Nothing less.

I swallow hard before I ask him about her, doing my best to keep my voice steady. "You two are back together?"

"Yeah, sorta." His tone changes, as if he's suddenly aware of all the ways this conversation can fly off the bend again. "We're trying. I was gonna tell you, I swear. It's just, it's not that serious yet." The panic is audible in his voice as he quickly blurts out the words. "Don't be mad. *Please*."

"Calm down, Hunt. I'm not mad. I'm happy for you." *Liar, liar, pants on fire.* I cock my head as I listen to his steady breathing through the phone. "That is, if *you* are?"

"I'll be happy when I have that belt around my waist in an hour."

I don't miss how he steamrolls over the question, but lucky for him, I don't even truly want to know the answer. "You will. You promise first round?"

"It will be over before you know it."

"Good." I smile. "Good luck, Hunt."

"Thanks, Charls."

Thirty minutes later.

HUNTER: *PHOTO*

CHARLOTTE: Told you, Champion. ;) Congratulations. Gold looks good on you.

HUNTER: Couldn't have done it without you.

CHARLOTTE: You can do anything you want, Hunt. When are you going to realize that?

HUNTER: Never. I need you to remind me for the rest of my life.

HUNTER

W E WALK IN, LAURIE'S high heels echoing in my ear with
each step, her arm linked to mine.

"Oh my god, Emily! Look at that!" She glances at Jensen's
date. After doing a shoot together, Laurie has been adamant
about setting her up with either Jason or Jensen, quoting *"we
can double date."*

"Damn, Toto. We're definitely not in Kansas anymore."
Jensen's eyes bulge at the skimpy dressed air acrobatic girls
hanging from the ceiling. The entire venue is decorated in the
Knights' signature black and white, while everyone in a suit and
tie blends right in.

Including me.

But on the inside, I feel like all these layers of fabric are
designed to be a deathtrap.

"Damn, I hate this damn tux." I pinch two fingers between
the collar of my dress shirt, hoping to relieve some of the heat
building in my chest. "Next time, only invite us if the dress code
is do-whatever-the-fuck-you-want-sexy."

Jensen cocks an eyebrow. "That still doesn't allow you to
come in sweats and a hoodie."

"Why the fuck not?"

"Because that would be a slumber party," Jason pitches in. "But I agree. Next time, I'm staying home if it requires us to dress up as monkeys."

"Damn, you two can whine," Jensen says as his eyes roll up. "I have had to do this bullshit once a month since I was eight. At least this crowd isn't filled with uptight politicians and their cookie-cutter wives. Besides, it's for charity. You wouldn't want the world to find out Hunter Hansen has a frozen heart that cannot even melt under the gaze of orphaned children?" His gooey eyes ridiculously stare back at me from underneath his fluttering lashes. *Fuckface.*

"I care about the kids," I rebuke. "But I could've done with a big-ass check and no tux."

"No such luck, Hansen." Jensen grips my shoulder, a shit-eating grin splitting his face, accompanied with a glint that screams trouble. "I'd much rather get tortured *with* you than without you."

"Don't you usually take Bodi to these things?" Jason opts, referring to Jensen's best friend since he was twelve.

"Yeah, but he went to visit his dad on the East Coast."

The three of us glance around the spacious room. Two open bars sit on either side of the room, while the front of the stage is conferred into a oak dancefloor. The rest of the space is occupied by two dozen tables, with medieval suits of armor helmets and big black and white feathers sprouting from the top as huge centerpieces.

"You'd think this is Robert Davis's third wedding," I mutter, referring to the owner of the team while we find our way to Jensen's table.

"Yeah, Davis doesn't have a budget for these things. Apparently, his first wife talked him into donating ten percent of his income to charity," Jensen informs, pulling out a chair for Emily, while I follow his example for Laurie. He's a fucking dickhead, most of the time, but it's in these moments that it's clear he wasn't raised in small-town North Carolina. No, Jared James Jensen's family is prestigious as fuck. "Said it was bad karma if he didn't."

We all sit down when a server appears, taking our drinking orders, and we chat a little until our drinks are placed in front of us. Laurie ordered a glass of Pinot Grigio or some shit, and she takes a sip before she almost gulps it all down.

"Oh my god... is that?" Laurie's eyes narrow, zoning in on a couple chatting with a man I recognize as Johnny Pearce, the GM of the team.

Emily gasps when she fixes her eyes in the same direction. "Nicole."

"Oh, you know Chad's wife? She's cool."

Two sets of evil eyes whip Jensen's way, and he winces from behind his bourbon. "Or not. Not cool, apparently."

"She's a shady bitch," Laurie blurts like a fire-spitting dragon. "We've both auditioned with Armani a few years back, but she stole the job from me."

"How is it stealing when you had to audition?" Jason says flatly, already bored with the conversation.

"*Because*... she didn't even know about the job until I told her about it," Laurie says earnestly, and even I see the flaws in that explanation.

"That's not stealing," Jason deadpans.

"It's still a bitch move," Emily counters with a resting bitch face, before she decadently lifts her glass of wine to her lips.

I see a dozen comments on Jason's lips, but I shoot him a stern look, silently telling him to drop it.

"Ladies, I don't care if you want to shoot daggers at Nicole all night, but behave. I don't want you to pull out your claws against my teammate's wife." His eyes fix on Emily while he links his fingers with her. A charming smile curls his mouth, but the dark expression in his eyes makes Emily shift a little in her chair.

"Of course not."

Squeezing Laurie's leg beside me, I nonverbally will her to look me in the eye to confirm the same.

Defiant as she can be, she keeps her gaze trained in front of her, feigning oblivion as I keep staring at her profile.

"Laurie?" I opt after a moment of silence.

Finally, she slowly turns her attention my way, followed by a roll of her sharp eyes.

"What?"

"*Behave*," I growl, digging my fingers a little deeper into her flesh.

"I always behave!" I just hold her gaze, shooting her a dull expression. She can be really sweet, bringing me my coffee in bed or cooking dinner after a long day at the gym, even though she can't cook for shit. But in public? Or with her friends? She can be as nice as a feral cat, claws and everything.

"Fine!" she mutters, then pulls my arm when the new Ed Sheeran song ricochets through the venue. "Hunter, please dance with me." Brown eyes peer up at me from underneath her fake lashes, and I let my gaze drop a little lower down the cleavage of her silver dress. The swell of her breasts lures me into the fantasy of ripping it off her body later tonight, but when they lower a little bit more to her bright red painted lips, it vanishes as quickly as it came. She's hot and fun. As much as people might not believe it, when it's just me and her, she's just a normal girl. Strolling around the house in yoga leggings and a hoodie, no make-up on, eating a bag of chips while watching some boring reality show. I live for those moments. It's the moments like this, when she's all dolled up and glued to her phone, that I'm wondering how the hell I ended up here.

"No thanks, honey. I'll pass."

"Oh, come on, you love to dance."

A crooked smile and a smart remark settles on my tongue, but I'm cut off before I can open my mouth.

"He hates to dance," Jason chimes in.

"He does not." I don't miss the fire in her gaze and simultaneously roll my eyes, already dreading what's coming. *Here we go again.*

"He'd rather run a stick up his ass than dance."

"Then why does he dance with me?" Laurie replies, trying to sound smug. Not sure if she means all the times she's been grinding her ass in my groin when we go out, but I wouldn't qualify that as dancing. More like foreplay.

"Clearly because he's whipped." Jensen smirks from behind his tumbler.

A humorless chuckle lifts from Jason's chest before he takes a sip of his drink. "More like chained," he mutters.

"*He's* in love." Laurie emphasizes every word, but Jason just throws her an unfazed expression and shrugs.

"I'm sticking with *chained.*"

"Definitely chained," Jensen agrees.

"You two are such assholes." She points her finger between the two of them, accompanied by a death glare that's supposed to scare them. It's cute, because all it does is fuel these two fuckers to keep pushing. Especially Jason. He has never made it a secret that he's not a fan of Laurie, and the feeling is completely mutual, if you'd ask my girlfriend.

"Never said I wasn't, sweetheart." Jensen laughs cynically, and Jason lifts his glass at her.

"What can I say? You bring out the best in me."

The air thickens, and from the corner of my eye, Emily shifts a little, uncomfortable in her chair, as Jason and Laurie are having their own personal pissing contest at who can look the scariest. Jason's features darken, though an evil grin haunts his face while

Laurie narrows her eyes in a lingering way. I'm torn between lifting to my feet and getting myself another drink or being the gatekeeper for these two. *Why can't they just get along?* Or at least fucking pretend they do.

"I'm not going anywhere," she finally declares. Her words are thick and heavy, a clear statement that runs deeper than just her potential departure when we go home.

Jason snorts. "Trust me, I know."

Laurie huffs next to me, and I rest my palm on her arm to ease her down a little. I'm not in the mood to pull my girlfriend off of my best friend because she's clawing his eyes out, and just one glance at her tells me she's ready to eat him alive.

"Okay, that's enough. Why don't you go get us a drink, and I'll meet you there in a minute." I send her a pleading look. Her red lips purse, as if she's contemplating what to do, before she flips Jason off and gets up.

"Are you coming, Emily?"

I release my pent-up breath when both girls walk away, and I snap my attention between my two friends like it's a goddamn tennis match.

"What the fuck is wrong with you? Both of you."

"What's wrong with us? You're dating her, man." Jason casually takes another sip of his drink, not hiding how he feels. In fact, it's dripping from his five o'clock shadow and blue eyes that are now as dark as the deepest point in the Atlantic.

"Jensen is dating her friend," I hiss. "I don't hear you complaining about her."

Jensen sputters, pointing his glass my way. "They are hardly friends. They run in the same circles. Unfortunately, the same that are dictated by my mother." He muffles the last words behind a sip of his drink.

"Not the fucking point," I hiss.

"Right."

"She's my girlfriend, guys."

"I get why you don't like her, although if you fuck this up, I will rip your head off." I glare at my best friend before jerking my head toward Jensen. "But what's *your* issue with her?"

His brows move to the top of his head, but it lacks a sincerity that tells me he definitely has an opinion on it. "Nothing."

"Uh-huh. Try again."

"Jesus, Hunt."

"What?" I snarl. I'm sick and tired of being the bridge between my friends and my girlfriend. A fucking wobbly bridge with holes and broken planks. Jason does his best half of the time, but it's more tolerating her than anything else, which, to be fair, seems to be the same situation for her. For some unknown reason, Jason and Laurie don't get along, and I've accepted it. But I will not accept them biting each other's heads off every chance they get. They can suck it up and play pretend for the common good. Meaning *me*.

"I don't have any issues with her." Jensen flashes me a dull expression.

"Great." I bring my glass to my lips, but before the honey-colored liquid can coax my tongue, Jensen adds, "I do have an issue with the two of you, though."

I look up at the strobes on the ceiling. "What do you mean?"

"Look, I'm just gonna say it. You two are toxic together, man." Now it's my turn to pull a face. "Don't look at me like that. She sucks the living soul out of you and not because her lips are always wrapped around your dick." He pauses, and my molars grind together at the way he talks about her, but I can't find an argument either. "Sometimes I wonder if you even like her."

"Of course I like her."

His intense gaze challenges me. "Name one thing you have in common with her."

Easy. "We hike together."

"Because you're forcing her," Jason says like a smartass, and I ball a fist to prevent myself from flicking my palm against his head.

"We both like to go out to dinner."

"She likes sushi, you like pizza from Donny's and hamburgers. She drags you to all these restaurants with tiny bites, when you just want a fucking steak."

"That's not t—" I'm cut off when Laurie appears on my side again, holding some kind of weird pepper thing wrapped in bacon in front of my face.

"Look, baby," she exults. "It's an amuse-bouche. You'll love it." Before I can decline, it's basically shoved into my mouth.

"Isn't it amazing?"

I nod, chewing the thing with a strained smile, and I can't avoid Jason's smug grin when she walks away again.

"*Chained*," he mouths.

I hate him.

The food is great, but far too small portioned for my appetite, so an hour later I'm feeding my hunger with my third whiskey, already planning on going to the drive-through for a burger when I get out of here. My eyes land on a blonde in a black pantsuit, her hair up in a classy bun. An intense glare is pinned on Jensen's profile, a smile etched in my face when I recognize her as the team's PR representative. Emily is sitting on his lap, his lips cascading up and down her neck, but by blondie's annoyed expression, she's clearly not on board with Jensen's PDA.

I lean in, close enough for him to hear me, but not loud enough for the rest of the table to register. "Why is PR girl glaring at you?"

Jensen's eyes roam to find her, then a crooked smile lands on his features before he whispers, "Probably because it's her favorite hobby. She loves getting pissed at me."

I want to ask why that is, but my attention is caught when everyone on the dance floor stops dancing.

"Isn't that McGee?" I question when one of Jensen's team-mates gets down on one knee and the whole room fixes their intention to the girl in front of him, who's already tearing up.

"What the hell?" Jensen mutters while Emily is squealing.

"Oh my god! He's gonna propose!" Laurie claps like a fucking seal beside me.

"Oh, for the life of me." Jensen's eyes roll to the back of his head. "I'm going to kill him," he mumbles, barely loud enough for me to hear.

"That's so romantic!" Emily and Laurie are both looking at the couple with complete delight, their eyes way too glazed over than they should be, considering it's not them getting the proposal.

McGee's girl screams yes, tears rolling down her face, and the whole crowd applauds when she jumps into his arms.

Laurie continues gushing, wiping the moisture from her eyes before she grabs my chin, bringing her lips to mine. "I can't wait until you propose."

My eyes fly open, the air stolen from my lungs. And not in a good way. I'm literally lost for words, but I'm saved from replying to it when she slaps Emily's thigh.

"Come on! Let's dance!"

I blink as they take off, then throw all the contents of my glass down my throat.

"Until I propose?"

"You're gonna propose?" Jensen snickers when he takes one look at my frightened expression.

I shake my head, putting my glass back on the table. "Wasn't planning on it."

"She sure as hell is."

I don't fucking care.

"Jensen, a word?" His blonde stalker appears next to him, sporting that same stern expression. Her brown eyes are gorgeous, smooth like honey, but the intensity of them makes me wonder if they are lethal.

"Oh, hey, blondie. Guys, meet Rae Stafford." Jensen glances up, then gives her a full once-over that's probably fueling the annoyance that flashes over her face. "Sit down. You look gorgeous."

"Please keep our relationship professional," she says as she takes a seat.

"I am. I'm just telling you how gorgeous you look. Nothing but professional. If I wasn't, I'd tell you what a great ass you have, or how I'd love to fist your blonde hair so I can—" Her hand is slapped over his mouth, her eyes squinting enough to impress me.

"Stop talking and do me a favor." Jensen's wide eyes peer over the rim of her palm, not moving a muscle until she sighs. "You can nod." Like a well-behaved puppy, he moves his muffled face up and down in agreement. "Great. Emily is your girlfriend, right?" Another nod. "Then why were you spotted with Jessica Graham last night?" Jensen's head jerks, but she shakes her head, holding a firm grip around his lips. "Never mind. I don't care. Just keep it in your pants, because people are questioning your integrity, and it will reflect poorly on the team." Jensen's eyebrows move up, clearly wanting to comment on the matter. "No, we're not going to argue, because you'll only piss me off. So I'm gonna go and you're going to keep it in your pants, got it?" When he finally nods, she lets go of him, then gets on her feet.

"Has anyone ever told you, you're intense as fuck?"

Rae feigns sympathy, peering down at him. "Ah, you want me to coddle you and shower you with kisses to make it all better?" she coos, to which Jensen looks up at her with gooey eyes and a hopeful smile.

"Yes, please."

Her glare springs back in place before she takes off again. "Behave, Jensen."

"Is she single?" Jason chuckles, bringing his glass to his lips.

"Don't even think about it, asshole." Jensen's possessive glare hits home, and Jason and I both wince, only adding to our amusement.

"What, you have a thing for her?" Jason asks.

"No," Jensen huffs. "I just want to make sure she doesn't cut off my balls. If you piss her off, she'll definitely take it out on me."

"Jared James Jensen, are you scared of that pretty blonde?" I joke.

"Have you seen that death glare she gave me? I'm freaking terrified of her." Then a smirk splits his lips. "Turned the fucked on, but terrified nonetheless."

50

HUNTER

THE NEXT DAY, I walk out of the house and into the yard. My bare feet welcome the warm tiles around the pool, a soft breeze ruffling my brown hair. Jensen is draped on a floating flamingo, eyes covered by sunglasses, glee etched in his fatigued features and typing away on his phone.

"Emily?" I lower my feet into the pool, taking a seat on the edge.

"What?" Jensen slowly pulls his attention from his phone, before locking gazes with me. "No. It's Rae."

The mischievous grin he's throwing at his screen purses my lips with suspicion. "Are you sexting with her?"

"I wish. She's mad at me." His entire stance tells me that he's not the least dissatisfied with that conclusion, and I let out a chuckle.

"What did you do now?"

"I might have been a bit flirty with Marie Louise Baker last night. People are complaining." Considering she's the wife of one of the biggest sponsors of the LA Knights, I can imagine the backlash that might have brought to Jensen's doorstep.

"You mean, her husband?"

A lopsided grin comes my way. "And Rae."

"What are y'all doing?" Jason's voice sounds behind me.

"Jensen is sexting his PR girl."

Jason drops down beside me, the water sloshing a little over my knees at the movement. "Oh, she's cute."

"I'm not sexting her."

"You're just pissing her off because you can?" My counter results in a full-blown evil grin, his eyes sparkling bright enough to show the excitement in his gaze from underneath his glasses.

"It's fucking fun, man."

"You're a sadist," Jason pitches in.

"Proudly. Are we throwing you a graduation party?"

"Nah, I'm good." Jason shakes his head, running a hand over his bare chest before he slowly rears his chin my way. "Are we throwing you an engagement party?"

"What? Fuck no."

"Oh, that's right," Jensen says. "Your girl dropped some hints."

"She didn't."

"She basically dropped a pink elephant into the room that says *please propose.*" His reply has me glaring at him, wondering how quickly he'd drown if I shove him off that bright pink flamingo and keep his head underwater, but I can't deny he's right. Laurie slipped that comment in like it was nothing, but I've barely had any sleep thinking about it. I never wanted to get married, and when I moved to LA, I thought I was safe from having to think about it until... forever.

"Whatever."

"Are you going to?" I don't have to move my head to know Jason's judgemental eyes are boring into my side.

"What?"

"Propose," Jason clarifies.

"It's not like the man has a choice." I pull a face at Jensen's revelation. "What? After a certain time of dating, it's kinda required."

"Where do you get this shit?"

"Being the son of a politician? Don't look at me like that. You know it's true. You've been living with her for a while now. Her dad likes you more than he likes her. I bet it will be no less than six months before he's breathing down your neck to make his baby girl an honest woman. If not for the happiness of his *baby girl*, at least for all the publicity it will give his business." Jensen pulls the words from his lips like it's nothing, but really they come at me like a fucking bulldozer. My chest tightens, and for a hot minute, I feel like my brain isn't getting any oxygen. It's no secret that Laurie's dad and I get along great. I know he was a big part in why Laurie and I started dating in the first place, but marriage? Is that really something that's inevitable? Green eyes that are not my girlfriend's flash in front of my eyes, and I shake my head to get rid of them. *Get a grip, Hunter.*

"Doesn't mean he has to do it," Jason replies with a shrug, and I want to believe him. I want to tell myself that I can keep going like this until forever, but just thinking about Laurie has me huffing in disbelief before Jensen speaks out loud what I already know.

"Can't avoid it forever. She ain't that kinda girl."

51

Charlotte

HUNTER LOOKS GREAT IN his three-piece suit, his brown hair not hiding below his signature snapback but pushed back in a cute crest. Laurie hangs on his arm in a white silk dress that hugs every curve of her body, her eyes smokey and alluring as fuck. She looks gorgeous. They both do. The little tug at my heart makes me believe I'll never really love seeing them together, but with every photo or TV appearance I see, it becomes a little more bearable.

"It's still fucking weird to see him on TV." Julie takes a sip of her wine from the other side of the bar, glancing up at the re-run broadcast of the Met Gala.

I pick up a glass, drying it with the cloth in my hands. "I know."

"We all know you are the bad boy fighter, but it's good to see you clearly have a soft spot. Are you in love?" My eyebrows lift up at the screen hanging above the bar, the question of the reporter catching me off guard. Hunter's hazel eyes grow big, but if it was fueled by fear, it quickly smooths back into a boyish smirk.

"Err, yeah, sure. What's not to love?" He tugs Laurie closer into his chest, a broad smile on her red lips.

"He's not very good with words, but we're madly in love." Her hand is draped over his heart, and I swallow away the nausea that now swirls in my stomach. Dread builds deeply, accompanied by something that can only be described as disbelief.

He loves her?

"Oh, shit." Julie almost chokes on her wine before her gaze clashes with mine.

"Did that just happen?"

"Can I lie?"

"No." I shake my head, fishing my phone from my back pocket. I have no right to have a racing heart and anger rising quicker than a fucking airplane for take-off, but I can't fucking help it. I still see myself standing on that sidewalk and him telling me he doesn't say those words. But clearly, that was a lie, wasn't it?

CHARLOTTE: You love her?

Julie keeps her eyes trained on me as I keep staring at the screen, waiting for those blue dots to appear.

HUNTER: What are you talking about?
CHARLOTTE: TMZ, asshole. I thought we agreed to share the important shit with each other?

"Jackass," I mutter, frustrated as fuck, then flip the screen to Julie.

"I'm sorry, girl," Julie offers with a pitying look on her face, and I let out a growl in response when my phone rings. I don't even have to look to know who it is.

"If you're going to throw some bullshit at me, saying you don't get why I'm pissed at you, you better hang up real quick, Hunter Hansen." I scowl, holding my phone against my ear.

"It's not what you think." The guilt in his voice is undeniable, but I'm not going to let him back-peddle out of this one.

"You didn't just tell her you loved her?"

8

"It doesn't mean as much as it does to other people. I don't even mean it. I mean, what is love, anyway? I like her, but love is a big word. I think." His voice sounds heavy, like he's barely believing himself, and I can't blame him.

Clearly, he's full of shit.

"Right, isn't that exactly why you shouldn't say them?"

"They caught me off guard. I didn't want to make it awkward."

I roll my eyes, his response not even surprising me. When it comes to his feelings, Hunter Hansen is the king of deflection, always trying to avoid whatever is going on inside of him. I could barely get him to talk about his mother, or the grief he was still carrying from missing his brother and father. It's the reason why him saying those words in front of a camera shocks me even more.

"Well, do you?"

"What?"

I let out a grunt, pinching the bridge of my nose. "*Love her.*"

"I'm not capable of love," he whispers, a sad tone shimmering through his voice.

"Will you stop lying to me? *Please?*"

"I'm not lying, babe."

"Everyone is capable of love, Hunter. Including you." I wish I could get through to him at some point, although the jealous streak inside me doesn't mind his explanation. Something I will smack myself in the head later for because Hunter and I are friends again, but this phone call makes it very clear we're nothing more than that.

"Maybe."

"Well, don't tell Laurie that. She won't appreciate it." I sigh, avoiding Julie's gaze. "Share, Hunt. That's the only way this will work. Just be my friend. That's all you gotta do."

"You're right, babe. I'm sorry. I'll share."

"Right. I gotta go now. I'm at the bar with Julie. We'll talk later?"

"Yeah. Of course."

"Bye, Hunt."

"Bye, Charls."

I throw my phone on the bar with a small thud, snapping my head toward Julie, who's looking at me with a face that tells me she doesn't agree with whatever he just said. I expect her to ask for a recap of the conversation, but she cocks her eyebrow with a frown on her lips, verbally kicking me straight in the gut with her question.

"I love Hunter. You know I do, but how long are you going to wait for that boy?"

"I'm not waiting for him." I turn around, pulling a bottle of tequila from the shelf and two shot glasses before placing them on the bar.

"Yeah, you are."

"He's my best friend, that's all," I say, shrugging my shoulders and pouring the translucent liquid into the tiny glasses. I silently laugh as the words roll off my tongue like I rehearsed it in front of the mirror, because it's the biggest lie I've ever told.

I love him.

I've always loved him, even though I keep telling myself he is my best friend. The smart thing would be to end this for good. To end our so-called friendship that we try so hard to keep alive, even though I know it's doomed to end in pieces either way, just like it did two years ago. But I can't break loose. I can't let go. I can't force him to swim on his own, because I'm terrified he'll drown, knowing I've been his lifeline since that day at the creek.

My heart won't let me live with that possibility.

"He's not. But you already know that."

"Shut up." I hold the shot in front of her nose, and she reluctantly reaches out her manicured fingers to take it from my grasp.

"You can't save him, Charlie."

I swallow hard, knowing she's right as my eyes well up. "I know, but I'm all he's got."

"He is going to drag you under."

Her words cut through my heart like a knife through butter, feeling like a junkie that refuses to go to rehab. Never wanting to really let go, always in need of the next hit, even though I know, one day, it will kill me. It's my biggest weakness. My biggest flaw, and maybe I'll realize it's my biggest mistake.

But my heart isn't ready to think about it.

"He won't," I say, closing my eyes, praying I'm right before I let the tequila burn another hole in my heart.

YEAR SIX

I KNEW I COULDN'T OUTRUN IT,
BUT I HOPED IT WOULD FLY OVER, LEAVING ME UNSCATHED.

*Do you think we'll ever
be okay?'*

52

Charlotte

I FELT IT LURKING in the shadows for months now. Ever since Hunter and Laurie announced to be madly in love on national television, I knew it was inevitable. But still, it totally caught me off guard.

"Hey, Hunt." I answer the phone, unaware of the trainwreck that's waiting to happen.

"Hey, Charls." His tone is flat. But I know this boy and I easily detect the hint of sadness in his voice, causing my heart to falter, and my feet actually stop in the middle of the pavement while I'm making my way to the grocery store.

The sun has my eyes squinting while my lashes flutter against the early fall wind.

"What's wrong? Are you okay?"

He chuckles, though not wholeheartedly, but enough to put me slightly at ease as I wait for him to disclose whatever is on his mind.

"I'm okay. In fact, I'm great." *You don't sound great.*

"You finally found an ice cream parlor that has clementine vanilla?" I joke.

"No." The brief silence that follows clouds my heart, and I can feel the hurt before he says the words outloud. "I'm engaged."

There it is. I knew I couldn't outrun it, but I hoped it would fly over, leaving me unscathed.

You know how in those movies, you see how everything around them seems to stop when the heroine gets news that turns her world upside down? I always thought that was just something they created for dramatic effect, to really make you feel connected to their emotions, that in real life, that doesn't happen.

Yeah, turns out, it does.

My head turns foggy as my vision blurs, and my heart starts to race like a thoroughbred. Parting my lips in shock, my mouth gets as dry as sandpaper while I feel the world around me rush by as if I'm just a bystander.

I feel so stupid. What did I expect? What did I hope? That one day he'd move back home? That his life in LA was just something temporary? That Laurie was just someone to pass the time until he came to his senses?

"Charls? You still there?"

Snapping myself out of it, I shake my head, trying to push out words in response.

"Engaged?" I repeat as steadily as possible.

"Yeah, I just asked her." It's just now that I register the muffled sounds in the background, like he's in some kind of restaurant. "She said yes."

His words start to sink in, and my face falls, my heart feeling heavier by the minute.

"Wow, Hunt. T-This is... great," I croak out. "Unexpected, but great. Congratulations."

"Thanks. I just wanted to tell you before she throws it all over Instagram, you know?"

"Right. Thanks. That's great, Hunt." I try to sound happy, but I know my words sound confused as fuck. "You're getting married."

"Yeah, can you believe it?"

"No. No, I really can't," I reply in all honesty.

For as long as I've known him, he doesn't make a commitment, can't say *I love you*, and doesn't believe love is for him. But in the last six months, he's shown that clearly isn't the case anymore. *That she changed him.* I want to be happy for him. But my heart is weeping.

"Me neither. I never thought I'd get married, but we've been dating for a while now. I know she's been waiting for it. At least now I won't be harassed by people asking me when I'm gonna pop the question." An awkward chuckle is audible through the phone, followed by a long sigh. "She doesn't want me calling you as much anymore, though," he admits, making my eyes widen, feeling like they are about to roll out of my head. "I told her we slept together. She's not comfortable with our friendship."

"Right. Yeah, that makes sense." My mind feels like it's about to explode, while I keep the phone tightly pressed against my ear, making it hurt a little. "So, no more Friday night calls?"

I admire the fact I can still push out words while it becomes harder to breathe with every second. *I'm losing him.*

"Just until she's more comfortable with you. I'm sure she will be, eventually." His voice is confident, almost determined. But let's be honest? It's the equivalent of seeing someone from your past in the coffee shop and saying you'll meet up soon. *It's never gonna happen.*

"Okay. That's okay. Yeah. Makes sense. I gotta go now," I blurt, feeling the desperate need to get myself out of this situation as soon as possible. "But I'm happy for you," I add.

"Thank you, Charls. That means a lot. Talk later, okay?"

I nod my head, though he can't see me.

"Yeah, sure. Talk later," I say, hanging up the phone, as I keep staring at the world passing by in front of me, wondering what the fuck just happened. Wondering why the sun is still shining bright in the sky, yet everything feels darker than it did five minutes ago.

53

HUNTER

"Y OU LOOK LIKE A circus monkey," Jensen snorts, barely keeping his whiskey in when Jason walks out of the dressing room with a deep scowl. It's as annoying as it is hilarious, because ever since I proposed to Laurie, it seems to be imprinted into his forehead.

"Come on, Hunt! It's fucking blue!" Jason screeches with clenched fists.

"Laurie doesn't want black at the wedding. Says it's the color of death." Not sure what it says about the thousands of people getting married every day that do wear black, but I don't care enough to ask. This is her day. If she wants us all to wear blue, we'll wear blue.

"Seems fitting," Jason mumbles.

"Oh, snap." Jensen is giggling like a little girl, and I throw him a death glare before settling it on my best friend.

"Jay, seriously? Can you just support me?"

His eyebrows move to the hairline of his blonde buzz-cut, fire flaring from his gaze. "I'm here in a baby blue tuxedo. *Baby blue*, Hunt! That's the definition of me supporting you."

"No, supporting me would be keeping your trap closed and not swinging all those digs at my head."

"It's hard when you see your best friend making a mistake." The counter is quick and harsh, coming from the depths of his frustration, I'm sure.

"Ouch, Mr. Spencer." Jensen pushes out a low whistle, but Jason just shrugs.

"What? He loves someone else."

Not this again.

"Can you please, for the love of fucking God, get Charlotte and me out of your head? It's not going to happen." Aggravation builds in my stomach, and I briefly close my eyes. I've had this conversation numerous times with him over the years, but lately, he keeps torturing me with it.

"You love her, Hunt."

"I do love her!" One drunken confession, and he just won't let it slide. I regretted it the moment I blurted out the words, and now Jason loves to remind me every chance he gets. I do love Charlotte. She's my best friend, and I want her to be happy; it's why I know it doesn't matter how I feel. "It's why I can't be with her. She wants a white picket fence in small-town North Carolina and a bunch of babies. Look at me? I live the jet-set life of LA," I tell them with my arms spread.

"But is that really what you want?" Jason frowns, and I let my hands drop to my sides.

That's the whole thing. It doesn't matter what *I* want. All that matters is what she wants and deserves. And I ain't it.

"Jason, there's a reason I moved to the West Coast. To get the hell out of North Carolina. That was the whole reason I started fighting, because I didn't want to stay."

"You didn't have a reason to stay."

"I don't have a reason now!" I snap.

"That's—" I cut him off before he can finish whatever is about to roll off his lips.

"Jason, you have to drop this! Charls and I are never going to happen, and I'd appreciate it if you'd stop making this any harder than it already is."

My raging eyes collide with his, both flaring with frustration, but it isn't until his softening yet cynical expression is aimed my way, that I feel something slicing through my heart.

"It's not supposed to be hard, man," he replies.

54

Charlotte

I T'S LATE.

A yawn escapes, the sound echoing through my bedroom while I wait for midnight to arrive so I can wish Hunter a happy birthday. But five minutes before, he beats me to it, and I settle into my pillow, a smile tugged between my teeth.

"Happy birthday, birthday boy."

"You sent me a Pink Snowball." His voice sounds dampened, yet completely in awe while music and voices are audible in the background.

"What else would I send you?"

"Designer clothes? A new watch? A car?"

"First off, Hansen. My budget isn't really equipped to send gifts like they do in LA. Secondly, that doesn't really sound like something you'd want for your birthday anyway." Sure, he likes flashy things, but I know deep down, he'd be cool with jeans from The Gap and driving his rumbling old truck. Or at least, I hope the boy that would love that is still in there somewhere.

I frown at his silence. "Are you okay?"

"Laurie gave me a new Rolex."

I gasp. "Oh, shit. Sometimes, I really forget how fancy you've become." I smile, even though I say it with a heavy heart, a feeling that grows more uneasy when it's followed by a loaded silence. "Hunt, I didn't mean to–"

"No." His voice is firm, before I can hear the ease slipping back in. "You're right. It's not something I'd ever want, but I guess that's LA life."

"Yeah, I guess so." The sound of breaking glass reverberates in my ear. "Where are you?"

"In the pantry."

"In the pantry? Of your penthouse?" A confirming hum slips over the line. "Why?"

"Laurie threw me a birthday party."

"Oh, that's nice." He doesn't reply. "Right?"

"I guess. I don't know half the people here."

For some reason, his hazel eyes flash in my mind with that boyish smirk I love about him, but it's like tiny needles are flying into my heart at the same time. As if I can feel his pain from across the country. "Are you drunk?"

He chuckles, curling my own lips. "Maybe a little," he confesses before a deep sigh rolls over the line. "Do you think we'll ever be okay?"

"What do you mean?" I ask, even though I know exactly what he means.

"You and me. Do you think we'll ever be who we were six years ago?"

I think long and hard before I answer, tiptoeing about how I should respond to this. "I don't think we can be, Hunt. We're not the same people anymore."

"I know." He pauses, and I hold in my breath as I feel my eyes well up. "Sometimes I wish I could turn back time. That we'd still be chilling at the creek every weekend, and I'd buy you books whenever I pissed you off. That we could go for ice cream and burgers and drive around late at night. That I'd never left." The air gets knocked out of my lungs at his last revelation, a tear escaping from the corner of my eye.

"You wouldn't have what you have now, Hunt."

I can almost hear him smile through the phone, and I close my eyes.

"I know," he answers, "but lately I wonder if what I have is what I want." I sniffle my tears away, telling myself to not read between the lines, but I can't. I can't help wondering what he's saying. What he's *really* saying. But before I can collect the nerve to call him out on it, a loud pound booms through the phone.

"Hunt, get out, man. It's your party." I recognize Jason's voice, and the sound of music and mumbling voices gets louder, telling me Hunter opened the door.

"I have to go, Charls."

"Okay, happy birthday."

"Thank you," he barely whispers through the phone before the line goes dead, and I'm staring into the darkness of my room, a weird feeling putting all my senses on high alert. Part of me wishes I didn't answer the phone. That I didn't hear what I just heard, because I know my mind can't erase the last five minutes.

That he'd never left...

Fucking hell.

55

Charlotte

I'M SITTING ON THE kitchen island, reading a book with a cup of tea, when my mother walks in. Her long blonde hair is perfectly styled, and she's wearing a gorgeous yellow sundress, shining like never before. She's been in remission for a long time now, and every day she looks better than the day before. She hasn't started working again, but she's enjoying her life, spending time with her friends and me. She even started cooking again a while back, and I'm enjoying every plate she puts in front of my face.

"Wow, Mama. You look amazing!"

"Thank you, my sweet girl. I feel amazing." She takes the stool next to me, grabbing my tea off the counter to take a sip.

"Do you have a date?" I ask, closing my book to give her my full attention.

"No, I'm just going to dinner with Margie from the gym. She was going on and on about this new place in Raleigh. She'll be here to pick me up in a minute."

"Sounds like fun."

"Yeah, I'm excited." She beams. "What are your plans today?"

"Jules is coming over. We're making cocktails and listening to the nineties top 100." I chuckle, right as my phone beeps.

"Hunter?" My mom's eyes widen with a hopeful look, one that pisses me off as much as it makes me sad. She's never made it a secret that she loved Hunter, but once again, lately, our time together, even over the phone, has become more and more brief. Our friendship is dying a slow death, and it makes me sad that my mama hasn't really realized that.

"No," I snort. Ever since he got engaged, we've barely been in touch, other than him asking what kind of suit would look best on him. I told him to go naked as a joke, but really, it was because I didn't seriously want to discuss anything related to his wedding. He's lucky I'm even going. God knows I'd rather skinny dip in the Antarctic.

"You haven't been talking?" Mama places a comforting hand on my arm when I push my phone to the side.

"Barely. His *fiancée* doesn't want us to talk too much."

"We haven't really talked about it, because I figured you need-ed some time. But how are you feeling about his engagement?"

Like shit? Like my heart has been ripped out of my chest and thrown into a shredder?

"Should've seen it coming, I guess."

"Maybe. But what are your thoughts?"

I sigh, knowing she'll never let me suppress my feelings about anything. When she was ill, I might have gotten away with certain things, but now that she's healthy and sparkling? Mama lets no moment pass where she can force me to face my fears and talk about my feelings.

"I want to be happy for him," I admit, really feeling it in my heart, because he deserves to be happy. "But I can't. I feel like he's making a mistake, because I don't like her. He deserves better. And when I'm being completely selfish? I hate her for stealing my best friend. Which is complete bullshit because it's him. He shouldn't give me that feeling. But I guess that's what happens when you fall in love? Your partner becomes more important than your best friend."

"Oh, please," Mama sputters. "You know he's not in love."

I give her a doubtful look.

"He's not," she repeats. "Let me tell you something about Hunter Hansen. That boy had a troubled youth, losing his father and his brother like that. Being verbally and physically abused by his alcoholic mama for years. Even though he feels love deep down inside of him, he believes he doesn't deserve it."

"He doesn't love. *His* words."

"Funny, because the first time I laid eyes on him, that's all I saw. *Love.* In fact, the love dripped from his face like a love-struck puppy."

"What the hell are you talking about, Mama?" I give her an incredulous look, the corner of my mouth rising because of her ridiculous words. If that was true, he'd be fighting for me instead of getting engaged to the girl he started fake dating a few years back. He'd give me the words I asked him for five years ago.

"He loves *you*, Charlotte. He has loved you since the first day he walked you home. He didn't even deny it when I confronted him about it on his eighteenth birthday."

Come again?

"You did what?! Are you serious?"

"As serious as my mama in her grave."

My eyes widen in shock, not knowing what to think of this. "He confessed he loved me when he was still here?"

"Pretty much. Look," she continues, "he thinks he doesn't deserve you. But trust me when I tell you, he loves you. It's written in his eyes. Even a blind man can see the love he feels for you. He's just a scared fool."

I stare at the countertop for a while, replaying Mama's words over in my head.

"If that's true... what do I do?"

"Nothing, sweetheart." She gets up and presses a kiss to my hair. "It will work out. Your souls are linked. They will never be able to stay apart for long." On that note, she grabs her bag from the counter, ready to head out, as if she didn't just drop a huge bomb in my lap. "I'm going. We might go for drinks later, so don't wait up."

I give her a small wave and mutter, *"Bye, Mama,"* still stunned about her confession. Part of me wants to believe it, meaning the big part pounding against my ribcage, but my mind is telling me to let it go, to stop hurting myself by thinking this is more than just friends. My heart is begging me to not let my mind get in the way, but too much has happened for me to fully give it control like that. He's engaged to someone else, for crying out loud.

Brushing my thoughts away, I get up, just as the doorbell rings, and head over to open the door.

"I brought food." Julie smiles wide, holding up a bag from the sushi restaurant.

"You're the best!"

She walks in, her denim playsuit snug around her hips, and I follow her to the kitchen, where she puts the bag in the fridge for later.

"Saw your mama heading out."

"Yeah, she's going out to dinner with a friend. She actually said something weird just now."

"Yeah, what's that?" She leans over the counter with an intrigued look on her face.

"She thinks Hunter is in love with me."

Julie's lashes flutter up and down, an anticipating look coming my way when nothing follows before she breaks out into a laugh. "That's it? Babe, the entire town thinks Hunter is in love with you."

"After all these years, still?" I ask, surprised. I can see how they did when we were still seniors in high school, but now? He's been living in LA for the last five years, and I've been... well, here.

"Well, maybe not everyone still believes that, but the ones close to both of you? Yeah, for sure."

"Do you?" A frown creases my forehead.

"Believe Hunter is in love with you? One hundred percent."

"What?!" I call out.

"Don't play dumb, Charlie. You might have needed some more time, but it was love at first sight for him."

"You can't be serious?"

"Dead," she replies with a straight face.

"He loves me. I know that. But he's not *in love* with me."

"Charlotte Roux, that boy has been in love with you since the day you first met. He's just too stupid to admit it."

My head is spinning, and I grab the cold surface of the counter, trying to keep myself on my feet. Sucking in deep breaths, I shake my head, needing a minute to process this.

Because what if they are right? What if he really loves me, but is too scared to admit it? Am I going to let that slide? See if faith one day brings us back together? I don't know. That's a huge gamble, and I'm not sure my heart can handle it.

"I'm gonna take a quick shower," I say, needing a minute to order my thoughts. "I'll be back in twenty minutes."

"Sure, girl."

A few hours later, I'm making our third cocktail with our bellies full of sushi while chatting at the breakfast bar. After the shower, I pushed my thoughts aside, not willing to address anything Hunter Hansen right this minute.

He can wait until tomorrow. But in reality? The possible truth in my mama's words has been nagging me more and more with each cocktail I pour down my throat.

Am I really going to just see what happens? He might not be fighting for me, but should I be fighting for him?

The doorbell rings as I'm finishing up our cocktails, while Julie is just staring at me like the lazy fuck that she can be.

"I'll get it." She gets off the stool, walking into the hallway to open the door as I stir our cocktails, throwing a lime wedge in there for good measure. I wipe my hands on a dishcloth, then pick up the glasses in excitement, ready to continue our girls' night on the porch. Hopefully talking to Jules about it will demolish some of my fear and help me make a decision about what to do with this new piece of information.

"Charlie?" Julie shouts from the front door, a slight panic in her voice that makes me pick up the glasses and head into the hallway.

"What?" I exclaim, looking at who's standing at the door.

I stop in my tracks for a second, narrowing my eyes, when I notice the two police officers standing on my porch, both showing me a troubled look.

"Miss Roux?" one of them asks as I slowly saunter their way, an ominous feeling washing my body when I feel the hairs on the back of my neck stand up, a shiver running through my spine. The air is sucked from my lungs while my feet feel heavy, glued to the hardwood floor.

"Yeah?"

"I'm sorry," he offers. His composed stance makes my eyes well up, a feeling settling in my gut that whatever comes next will turn my world upside down, and I swallow hard to brace myself. "It's about your mother. She was in an accident."

"Oh my god." Julie gasps, bringing her hand to her mouth. "Is she okay?"

But one glance at the look in his eyes, and I already know the answer to that question. I know they don't grace you with a personal visit unless it's bad. Really bad. But mostly, it's the heavy feeling in my bones that tells me everything I need to know before he voices it. The feeling that's pulling me under, though I'm doing my best to stay afloat. *Don't say it. Don't say it. Please, don't say it.*

"She didn't make it."

When the words are pushed through his lips and into the world, it feels like an energy field slams into me. I hear glass splintering around me as my body connects with the cold floor, knocking me out.

And everything goes black.

56

HUNTER

T HROWING MY PHONE AND keys on the counter of my kitchen, I look up at Laurie, after a long day of boring sponsor meetings and an excessive work out. Her flawlessly styled hair frames her almond-shaped face, being very much the epitome of one of those Instagram-perfect girls. She's standing on the other side of the marble white kitchen island, doing probably exactly that. Wasting time on Instagram.

Call me old-fashioned, but I'd rather spend my time with my real friends than my virtual ones, knowing my two million Instagram fans don't mean shit.

"You wanna order a pizza?"

She catches my eye, turning up her nose, then brings her gaze back to her phone.

"Ew. No. Order me a salad or something."

Rolling my eyes, I let out a deep sigh, walking to the fridge muttering, "A little bit of carbs won't kill you."

"No. But my personal trainer tomorrow will," she snarls.

"Right." I pull out a bottle of water, then put it on my lips, when my phone starts to buzz its way over the countertop.

"Who's that?" Her head snaps up. Suddenly, her focus is no longer on the screen in front of her.

Taking a step forward, I stretch my neck, and automatically, a smile appears on my face when I read the name.

"Charlotte."

"Ugh!" Laurie huffs, sending me a disappointed glare. "We discussed this, Hunter. Why is she still calling you?"

"Because she's my friend," I say, irritated, taking another drink of my water. "Besides, we discussed that I wouldn't talk as much with her. I never said I was going to stop talking to her. I haven't spoken to her in three weeks. She's probably calling to catch up." I don't mind taking her feelings into consideration after she found out Charlotte and I have a history that was a bit bigger than I told her at first. I wouldn't be happy if she still talked to her ex either. But Charlotte is my friend, first and foremost. I'm not giving that up. Not even for my fiancée.

I reach over the counter to grab it, stopping in my movement when Laurie opens her mouth with a big scowl.

"Well, you're with me now. You can play catch up with her tomorrow."

"What's the problem, Laurie?"

She folds her arms in front of her body, making me roll my eyes at her childish behavior. "The problem is you talking to some other girl when you're with me." The buzzing sound of my phone stops, showing the missed call, before it almost instantly starts to ring again.

"She's my best friend." A worried feeling trickles down my skin, wondering if maybe Charlotte's calling for something important.

"And I'm your fiancée." Laurie pouts. *Goddamnit.*

"Exactly. Why are you being all insecure about this?" I look at the phone, dying to pick it up.

"Because you two have a history. I don't trust her." I quietly watch her for a few seconds when the buzzing stops again.

"What is not to trust? She lives on the other side of the country?"

"I don't fucking care!"

"Do you trust me?" I ask, when the phone rings again, balling my fists to stop myself from answering.

"Yeah." She says one thing, but her eyes clearly express something else. I'm not even gonna point that out.

"We're just friends. Nothing is going on between us."

"Fine," she snaps, "but in that case, your *friend* can wait until tomorrow."

As much as she pisses me off, I've had a long day, and I don't feel the need to get into this now, knowing there's some truth to what she's saying. I'm going to marry her. She should come first. Because at some point, that happens in life. You settle with a partner, get married, and they become your center of attention. But I'm not sure if I'll be able to push Charlotte away like she wants me to. I owe her too much. She saved me, acting like my light when I couldn't see the end of the tunnel.

"Please?" Laurie gives me a pleading look, slightly turning me on when her lashes flutter at me, a grin forming in the corner of my mouth. The phone stops ringing, and I grab it, sauntering toward her with a seductive smirk on my face, before it starts ringing in my hand again.

"Fine," I say, cupping her face as I press a kiss to her lips. "Just let me send her a quick text, and then we can order some food."

"Fine." She rolls her eyes.

HUNTER: I'm in the middle of something. Will call you later.

"Happy now?"

"Yes. Now kiss me." She beams as I throw my phone on the counter again, covering my mouth with hers, and it doesn't take long until our kisses become more demanding, making my dick twitch in my jeans.

My hands explore the rest of her body, getting more turned on by the second, as I push that other feeling away, something fierce.

The feeling that I've just made a huge mistake.

57

Charlotte

S TARING AT THE CASKET being lowered into the ground, I feel
nothing.

Blank.

Hollow.

When you are younger, you think your parents are invincible.
Superheroes. You don't think about them dying long before you
have kids of your own, and until you're completely independent.
Not for me. I've known my mama could leave me since I was
eight, preparing myself for that day to arrive sooner than I'd
ever have kids. But now I realize you can never really prepare
yourself for it. That's bullshit. A white lie, you tell yourself,
hoping you'll be fine. Well, the truth is—I'm not fine.

I'm not okay.

I feel like a failure.

I took care of her as best as I could, thinking it would make a
difference in my future. But the knowledge that my mother will
never come back has opened my eyes to something I should've
seen from the start.

That I was always gonna fail.

I failed to keep her safe.

"Have you heard from Hunter?" Julie hands me my glass, taking the seat in front of me on the screened porch.

I let out a snicker, though there's nothing funny about it.

"Of course not. Bet you that Instagram-addicted bitch won't let him." I sound bitter, and frankly—I am.

I tried calling him a bunch of times, the night those police officers crushed my world in two. Even after he sent me a text to say he was busy, I brushed the rejection aside because I simply needed him. I needed my best friend to tell me everything was going to be alright. That I could get through this even though I had no clue how. But he never answered, and he never called back.

"It's been a week. He just left you hanging after you called him God knows how many times?"

I shrug my shoulders, my face filled with fury. After the funeral, I cried for days, not letting any other emotion in than grief. I didn't eat, didn't shower. Suddenly, there was no more reason to get out of bed. But in the last twenty-four hours, my grief has been replaced by anger. Straight up burning flames of fury that are directed toward Hunter Hansen.

"Did you text him? Saying what happened?" she asks carefully.

"No!" I bark, lifting a reprimanding finger in the air. "And neither will you! If that asshole doesn't think I'm important enough, he doesn't need to know shit." I don't expect him to be at my beck and call whenever I want. I know he has his own life. But up until now, I truly thought we were still friends. That I could still call him and he'd at least listen to me, no matter how random or silly it might seem. I shouldn't have to tell him my mother died over a text message. No, he should pick up the goddamn phone. Surely calling him ten times in a row screams important, right?

"Okay. Okay." She throws her hands up in the air in surrender before moving forward, her elbows resting on her knees as she locks her gaze on mine.

"But you gotta end this, Charlie. He's killing you inside. You can't be friends if it's going to keep hurting you like this. He's *not* your friend. You gotta stop trying."

I ball my fist, wanting to punch something, knowing she's right.

Fuck this shit and fuck him.

"I know."

HUNTER

W E'RE WATCHING A MOVIE on a Wednesday night, when I hear Jason gasp next to me, glancing at his phone. "What the fuck?"

"What?" I ask.

His eyes grow wide, an amused grin on his face, and I give him a bored look, assuming he's gushing over some chick again.

"Charlotte is here."

"What?" I repeat while my heart feels like it's jumping out of my chest, a small smile tugging at the corner of my mouth.

"She's standing in front of the gate, demanding I send you out."

"How does she even know I'm here?"

"Lucky guess?"

I rub my hand over my face in confusion, wondering if I missed something, then look at my friend quietly as I get up to walk out the door. Wearing nothing but sweats, I punch the code of the security system to open up the gate door, then walk out on my bare feet.

The white concrete feels cold underneath my skin, while the sun is about to set between the hills in front of me. A smile splits my face when I watch that dark blonde wavy hair walk through the gate, a taxi still parked in front.

"Well, this is a surprise." I walk toward her, my arms wide, ready to pull her into a hug until I notice the scowl on her pretty face. My gaze roams over her entire body, slowly registering the cloud of thunder she's approaching me with. She's wearing a pink sweat suit, with bags underneath her eyes that furrow my brows with worry, and when I can take a closer look, her hair seems messier than I've ever seen it before. *She looks exhausted.*

"Are you okay, Charls?"

"My mother died," she blurts, her clear-water eyes shooting daggers at me with an ice-cold expression. *What?*

A tightness forms in my chest instantly, nausea piling up in my stomach as my eyes grow wide. That's not possible. She was doing better. I would've known if she was sick again. Charlotte would've told me.

"What? When? I thought the treatment was going well." My voice cracks as I bite my lip, not understanding what's going on. Hoping this is a joke, a mistake, or whatever it could be to make it not true. Because there is no way. There is no way I missed this. But guilt also scrawls up my spine, knowing I haven't been there for her lately.

"It was," she sneers. "She was going to fully recover. Was finally strong enough to enjoy life again."

I swallow hard; the blood rushing from my face, softly shaking my head.

"I don't understand."

She gives me a false smile, and I can literally feel my heart break, witnessing the hurt in her eyes as they well up. They are lethal to me, effectively killing me from the inside out.

"She got hit by a truck driving home. He was drunk."

No.

"Charls."

No, this is not true.

"Don't." She raises her hand, closing her eyes to take a breath, before they open again.

"When?"

"Last week." Her voice shakes as she gives me an intense stare that scares the shit out of me, a cold chill covering my shoulders like a wet blanket. "You know? That time that I called you excessively because I needed you and you texted me, *I'm in the middle of something. Will call you later*? And then you didn't. You brushed me off like some annoying little girl, begging for your attention." She clenches her jaw, and her nostrils flare as her voice becomes louder with every word. "But really, I was begging for my best friend, because I needed his comforting words. His smile to brighten up my now pitch-black world. I needed one of his lame jokes to make the pain in my chest lift for just one second. I needed you, goddamnit!" she shouts, her pain hitting every single one of my organs with slicing realization.

Heat creeps up over every inch of my skin, a sheer contrast with the shivering of the bristle hairs on my back. My eyes go wide, letting out a strangled cry when I realize exactly what day she's talking about. *No. No. Fuck no!*

"You missed the fucking funeral, asshole! You know the funny part? I've waited for my mother to die since I was eight. I prepared myself for years, waiting for the train to arrive at the station, and when it did, it still hit me in the fucking face."

"I-I'm *so* sorry," I push out, dragging my hands over my face, before I reach out for her to give in to my need to hold her against my chest while cursing myself. I should've listened to my gut. I should've told Laurie to get over her insecurities.

I should've answered the goddamn phone!

"Don't touch me." She slaps my hand away. "Don't touch me when you're still too much of a coward to say it!"

"Say what?"

She raises her chin in the air, a scowl in place. "Tell me you love me. Tell me you love me, because I *know* you do! We keep pretending we're friends, when we've always been more than that. You *love* me. Admit it."

Processing her words, I stare at her, the wind of the hills gushing through my messy hair, feeling an aching pain in the back of my throat.

I want to give her those words and make it all better. I don't know shit about love, but if there is anything that comes close to it stored inside of me, it's reserved for her.

And only her.

No one compares to her, and I know it.

She's the only thing that ever made me doubt taking that leap of faith, willing to risk it all. I might be engaged to someone else, but most days, I don't even know why, because Charlotte still lingers in the back of my head, deep in my soul, a part of me. But crossing that line means there is no way back.

She will expect everything from me.

And she deserves it all. She deserves better.

"Sometimes love isn't enough."

She shakes her head. "For who? For me? Or for you? Because I never asked you for more. I don't give a shit about your money, your cars, the life you're living. For me, love is enough. *You* are enough. It's you that needs more than that. It's me who isn't enough for you. It was never the other way around. Tell me, Hunter!" she demands, her voice becoming more frantic with each sentence while her eyes turn glassy. "Tell me we are going to cut this bullshit right now and admit you love me, or I'll walk away once and for all. I can't do this anymore. I can't keep pretending. Tell me you love me, or set me free. Let me go. *Please.*" Her pleading look is devastating.

"Charlotte." I don't even know what else to say as I feel her slipping away, knowing this is the end, yet praying it isn't. My heart pounds a few times, loud and painful, before her humorless snicker hits me in the face.

"You know, one day you are going to look around, thinking what the fuck am I doing? And my face will appear, telling you I told you so."

"What do you suggest I do?" I ask, my hands tucked inside the pockets of my sweatpants. My mind goes back to the moment I heard Logan and my dad were in an accident, feeling the exact same way right now.

Helpless.

Alone.

Unworthy.

"None of this would've happened if you would just get your head out of your ass and come home!"

"Come home? I'm engaged."

"So? We both know she doesn't mean shit to you." She cocks her eyebrow, folding her arms in front of her body.

"That's not true." I shake my head, not sure why I keep lying to her. *To myself.*

"Yeah? Is that why you are hanging out with Jason five nights a week? Why you sleep more in your old room in this big ass house than sharing the bed with your *fiancée*?" She fiercely holds my gaze, pointing at the glass house, and I just stare back at her. "Tell me I'm wrong, Hunt! Tell me I'm full of shit and that you love her. That you want to grow old with her, have a bunch of babies and sit on a porch with her when you're all gray and wrinkly and I'll leave right now. *Tell me!*"

I can't. But I can't give her what I want either.

"I have nothing left there. What's there to come home to?"

"Right." Her face falls, and I close my eyes as I pinch the bridge of my nose at my poor choice of words.

"Charls, I didn't—"

"No, you completely made your point." She smiles sadly, her green eyes dejected.

"See, that's exactly it," I yell, my frustration tipping over as I throw my hands in the air. "I screw up anything that comes remotely close to love."

Her lips are firmly pressed together. "It's only eight letters, Hunter."

"But they are not made for me!" I bawl.

"It's funny." A laugh leaves her lips, yet her eyes don't join them. They stay as vicious as the devil himself, bringing me even more of a clarification of the finality of this conversation. "You get your ass kicked for a living, and you have more money in the bank than you can spend, but you don't have the guts to face your biggest fear."

She's right. I'm a coward. There's no sense in denying it. But I'd rather be a coward than hurt her any more than I've already done.

"Love is not made for me." I shake my head.

"Goddamn, Hunter! That's not a choice you get to make! You can't decide if love is for you or not. It just *fucking* happens."

"You deserve more, baby!!" My voice breaks, shouting out the words that have been running through my head since the first day I met her. "You deserve a good guy, someone who would do anything for you. Who will keep you safe and chase your demons away. Who will give you a family! That's not me. I am the villain in this story. The fighter. The rebel. Destined to break your heart because I don't have one anymore. You deserve more than my broken soul."

Her head tilts, taking in my words. "What if there isn't more for me?" She waits, then shakes her head. "Don't answer that question."

"There is more for you, Charls. One day, you'll run into some good guy, with a good job, who makes you laugh, and gives you everything you need."

"I need *you*, Hunter," she hisses, rage radiating from her gorgeous eyes. "I've always needed *you*. But it turns out, you'll always need everything else."

It feels like a knife cracks open my chest and slices right through my heart. If only I was selfish enough to tell her she couldn't be more wrong. "I'm so sorry, baby."

"Yeah, so am I." A tear runs down her cheek, making me inhale a sharp breath, my heart pounding against my chest. "But you know what? I owe you a thank you. Because I finally realized that it's what I've been doing my entire life. Taking care of everyone. Always ready to drop what I'm doing to do whatever everyone wants, even though I want to do something completely different. Feeling like it's my sole purpose to help everyone around me. But it's not. I get that now. I'm done with taking care of everyone else, when the only one I should take care of is me. So thank you. You made me realize that I shouldn't expect anything in return, making it that much easier to focus on myself." She gives me a coy smile through her tears. "Have a nice life, Hunter Hansen. You deserve the world. And I mean that. I'll see you in another life."

No.

She turns around, strutting away from me, and without thinking, I follow her tracks, pulling her back by her arm when we reach the sidewalk in front of my gate.

"No, don't leave," I yelp, desperate. Not even knowing what I will do without her. I've tried that. We didn't speak for a year, and I felt numb the entire time. Like someone took away a piece of me. I don't deserve her, but I can't fathom the thought of not having her in my life either.

"Don't touch me!" She tugs her arm free as she glares up at me. "And don't follow me. Don't call me. We are done, Hunter. It's over." With big and determined strides, she walks back to the taxi, ordering the driver to leave.

It's over.

The words echo through my head, keeping my feet glued to the pavement, not knowing what to do while the car starts to move. *No. No. No.*

"Charls," I bellow, feeling the panic creep into my body, pulling on my hair. "Charls! Charls! CHARLOTTE!"

My voice sounds more frantic every time I call out her name, but the cab keeps going, disappearing around the corner and leaving me on the sidewalk as the world blurs around me.

I don't know how long I've been standing there, looking at the corner she disappeared around, but when I turn my head, Jason is standing on the front steps of the house, his hands tucked into his sweats with slumped shoulders. His expression is sympathetic, telling me he witnessed the entire thing.

"Did you know?" My chest slowly moves up and down, my eyebrows knitted together as I hold my best friend's gaze, wondering if he kept this vital piece of information from me. But my lips part with relief when he shakes his head, confusion etched in his dark blue eyes.

"No. She didn't tell me either."

I squat down, burying my face in my hands. I haven't cried since the day I lost half my family, but it's like a dam has broken, my torso shaking with every sob that comes out. How did I screw it up this bad? I have everything I ever wanted, yet I manage to lose the one thing that really matters. I'd give it all up if it means I can be a better man for her.

I feel like a mess, functioning on autopilot, when Jason hauls me up and drags me back into the house. My vision is blurred, my throat sore, and when my gaze lands on the bottle of Jack Daniels sitting on the counter, I swipe it up. I screw off the cap, then take a big swig. The burning liquid surges through my gullet, and I close my eyes, waiting, hoping, praying it will take away some of the pain.

When they fly back open, Jason is giving me a stern look, standing on the other side of the island. "What?"

He doesn't reply, but just shakes his head with a look that questions my sanity.

"She's my best friend, Jason. And I'm supposed to be hers, but I'm too much of an asshole to answer my phone when her motherfucking mother dies!" I rub the back of my neck, having no clue what the fuck I'm doing.

"She has never been your fucking best friend!" he snaps, incredulously. His features harden, and the look in his eyes tells me it's a good thing there's two square feet of marble between us, or he would've launched at me. "Don't you dare keep feeding me that lie!"

"It's not a lie," I counter, a little less fire in my voice as I bring the bottle to my lips again.

"Bullshit. You keep pretending that she's your best friend and *maybe* you've got feelings for her, when really, you've loved her since day one. *Day fucking one, Hunter.* This isn't some best friends to lovers bullshit. You and Charlotte? That's fucking love at first sight."

"It wasn't love at first sight for Charlotte." I huff, rolling my eyes at his comment.

"I wasn't talking about her."

I frown as I look at him with a dazed face.

"You think I didn't notice the secret glances since freshman year? And when you and her finally started talking, there was only one thing that was important. You bent over backwards to make sure you could spend time with her every chance you got. It was fucking annoying, but you've loved her from day one, asshole!"

He stays quiet, and I can feel how his eyes are boring through me with a scowl in place. I swallow, then stare at the infinity pool in the backyard to avoid it.

"She called me," I confess in a monotone voice. "And I ignored her, because Laurie didn't want me to talk to her." I croak the last of the admission, rubbing my eyes with my hands, trying to push the emotion away. I knew it was the wrong thing to do, still regretting it the next day. But now I hate myself for it. Hate that I listened to Laurie's insecurity when I knew something was going on.

I'm an asshole.

"That's fucked up, Hunter."

"She hates me now."

"Yeah, well, you break it, you buy it, man." A cynical chuckle leaves his lips, and I snap out of it, shooting him a glare. "I'm not joking. You fucked up, big time. Now fix it. Stop acting like fucking Big Bird, putting your head in the ground, and sign that fucking deal. You've been dying since you first laid eyes on her."

"Why you talking about my girl like she's a fucking business transaction?" I sneer, not liking the fact he talks like it's all so simple.

"Because you do weird stuff like call her 'my girl,' but then freeze when I tell you to fucking go and actually *make* her your girl. You're engaged to someone else! She's not *your* girl. But you can make her."

I blink, staring at Jason in silence, my chest moving up and down rapidly as his words seem to cut through my body like the needle of a tattoo machine. Annoyingly. Harrowing.

"What are you so afraid of, man?"

"That she'll leave. *Permanently*," I admit. "That one day, I'll wake up, and she's not there. Gone, like *them*."

"She won't leave willingly. Not you. She'll never leave you. So, if you are scared of her leaving like your brother and your father? Then yeah, that can happen. But is the chance of that happening scarier than living without her?"

There are a lot of things going through my head right now, but it's mostly, it's panic. Panic of what the fuck have I done? Panic at what the hell am I doing? Panic at how the fuck can I fix this? Panic at the thought of my heart physically jumping out of my chest as I feel it pound against my ribcage like it's in a damn hockey game. The thought of losing her feels like a tight grasp around my throat, suffocating me more by the second.

"I don't deserve her."

"You're right," he says with a matter-of-fact tone, "you don't. Especially not after tonight." He pauses, and I close my eyes. "But if you are just half the man I think you are, you'll use the rest of your life to become the man she *does* deserve!"

My eyes fly open, colliding with my best friend's features that scream something like *duh, asshole*.

"She deserves better. But she wants *you*," he adds. "Are you really going to quit the best thing that ever happened to you?"

"No," I cry out, running my hand through my hair, releasing out a feral moan, then letting my feet carry me to the couch with the bottle in a tight grasp.

"So, what are you going to do?" Jason calls out behind me.

"Numb the pain."

"Are you going to win her back?"

"Ask me again when I'm too shitfaced to lie to you about it."

YEAR SEVEN
ELEVEN MONTHS LATER - PRESENT DAY

I CAN'T PRETEND HE DIDN'T BREAK SOMETHING BETWEEN US,
AND FRANKLY,
I DON'T WANT TO ANYMORE

'You can't do this'

59

HUNTER

A BIG GRIN SPLITS my face when I spot her wavy long hair at the bar. She's chatting with Julie, and I stand still for a moment, taking her in. My heart speeds up, and it feels like time slows down as a feeling of comfort sinks into my legs.

It feels like home.

I saunter toward her, and Julie's eyes grow wide when she notices me standing beside Charls. When Charlotte becomes aware of Julie's shocked, yet amused face, she freezes for a moment, probably refusing to turn around.

"Hey, babe." I place my body only a foot away from her, not wanting any more distance between us.

She turns around, meeting me with her gorgeous eyes that are now doing their best to glare daggers at me. But I see the glint of excitement. It's small, but it's there, and I'll take it.

"What the fuck?" she screeches.

"What's up, Julie?" I glance over her head, giving Julie a short nod. I'm sure she would be hitting me over the head with something if I totally caught both of them off guard, but Jason was smart enough to give Julie a heads up that we were coming into town and that I was on a mission. Jason disclosed she blurted out the words "asshole," "motherfucker," and "jackass" multiple times but, ultimately, she's seeming to give me a shot.

"Hey, Hunt," Julie drawls, and I put my focus back on my girl. Her eyes have lowered to my lips, and I bite it in amusement, followed by satisfaction.

My first impulse is to take her in my arms and kiss her until sunrise, but I know patience is a virtue. Gotta take my time, to show her I'm not going anywhere; otherwise, she'll use every chance she can get to run away from me.

And I can't blame her.

By the time she left California eleven months ago, I was drunk as a skunk, and Jason allowed me to go on a bender for three days. I say "*allowed*," because even though he had a constant scowl on his face, he stayed with me, preventing me from killing myself with my stupidity. Coming with me to every club, making sure I didn't choke on my vomit, and to keep me out of any more trouble. After three days, he locked me in my room, forcing me to sober up and sleep it off. By the time I woke up after twenty-four straight hours of sleep, my head felt as bad as my heart, and I just stared at the ceiling for hours until he came in with a burger and a bottle of water.

"Are you done drinking yourself to death?" he asked. I kept my gaze fixed at the ceiling, answering with a simple yes.

"So what's the plan? Because I've been waiting for you to get your head out of your ass for years, but no fucking luck. You've had three days to wallow in your shit, but I'm done being your babysitter. Figure your shit out and get your fucking girl back, man."

"I will." It probably wasn't the response he was expecting because when I finally let my gaze connect with his, it was washed with surprise.

"You will?"

I nod.

"How?"

"By doing the right thing."

8

"What is the right thing?"

"Breaking off my engagement and fighting for what I really want."

It's funny how all those fucking cliches are annoyingly true. Now that the finality of Charls's words started dripping in, no longer clogged by the alcohol, I finally saw what I was missing.

The thought of marrying Laurie freaked me the fuck out, and all I could see if I looked at the future was Charlotte.

Her beaming smile looking at me when I wake up in the morning.

Her comforting words when I have a bad day.

Her sweet giggles and banter filling up my life.

It's Charlotte.

After I broke off my engagement, I wanted to jump on a plane to North Carolina to beg Charlotte to forgive me, but I knew I had some shit to process before I could give her even a fraction of what she deserves.

I'm not there yet, and chances are, I might never be, but I had eleven months to come to terms with at least half of my demons, and I'm not willing to give up on us. Charlotte once told me all she needed was me, and I'm willing to give her every single part of me.

"How are you?" I ask.

"Fine," she replies, averting her face, pretending to be indifferent. "You here to visit your mom?"

I place my elbow on the bar, looking at her with a smirk.

"Nah, I'm staying."

"You're what?!" she snaps, her eyes briefly ogling me before she returns to her glare. "Why?"

"Because I have unfinished business in this town." I grab her glass out of her hand, making sure our skin connects for longer than necessary while I keep staring at her, taking a sip.

"You better be talking about your mom, Hunter Hansen."

"She's the reason I left," I explain. "*You* are the reason I'm back." Emphasizing my words, I place my hand on her thigh, then put the glass back in front of her.

"No, you're not."

When she dismisses me by putting her attention somewhere else, I lean in close enough to count the small freckles on her cheek. "I know it took me a while, but I'm back."

"Good for you," she sneers.

"I want another shot," I demand.

"At what?" she asks, still refusing to look at me.

"Your heart."

"I have a boyfriend," she scolds, snapping her head back toward me.

God, she's gorgeous when she's all fire.

"We both know he doesn't mean shit." I grab her glass from the counter once more, taking another sip like the arrogant asshole I am.

I have to admit, finding out she started dating a few months ago was a minor setback. I locked myself in the gym for three days, beating the crap out of the punching bag, getting all my frustration out until I decided I didn't care. It didn't matter. She could be married with a bunch of kids right now, and I'd still fight for what's mine.

And Charlotte Roux is mine.

Plain and simple.

"*You* don't mean shit," she counters, making me chuckle.

"And your pretty eyes tell me you're full of shit."

"Stop flirting with me."

"Never." I wink, holding her gaze until she rolls her eyes.

"What do you want, Hunter?" Her eyes move to her glass, and she casually picks it up to swirl the contents around the tumbler, faking her disinterest.

"Eight dates. One each for every year that I should've made you mine and didn't, and then one extra for the years we'll have in the future."

"What? No! I have a *boyfriend*."

"Who cares?" I tilt my head, rolling my eyes.

"I do." She points her thumb against her chest. "And I bet he does, too."

"I'm not going anywhere, babe." The statement is simple and clear, and I mean every word of it. She can push me away for as long as she wants. But even if it takes me until we're old and wrinkly, she's my girl, and I'm gonna get her back.

She sighs.

"You can't do this. You can't just barge back into my life like that. Expecting everything to be all good."

"I know, but I'm fucking doing it, anyway." I hear Julie snigger behind her, and I keep staring at Charlotte's cheek, until finally our eyes lock. The tension rises, and I can see the frustration etched in the blue-green gradient of her eyes. "Eight dates, Charls. Eight dates to convince you to give me another shot. If you still want me to leave after those eight dates, I'll be gone. I promise."

She shakes her head.

"No dates."

"Babe," I plead.

"Fuck no! That ship has sailed, Hunter." She keeps staring at me fiercely, then her pinched lips soften a little. "But I'll give you eight days to convince me you're still my friend."

Fuck that is the first thing that wants to fall from my lips, but I hold back. *Patience.*

"*Best* friend," I reprimand.

"Let's just start with friends, okay?"

No. Not fucking 'okay'. But considering I've torn her heart apart and haven't seen her in almost a year, I guess I have to count my blessings. One, being the fact that she hasn't hit me yet in the first place. Two, the small win that she's actually agreeing to *something* instead of nothing.

"Fine, but we are calling them dates. And I want eight full days, morning until evening."

"Oh God, what the fuck will I tell Ben?" She throws her hands up in the air, defeated.

"Tell him your *best friend* is back in town."

"You're not my best friend until you've proven yourself," she scolds.

Rapidly, I circle her waist with one arm, pressing my body flush with hers.

"Before those eight dates are over, I will have proven to be so much more than your best friend, babe," I groan against her ear, then place a peck on the soft skin of her cheek. "I'll see you soon."

When I let go of her, she's looking at me with lust in her eyes.

Oh, yeah, she's still mine.

"Asshole." She glares while I back away with a smirk.

"I am. But I'm *your* asshole." I wink, then turn around to walk out of the bar.

You can't hide from me, Charlotte Roux.

60

Charlotte

I SLEPT FOR TWO hours.

That's it. That's all my mind allowed me to have after the day I had yesterday.

I anticipated it.

In fact, the reason I went out with Julie was to make sure I'd get some sleep after a few drinks, trying to forget the experience I had earlier in the day. But Hunter Hansen strolling into the bar like it was nothing totally fucked up any chance I had at sleep.

I can't believe he's back.

For *me*.

I planned to be staring at the ceiling, wondering where this experience would leave me and Ben, but instead I've been staring at the white plaster thinking about the man that doesn't deserve a single one of my thoughts.

But here we are. Tired as hell, frustrated as fuck, and desperately trying to escape in some kind of MC novel. I manage to let my head disappear inside the pages for less than five minutes before the rumbling sound of an old truck snaps me out of my book.

Fucking hell.

I don't even have to wait and see who drives around the corner, because deep down, I already know. I already know there is no chance in hell he would've sold the truck that holds so many memories. Not to mention the fact that I'd recognize that sound anywhere. My head peers down again, my eyes trying to focus on the letters in front of me when I ignore the truck parking in my driveway.

I quickly glance up, confirming my suspicion, when I notice Hunter sitting behind the wheel with a black snapback on his head. His hazel eyes look vibrant as hell through the windshield, way too perky for my taste, acting as more motivation to ignore his presence altogether.

Maybe if I just pretend he's not there, he'll leave.

Pursing my lips in annoyance, I roll my eyes, waiting until I hear his footsteps saunter down the path toward the front door before he ambles up the porch steps.

"Hey, babe." He crosses his arms in front of his body, resting his hip and shoulder against the porch post while his lip curls in a smug smile. My eyes continue dancing over the letters on the page, but I fail to register even a single word.

"You can't ignore me, Charls."

"It worked for eleven months."

He scoffs, amused. "That's because I allowed it, baby. You know that."

Arrogant motherfucking asshole.

"Don't you have to get back to LA for a fight or something? Entertain all the fancy people you hang out with now?"

"I'm on hiatus."

Of course he is.

I can't resist lifting my eyes to his, and I instantly regret it. His gaze tempts me with little sparks of joy, hypnotizing me like fireflies in the night.

"What are you doing here, Hunt?" I scowl.

"Came to see you."

I let out a sigh, slamming my book closed, and throwing it on the wooden planks with an audible thud. My eyes lock with his as I mimic his stance, crossing my arms.

"You can't just appear on my doorstep."

He just laughs.

"I mean it, Hansen!"

"Is that some kind of thing?" he asks, with a dull look on his face, silently calling me out on my bullshit. It's like I'm thrown back into time, that cocky son of a bitch like a blast of my past to fuck with my head. "Because I just did."

"Shut up, smartass. What if my boyfriend was here?"

His eyebrow raises in confusion, before the corner of his mouth softly starts to tug on his lip. "You mean, he isn't?"

"No."

He purses his lips, clearly doing his best to suppress a smirk. "So, you're not living with him?"

"You didn't know?"

"No." He casually shakes his head. Somehow that makes it even worse.

"You just dropped by, even though he might be here?"

"I don't care if he is," he huffs, making my jaw tick.

I hate him.

"Hunter!" I growl.

"What? Friends, right?" He cocks his eyebrow, daring me with his piercing eyes. "Nothing to hide if we're just friends, Charls."

I stare at him, too pissed to say a word, too annoyed with myself to admit he might be right. I hate and love his arrogant stance, loving him for it when he's that confident ass who woos me off my feet, but hating him when he's using it against me to get his way. I've never been able to resist anything that revolves around Hunter Hansen, and apparently, him ripping my heart out didn't change that one bit. Because here we are, and instead of throwing my shoe at his head, I keep my stance statue-still. If anything, I have to keep myself from jumping up and wrapping my arms around him. Because fuck me, I can play hard to get all I want. But deep down inside, I missed him like crazy. I missed my *best* friend. It's been eleven months, but looking at him now, it feels like eleven minutes.

Every single time the darkness of losing Mama got a hold of me, he was the one I wanted to call. And every single time, my heart broke a little more because he wasn't there. Now he's here, and I don't know what to make of it. I keep begging my heart to keep the gates closed, but no surprise there, she's stronger than my mind, who's the sensible out of the two.

"Or are we more than friends?" he dares.

"No."

"Well, you've never been bothered by me stopping by unannounced."

"I am now." I swallow the rest of the words that are on the tip of my tongue, while he slowly pushes off the porch post, sauntering toward me. He stops in front of me, looking down with a lustful stare that makes me swallow hard, before my lips part, and I push out a breath.

"Let me rephrase that. I never cared if you didn't want me to come over unannounced."

"Glad to see you are still an asshole." I avert my gaze, dropping my focus back to my book on the floor, as if it will help me ignore him. Like he'll actually leave if I just don't acknowledge his presence.

Hunter Hansen has always been in my personal space, long before we crossed the line we should've never crossed. I'd be stupid to think this time things are going to be any different.

"Come on, let's go." He offers me his hand, and I eye it with a glare, turning my head back to my book.

"No."

"Charls," he groans as he lays his hand on the nape of my neck in a dominating way, giving me a slight heart attack. He's always been a bit demanding, but fuck me, this is new.

My traitorous vagina springs to life as my pulse starts to throb underneath his touch. He softly squeezes, forcing my head to look up at him as I clench my teeth.

Shit, I'm in trouble now.

"I forgot how sexy you are when you're pissed at me." He licks his lips, then drags his teeth over his lower lip, and I know he's not joking. He's dead serious.

"No, you didn't."

"You're right, I didn't." He grins.

"Stop flirting with me," I say through gritted teeth, trying to push those lustful feelings away.

"You agreed to eight dates. This is the first. Come on. Let's go." He lets go of my neck, offering his hand once more. Even though he doesn't deserve my attention, my heart's been dying for his affection ever since the last time I saw him.

"I don't want to," I say, folding my arms in front of my body like I'm some damn toddler.

"I know. But you can walk, or I'm picking you up and putting you in my truck myself. Your choice. I prefer option number two."

"I have to work today."

"No, you don't. I have your schedule."

"What?! How?!"

His mouth playfully curls. "Julie."

That damn little traitor.

"Where are we going?"

"You'll see."

Rolling my eyes, I then slam his hand out of the way and get off the swinging bench, stomping off the porch. He follows me with a loud chuckle, until I glare back at him, and he lifts his hands in a placating gesture.

I should've never agreed to this.

I should have slapped him and told him to fuck off, but the bastard caught me at a vulnerable moment. A moment when I barely had the strength to pick up my glass to let my grief settle in my veins, let alone resist the everlasting charm of Hunter Hansen.

I walk toward his truck with a big stride forward, then get into the vehicle like a moping teenager forced to tag along with my mom, while he rounds the truck to get behind the wheel.

Leaning on the center console, he looks in the rear mirror while a whiff of his citrus, woodsy cologne hits my nose, fogging my brain before driving onto the road.

Oh, damn.

He's smart enough to keep his mouth shut, even though I can see him glance at me every now and then, making it damn hard for me to not snap at him.

We drive for about five minutes until he pulls his truck into the parking lot of the Burger Shack, and I snap my head toward him.

"Seriously?" I screech.

The last thing I wanna do is relive old memories with the man who all tainted them with his asshole behavior.

"You wanna go in, or eat in the truck?" He shrugs, unimpressed by the scowl on my face.

Part of me wants to scream at him, asking what the fuck he thinks he's doing. Hating him for triggering the memories he knows mean the most to me. Hating him for thinking he can just waltz back into my life, like he didn't rip my heart out of my chest. But the other part is tired as fuck.

Tired of fighting life.

Tired of wondering *what if?*

Tired of ignoring him, when all I wanted was to share every hard part of my life with him.

I let out a big sigh, turning my head back in front of me, staring out of the window while he's waiting for me to tell him which way to go.

"In the truck," I finally say, with mixed feelings. My heart feels like it's coming home after a rough day at work, into the comfort of your favorite blankie, while my mind shouts at the familiarity he's creating. Realizing it's going to be a fucking challenge to keep Hunter at a safe distance after these eight days.

He hums something in agreement as he turns his truck into the drive-through, ordering what we used to so many times before, as if we never stopped. A few minutes later, I take a bite of my burger, then close my eyes, feeling seventeen all over again, while a small smile lifts my lips.

This shouldn't feel so good.

I turn my body toward him, pressing my back against the door while I rest my head against the window. He gives me a coy smile as he does the same, mimicking my stance. I eye him, pointing out all the differences in my head. He's bigger, broader than seven years ago. His features have matured in a fucking sexy way, his chiseled arms now covered with more tattoos than before. But it's his eyes that captivate me with even more gravity than it felt like when I was seventeen.

Like they hold more depth.

"Wanna play a game?" he asks between bites.

I look at him with suspicion.

"What kind of game?"

"Twenty-one questions."

"Fine," I reply, thinking there is no harm in that. "Three passes, though."

"Cool. You can go first." He nudges his head toward me, while he takes off his snapback and throws it on the dashboard, then runs his hand through his messy hair. My lips absentmindedly part, glancing at the thick veins on his biceps.

I take another bite of my burger, wondering what I should ask him.

"Have you already visited your mother?" I ask, thinking I'm not ready to ask the deep questions.

"I'm staying with her," he confesses, giving me a look, as if he can't believe it himself.

"You are?" My eyebrows raise in surprise. "Why?"

"I've paid off her mortgage. It was the least she could do when I told her I needed a place to stay."

"Why didn't you just buy a house if you're planning to stay?"

He raises his finger in a reprimanding way.

"Na-ah, that's another question. My turn," he says, handing out half of his burger for me so we can switch.

"Are you going to keep living in your mom's house?"

The question slightly makes me gasp for air, because it's one I don't have an answer to.

"I don't know. I haven't decided yet," I confess, causing him to give me a sympathetic smile. I've been thinking about it a lot, but even though it's been almost a year since my mom passed away, I'm still not any closer to making a definite decision about it. Part of me wants to stay, doing my best to keep every memory of my mother intact, not willing to give it up just yet. While the other feels like I need a fresh start, to start my own life instead of continuing on with my old one.

"My turn. Why are you really moving back?"

It's a tricky question, because while I think I want to know the answer, the answer he gives me might not be what I want to hear if it means he's going to move through my life like a hurricane, destroying everything I've built since I lost Mama.

Not that it's much, but still.

He lets out a sweet chuckle that strokes my ears, a sweet smile splitting his face.

"Because you're here," he states matter-of-factly.

"Shut up, Hunt," I growl, even though my heart is jumping for joy inside of me, giving myself a silent slap on the wrist, reminding me that I have a boyfriend. One who's handsome, sweet, and loving, supportive, and most of all, who didn't leave me when things got hard. If anything, he was too understanding, getting on my nerves with the amount of love he had to give me.

"Just because you don't want to hear it, doesn't mean it's not true, Charls. I'm here for you. *I'm here to stay.*" He stares at me, as if he wants to make sure I hear every word, letting them sink into every fiber in my body.

"Also, it's October, so don't even dare to try to avoid me on my birthday." A judgy frown creases his face, and I roll my eyes.

"As if I would ever forget your birthday." He knows I wouldn't. No matter how much he might have pissed me off through the years, I'd always wished him a happy birthday at midnight. Sometimes with a kiss, sometimes a heart, and once or twice with an emoji flipping him off, but I always remembered. Like a fucking timer that goes off in my head every October, pun intended.

"You won't forget, but this year, I'm not settling with a text and a fucking emoji," he scolds.

"Whatever. My turn. Why did you break up with your *fiancée*?" I joke, even though we both know it sure as fuck ain't no joke. I read all the gossip magazines about it, because, well, I'm only human, but I knew most of it was superstar Laurie playing the victim. She told everyone who wanted to listen to her shit about how Hunter cheated on her. Multiple times. I know Hunter. He's an immature asshole most of the time, but he doesn't cheat. His heart is too pure to do that.

"I didn't cheat on her, like she's saying, if that's what you're asking."

"That's not what I'm asking." Hunter's ego is too big to cheat on anyone. If he wanted to sleep around, he would just tell Laurie to take it or leave it.

"Then what are you asking?"

"Why did you two break up?"

"She wanted marriage and kids, and I didn't."

"Not now or not ever?" I curiously tilt my head.

"Not with *her*." I don't miss the way he's trying to bore his gaze into mine, his eyebrows up as if the answer is obvious.

"Why not?"

"Because she wasn't you." He shrugs, crushing my chest with lightning speed.

Hot damn, I forgot how fearless he can be when he wants to be. How blunt, if he's feeling confident and in control. I expected something between the lines. After all, he made it no secret that I'm the reason he's back in Braeden, but for some reason, I wasn't expecting that.

"Oh, please. Stop with the fucking flirting." I roll my eyes to hide the melting of my heart, bleeding out of my cracked rib cage.

"Stop asking the questions you don't want to hear the answers to."

I narrow my eyes at him, pursing my lips before I recover my face, giving him a fake smile as I take a bite from my burger.

"Right." He shakes his head, an annoyed look stealing his features.

I'm frustrating him. *Good.*

I can see it in his entire stance. He's used to getting everything he wants from me, anything he needs, with me jumping up to give it to him. Because that's what I do. It's who I am, and I wouldn't change it for the world. Yeah, I'm a nice girl. I do my best to help every single person who matters to me, but I'm not some kind of doormat.

My heart might still love him without a doubt, but I'm team head right now. Wanting him to fucking show me why I should still consider him my friend.

Meaning—I want to make him grovel until his knees are bruised.

"My turn." He makes a ball of the paper that was wrapped around his burger, after he popped the last bite into his mouth. Talking to me with his mouth full, like the true barbarian that he is.

"Why don't you have a dog?"

The question surprises me, and I let out a full laugh until I notice the beaming smile on his face. Realizing my mistake, I lower the corners of my mouth as I eat the last bite of my double cheeseburger.

Taking my time, I slowly chew the last of it, intently making him wait a little longer before I answer. I was aiming for a roll of the eye, an annoyed huff, maybe even a *fucking hell, Charls,* but he keeps his eyes locked with mine, looking at me while I swallow the contents down my throat, as if he can't wait to see me swallow something else. I inhale deeply, trying to push away whatever feelings the look in his eyes is giving me, then shrug my shoulders and answer.

"It didn't feel right."

"Why is that? You wanted a dog for so long. I figured as soon as you got the chance, you would run to the shelter, giving yourself a fur friend."

The features in his face are soft, reminding me of years ago, the first time we met.

"I thought about it," I confess, fumbling with the sharp edge of my nail. "I even went to the shelter about a month after Mama died. But it didn't feel right. I couldn't pick one by myself, so instead I walked right back out. Never went back, even though the thought still crosses my mind now and then."

He reaches out his hand, grabbing mine before he links our fingers, the move making me look up at him. I expect him to say he's sorry or some other bullshit I'm not ready to hear, but I watch him while the corner of his mouth lifts a little as he squeezes my hand.

"You'll get one. When you're ready. When it's the right time."

Without thinking, I smile back at him, a warm feeling forming inside of me.

"I know."

He lets go of my hand, the stern look in his eyes telling me he doesn't really want to.

"Look, I know you're not ready to talk yet." My lips part to respond, but he places his hand over my mouth, and his warm skin on my lips makes me blink in shock. "And that's okay. I can't blame you. We don't have to dig out the deep stuff. Just spend some time with me, okay? That's all I ask." I can see the corner of his eyes grow moist, while he inhales loudly through his nose, then pushes out a troubled breath as he lowers his hand again.

I want to tell him to fuck off.

But I can't.

I can't, and at this point, I'm wondering if I ever will.

If I will ever be strong enough to resist Hunter Hansen in any shape or form.

"Okay."

61

HUNTER

CHARLOTTE ROUX IS NO longer the sweet little girl she was in high school. Her entire stance has closed off, determined to make life difficult for me, but even though it pisses me off, it also fucking turns me on.

I already knew that, but the last few years I've not been on the receiving side of her sass, aside from our world-shattering breakup, and fuck me, it makes me want to shut her up with my lips.

"My turn." She unbuckles her belt when I'm parked in front of her house again, turning her body toward mine while I wait in anticipation.

"What was your eighteenth birthday wish?"

I let out a loud groan, moving my head toward her as I gave her an incredulous look.

When I made that wish, I never expected it to come true.

It did.

Faster than I anticipated, but it left even quicker.

"You can't do me like that, babe," I plead, making her chuckle softly, the curiosity dripping from her face.

"Answer it, *fighter boy*." She wiggles her eyebrows while her tongue darts out, daringly licking her lips. Her stance has opened up in the last half hour, as I just drove around with her like we were seventeen again. I thought about going to our spot at the creek, but after the number of glares she gave me when I showed up on her doorstep, I figured that might have been pushing it too hard.

"Pass," I blurt.

"No!" she shouts through the car, laughter audible in her voice as she points her finger at me. "You had your passes. You've gotta answer this one!"

I narrow my eyes at the girl who clearly likes to torment me in any way she can, while the corner of my mouth curls in an amused smile.

"You like to make life difficult for me, don't you?"

"Maybe." She shrugs, making me want to kiss the devilish grin off her face, and I let out a deep growl, turning my focus back to her.

"I can't believe you're going to make me say it."

"Are you kidding me? I've been dying to know for years, Hansen."

I look up to the ceiling before I close my eyes, enjoying the fact that she's joking with me. Clearly, she has no clue what the answer to that question is.

"Spending the night with you," I blurt.

Her eyes widen, her lips parting, forming a silent 'O'. Shock glimmers in her eyes, and I swear I can see the hue change on her cheeks.

"Right." She averts her gaze, not wanting to go into it any further, and I press my lips together, suppressing a smile.

"Let's keep going," I say, hoping to maintain the relaxed energy she's been giving me. "Once upon a time, you told me you wanted to travel. Where to?"

She gives me a grateful look, relieved I don't push for her reaction to my answer.

"Spain."

"Yeah?" I smile.

"Oh yeah, I want to dance flamenco, eat tapas, and taste *real* Sangria. Not that shit we have in the grocery store." She turns up her nose, and I smile, knowing exactly where I'm gonna take her when I get the chance.

"Okay, next one." Her face lightens up a little bit more with every question, and the victorious feeling inside of me grows bigger as the game progresses.

"You have to pick: never fighting or never eating clementine vanilla ice cream."

I give her an incredulous look.

"Are you shitting me?"

"Answer it!" Her smile splits her face, a bright look in her eyes.

"Charls," I growl.

"Answer it!" she repeats, amused.

I rub my neck, pursing my lips, until I answer with a long sigh.

"You know I'm not giving up ice cream."

Her shoulders shake with laughter, a smug grin spreading across her cheeks.

"Glad to see some things never change. Guess I figured out your guilty pleasure."

"A hundred percent," I admit. "I can't live without ice cream."

"Who can live without ice cream?" she says, pulling a face in that cute way she does.

"Not us, babe. Not us."

"Right." She smiles, then glances at her front door. "Well, I guess I should be going. Early day tomorrow."

I know she has nowhere to go, but I don't call her out on it, happy with the few hours she gifted me with today.

"Yeah. I guess so."

She lets out a deep sigh, giving me a tight smile as her fingers reach for the handle of the door. It takes everything I have not to pull her back and against my chest.

"I guess I'll see you around?" A hint of kindness is visible in her eyes, and I take a snapshot of it in my head, wanting to make sure I remember that look on her face when she's pissed at me again.

"You bet, babe."

She opens the door, lowering her body onto the concrete, before she gives me another stern look, the door in her hands.

"Just call me next time, okay?"

I suppress the smug grin that wants to appear when I hear her saying "next time," so instead I give her a small nod, doing my best to show her I'm serious.

That I'm listening to her.

"Okay, Charls. I'll call first."

"Thank you," she says, closing the door behind her, and I watch her walk away toward her front door. I don't want to drive away, but I know I have to. I need to give her just enough time and space to make sure she'll keep me around, just long enough for me to fix everything I've broken. And it's a goddamn long list.

"Hey, Charls?" I bellow through the window after I lower it with the button on the center console.

She turns around with those mesmerizing eyes, instantly capturing my attention while her dark blonde waves bounce around her head, giving me a questioning look.

"Thank you for tonight."

A smile forms on her lips. "You're welcome, *asshole.*"

She turns back around, moving into the house while I make my way out of her driveway, knowing I will sleep better tonight.

Knowing I'm making progress.

Seven more dates to go.

62

HUNTER

"**I**'M IN FRONT OF your door." The next morning, I sit in my truck in her driveway, looking up to the window of Charlotte's room. I have no idea if she still sleeps there, but I keep my eyes focused on the glass, waiting for her to appear any second now.

"What?!" she screeches in a sleepy voice. "You said you'd call first!"

"I'm calling now."

"I hate you," she says, and I can feel her glaring through the phone, a chuckle escaping my lips. "What time is it?"

"Five-thirty."

"What?! The fuck, Hunter! Why?!"

"You agreed to full days. You only gave me a few hours yesterday. I want a full day today."

"It's the middle of the night." I can hear how she's drifting off again, so I push the horn of my truck to make sure she stays awake.

"Dear Lord!" she yelps, and I snicker. "What is wrong with you, Hansen?"

"If you're not out in ten minutes, I'm coming to get you."

"What? No!"

"Then get out of bed, get dressed, and get out of here. We're running late."

"I hate it when you're cryptic," she growls.

"Nine minutes, Charls."

"Fine! I'll get up," she huffs.

"Wave in front of the window."

"What?"

"Wave in front of the window," I repeat, rolling my eyes.

"What? Why?"

"Because I know you. You're going back to sleep if you don't get out of bed right now. I need proof. Get out of bed, or I'll come get you."

"No, you won't!" A slight panic is audible in her voice, and a smile splits my face.

"You know I will."

She stays quiet, as if she's contemplating her chances, then lets out a deep grunt.

I can hear her get up, stomping across her room, until her scowling face appears in the window.

"Hey, babe," I sing, giving her a playful wave.

She flips me the bird, then disappears out of my sight.

"I'll be right down, *asshole*." Before I can reply, she hangs up, cranky as ever.

She never was a morning person, always bitching at me if I picked her up at dawn to take her somewhere for the day. But even though she'd hate me in the morning, she always loved the adventures we'd go on together, and I hope this will be no exception. Besides, I'm sure her "boyfriend" will want to snatch her time sooner or later, so I might as well get ahead to really show her I'm back for good. I've wasted enough time already.

Ten minutes later, she opens the door on the passenger side of my truck, still glaring as she drops herself in the seat, buckling up. Long legs taunt me from under her denim shorts, and for a split second, I'm happy her torso is protected from the early morning crisp weather behind a hoodie, because my dick would be getting highly uncomfortable if I see more skin.

"You ready?" I beam, starting the engine.

She slowly turns her head, cocking her eyebrow, her eyes still shooting daggers.

"You got food?"

I reach behind her seat to grab the bag of donuts, tossing them into her lap, then I open the center console to grab out a small thermos.

"Better now?" I hand her the thermos, her eyes going from the thermos to me.

"Depends. Tea?"

"Orange and ginger."

She purses her lips, and I can see the features in her face soften a little when she grabs the thermos out of my hand, then reaches into the bag to choose a donut. As we drive off, I glance at her, watching as she sinks her teeth into the glazed dough when I get on the road and hit the throttle.

"Better," she says, her mouth full of donut, as she closes her eyes to savor the taste, and I shake my head with a smile.

We drive in silence while she eats her breakfast, and I enjoy the peace. Nostalgia shivers up my spine.

Fuck, I'm a lucky bastard.

Eleven months ago, I didn't know if I'd ever have these moments again, and therefore I appreciate them even more.

"Where are we going?" she finally asks after finishing her donut.

"You'll see." I wink. Her eyes roll in reply, but the annoyance from earlier has totally simmered away.

When I drive into the mountains, she turns her head toward mine, and I glance at her again, before putting my focus back on the road.

"Are we going to the quarry?" Her voice is soft and uncertain, enough to make my heart crack just a little.

"Is that a bad thing?"

She shakes her head.

"No. I just haven't been back there since—" she whispers, fiddling with her fingers as she stares out of the window. "Well, since that day."

Her eyes lock with mine, and I can see the pain laced there before she gives me a sweet smile. It guts me that I hurt her. That I brought her so much pain. The tension in the cab rises, and I suck in a deep breath, then make a bold move by laying my hand on her neck, hoping she won't shut me down.

"Neither have I," I confess, as I rub the back of her neck with my thumb, a comforting feeling settling inside me, grateful she's letting me touch her.

"You haven't?" She frowns.

"No. Didn't feel right to go without you after that day. The creek is our spot. But the quarry... the quarry is special."

Because you are special.

I let go of her neck, not wanting to push my luck, putting my hand back on the wheel.

"But that's your family spot."

"I know." I shrug. "But my mom ain't gonna come with me, and I don't want to share that spot with anyone but family."

"I'm family?" She frowns, a spark of hope in her voice that bursts my heart into flames.

"You've always been more than that, Charls." Fixing my attention back on the road, we continue the ride in silence as she keeps staring out of the window.

I realized a lot of things in the last few months. One of those things is how important Charlotte has always been to me. Ever since the accident, I've felt alone, nothing more than an orphan trying to get through life. My mom didn't give a shit about anything other than the bottle in her hand, and she made me feel like a burden on a daily basis. I knew I wasn't worthless, but I felt damn alone trying to survive in a violent household.

Until Charlotte.

She changed my world in so many ways. She gave me the feeling I wasn't alone. She gave me the feeling I was enough. She made me feel loved. She changed me, taught me to always keep going, and to never give up hope. She taught me life isn't black and white for anyone, and even though my mom treated her like shit, she always tried to make me look at the good memories that my mom was a part of.

She's the most beautiful person I've ever met, and from that first day at the creek, I knew I didn't want a life without her. I'm the luckiest bastard in the world that she gave me even an ounce of her attention, and I see that now. It took me seven years to actually man the fuck up and admit it, but I refuse to live without her.

She's my family.

Whether she likes it or not.

Fifteen minutes later, I park in front of the path and we both exit the truck. Grabbing my bag, I walk to the tailgate, then follow Charlotte as she slowly starts the walk to the quarry. The dawn is completely set, but the humidity of the trees around us chills my bare arms. The peace in the woods calms my senses, a satisfying smile forming on my lips at the sight in front of me. I stare at the back of her wavy dark blonde hair in silence, admiring her luscious curves. She's matured over the years, becoming less girl and all woman. I noticed every time I'd see her again, but always tried to push it away because of our *just friends'* agreement, thinking we could never work, both living on different sides of the country. This time I'm only holding back because she still has a boyfriend, but I have every intention of feeling that peachy ass under the palms of my hands before these eight dates are over.

"Stop staring at my ass." She stops, her hands on her sides, turning her body toward me, then takes a step back to let me pass her.

"I wasn't staring at your ass," I lie with a smirk, strolling closer.

"Whatever." She rolls her eyes, and I take another step, crowding her personal space. Her gaze grows big, and I notice her swallow hard before her lips part when our faces are only three inches apart.

"I wasn't staring." My breath is fanning her face. "I was thinking about how much I'm gonna enjoy feeling that sweet ass in my palms again."

"Hunter! What is wrong with you?"

She slaps my chest with a shocked scowl on her face, mixed with an excitement that makes me laugh. She's failing if she thinks she's selling her indignance.

"Just voicing the inevitable, babe." I lick my lips, then softly brush past her, leaving her frozen in the same spot.

"Stop flirting with me," she growls, following in my tracks with big stomps.

"Not gonna happen, Charls."

"You're impossible!"

"Yup," I retort, popping my 'P', making it softly echo through the woods, a smile plastered on my face.

She can deny all she wants. She can tell me she has a boyfriend a hundred times, but I see the look in her eyes. What we used to have is still there. I just need to convince her to give me another chance, to make her trust I will never hurt her the way I did ever again.

To show her I'm in it for the long haul this time. *Till death do us fucking part.*

When we reach the quarry, the sun is appearing behind the trees, softly warming my skin as I set up the blanket I brought with me, then take off my shoes and lie down. She's standing beside me, her hands tucked into her sides again.

"You know if I lie down, I'll probably fall back to sleep again, right?"

I fold my hands in front of my chest as I look up at her. "I know there's a possibility."

She narrows her eyes at me in suspicion, as if she's waiting for me to throw out another flirty comment, then lies down next to me when I keep my mouth shut. I can't resist, though.

"But I can think of a few ways to keep you awake."

She groans.

"Stop. Flirting. With. Me."

I roll onto my side, my head resting on my elbow, while I get a little closer to her. She snaps her head toward mine with the same wide eyes as a few minutes ago, her lips trapped between her teeth.

"I would. But I know you. You don't really want me to stop." My eyes move back and forth over her pretty face, and I resist the urge to stroke her small freckles with my thumb.

"I have a boyfriend, Hunter," she whispers.

Clenching my jaw, I grab her hip in frustration, roughly digging my fingers into her jeans, desperate to feel her skin against mine.

"Trust me, that's the only reason I haven't kissed you. Yet. But we both know it's going to happen, anyway. I'm patient. I can wait. I *will* wait. But not because I want to. I'm not gonna stop saying the shit I wanna say to you. Never have, never will, Charls." I let go of her, then lie back down again, looking up at the sky. I feel her studying my face, before she mimics my stance.

Her not responding tells me enough, but I don't want to push her for more before she's ready, so instead, we both keep staring into the sky, while the sun vanishes the thick tension between us, until a few minutes later, we're back to our comfortable selves.

"Are you gonna sell your mama's house?" I ask, reaching out my hand to link it with hers, showing her I'm here. I know it's a bold move, but I've got to where I am today by being bold. Taking risks. Every form of affection I display toward this girl, *my girl*, is a risk. But it's a risk I'm willing to take, because I need her to know I'm here. I'm here through the good, and the bad, the easy parts and the hard, assuming this question is one of the hard parts.

She glances at where our hands connect, then looks back up, not saying a word about it.

"I've thought about it. But I can't say goodbye."

"Do you want a family in that house?" Her free hand moves to her stomach, cradling it a little, until her eyes find mine.

"I think I do," she admits with a coy smile. "That house is filled with memories, and I think by raising my own children in the same house, they still get to know Mama a bit, you know?"

I softly squeeze her arm, shooting her an understanding look.

"I think she would've loved that."

She lets out a sigh, the muscles in her face relaxed, putting a smile on my face.

"I forgot how peaceful it is up here."

"I know. I've missed this." My thumb gently swipes up and down her skin.

"Me too," she admits.

"Yeah?" I know she isn't just talking about the quarry. I know she can feel our connection growing again.

She nods her head, then quickly averts her gaze.

Last night it took me a while before she relaxed, but it seems like I'm making progress even quicker today. I get up, taking off my shirt while she eyes me with confusion.

"What are you doing?"

"Let's go for a swim."

"I didn't bring my bathing suit."

"So?" I bellow, taking off my shorts with a smirk on my face.

"Oh God, Hunter. Please don't tell me you're gonna do what I think you're doing?" The words have barely rolled off her tongue when I reach for the rim of my boxers, and push them down to my ankles, then step out of them with full confidence.

"For fuck's sake, Hunter. Don't. *Please*. Put your boxers back on." Her screech flies over the water while she holds her hand in front of her eyes, and I let out a laugh.

"Come on, Charls. We're only young once, right?"

She gives me an *are-you-shitting-me* look, locking our eyes before she can't resist any longer, and they glance back down. She grinds her teeth, then places her hand back on her eyes with a cry.

"Hunter!" She drags out my name with a pleading tone, and it widens my eyes when I feel my dick twitch in response, wishing she was calling out my name while I'm buried inside of her. Time to cool off. *Literally*.

"Suit yourself," I blurt with a cocky grin, walking toward the edge of the water. "I'm going in. Just join me when you've found your big girl pants."

"Shut up, asshole!" she calls out, watching my bare ass walk into the water.

When I'm fully in the water, I turn around, gazing up at her with a smug look on my face.

"Come on, babe. Get in."

"No."

"It's nice."

"It's almost October."

"And it's still eighty degrees. It's not cold, I swear." Okay, my hard-as-a-rock nipples beg to differ, but let's pretend that's not happening. "Live a little, Charls."

She's looking at me with a skeptical expression until she lets out a deep sign, and I know I've got her.

"Turn around," she orders, drawing circles with her finger in the air. "And no peeking!"

I do as she says with a huge grin on my face, hearing her undress behind me.

Waiting patiently, I take a deep breath until I register the moving water.

"Can I turn around?" I make a slight move to glance behind me, simply because I can't resist.

"Don't you dare, asshole!" she barks, and I chuckle, loving how she's getting all worked up.

"Okay, you can turn around now."

I turn around, looking into her blue-green eyes, sparkling even more because of the reflection of the water on her face. Her shoulders are above the water, and I can see the curves of her breasts as she waves her hands through the water, the bottom of her hair swaying through the surface.

"Hey."

"Hey." She smiles.

"Cold?"

"A little."

"You're gorgeous."

"Stop flirting with me." She rolls her lips, our eyes locking, peering at each other as if an invisible cord connects us.

"I'm not." I keep a straight face, showing her I'm serious, and her lips part, breaths becoming shallower. The tension builds, rapidly and steadily. It's undeniable and impossible to brush aside. But even though I want to close the distance between us and wrap her in my arms where she belongs, I don't.

Not yet.

"I'm not gonna try anything, Charls." I shake my head.

I'm not going to push her to do something she's not comfortable with. I waited seven years. I can wait a few more days, or weeks, or months, or however long she needs.

But really, I'll wait forever if I have to.

Her eyes keep piercing through me, drumming up my heart beat a little faster.

Finally, the corner of her mouth quirks, and her muscles relax, the tension transforming into the comfort that represents our friendship.

"How's your mother?"

I chuckle as I lift my snapback from my head, throwing it back onto the pebbles on the shore, then run a hand through my short hair.

"How is it she's been treating you like trash since you met her, but you still ask how she's doing?"

"I don't know. Because I'm nice?" She shrugs, her eyebrows raised in question.

"You are nice, Charls. You're *too* nice." I hold her gaze, until lips purse with somewhat of an agreeing hum before I continue. "She's good. Still the Wicked Witch of the East, but she's good."

She cocks her head, narrowing her eyes at me.

"What?"

"This is the first time in all those years that you're not talking about your mother in a bitter tone."

My brows raise, a smug grin forming on my face. It's been ten years, but yeah, I feel proud when I think of my mother. Not our relationship, as that's not something to be proud of, but I am proud of how I did my best to accept the situation. How I found a little bit of peace amongst the chaos. Pushing my bitterness aside so it wouldn't consume me.

"I know."

"What happened?"

I take a step closer, less than a yard away from her, and I hold still, the water showing small ripples as I wait for her response to my movement. When she just blinks her lashes at me in anticipation, I open my mouth.

"I went into therapy."

"You did?" I nod.

"Mmhmm, I thought it was finally time to get rid of my demons. Go through some old pain. Figure some shit out."

"Why?" Her gaze is open and interested as I take a deep breath to answer her question.

"Because eleven months and fourteen days ago, something happened. Something that fucked up my life, and I knew I needed to fix it. But first, I had to fix myself."

Her eyes slightly widen, and she bites her lip, her hands suddenly frozen on top of the water.

"So, I did," I continue, ignoring her reaction. "I didn't drink for six months, upped my workout schedule, and I went to therapy. She helped me deal with the death of my dad and Logan, and helped me find a way to live with my mother, without anger."

"I don't know what to say. That's amazing, Hunter."

"Thanks, Charls." We stare at each other, smiling, the memories of our last time here rushing through my head. The warmth of her body against mine, her cheek resting on my shoulder. My arms wrapped around her back. *Our first kiss.*

She splatters water toward me with a soft giggle, as if she can read my mind. "Don't even think about it, Hansen."

"Think about what, Charls?" I mimic her move, splashing water in her face, and she lets out a playful squeal before our movements erupt, splashing as much water at each other as possible, letting out cries of laughter in between.

Finally, I leap forward, automatically making her turn her back toward me with a shriek, trying to get away as my arms circle her waist. My bare chest connects with her back, and my cheek rests against her hair as I hold her in a tight grip, our laughs slowly growing quiet. Feeling her skin against mine, I realize the mistake I made when my dick presses against the cheeks of her ass, eager for more. My lips part as I let out a deep breath against her ear while my heart rate speeds up. Not willing to let go, though scared to stay in the same position.

I can feel the resilience die down as I hold her, a flutter going through my stomach when I put my lips flush with her ear. Eleven months ago, I'd take my chance and make full use of the open window. But I'm adamant to not screw this up, and take my time to show her I'm in it for the long haul.

I can be patient.

"I'm dying to kiss you, but I won't. Not until you're ready."

She gasps for air at my words, then pushes out a deep breath.

"I'm going to count to three, and let go of you. Then you're going to get out, and get dressed again, okay?" I whisper.

She nods in agreement, and I dip my chin, pressing a lingering kiss on the crook of her neck. When my lips land on her skin, she sucks in another sharp breath, then holds it until I start counting.

"One. Two. Three." I let go of her warm body, then move around her to give her the privacy she needs to get out of the water. Frustrated, I close my eyes, blowing out a breath, but chuckle when she gets out of the water, muttering, "Always a tease. *Asshole.*"

"Don't tempt me, Charls." I laugh, shaking my head in surprise at her comment. I can feel her walls crumbling down more by the second, making me even more confident about me and her.

"No! Don't tempt *me*, you jackass!" The edge in her tone twists my attention to her, my jaw dropping at the sight in front of me. Her upper body is fully above the water, her tits staring back at me, perky and taunting as hell. Wet blonde hair covers up her nipples, but I can see the hard nubs peeking through her strands. She looks sinfully gorgeous, and all I want to do is take her face in my hands and pull her lips to mine. But the death glare in her green eyes holds me from moving a single muscle, and I realize my confidence was short-lived.

Shit.

63

Charlotte

I T'S WEIRD HOW MY emotions can go from full contentment to fuming within a heartbeat. But to be honest, it doesn't even surprise me. This is Hunter's biggest talent. Making me feel happy one second and completely incredulous the next.

"This is what you fucking do!" I fume, and his brown eyes fill with guilt. "You make me cross the line and then you push me away!"

"Do you want me to kiss you?" His lips spread in a grim line. "Because I fucking will!" He takes a few steps forward, enough to let the V of his hips appear from below the water. My breath falters, suddenly aware of the fact that I'm still naked.

"No! That's not the point!" I quickly turn around, stomping onto the cobblestone.

"Then what is the point?!"

I pick up a towel, covering myself up with it, then ignore him strolling closer, butt naked, with an attitude as if he's fully dressed. I hate him. I hate him and I hate even more how fucking good he looks with water dripping down his skin.

Cocky son of a bitch.

"The point is that you're an asshole."

He scoffs. "Gee, Charls. Original. Tell me something I don't know."

"Argh, you piss me off so much!"

"I know that!" He yanks the other towel from the ground, rubbing it over his wet hair, not even pretending to rush to cover up his goddamn junk.

"Then stop pissing me off!"

"I don't know how!" His motions stop, a pained expression hitting me like a ton of bricks as his voice softens. "Tell me why you're mad at me."

Grunting and growling, I fumble with the towel around my lady parts, trying to put my underwear back on. "You wanna know why I'm mad?" I shout. "I'm mad because my world turned pitch black, and you were gone! I'm mad because you stir up all these old feelings. I told you last year I was done! It was over! But here you are, confusing the fuck out of me. *Again!* You're like this old dog who never loses his tricks."

"Better be a fucking Bull Mastif then," he mumbles, pulling his boxers over his hips.

"Hunter!"

"I'm kidding! Sorry!" Our gazes stay locked, both filled with fire. My attention drops when he pulls his teeth between his lips, then whispers, "I fucking hate how I broke your heart."

"See, I don't believe you anymore." I point my finger at him. "*You* did that. Once upon a time, I'd trust you with my life. Now I don't trust you as far as I can throw you." I continue putting on the rest of my clothes, too angry to look at him.

"I know I did. But I'm going to try to fix it for the rest of my life."

"Why?!" I snap my gaze back up.

"Because I love you!"

For at least five seconds, my gaze travels up and down his haunted expression. Pebbles coat my skin, and I'm pretty sure it's not from the water. Disbelief has my heart stuttering as I shake my head, putting on my shoes.

"No. *No*. You don't get to tell me that! You don't say those words! You said them to her, but you refused to say them to me! You can't say them now like suddenly they mean something!"

"I never said them to her. I never denied it, but I never flat out told her I loved her either." He pulls his shirt over his head, then runs a hand through his dampened hair. "I couldn't. Because I didn't. I lo—" I cut him off before he can repeat it again.

"No. No, I don't want to hear it. It took me six months to function, Hunter. I'm finally alright. You can't fuck up my life again. I won't let you." I bravely let out the words, but sadness fogs my eyes, out of my control. My throat hurts from trying to hold back my rampaging emotions as I get up, pinching the bridge of my nose. *Good luck there.*

"Babe."

I lift up my gaze. "You weren't there." The worst week of my life, and he wasn't there for me. He was supposed to be my friend. "She died and I needed you. And you weren't there. Every single time you didn't answer your phone, I fell deeper and deeper into my sadness. You can't undo that."

"I know." The light goes out in his eyes, simmering with regret, but it all means jack shit right now.

"You missed the funeral."

"I know."

"She loved you, you know." Despite his asshole behavior, my mama loved him like a son. Sometimes it was frustrating, especially the moments I wanted to strangle him, but I couldn't blame her either.

"I know." Silence grows between us, then I catch movement in his lips. "I-"

"No," I interrupt. "I don't want to hear it." I don't want an explanation. I don't want an apology. I'm not ready for it.

"Okay. What do you want?"

"Take me home."

Hurt flashes in his hazel-brown eyes, but finally, he gives me a curt nod, then puts on the rest of his clothes.

The drive back into town is silent. Awkward. But at this point, I'm too tired to care. A few moments my thoughts drift to where my eyes well up, but I manage to keep the tears at bay, pushing them away with the anger still bubbling inside me.

I can't pretend he didn't break something between us, and frankly, I don't want to anymore.

A while later, he parks in my driveway. The house looks exactly the same as it did seven years ago. White with blue windows and rose bushes wrapped around the porch. A gnome that I broke playing in the yard when I was eight. It's home, but even though the exterior hasn't changed, the feeling I have looking at it has changed all the more. I know that when I walk over that threshold, emptiness will wait for me, and for the first time since Mama died, I don't want to go in.

But I know I have to.

I step out of the truck and catch Hunter doing the same before I can shut the door.

"Stay," I order.

He turns around, half his body still inside the truck. "Charls, I–"

"No, Hunter." I'm adamant about this. The last thing I need is him giving me even more to think about than I already have. "I meant what I said. I don't want to hear it. Maybe someday. But not now. Not today. I've had a very shitty week, and you keep pissing me off, and I just can't deal."

"Okay," he agrees, then sits back in his seat, closing the door. "What can I do?"

"Leave me alone." The expression that washes his face tells me that's the last thing he wants to do, but it's what I want. It's what I *need*. "Please."

I don't wait for his reply, but close the door, holding his gaze. Tormented eyes stare back at me through the window before his chest moves up, sucking in a deep breath. Never deviating his eyes from mine, he backs up his truck. I wait until he turns the vehicle back on the road, then drives off, and I finally let myself collapse.

My knees fall to the gray concrete, my tears slipping out one by one. The pain that's pulsing through my veins demolishes all the restraint I had, and for a few minutes, I just sit there, letting myself drown in my own sorrow, as if an unexpected rain cloud has broken above my head.

I wish it was all different. I wish I could forgive him and we could pick up where we left off, but even if I could, where would that put us? Back to being friends once a week? Where we'd catch up and he'd start dating some other Laurie? Or would we continue what we had before he moved to LA? In my head, neither is an option, because number one I'd never want to relive and the other isn't possible... because we aren't teenagers anymore. He might be the same old dog I accused him to be, only richer and famous, but I'm definitely not the same.

But this time he said I love you.

The thought jams into my head like it's not my own. I can hardly believe he actually said that those eight letters. I'd like to tell myself I misheard, that it was my imagination, but his haunted eyes seared through mine, selling me every word with an urgency I've been waiting for since the first day we've met. *He told me he loved me, goddammit.*

Fuck him, for knowing exactly what to say at the right moment.

Fuck him, for messing with my head again.

Fuck him, for finally doing it in the right way.

And fuck me for actually wanting to believe him.

Rubbing away the moisture from my jaw with the back of my hand, I blink the rest of my tears away when my eyes land on the little piece of plastic in the driveway. Still sniffling, I get up to take a few steps, then pick up the black credit card that sure as hell isn't mine. *But I know whose it is.*

It must've fallen out of his pocket when he opened the door and the good girl in me is already fishing for her phone from the back of her shorts to give him a call.

But when I see his name on my screen, I hesitate, the credit card in hand.

I'm not vindictive.

I'm really not.

But Hunter doesn't play fair, so why should I?

Besides, like I said, I'm not the same girl I was seven years ago.

64

HUNTER

"S O, I TAKE IT's going well?" Jensen doesn't even try to hide his laughter that's now echoing through the phone. My eyes are trained on the Candince Swanepoel poster on the wall, making a mental reminder that I need to give this room a makeover. Part of me feels nostalgic staying in my childhood bedroom, but the other part gets depressed being catapulted back in time.

"She hates me."

"Well, she does have a good reason."

"You're not helping." My legs are stretched out before me, my back pressed against the headboard.

"I know. But I'm having so much fun with this."

"Shut up." I bite my smile away. *Hockey dickhead.*

"So, what's the plan?" he questions when he's done cackling.

I rub a hand over my face. "I don't fucking know. Give her a few days to cool off and try again?" What else can I fucking do without her trying to rip my head off?

Jensen snorts, and I roll my eyes prematurely, knowing some kind of bullshit answer will come from his lips. "What are you, a fucking pussy? Come on, you're Hunter Hansen. You don't sit around and wait. Didn't you say she has a boyfriend?"

"Yeah."

"Can't give him too much time to swoop in and save the day."

Not gonna lie, that's definitely something I want to avoid. "What do you suggest?"

"Take what's yours."

"I'll only piss her off more."

Another snort. "Like that ever stopped you."

It didn't, but I now see how that was my mistake. I walked into her world like a damn hurricane multiple times, never giving her any time to adjust. The amount of hot and cold moments is a fucking disgrace. I keep saying she deserves better; well, pushing her before she's ready is part of that.

"I want to do it differently this time. You know, not screw up for once?"

"Oh, so the goal is to *not* screw up?" Sarcasm is dripping from his tone. "I wouldn't know how to do that because if I have to believe Rae Stafford says, I keep, and I quote, '*screwing shit up without even trying.*'"

And just like that, amusement flips from him to me. "PR girl giving you a hard time again?"

"You'd think I'm not even allowed to talk to women if I have to go off of her judgment."

I cough out a laugh. "You don't talk, Jensen. You balance on a fine line between talking and verbally cheating."

"I'm a flirt, what can I say?" he says in a playful tone, when a beep slips in my ear.

"I'm getting another call. Talk later." Without waiting for his reply, I switch the call, the screen lit up with my accountant's name.

"Hello."

"Good afternoon, Mr. Hansen. I got a call from the credit card company because, apparently, a large transaction was done last night. I want to verify with you this is correct." I detect a little worry in the old man's voice, spiking my own.

"What kind of transaction?" I realized last night my credit card was no longer in the pocket of my sweats, but I was too lazy to really search for it, figuring I'd have all day to do so. Now, I'm wondering if I should've blocked it right away.

"Fifty thousand dollars to the Braeden Animal Shelter." My eyes feel like they are about to roll from their sockets as he continues. "I checked the company details, and it's a non-profit organization in North Carolina."

At first, I'm shocked, barely registering what he's saying, but then it clicks.

"What organization was that again?"

"The Braeden Animal Shelter in North Carolina."

"Fifty thousand dollars?" I blurt. "Jesus. Is there a comment with the transaction?"

"Yes, sir. It says: Hopefully this will make those old dogs feel more comfortable."

A full laugh rumbles from the base of my chest, relief lifting the heavy feeling I've been carrying around since last night. *That little brat.*

"Fifty thousand dollars to the Braeden Animal Shelter, huh?"

"Yes sir. Is this correct?"

"Yeah, it's correct."

"Sir, are you sure I can approve the transaction?" the old man asks, still with a load of reluctance.

"Yes, it's fine. Thank you for calling." I hang up, contemplating how to react to this act of war from my girl. I want to be angry as fuck for spending fifty grand without telling me, but truth be told, I can't find an ounce of rage inside of me. If anything, she just gave me the answer that I've been looking for while it was me and my insomnia the entire night. She thinks she pissed me off, but all she did was show me that she still cares.

And that's all the motivation I need to not give up.

65

Charlotte

SITTING ON THE SWINGING bench on the front porch, I stare at the pink peonies placed on the table. With pursed lips and arms crossed in front of my chest, I keep flicking my gaze between the flowers and the eight books neatly tucked into a box with the spines up. They are all wrapped in craft paper, each of them showing a letter in the middle.

I am so sorry, it spells.

Asshole. Since when is he aiming to be all cute and shit?

I've been staring at it for ten minutes, contemplating whether to take the gifts or leave them as they are until I get the chance to shove them back in his face.

Finally, I decide to put the decision off until later and grab my laptop from the other side of the bench, then get up to take a seat on the screened porch out back instead. This way, any *unwanted* guests have to ring the doorbell first.

I'm grateful my mother left me taken care of. When she died, I had no clue how I was going to pay for the mortgage with my bartending job, and because I took care of my mother, I didn't look for a better job after graduation. But thankfully, her lawyer quickly informed me that she paid off our house when my grandfather died, had health insurance, so her illness didn't result in any debts, and also had some stocks that she had liquified the last time she got sick, making sure I could grieve and figure out life for the next few years without worrying about money after she died.

I still work at the bar two nights a week to have a reason to leave the house for anything other than groceries, but I spend most of my days reading and writing.

Or attempting to write. I've started numerous stories in the last year, but for some reason, I have a hard time finishing them.

Every time my mind comes up with a new story, I type away as if my life depends on it, before telling myself it's shit, and throw it all out. If I wrote on a typewriter, there would be wads of paper piling up around me.

"Dang it!" I exclaim, slamming my notebook shut when I delete my words for a second time today. Throwing the device on the chair next to me, I put my arms over each other like a grumpy kid. As expected, my mind wanders off to the person who makes it impossible to concentrate ever since he strolled back into town like he belongs here. He doesn't. *At least not anymore.*

Being so close to him yesterday fucked with my ability to sleep, because my mind and my heart keep fighting each other, driving me nuts. "Julie bought you flowers and books?"

I grab my heart as I jolt in my seat, then snap my head toward the door. Ben throws me a devastatingly sweet smile that would've melted my iced-out heart six months ago, but now it just irritates me as he closes the door behind him.

I never should've given him a key.

"What?" I ask, confused.

"The flowers?" His thumb points over his shoulder. "Out front?"

"Oh, right." *Shit.* "Yeah, Julie."

"That's sweet of her." He walks toward me, still wearing his navy-blue coaching outfit as he leans in, planting a kiss on my lips. There was a point in our relationship when I thought I felt butterflies. A tingling feeling when he kissed me. But now?

Nothing.

"Are you okay?" He gives me a pointed look as he takes my laptop and sets it on the table before sitting down.

"Can't seem to get on with writing today."

A big, calloused hand lands on my knee. "It's okay. You'll get over this, and you'll get your mojo back."

I know he means well, trying to support me, but him referring to *this* as something I'll get over instantly raises my anger. Like it's an inconvenience that I need to treat as a hurdle.

My hands start to itch, and I rub them over my black jeans while he lovingly brushes a strand of hair behind my ear, when really, I want to slap his hand out of my face, because in my head, they are the wrong hands.

Damn you, Hunter, for screwing with my head.

"Maybe," I mumble instead.

"How are you today?"

Keeping quiet for a while, I avoid his gaze that fixates on the side of my face, before I finally shrug my shoulders.

"Fine. I guess."

"It's okay to not be okay, Charlotte."

I can't help but snort at his yoga-like mantra.

What about contemplating if you should break up with your boyfriend because your ex, correction, *best friend*, is back in town? Is that also okay?

He brushes his fingers through my hair, and I close my eyes, wondering if we will be one of those couples who will get better out of this? If it will grow us stronger or tear us apart.

Wondering if I'd be as agitated as I am now if it was anyone else saying the same thing.

If anyone else brushed his fingers through my hair. I don't want to know the answer to that question.

"What did you do yesterday?" he follows up when I don't reply.

"Spent the day with a friend."

"Julie?"

"Actually, no," I confess.

He raises his eyebrows in question, and a feeling of guilt showers my body as I awkwardly look at him, quickly recalling my day with Hunter.

"So, I used to have a best friend..." I start with a cautious face.

"Other than Julie?" he asks, as I nod in response. "And she's back in town?"

"*He* is."

He frowns in surprise, then gives me a sweet smile that I wasn't expecting. "*You* had a guy best friend?"

"Yeah, his name is Hunter. We spent most of our senior year together."

"I've never heard you talk about him." His stance is open, and his face interested, making me a bit unsettled, not knowing how I even want him to respond.

"We kinda drifted when he moved to LA after graduation. He just moved back."

"That's nice. Can't wait to meet him."

"Right." I get up, needing some space, though I don't know why. "I'm going to take a shower."

"Alright, wanna have dinner tonight?"

"Actually, I think I'm gonna head to bed early, watch a movie."

He gives me a troubled look, filled with sympathy, pissing me off even more. He's the perfect boyfriend, supporting his girlfriend after a traumatic event, but I just want him to be angry, mad. I want him to scream with me, but then that's a lie, because really, I just want to be alone.

"Are you sure you are okay?" He gets up, closing the distance between us, rubbing his hands up and down my arms.

"I need a break." The words are blurted out before I can even process them.

Dark eyes look at me through thick black lashes. "From us?"

"From life. But yes, also from us."

The last few days have been confusing as fuck. I was already feeling like shit, and now Hunter being back in town is fucking with my head, with no way to fix it.

But I don't want Ben to fix it either. I want to wallow in my misery, with a bowl of ice cream, trying to figure out all the shit going on in my life. *I just want to be alone.*

"I know you're going through a rough time..."

"It's not just that. It's everything. I just need time. *Alone.*"

I can see he wants to argue with me, but I push out the air from my lungs when he nods.

"Okay." His forehead rests against mine, then he presses a chaste kiss to my lips. I pray for a tingle, a curl of my toes. *Anything.* But all I get is more doubt when I feel nothing.

"Can I call you?"

"Yeah."

He stares down at me, his hand softly going through my hair affectionately, the thing I loved about him. We met at the bar, where he came in with his co-worker from one of the local elementary schools a few towns farther away. He's the baseball coach of the high school, and he looked damn sexy walking in with his black sweats and black t-shirt. His black hair was a little longer on top of his head, and messy from a day on the field.

He instantly caught my eye.

The next day, he took me on a date, and I loved how he kept running his hand through my hair, in the most endearing way, actually asking him to keep going.

Now I just want him to stop.

To stop touching me.

To stop talking to me.

To leave me alone.

"I'll call you tomorrow." He presses a kiss against my forehead, his hand resting on my neck. "Get some rest."

"I will." A strained smile lifts the corners of my lips before he disappears into the house. I keep my ears perked, and when I finally hear the sound of an engine, I let out a relieved breath, dropping myself back on the couch with an uneasy feeling flipping my stomach.

What the fuck are you doing, Charlotte?

66

Charlotte

I MUST'VE FALLEN ASLEEP, because an hour later, I blink, needing a moment to readjust to my surroundings. Yawning, I stretch my arms above my head, then rapidly drop them when I hear something fall on the front porch. I get up with a little reluctance, moving to the front of the house. The sounds of metal twisting over metal create a frown on my forehead, until I glance through the peephole of the front door.

"What the fuck?" I whisper.

Hunter is standing on some utility steps, looking mighty fine in his jeans that ride low, and a white shirt that shows off his tattoos. His hair is covered with his signature snapback, but it's the muscles in his back that are begging to be touched as he lifts his arms to change the lightbulb of my built-in lantern lamp hanging above the porch steps.

"What are you doing?" I ask when I open the door.

That boyish grin flashes over his shoulder, making something flutter inside me. "Fixing your lamp. I saw it flickering yesterday."

"Why?" My lashes lower in suspicion.

"Because it needed to be fixed?" he says with a know-it-all voice before he continues with his task on hand, since apparently, he's now adding handyman to his resume. "And I wanted to see you," he states, as if it's the most normal thing to say.

"I thought we agreed you'd call first?" I scowl.

"I did."

I fish my phone from my back pocket.

Missed call: Hunter.

Shit.

"I thought you were ignoring me."

"I did say I wanted to be left alone." Is it possible to love and hate someone's annoying traits at the same time? I want to strangle him for not listening, but I would be lying if I didn't appreciate his stubbornness a teeny tiny little bit.

"True," he agrees, closing the lantern again before screwing it shut, "but I also know you're not the girl who likes to be alone when she's sad. Even though I'm the one who's responsible for it in the first place."

"So, you came and forced me to talk to you?" I cock my eyebrow, doing my best to keep a straight face when I feel the corner of my mouth wanting to curl up.

Stubborn fucking asshole.

"Of course. But turns out, you weren't ignoring me after all."

"No, I wasn't." I take the few steps to my swinging bench, letting out another yawn.

"Were you sleeping?" I don't miss the apprehensive twitch of his brow while he throws his screwdriver back into his toolbox.

"Didn't really expect you to own a toolbox," I tell him, rocking the bench up and down with one foot on the ground.

"Found it in the shed. I guess it's my dad's."

I study him intently, my arms crossed in front of my chest with my lips pressed together to hold back the smile that's lingering like a balloon that's waiting to pop.

How is it that I send my boyfriend away, wanting to be alone, yet my heart is dancing for joy when Hunter is crossing every boundary there is? Showing up unannounced for the third time in forty-eight hours, doing sweet things like fixing my porch light, relentlessly letting me relive old memories I assumed were tucked safely in a vault, never to be opened again.

"Thank you." I gesture above his head. "For fixing the light."

"Anytime, babe." Slowly, but with deliberate steps, that for some fucked-up reason take my breath away, he closes the distance before lowering himself next to me. There's at least a foot between us, but he's still close enough to let his scent level in my nose, and like a junkie, I breathe in deeply.

"Where's the dog?"

My lips frown. "What dog?"

"The dog you picked up from the animal shelter?" I pull my lip between my teeth when he pauses. "I figured for a fifty-grand donation, you at least got yourself that dog you finally wanted."

I notice him grinning from the corner of my eye, but I keep a straight face for as long as I can. "Couldn't find one that clicked with me."

"Hmm, shame."

"I know." I swallow back the giggle, then amusement slips through my teeth. "You want it back?" Putting words into action, I pull the black plastic out of my jeans, then hold it out to him.

"Nah, keep it." *I'm sorry, what?* "Spend it all, for all I care. It's all yours once we get married anyway."

"We're not getting married," I huff, even though my stomach flutters, working against me.

He ignores my reply and instead pulls a velvet bag from the front of his jeans. It's turquoise, with black letters embedded that say Tiffany & Co. *Oh, boy.*

My eyes grow big, my lips parting in shock. "You're not fucking proposing, Hunter Hansen!"

He hoots out a laugh, clearly aiming for that response. "Don't worry, I'm saving that for when you're not mad at me."

"That might take a while," I mutter, as I watch how he drops a small necklace in my hand. I stare at the silver pendant in awe, my throat closing a little. It's a small heart, with stitches cut through the middle, the edges rough, reminding me of my own. "Oh my god," I whisper.

"I bought it with my first paycheck."

I collide my gaze with his. "But that was years ago."

He nods, rolling his lips together. "I wanted you to know my heart was yours, beat up and crushed. But I never found the right time to give it to you."

I drop my gaze back to the metal in my hand, wondering what changed.

"I'm not going anywhere," he says, as if he can read my mind. "I just want to be part of your life. And if that means I have to be the best friend, I will be the best friend. If you're happy with Ben, I'm fine with that."

I pull a face. "No, you're not."

"Not one fucking bit." He adamantly shakes his head, and I laugh. "But you're in charge."

My chest rises up as I inhale deeply, then toss him a small smile.

"Thank you. It's beautiful." I put it on my neck, then fumble with the pendant between my fingers.

I'm not sure how to feel about his explanation, but having a piece of him hang around my neck swells my heart more than it should.

"What has you sleeping in the middle of the day, Charls?" The look on his face is genuine, with a glint of worry in his eyes as he drops his calloused hand on my thigh. "You okay?" The heat of his palm burns through the fabric, sirening me to tell the truth. My cheeks curl, loving how he shows me he cares, before my face falls when I realize Ben did the same thing an hour ago. *You know? The man who's supposed to be my boyfriend?*

"Hey." He squeezes my knee, narrowing his eyes at me. "Talk to me."

"I'm fine. Really. Just tired."

He gives me a knowing look, telling me he doesn't buy my bullshit, then gives me a smile, indicating he'll let it slide for now, and I give him a thankful look. "Let's get out of here."

"Go where?"

"The bowling alley." He smirks.

"It's two p.m. on a Tuesday?"

"So? Who says you can't go bowling on a Tuesday? Let's go."

When he first said he wanted to go to the bowling alley, I rolled my eyes at him, knowing he's using this strategic trip down memory lane to get back in my good graces. But as much as his tactics annoy me a little, they're also working.

They remind me of the fact that my happiest days were with him, and I'm in desperate need of some happy days with last week's event still hanging above my head like a thundercloud.

We walk into an almost empty bowling center, with only a kids' party on one of the first lanes, and I glance around, following Hunter toward the counter.

"Hi." He volleys the blonde girl behind the front desk one of those panty-dropping grins, and her jaw falls to the surface, looking at him with wide eyes. "Can I get a lane for two?"

"Oh my god. You're Hunter Hansen. I heard you're the new boss."

Wait, what?

"Yeah." He carefully glances at me while I stare at the situation unfolding in front of me. "But can we keep that quiet?" He winks at her, and instantly my eyes roll to the back of my head.

She lets out a muffled shriek, placing her hand in front of her mouth.

"Of course, I understand," she says, as she taps stuff on the register. "That will be twenty bucks for an hour."

Hunter grabs a hundred-dollar bill out of his pocket, leaning in as he hands it to her.

"Thank you for your silence." He looks at her name tag. "*Kirsty*."

She blushes, letting out a giggle.

"You're welcome. You've got lane ten, away from the kids' party."

"You're the best, Kirsty." Hunter taps the counter, then makes his way over to lane ten on the other side of the bowling center. I give the star-struck girl a knowing smile before I follow Hunter, who lowers the snapback on his head to hide his face a little.

"What's that about you being the new boss?" I frown, trotting behind him.

"Nothing. I made some investments. This was one of them."

"Wait, so did you invest in this place, or did you buy it?"

"Isn't that the same thing?" he bellows over his shoulder.

"That depends entirely on the amount of money you *invested*." His silence is answer enough. "Oh my god, Hunter! Did you buy this place?"

"Maybe?"

"Why?"

"The owner wanted to sell. I bought it." He shrugs, as if he just bought a loaf of bread instead of a bowling alley. One that is part of half the youth in Braeden. If not more.

B. LUSTIG

"So that's what I'll be dealing with when I take you back?" I joke. "Bowling night with the boss? Women dying for your attention?"

He abruptly turns around, making me crash into his chest, and I look up at him with wide eyes.

His eyes darken as I realize my mistake, and he grabs the side of my belly in a possessive way, his gaze moving back and forth over my face.

"*When* you take me back, Charls?" *Poor choice of words, Charlotte.*

"As friends!" I blurt, almost choking over my own words. "As friends!" I push him out of my space, walking past him as my heart pounds in my chest like a sledgehammer.

Shit.

Pretending I didn't just make the stupidest comment ever, I change my shoes, ignoring the smug grin on his face before getting up to set up the lane.

When I'm done, I turn around, our gazes instantly locking.

"You're up, famous boy."

He stands with a troubled look on his face, closing the distance between us once more. He crowds my space again, but this time, it's not in an intimidating way, as the features in his face soften when he's right in front of me.

"No," he says from under the rim of his hat, "I'll make sure you won't have to deal with that *when* you take me back."

I clear my throat, no clue how to react to that.

But he doesn't wait as he moves past me, grabbing a bowling ball out of the ball rack, then he gives me a smug grin before throwing it down the lane.

Strike.

He quietly dances, moonwalking down the lane, and I let out a laugh. He wiggles his eyebrows as he walks back while I move to the ball rack to choose a ball for myself.

"You want to make this more interesting?"

"What? You gonna give me a date so you can bully him away?" I give him a sweet smile, fluttering my lashes at him.

"You wanna call your boyfriend?" he challenges, and my face turns sour.

"No," I reply, taking a step forward to throw the ball down the lane in a perfect line.

Strike.

"Yes!" I jump up, clapping like a seal, then dance back to the bench, as Hunter starts a slow clap.

"Well done, Charls. Have you been practicing without me?"

"Maybe."

I try to walk past him, but he snatches my wrist, quickly tugging me onto his lap.

"Tell me about your boyfriend."

My first reaction should be to get off, telling him he needs to stop blurring the lines. But the scent of his cologne intoxicates me, keeping me in place as he starts to brush my back with the tips of his fingers, and a shiver runs down my spine.

"What do you wanna know?" I frown, as my wrist is still wrapped in his warm palm, burning me with the scorching feeling it leaves.

"Everything."

I sigh, enjoying his hands on my body, cataloging every inch he touches. "His name is Ben. He's twenty-six years old, and a baseball coach in Kallhaven. We met at the Nomad. He has black hair and blue eyes."

"Not that. Fuck that shit. I want to know why you *love* him."

Surprised, I look at him, keeping quiet because I don't know what to say.

"I-I-I don't know," I finally confess when his hand reaches up, taking a hold of my chin.

I can see his Adam's apple bobbing in his throat, as if he's swallowing his desires away, and we keep our eyes locked for God knows how long until my buzzing phone snaps us out of it.

Clearing my throat, I grab my phone out of my back pocket, closing my eyes for a second when I read the name on the screen before I answer it, covering Hunter's mouth with my hand.

Great timing.

"Hey, Ben," I say, keeping my eyes locked with Hunter, softly growling.

"I know you wanted space, but I just wanted to make sure you're okay?" Ben's friendly voice asks.

"Yeah, I'm okay."

"You're going to call it an early night?"

"Yeah." I nod. "I'm just going to watch some movies for the rest of the day, order some takeout, and go to bed early." Hunter's eyebrows raise at my lies, and I'm scolding myself for letting them leave my mouth so easily.

The line goes silent until I hear Ben let out a troubled sigh.

"You don't have to do this alone, you know? We're in this together."

His tone is annoyed, and I clench my jaw.

"I know," I say through gritted teeth, "but I want to be alone."

"Okay," he says quietly. "I'll call you tomorrow then."

"Alright, bye." I hang up, pushing it back into my pocket, then lock my eyes with Hunter's again. "Don't judge."

He stares up at me, brushing his nose against mine.

"I won't. You want me to take you home, though?"

I think about it. Going home is the safe choice. It's what I should do and what I told Ben I'd be doing. But the longer I'm in Hunter's presence, the more vocal my heart seems to be.

"No. I want to stay here."

67

Charlotte

"SO YOU AND BEN are on a break?" Julie's arm is curled around mine as we trot down the street. The fall has barely set in, and a soft breeze rustles through the trees that are standing firm and opulent on Main Street as we head toward the local bookstore.

"Well, I don't know about that. But I did tell him that I needed a break."

"And then you went bowling with Hunter." There's a bit of ridicule in her voice.

"Yes. Oh my god, I'm such a harlot." Actually saying it out loud, I realize how ridiculous it sounds. But the weird thing is, even though I should feel embarrassed about hanging out with a man that isn't my boyfriend, I don't. It feels completely normal to go bowling on a midweek afternoon with Hunter Hansen. Which is a clear red flag that I'm in some serious danger. *SOS.*

"Did you sleep with Hunter?"

"What? No!" I hold back the fact that my vagina was practically begging me to cross that line too, but we kept it all PG-13.

"Kiss him?"

"No." I wish. *Shut up, Charlotte.*

"Then you're not a harlot," she states matter-of-factly, something I'll happily agree with. I was just reliving old memories with an old friend, right? Nothing bad about that.

"Still can't believe you spent 50k on his credit card."

I lick my lower lip with mischief etching through. "I thought he was gonna cancel it and yell at me." I was planning on it. I wanted to fight with him, just to have a reason to shout in his face about all things petty. Is it childish? For sure. Do I care? Nope. I've been the good girl for years, so I just wanted to be the bad girl for once. Spending fifty thousand on Hunter's credit card sounds like my kinda bad way more than pole dancing in the strip club two towns over.

"*Puh-lease*," Julie scoffs, "at this point, you can buy a million-dollar mansion and he'd still be worshiping the ground you walk on. Remember, he's here for *you*."

"We're friends, Jules." I wonder how long I can keep saying that until I start growing two heads. One that tells the truth, and one that is all too good at lying.

"He's not here to be your friend, Charlie."

I shake my head, our hips moving in unison with each step, the bookstore in sight.

"Change of subject. Are you coming for fun, or do you actually want to buy something?"

"I want to buy that book about Ikigai."

I give my best friend a side-eye. "What is that, Thai food? A Chinese game? A new dating method from Europe?"

A grunt rolls over her taut lips. "I wish. Find me some Italian men."

"You like blond men."

"Not true."

"All your boyfriends have had blond hair," I deadpan, while her eyes move to the sky to think it over.

"That's not—*damnit*," she mutters when she realizes I'm right. "Anyway, it's your reason to get out of bed."

"Cryptic, but okay."

"It's the one thing you're good at, have passion for, and you can actually make money with. It's Japanese. We should all find it to truly be happy in what we do."

"Sounds complex." I just want to figure out what the hell I'm going to do with the weird feelings that are bubbling up ever since a certain person strolled his ass back into town.

Julie shakes her head with her eyes rolling to her lashes, as she opens the door of the bookstore, and the bell rings above our heads. "It's not, I'll show y—"

"Hunt," I cut her off, holding still in the doorpost before I take the final steps inside with a frown creased above my green eyes. He's standing behind the register in the back of the small store, looking like he belongs there. He doesn't belong there. If his broad, bulky, and sexy sculpted body isn't a clear indication he prefers a gym over a bookstore, his awkward stance is a dead giveaway. "What are you doing here?"

"Oh, shit." A guilt-ridden expression mars his face, only fueling my confusion. "Err, helping out?"

"Helping out with what?" I plant my hands on my sides, taking him in from head to toe. His chiseled muscles are taunting me like ice cream on a hot summer day, the way his t-shirt hugs the rest of his torso, and those playful hazel eyes that stare back at me from underneath his backward snapback pull me in. The entire sight boils my blood in a way that literally burns my center alive. *Why does he have to be so hot?*

He quickly roams around the room, then grabs the two books that are sitting on the counter. "Errr, sorting." He nods, as if pleased with this bullshit explanation. "Jessa received some heavy inventory, so I figured I'd give her a hand."

"A hand?"

"Uh-huh."

I'm about to call him out on his bullshit, when the sound of the toilet flushing in the back catches my attention, and his lashes lower. He pulls his lip between his teeth, seductive as hell, though he isn't even trying, and I lift my eyebrows in question.

"We have to re-do those toilets, man." Jason walks out the back, as if he's done it a hundred times. "They look like the founding fathers of Braeden still drop number twos in there." His gaze moves up, eyes wide like Bambi in the fucking headlights.

"Julie. Charlotte. Hi," he says, sharing a little uncomfortable glance with Hunter.

"Okay..." Julie throws both men suspicious eyes, her finger up accusingly. "It's weird that you two are standing in a bookstore."

"What the hell?"

"Here are the books, sir. All up to date and ready for your accountant."

I blink, until suddenly, it hits me. "Oh my god. You bought the bookshop?!"

A sheepish grin curls his mouth. "May—"

"Oh, look at the time!" Jason cuts him off, pulling him away from the counter. "Sorry, man, we got that call you can't get out of, remember?"

They brush past us, suddenly in a hurry, as if their pants are on fire, and Julie and I keep our eyes trained on them, twisting our bodies simultaneously with their movement.

"Yeah, the call." Hunter points to Jason, then the door, then throws me another grin that's filled with the lies that are burning down their ankles.

"Sorry, girls, nice to see you! Talk soon!" Confused, I let them leave, watching them dart over the cobblestone until they are out of sight. Julie and I exchange a look, then I turn around to Jessa.

My frown is peering into her innocent baby browns, a little lamb unaware of anything that conjured my puzzled expression. "What?"

"Jessa, did Hunter buy the bookshop?"

"Yes." *What the hell?*

"Why?"

The teenager shrugs. "Mrs. Henley wanted to sell and retire in Florida. Apparently, Hunter made her promise a few years ago that she'd call him if she ever wanted to sell. So she did."

Julie takes a step forward. "Wait, when did she sell it?"

"About six months ago?" Her expression lights up. "Hunter made me manager since I'm taking a leap year."

First the bowling alley, and now the bookstore? That makes no sense, considering he only touches a book to buy me one...

With lashes high, I gently turn my head to Julie, whose confusion is replaced by a smug grin. "I guess *fighter boy* is planting his roots in your garden."

68

HUNTER

I GLANCE AT MY watch, then glance at Jason as we sit around the bonfire at the creek. The sun is setting, and I stare into the dancing flames while I listen to the crackling sound of the fire.

"Are you sure she's coming?"

"Relax, man. Julie said she'll make it happen. I'm sure they'll be here any minute now."

The last few days, I left her alone, hanging out with Jason for a bit. Which was almost impossible when she walked into the bookstore, looking all gorgeous and unbothered like she did in high school. She looked a little less tired than the days before and her gorgeous green eyes sparkled with enough mischief to light me up from the inside out. It was fucking hard to not text her or drive to her house later that night, but the last thing I want is to spook her again. The fact that she's letting me get as close as I did is motivation enough to not rush my desire to claim her. But I can feel the truth. I'm still under her skin, like a tattoo, unable to get rid of. Just like she's on mine.

When I hear a car approaching, I snap my head up, noticing Julie's red Jeep park next to my truck. I straighten my back, watching Charlotte give her best friend an accusing glare before her eyes roll back and a smile slips through as she exits the car.

"Looking for a loophole to get me out here, Hansen?"

"It was his idea, I swear." I point at Jason, then lift my hands in a placating gesture. "But you don't hear me complaining."

I get up, smirking, as she walks toward me, and I wrap my arms around her, burying my nose in her hair. Breathing her in, my heart instantly calms down, because all is well in the world when she's with me.

"Hey."

"Hey."

"I've missed you," I confess, pressing a kiss on her forehead.

"I missed you too," she whispers with her gaze low and a little flushed, looking up at me through her lashes. A fuzzy feeling forms inside of me as I throw my fist in the air in my mind, considering that a win.

Jason plucks another beer for me and him from the cooler he brought, then grabs two red cups to make rum and Cokes for the girls.

"God, I feel like we're back in high school again," Julie says, taking the cup from his hand. We all take a seat on the logs around the fire, drinks in hand. It's eerie to think how much time has passed, how much has happened, yet when I look at Charlotte, I feel exactly the same.

She sits down next to me, while Julie takes the seat next to her, placing the girls in the middle, and Jason on the far end of the log. The sun is about to set, the crickets are starting up their evening concert, and I'm seriously wondering when was the last time I felt as content as I do now.

"Sometimes I wish we still were," I mutter, taking a pull from my beer.

"What?" Jason yelps. "Are you crazy? You'd rather be broke and insecure again?"

"When is Hunter ever insecure?" Charlotte turns her head to Jason with an incredulous look.

"When it comes to you," he counters, and I close my eyes in annoyance as the girls giggle beside me.

"Way to set the mood, Jay." I raise my beer at him with a slight glare.

"Oh, whatever. It's not like it's a big secret between the four of us." He rolls his eyes, and I can hear Julie chuckle at his words. "Let's play a game! Never Have I Ever! I'll start."

Jason's eyes glance over at all of us as the corner of his mouth curls into a grin.

"Never have I ever—gotten a tattoo."

We all take a sip of our drinks, and my eyes roll out of my sockets, realizing what this means.

"Wait, what? You got a tattoo?" My eyes peer at Charlotte as she presses her lips into a flat line, then closes her eyes and nods.

"What!" I exclaim. "Where?" I remember every inch of her body, and my dick twitches in longing to have a fresh look now that apparently her body has changed with something I'm not aware of.

She lifts her shirt up with a strained expression, and I read the lines on the side of her belly that make me gasp for air: *Love is enough*.

"When did you get this?"

"Six months ago," Julie blurts, taking another sip from her drink.

Charlotte looks away, and I drag my hand over my face as guilt washes over me. It's a sentence that has haunted me ever since she left me on that sidewalk almost a year ago. *"For me, love is enough."*

Her eyes lock with mine, a serious look swirling there, and I keep a straight face as the tension rises between us. It steals the air from my lungs, and I lift the bottle to my lips again to calm my pounding heart.

"Okay," Julie muses, to snap us out of it. "Your turn, Hunt."

I purse my lips, acknowledging Julie's grim expression, then look up at the sky to think of a question to lighten the mood.

"Never have I ever—used a fake name." Everyone but Charlotte takes another drink, and Julie turns her head to Charlotte incredulously.

"Come on, Charlie. You've never used a fake name? Not even with a guy at a bar?"

"I don't see why?"

"Because it's fun." Julie blinks.

"Because it's convenient at times," Jason chimes in.

"How is that convenient?" Charlotte rolls her eyes.

"Because you don't want to get abused by groupies," I add, taking another pull from my drink.

"Arrogant much, Hansen?" Julie wrinkles her nose at me.

"He was born like this," Charlotte counters, giving me a side glance, and I roughly grab her neck, my eyes narrowing while I look at her.

"Don't make me show you just how arrogant I can be."

"I already know." She licks her lips with a daring glare that has me growling at her through gritted teeth, a small smile hiding in the corner of my mouth. Fuck, she makes it so hard to take it slow if she's going to keep tempting me with those *fuck-me eyes.*

"Oh God, get a room, you two." Julie glares. "Charlie, you're up."

Charls's eyes dart away, and I let go of her again.

"Never have I ever—peed in the shower." Jason and I both take a sip, making the girls cry out.

"Eeew, you guys are disgusting," Charlotte bellows.

"What? Why? It literally washes away." I chuckle, throwing my hands up in question.

"You're such typical guys," Julie quips.

"Well, thank fuck, or you'd rather me wear a dress?" Jason gives Julie a mocking look, grinning.

"I accept you as you are." She jokingly shrugs, and we all start laughing. "Okay! My turn! Never have I ever—lied to someone in this group." She gives us all a smug grin, moving her head back and forth between all three of us, as I take another pull to answer her question.

"What?" I howl. "I'm really the only one?"

They all hum in agreement, and I roll my eyes at them.

"Whatever. Jason, you're up."

"Never have I ever—fallen in love at first sight."

Jason and I both take a sip, and Julie snaps her head from left to right.

"I know why you are drinking." She points an accusing finger past Charlotte's flushed cheeks, then flips it to Jason. "But who are you talking about?" We all stare at him, wondering who he's talking about.

"No one, never mind," he mumbles, then gives me a pleading look to keep the game going. I shoot him a questioning look before continuing the game when he slightly shakes his head.

"Never have I ever—gone skinny dipping." Charlotte's head slowly turns my way, a scowl on her face. "Drink up, Charls." I chuckle, taking a drink.

"Asshole," she mouths, glaring.

"Wait, *you* went skinny dipping? When was this?" A confused look appears on Julie's face. "Like, in high school?"

"Okay, next question!" Charlotte calls out. "My turn! Never have I ever—kissed a celebrity."

Everyone but Julie takes a drink, and Jason wiggles his eyebrows at her. "You know, I'm sorta a celebrity now. Being Hunter's agent and all."

She playfully pushes his face away when he leans in. "I dated your brother, you fool."

"I hate my brother and he hates me."

"Which will only become worse if he finds out you're trying to kiss his ex-girlfriend."

"I don't care." The expression he's tossing her confuses even me, because is he serious? I know they've been friends for years, Jason being there for her when Jackass Jacob broke her heart again, but the look sprouting from his blue eyes right now has me wondering if it's anything more than that.

"Oh, come on!" Jason's playfulness slides into his features again, lips puckered. "Just a little kissy kissy?"

"Are you crazy? I have no clue where your lips have been!"

"I know where they haven't been." He lowers his voice, a flirtatious look on his face that makes Charlotte and me laugh out loud.

"Oh, no. We are not going to do that flirty talk again like these two." She gets up, walking to the log on the other side of the fire, demonstratively crossing her arms in front of her chest.

"Wait, what?" Charlotte says at the same time I blurt, "Again?!"

"You know I can still grab you over there, right?" Jason deadpans, with an amused spark in his eyes.

"Whatever. Never have I ever—had sex in a public place," Julie blurts, ignoring Jason's lame attempts to flirt with her, and our incredulous, narrowed gazes. Brushing it all off with a small laugh, Charlotte and I exchange a conspiring look before taking a sip from our drinks. After that night on the tailgate of my truck, I have never had sex with a girl outdoors again, not wanting to taint one of my best memories by blurring it with other girls.

"Have you never, Jules?" Jason questions in surprise.

"Have you?" she blurts in a harsh tone.

"Nah. But I'd like to. Wanna change that?" The mocking look on his face makes me silently chuckle, while Charlotte watches them with a smirk on her pretty face.

"No," Julie says, a scowl in place.

"Fine."

"Is this what we sound like?" I point my finger at Charlotte, and I instantly regret the question when they both bellow in sync.

"Yes!"

"Right," I mumble, with Charlotte giggling beside me, and I give her a soft push.

"Okay, my turn. Never have I ever—kissed my best friend," Jason calls out, and my heart stops for a beat.

"I'll smack those shady grins off your faces if y'all don't drink real quick," Julie says with a reprimanding finger in the air toward Charlotte and me. We both take a drink as we feel the tension closing in on us.

"Good," Julie says, then gives me a *do-something* look, and I glare at her in response. Looking up at the sky, I think of a question I'd want to know the answer to. I know one, although asking it feels as much as looking for an answer as confessing my own shit. I'm ready for it, but I'm still unsure about her.

When I finally decide to go for it, I glance at Julie, who's giving me a wink of encouragement before I open my mouth.

"Never have I ever—been in a relationship with the wrong person." I quickly take a pull from my beer, avoiding Charlotte's shocked gaze burning through my skin. Locking my eyes with Julie, she gives me a smug grin, then points her attention to Jason.

"Jay, can you help me with my Jeep? I heard something rattle on the way over here."

"I don't know shit about cars, Jules." He gives her an incredulous look.

"You can look anyway," she says through gritted teeth, her eyes glaring at him as she softly points her chin at me.

"Oh, right." He jumps up, giving me a wink, then follows Julie back to the cars.

"Yeah, real subtle," Charlotte yells at their backs, and I let out a laugh, throwing my arm over her shoulder. My hand starts to rub her arm, feeling the goosebumps under my palm.

"Are you cold?" Not waiting for her answer, I grab the hem of my hoodie, pulling it over my head. "Arms up."

She puts her red cup on the ground between her legs, then brings her arms up so I can help her put the hoodie on while I place one of my legs over the log so that I have a leg on either side of hers. I smile when her gorgeous head pops into the hood with a sweet look.

"Better?"

She nods in agreement, and I wrap my arm around her neck. "Come here."

Tugging her back against my chest, she mimics my stance, bringing one leg over the log so that she can settle against my body. I wrap my arms around her waist, pulling her closer, pressing a kiss on her hair.

She lets out a long, content sigh, placing her warm hands over mine, resting her head against my chest.

"You know at some point you have to tell me about whatever is going on with Ben, right?"

"What do you mean?"

"I know there's something you're not telling me. Something that's making you lie to him. You don't lie, Charls," I point out.

"Yeah." She pushes out a breath, not even denying it. "I know. You know at some point you have to tell me what happened with Laurie?"

That's easier than she might think.

"Nothing to tell. We started dating for publicity, and before I knew it, we became something bigger than that, which never should've happened. *I* should've never allowed it to be. It was a bullshit relationship that I stayed in because I thought it was expected of me. I never loved her, and when I realized that, I ended it."

"That simple, huh?"

There's skepticism in her voice, and I can't blame her. But it's the truth. I didn't see it at first, but my eyes are wide open now.

"That simple, babe. I can never put anyone before you. And I'm sorry I gave you the feeling that I did."

I can feel her chest moving up and down calmly, our hearts beating simultaneously, like they're supposed to.

"It's okay. You're an asshole." She turns her head toward me with a beaming grin on her face. God, I missed that vibrant look in her eyes. "But I forgive you."

Holy shit. Every muscle in my body freezes for a second, before my heart continues to beat and I blow out a pent up breath that feels like it was stuck for years. *She forgives me.* It's more than I deserve and tempting as hell to push my lips against hers, but I manage to resist the urge.

"Is that so?" I tickle her side, and she lets out a shriek.

"Stop that!" She laughs, and it's music to my ears. "Asshole." I can't believe I almost lost this. I almost lost *her.* She settles back into my chest, and we stay like that for a while until I bring my lips flush with her ears.

"Do you know how hard it is for me to not kiss you?"

She gasps for air, letting out a troubled moan.

"Hunt," she huffs, and I'm not sure if she's begging me to cross the line or pleading with me to stop. "Stop flirting with me." Her voice is uncertain and needy at the same time.

"I don't think you really want me though, Charls," I whisper, thinking back to the last time I had her wrapped in my arms at a bonfire.

"Doesn't matter what I want."

My hand grabs her chin, softly forcing her to look at me. The world around us goes silent as we look into each other's eyes, our lips almost touching.

"What you want is all that matters, Charlotte Roux."

I'm tempted to close the distance between us, pressing my lips against hers, and the asshole in me is screaming at me to just do it. But I know why she's still hesitant. I know she still has that loose end to let go of, and I can't push her into that. It needs to be her.

"I don't know, Hunter. The world has felt foggy lately, except for the moments I'm with you. But I-I—I just don't know. It shouldn't be this way." The tone of her voice is sad, and I feel my heart crack a little listening to it. Hating that I'm the variable in this situation.

"Yo, fuckers!" I hear Jason shout behind us. "Let's go hang out at the bar. I'm getting eaten by mosquitos over here."

Realizing the moment is over, I take a deep breath before pushing it out, squeezing her tighter, pressing a kiss on her cheek, then I rest my forehead against the back of her head.

"Let me make one thing clear, babe. I'm here to stay. I know I said I want you to be happy, and I'll be your friend for as long as you aren't ready to give me any more than that. But I'm not here to be your friend. I'm a persistent asshole, and I'm going to keep trying until I gain your trust again and you give me what I want. Because I want to give you everything. You're all I see." I pause, pulling my arms tighter around her torso. "I *need* you," I disclose, then give her a slight push to get up.

"Trust me," she says when she's on her feet, looking at me with those piercing eyes. "I know."

69

Charlotte

"I HAVE A CONFESSION to make," Hunter says when we approach the ice cream shop. My eyebrows knit together, worry swirling in my stomach until I see the mischief in his gaze.

"Okay..."

"It's mine." He comes to a halt in front of the shop, his back toward the building, his front fixed on me.

"What do you mean?"

He throws his thumb over his shoulder. "It's mine."

I blink, glancing inside where Moira is placing a few containers of fresh ice cream into the cooled display. At first, I'm not following, but when our gazes collide again, my lips slowly but surely form a big 'O'.

"You bought the ice cream shop?" He nods, and I wonder why I'm still surprised. Not sure what his tactic is, but he is clearly on a mission to buy half the town. "What else did you buy?"

"The Burger Shack."

The Bookstore, the Burger Shack, the bowling alley, the ice cream shop...

"Are you kidding me?" I gasp when it hits me that it's all the places we used to come together. "Why?"

He steps into my space, grabbing my hips as he jerks me against his chest. His lips come awfully close as he peers down at me, my heart purring in delight.

"I didn't know how hard you were going to make it for me. But I knew you'd never leave this place. So, I set down my roots by buying property all over town. This way, you had no choice but to talk to me at some point."

"What about your career? The fights?"

He shrugs. "I'm not going back to LA. If they want to fight, I'll do it right here. I'll train here in North Carolina. I'm not leaving you again, Charlotte."

Forget my heart purring. It's screaming at me, as if she's at a Taylor Swift concert.

"You're crazy," I muse, breathing the same air as we look into each other's eyes.

"No, baby." His breath feathers over my lips, the heat of his body messing with my brain. *"I'm in love."* My lips part, and for just a split second, I think he's going to throw all the hesitation away and kiss me, but instead, he grips my neck, moves his lips to my forehead, pressing a scorching kiss on my skin.

"Come on, baby." He tugs me with him as we enter the store, the warmth of his kiss still burning on my head.

I look at Hunter ordering for us with a smile that I can't seem to wash off my face.

This all feels better than it should. In fact, when Hunter is around, I feel like me, and I haven't felt like me in a long time. My mind keeps telling me to keep my distance, but I can't say no to Hunter Hansen. As soon as he throws that boyish grin in the mix, and shoots me a wink—I'm gone.

A druggie hooked.

He's looking handsome as fuck, wearing some dark jeans and a navy-blue t-shirt that hugs his broad shoulders, showing off his tattooed arms. His snapback is on his head, backwards, and I breathe in the smell of his woodsy cologne every chance I get.

"Clementine vanilla, and cookies and cream for my girl here." He shoots me another wink, clearly oblivious to what it does to my heart, handing me my ice cream before he throws a ten on the counter. "Thanks, Moira!"

"My pleasure, Hunter!" The old lady giggles, with a spark in her eyes. This is probably the highlight of her day, and it's cute he gives her some attention, making her feel special.

Because that's who he is. Deep down, his cold, stubborn heart has so much love to give to the people around him. I think it's why I fell in love with him in the first place. Because underneath all his rough, calloused exterior, he's one of the good guys. He just never shows it unless you earn it.

He offers me his arm, and I softly graze the tattoos on his skin with one hand, then link my arm holding the cone with his as we start to walk down the pavement.

"Does Jason have a thing for Jules?" I think back to the banter that went down between the two of them, wondering if that might mean more.

"I honestly don't know. Does Julie have a thing for Jason?"

Shaking my head, I bring my cone to my mouth, licking the cold sweetness. "Not that I'm aware of."

"I don't know," he quips, a smile creasing his handsome face. "I thought I saw a few longing looks coming from Jules at the bar. And I know what those look like."

"Oh, please, hold up, everyone! It's Hunter Hansen, the master of longing looks," I mock with a deep voice. "Julie sure as fuck doesn't look at Jason like your groupies do."

"I wasn't talking about my groupies."

"No, then who?"

"You." His tone is one of triumph, making my jaw drop with an incredulous look.

"What? I don't give you longing looks."

He taps his cone on my nose, making me squeal, then presses me against the wall of the hardware store, his eyes roaming my face.

Abort, abort, my head yells at the same time my heart wants to break through my ribcage.

"I don't know, Charls." I can feel his breath fanning my face, a tingly feeling developing between my legs. "You look pretty *longing* right now." *Oh, shit.*

"Stop flirting with me," I huff, dying to taste him as I try to ignore the ice cream on my nose, dripping onto my lips. When he's on my shit list, his hot and cold behavior pisses me off something fierce, but fuck, when I feel him this close, all up in my space, I never want him to leave. I want to wrap my arms around his tattooed chest and never let go. I want to show him all the love I've always had for him, even when he didn't think he deserved it.

Fuck, I love him.

He chuckles, as the corner of his mouth curls up in that boyish grin that melts my walls quicker than I want them to.

"Never, babe."

He leans in, and I suck in a breath, parting my lips while he slowly licks the ice cream from my nose. Heat flushes my neck in desire while I close my eyes as he migrates an inch down, his lips brushing mine, giving the smallest peck, and wiping away the clementine vanilla.

Slow.

Affectionate.

Sizzling.

And silently making me beg for more.

When he straightens his neck again, locking his gaze with mine, he bites his lip with a smug grin.

"Told you clementine vanilla is still my favorite flavor."

Consequences be damned, I bring my cone to my face, looking up at him through my lashes, then part my lips, dragging my
tongue seductively over my scoop. "I don't know," I say, my tone
turning husky, "I'm really craving cookies."

His eyes darken as he swallows hard, and we stand like that
for what seems to feel like forever; the world blurring around us,
and the sound of everyday traffic muffled to a minimum while
our lips almost touch.

"What the fuck?!" A familiar voice pulls me from our bubble,
and I turn my head, my heart stopping when I look at the glaring
face of Ben.

Oh, no.

"Ben!" I glance at Hunter, who presses his tongue against his
cheek with a scowl as he takes a step back, clearly not wanting
to, the muscles in his arms tightening.

I give my boyfriend a tight smile as guilt washes over me. *Oh
my god, what have I done?*

"Is this your *alone* time?" he roars.

"Hunter actually just tried to cheer me up by buying me ice
cream. Ben, this is Hunter, my best friend. Hunt, this is Ben.
My..." I can barely get the word out of my throat, because I
know it's a lie, but what does one call someone when you're on
a break anyway? "...boyfriend." Hunter offers his hand, though
not wholeheartedly, but Ben just glares at it, then turns his focus
back to me.

"You always kiss your best friend?" he snarls. I hate the level
of contempt that's showered onto his features as he stares back
at me with daggers in his eyes. But I know I deserve it. I know
I've crossed a line I shouldn't have, regardless of how I feel.

"No. Yes. No. I don't know." I shake my head, glancing from
Ben to Hunter and back.

"Fuck this, Charlotte. Here I am, giving you space, thinking
we'll work it out. But really, you're here kissing other guys."

"Yo, that's all me, man," Hunter replies, hands up. "I over-stepped. I apologize."

Ben ignores Hunter, taking an angry step closer to me.

"You know you're not the only one losing here, *Charlotte*." His tone is condescending, bringing a shiver down my spine, and not in a good way. "This happened to both of us, yet you are the one being a selfish *bitch* about it. So much for me trying to do the right thing, huh?"

"Hey!" Hunter barks, giving Ben a nudge to get him out of my face. "Don't talk to her like that."

"I'll talk to her however I like."

"Guys," I plead.

A smile that doesn't match his eyes land on Hunter's face, and he clenches his jaw, taking an ominous step forward. He softly moves me out of the way, getting into Ben's face while throwing his ice cream to the side as he balls his hands into fists.

I know this look.

It's the look that gets him into fighting mode, preparing him to rip someone's head off. Preferably as fast as possible, and without mercy.

"Hunter," I call out.

"You might wanna reconsider your words before I teach you just exactly how to talk to her, *loser*."

"Hunter!" My hand lands on his chest, pushing him away from Ben as he keeps glaring at him. "Stop! Just stop!" He quickly glances at me, acknowledging my words, then I spin to look at Ben.

"I'm sorry, okay? I'm hurt and confused as fuck. Yes, Hunter overstepped there..." I hear Hunter huff behind me. "But I'm as much to blame. Hunter and I didn't leave things on good terms, and we're trying to work it out."

"By kissing?!" Ben blurts incredulously. "You said you needed some space to figure shit out. I thought you meant us! Not to rekindle an old flame with the guy who's clearly *not* your best friend!"

Julie was wrong. I'm definitely a fucking harlot.

"I do."

"You told me he was your best *friend*."

"He is." I sigh, pinching the bridge of my nose, reprimanding myself for the mess I've put myself in. "I just—I don't know, okay?"

"You're so full of shit, Charlotte. Didn't pick you for a cheater."

"I'm not!"

"Fine!" Ben snarls. "You pick then. Me or him." The moment I realize what he's saying, I gasp for air, shaking my head.

"She doesn't have to do anything," Hunter says over my head.

"Yes, she does! Because I'm not going to compete with some low-life scum." Ben glares at Hunter from head to toe, and I can hear Hunter growl, taking a step forward. I keep my back in front of him, making sure I stay situated between the two men.

"Do you even know who I am?" Hunter grabs the back of my shirt, letting me know he's got me.

"I don't give a shit who you are. But you're clearly more than best *friends*. Choose, Charlotte! Me or him." I look at Ben, the frustration dripping from his face, and I can't blame him.

He doesn't deserve this. He's been trying to make me happy for the last six months, doing everything in his power to support me in everything. But he's been running a race he can never win. He's competing for my heart, but my heart is not a prize that can be won. My heart is something I don't control, no matter how hard I try. That has become more than clear since Hunter moved back home.

I feel my eyes well up, and I shut them with a sigh, then take a deep breath. When I open them again, I look at a disappointed, still glaring Ben.

"I'm sorry, Ben. It's me." Internally, I roll my eyes at my own words, knowing how lame this sounds. "I think I should be by myself for a while." I run a hand through my silky hair. "You and me? What we have been through? I didn't want it. Our relationship went from casual and fun to serious and permanent in a very short time, and I wasn't ready for it."

I push out the words, scared I might chicken out while I keep staring at the hurt in his eyes.

"I've—I've—I have shit to work out. I need to figure out what I want." I turn my body so I can look at both of them.

Hunter's eyes darken in question, barely noticeable for anybody else but completely clear to me, as if he's tapping into our unspoken connection, asking me if I'm okay.

"I need time. I need to think. I-I need to go." I ignore Hunter's gaze, as I give them both one last glance, then strut off while tears start to run down my face. I hear Hunter call out my name, but I keep walking, knowing I need to be alone right now.

What the fuck are you doing, Charlotte?

I'm not the kind of girl who messes around with two guys. I don't do that. I'm an honest girl. It's the one thing I've always been unapologetic about. Honesty and trust are of the highest on my value board, and don't go kissing men who aren't my boyfriend. But my throat turns sour, realizing I just came damn close, and my heart doesn't even regret it.

"I have a hangover, Charlie. A bad one." Julie's groggy voice comes over the line.

"I think I just broke up with Ben." My voice is etched with emotion, and I wipe away the tears with the back of my hand.

"So, the temporary 'break' turned into a permanent breakup?" Though she sounds exhausted, there's no surprise audible in her tone when she continues after I grunt something in confirmation. "Because you're in love with Hunter?"

"What?!" I blurt incredulously, a bit angry and still sniffing. "Why don't you even sound surprised about me breaking up with Ben?"

"Look, Charlie," she says, sympathetic. "As much as I like Ben, you're fooling yourself if you think he could ever make you happy."

"What do you mean?" I know very well what she means, but up until now, I was too much of a coward.

"Charlie, you've always been in love with Hunter. Ben was a rebound. A rebound who almost got completely out of control, and to be honest, I'm sorry that happened to you. But I'm glad it did."

I start sobbing again, that horrible morning still carved into my membrane, and I hear her let out a deep sigh.

"I'm sorry, Charlie. I know you're hurt, but you gotta take the risk. Give Hunter a shot."

"I've taken the risk. Twice! And it crushed me!" I shout, throwing up my hands in despair. A brick lays in my stomach, and my feet seem to feel heavier with every step I take. "And last week, it crushed me again just thinking about him when he wasn't even fucking there!"

Sometimes I wonder if he hurt me beyond repair, but then he sauntered into that bar, and I swear my heart somehow found the strength to glue parts back together without my permission. I try to keep my heart chained and behind bars, but the little bitch keeps growing stronger and stronger, and I don't know how to make it fucking stop.

I can't lose him again.

"And not being with him is still crushing you. Look, not to sound like a fucking fortune teller right now, but I think there's a reason he returned that *exact* day. Life's throwing you the bone you've been waiting for. *Take it.*"

"I'm scared, Jules," I croak out. My mind is scrambling, because at this point, I don't even know what exactly I'm scared of anymore: being with him or being without him.

"I know, girl. But so is he. You can be scared together. He's an asshole. But he's always been *your* asshole."

70

HUNTER

I'M IN MY TRUCK, pissed at myself for kissing Charlotte when she isn't mine to kiss.

Not yet anyway.

The dial tone echoes as I wait for Jason to answer the phone.

"What's up, Hansen?"

"I fucked up."

"Why?" His voice sounds bored, and I rub the back of my neck.

"We went to get some ice cream, then I kissed her... at the same time we ran into her fucking boyfriend."

He lets out a full belly burst of laughter, and I roll my eyes, unamused.

"Talk about bad timing, playboy."

"Shut up."

"How did she react to you kissing her?"

A fluttering feeling forms in my gut, my heart rate speeding up in excitement, thinking back to my lips on hers. It was only brief, a slight brush of our lips, but fuck me, I was ready to dive in for more if that damn guy hadn't shown up.

"Like she wanted more." I chuckle before my face falls a bit. "But then he got into her face, I got into his face, and she snapped. Then she walked away. I wanted to take her to the shelter to get a dog."

"She walked away?"

"Yeah," I reply, dragging out the word. "I guess it was more like storming off? And I'm pretty sure she broke up with that douchebag."

"Wait, what? She broke up with him on the sidewalk?"

"I don't know!?" I blurt, confused. "She was like: *I need time. I need to be by myself after what happened.* And I have no clue what that means. I wanted to go after her, but I don't know."

"Where was douchebag Ben?"

"Still glaring." I huff. "I wanted to punch him real bad. Thinking about how he's been kissing my girl for the last few months, but instead I punched a trashcan and walked to my truck."

"Really?" I can hear the shock in his voice, slightly pissing me off.

"Yes, *really.* Can't have that fucker calling TMZ, saying he got punched by Hunter Hansen. Gina will have a fit."

"But your lawyer will have a blast?" he jokes.

"You're enjoying this way too much."

"Oh, come on. You got what you wanted! She broke up with him. What are you still moping about? You got the girl."

"I didn't *get* the girl. She stormed off!" I correct.

"So, go get her! Where the fuck are you waiting for?!"

"She didn't seem like she wanted me around right now."

"Like that ever stopped you," he says flatly.

I groan in frustration, biting my lip.

"I don't even know where she is."

"For fuck's sake, Hunter. I'm sure you'll know where to find her." He stays quiet, and I know I'm acting like a scared little boy. Everything I've done the last year was for this moment, facing my biggest fears, and winning my girl back. And now that's finally here—I'm scared as fuck.

"You're gonna chicken out now? We moved back to this one-horse town to back out now? I saw the way she looked at you last night. The two of you are endgame."

"Something is holding her back. Like she's scared to open up to me again."

"Then convince her otherwise. Show her you're legit this time. Either way, you should hang up the phone and talk to her instead of me."

"Right." I smile.

"Cool. Call me after." He hangs up the phone as I stare out onto the street, thinking about where she could be. When I start driving in the direction she stormed off in, it only takes me a minute to realize where she went, and I park in front of the cemetery two minutes later. Walking through the gate, I quickly notice her on her knees in front of her mama's grave, and the sight of it makes goosebumps pepper my skin as I approach her. *I'm not giving up now.*

71

Charlotte

A<small>FTER HANGING UP THE</small> phone with Julie, I kept walking, trying to process my thoughts, until I found myself walking
through the gates of the cemetery. The freshly cut grass seems
to calm my nerves a bit as I head to my mother's grave. I crouch
down, reading her name while my fingers brush along the cold
stone.

Elizabeth Roux.

There's a fresh bouquet of pink roses put in the vase in front of
the headstone that isn't mine, and it warms my heart that there
are still people visiting my mother's final resting place.

I let out a deep sigh, wiping away the final tears, looking up at
the sky.

"Hey, Mama," I start, a sad chuckle escaping my lips. "I fucked
up. I fucked up big time, and I don't know what to do."

My eyes land on the pink roses.

"The last few weeks have been terrifying, realizing I didn't
want whatever I had with Ben, but as much as I love my time
with Hunter—it also terrifies me. He can break me, and he
almost did before." I keep quiet, my hands in my lap, silently
wishing she'll give me a sign.

When I left LA almost a year ago, I was broken. There was
a part of me that was relieved. I found the strength to tell him

how I felt once more, combined with pride that I took the risk of putting my heart on the line. But as I offered him my heart, he didn't have the courage to grab it, and it felt like it turned into ashes in the palms of my hands. I got back into that cab feeling ten pounds heavier than when I arrived, already adding to the weight I've been carrying since the funeral, then I called Julie to tell her what happened. My throat was aching from crying, and I started sobbing again while telling her everything. By the time I came home the next morning, my tears dried up, and I was left with a throbbing headache and a hollow feeling inside. Feeling like I just lost the most important people in the whole world.

In the same month.

I understood, and felt the finality of it all, and it was consuming me with no clue how to keep going. At some point, I got out of bed, started eating again, and did my best to feel alive. It took me a while, but after a few weeks, I got my routine back and found ways to get out of the house. I was able to push the hurt to the back of my mind, because he was on the other side of the country, and I wasn't confronted with him all the time. Other than the shit in the media that I heavily avoided. I was able to find joy in the memories Mama and I had, while also breaking down by the emptiness she left around the house. It was my own personal hell that I crawled out of until I met Ben.

Suddenly, he gave me a reason to smile again. A reason to do more than just eat and sleep my way through life. I was even able to convince myself that I fell in love with Ben after a few dates.

But Julie is right.

I have been in love with Hunter since the first day we met, and even though I wanted to move on so badly, I knew it would always be a struggle if he ever reappeared in my life. That wasn't going to happen, though. Because he was engaged, he had nothing to come back to North Carolina for, and his life was in LA. There was no way he was going to settle in Braedon and contact me again after everything I said to him.

And then he did.

"I wish you were still here, Mama," I whisper into the waft of the air.

"I had a feeling you'd be here."

My head snaps to the side, and I'm met by Hunter's regret-ridden eyes, his hands tucked into his jeans. Gone is his confidence. Standing in front of me is the troubled teen he was when we first met.

I look back in front of me, my eyes roaming over the letters of Mama's name.

"Someone bought her fresh flowers."

"I know. I did." He moves a little closer, and I look up at him, peering down at me with a kind smile.

"You did?"

He nods with a hum, my brows creasing together in question.

"Your mom sent me a letter, you know?"

"A letter?"

He hums again, the corner of his mouth lifting slightly.

"It was sent to me by her lawyer, six weeks after you left LA."

72

HUNTER

S HE SHAKES HER HEAD in confusion.

"She never told me."

"She wrote it the last time she found a lump. I guess when she thought she wasn't going to make it."

"What did it say?" She presses her lips together, the anticipation washing her face.

"The short version? That I should stop convincing myself that I didn't deserve you."

Another tear escapes the corner of her eye as she tries to muffle a sob, and my hands itch to cup her face to kiss it away.

I swallow hard, telling myself this might be my only shot.

"Your mama called me out that night on my eighteenth birthday. Telling me I was full of shit."

"Hunter." Despair etches her voice, and I keep my mouth shut. "I can't do this. Not again. Not when I'm barely recovered from the last time. You didn't want me."

"That's not true, Charls. I've always wanted you."

"Yet, you got engaged to someone else!" Her greens are laced with nothing more than sheer hate and disappointment. "Pretending you were in love with her!"

"That meant nothing." I shake my head.

"No! That meant everything. You gave her what I'd been begging you for!" she bellows firmly. "I don't want to hear it anymore, Hunter." She gets up, and I can see the anger on her face. "This is what you do! You walk into my life whenever you want, and you walk right out when you want to. I can't handle it anymore! I don't want to handle it anymore. I meant what I said to Ben. But the same goes for you. I need time. I need *space*."

She pushes the last word out with a growl before she walks past me to leave.

"Don't go." I grab her arm, bringing my face closer to hers. "Talk to me. You *have* to talk to me."

"I wanted to talk to you eleven months ago, but you didn't have anything to say," she spits, her eyes shooting daggers, and I can actually feel them pierce through my heart one by one. I want to tell her that I was stupid. That I was an asshole, too afraid to admit what I've been wanting to admit for so long. But before I can reply, she opens her mouth again while a breeze blows a few strands of her hair in front of her face. "I wanted to talk to you the summer after graduation, but you didn't have anything to say, *Hunt*."

I clench my jaw, frustrated when I feel her slipping away.

"I have something to say *now*."

She pulls her arm free, giving me a push with an ominous glare.

"And *now* I don't want to hear it!"

"Charlotte!" I shout when she walks aways from me again.

"No!" She spins, pointing a finger at my chest. "Ever since we became friends, my world has revolved around you. Around *us*. Right now? It's about me! And I don't want to hear it. I just fucking want to be left alone," she growls, then starts marching through the gate.

I let out a feral roar, looking up at the sky, not knowing what to do. The sun warms my face in a soothing way, but inside it feels like I'm suffocating. That strong feeling of something dying inside of me I had when she left me on the sidewalk a year ago.

When I arrived back in Braedon, I felt confident, ready to do whatever it takes. Now, I'm seriously questioning if I should let her go. But the thought also makes my heart tighten in my chest. We have this unspoken connection I don't think will ever disappear, but what if that's all that's left? What if she really just wants to be friends because I broke any other feelings she might've had?

Dragging a hand over my face, I look at the headstone, thinking back to the letter Liz sent me.

We both know you will never love anyone more than you love my daughter, she said. And I know it's true. After Jason forced me to pull my head out of my ass, I was ready to go to war for her heart. Receiving Liz's letter pushed out any doubt I felt. But standing here, alone, makes the uncertainty rush through my body all over again.

I pull out my phone, needing a tiny push to keep going.

HUNTER: She doesn't want to talk to me.

I wait, staring at the screen, until those three dots appear.

JULIE: She's hurt
HUNTER: Should I let her go?
JULIE: Hunter Hansen, you are not the insecure asshole you pretend to be. Stop asking me stupid questions and get your girl back.

I chuckle at her reply, giving another glance at Elizabeth's grave.

"I'm gonna get my girl back, Liz. Wish me luck."

73

Charlotte

I've been sitting on the porch steps for ten minutes, replaying the last hour in my head, when Hunter parks his truck in my driveway. I knew he would. I wish he would respect my desire to be alone almost as much as I want him to be here. Because as much as I'll never be ready for this conversation, it's as inevitable as the moon appearing within the next few hours to announce the nightfall.

Giving me a blank look, he gets out of the truck, running a hand through his hair.

He slowly walks toward me with tentative steps, and I reach up my hand to make him stop, knowing I will break if he comes any closer. I will cave before I say everything I need to say. He gives me a troubled look, tucking his hands in the pockets of his jeans.

"At first, I thought losing you was the worst day of my life." He swallows, his lips in a flat line. "Then I thought it was Mama dying. Then I flew out to LA, and literally felt my heart pulled from my body when I said goodbye to you, *again.*" I shake my head, my voice cracking as my eyes well up. "But I was wrong, because the day you came home was the worst day of my life."

I can see uneasiness painting his face, though I'm sure not for the reason I have in my head. "Why, babe?"

I wet my lips, pressing them tightly together while I close my eyes to prevent the tears from running down my cheeks. *Not yet.* Not until I've said it all.

"Hey, talk to me." He squats in front of me, too close for me to stay indifferent, grabbing my knees with a desperate look on his face.

"I can't."

"You can always talk to me," he says with a choking voice, squeezing my knees in encouragement.

His words make me remember how I used to tell him everything, feeling completely comfortable with him. I've confessed I loved him multiple times, and he never said it back until it was too late. He never told me how he felt, not even when I needed it the most. Can I believe him now?

Can I trust him like I once did?

Can we ever grow from the pain and chaos we created?

I want to be brave once more, thinking I have nothing left to lose, but I don't know if I can handle it again.

"I'm scared," I confess, a tear staining my cheek. "Scared that if I give you all my secrets, you won't stop until you have my heart. And I can't lose that again."

He nods, but I can see the fear in his rapidly blinking eyes, his shoulders tightening.

"I know, Charls. I know." He pushes a strand of hair behind my ear. "And I'm not going to pretend I'm here for anything else but your heart. But I'll be working every day for the rest of my life to show you I will protect it with everything I got from this day forward. On *your* terms. *Your* pace. You don't have to tell me anything until you're ready."

"What if I'll never be ready?" I whisper.

He looks up at me, the determination in his eyes mixed with sincerity, that wraps a blanket around my heart. "I'll still be here waiting."

The muscles in his neck tighten, his jaw ticking. He's prepared to fight. To wait, wait until the end of time if he has to.

"I had a miscarriage." Speaking the words out loud hurts, a physical pain going through my chest when I think about the life I've lost. But it feels liberating at the same time, setting me free as I release the secret I've kept to myself, even though I've been dying to tell him.

"What?" His eyebrows squish together, as he runs a hand through his hair in confusion.

"The day you came home, and found me in the bar. I was eight weeks pregnant. Or I was, up until that morning."

He gets up, looking at the sky, curling his arms above his head as if breathing is too hard of a task, then locks his gaze with mine.

"I'm so sorry." His voice cracks with emotion.

I shake my head with a bitter smile tugging at the corner of my mouth. "That wasn't the worst part," I confess, staring at the grass of my front yard.

I wish that was the worst part.

Normally, I enjoy the smell of fresh grass and the roses in front of my porch, but right now, my senses seem to be numb. Not registering anything other than the pain inside burning around my organs.

"It was the part where I was relieved," I continue, not being able to control my tears any longer. "Thanking God on my bare knees for saving me, but feeling like fucking trash for thinking it. Grateful that I didn't have to carry that burden for the rest of my life, but loathing myself at the same time."

"What burden?"

My eyes lock with his, wanting to make sure he hears every word I'm saying. To feel the gravity of my confession, hoping he now realizes exactly how much I've always loved this troubled boy.

"Looking into my child's eyes, wishing they were yours." His face turns as white as snow as he pulls his hair in frustration, sucking in a sharp breath.

"Charls."

When I know he's heard me, *really* heard me, I keep going, knowing I have to push through now. There's no back-peddling from this.

"For four weeks, I cried my eyes out, telling people it was hormones, when really, I couldn't bear the thought of carrying a child that wasn't yours. And then when I lost it, I felt emptier than ever, feeling like my life wasn't even worth living." The tone in my voice becomes more frantic and angry with every word, yelling everything I have left to say. "Because I wondered if I killed my own child by wishing I wasn't pregnant! But then, when my prayers were answered, I regretted every second of it. And I hate you for it. Because that should've been you. That should've been our baby!" I shout, pointing my finger at him in agony. "And now it's too late."

I bring my hands up, covering my face.

"It's too late, Hunter."

"It's never too late, Charls," he counters.

"How can you say that?" I bellow with frustration, my ass still firmly planted on the wood of the steps, not sure I can stay on my feet if I get up.

"Because sometimes you realize you're too late, but you pray life is on your side, giving you another shot."

"This is not high school, Hunter!" I give him an incredulous look, staring at his pained expression when he brings up his hands in despair.

"I know. I'm sorry. I'm sorry I had to lose you before I realized I can't live a fucking day without you. It's not that I don't want to. I do. I want to let you go so bad, knowing I will never be good enough for you. But I can't. My heart stops beating when I'm not around you. My life is nothing more than an empty vessel without you in it. I know I should've stayed. I'm a fucking idiot. And now I'm here trying to hold on, when you have already let go." I keep staring at him, while my shoulders shake from the tears that come down in bucketloads. "Ever since you walked out that day, leaving me completely lost on the sidewalk, I've realized you've been my lighthouse since day one. Preventing me from crashing into the fucking rocks that life keeps throwing me. But I get it now, I see it now." He nods.

"*See what?*" I push out.

"I have to crash through the rocks to get to you. I've been holding on to you like a life jacket, treasuring you as my beacon in the dark, when really, I want to hold your hand and walk in broad daylight for the rest of our fucking lives. It's you. It's *always* been you."

I shake my head, my heart aching, hearing him, but still hesitant to fully open the door.

"If it's not you, it's not anyone. I've always wanted the world, fighting anyone who dared to get into that cage with me to get there, but when I got it, I lost you." His eyes are reddened with emotion, showing me that lost boy I met all those years ago. Pretending to have figured it all out, but really, he's just desperate to be held.

To be cherished.

To be loved.

"You once asked me what my dream was, and I told you I didn't know. That was the only lie I ever told you, because from the moment my eyes met your green eyes that day at the creek, it was you. *It has always been you.*" His footsteps getting closer sound terrifying, holding a tight grip on my heart when he falls to his knees, placing himself between my legs while softly peeling my hands off my face. I sob when he looks me in the eye with a pleading stare, holding my hand in his palm. "Ask me what my dream is, babe."

I shake my head, diverting my gaze, scared as fuck to do as he said. "Ask me what my dream is. Please." He cups my face, pressing his forehead against mine. "Charls. *Ask* me."

"What is your dream?" I whisper breathlessly.

He lets out a relieved sigh. "My dream is a house with a white picket fence and a big porch, where my wife can write all the stories that are stuck in her head while the kids are in school. I will forget our anniversaries, but she will forgive me because I make up for it the rest of the year. After the accident, I thought my dream was to be free. That all I ever wanted to be was the best fighter in the world. But now I know that all I ever wanted was to be yours. I love you, Charlotte Roux. I love you, and I'm going to keep telling you for the rest of my life, whether you want to hear it or not. I don't give a shit about Ben, or whoever wants to steal you away from me. I will fight for *you*. I will fight for *us*. You are mine and you know it."

And with that, it's gone. My heart is slipping out of my chest and into his hands, forever at his mercy until the day I die.

There is no way back.

This is final.

This is *it*.

Hunter Hansen is it, and there is no use denying it. I've been trying to deny it for years, but I never stood a chance. He's melted so deeply into my core that his soul is merged with mine. Two kids with our hearts on fire and nothing that can stop us from burning together.

I rest my hands on his neck, my painful tears being replaced by tears of relief. The extra weight that I've been carrying lifts off my chest when I finally nod.

"Do you hear me, Charlotte Roux? You. Are. Mine," he growls against my lips. *I'm his.* I could never be anyone else's.

8

"I'm yours." I press my lips against his as hard as I can, feeling how the darkness finally escapes my body when his arms wrap around me. With his mouth covering mine, I finally find what I've been looking for all those years.

He finally gives me everything I'll ever need.

74

Charlotte

H E PICKS ME UP, wrapping my legs around his body while
we explore every inch of each other's mouths. Walking
us back into the house, his hand fists my hair so he can deepen
our kiss in a demanding way.

The bulge in his jeans presses against my center, and I moan,
thinking about how I want him to stretch me as wide as possible.
How I've been longing for that day for years. His cold hands
snake under my shirt, and everything seems to blur around me
the longer I hold on to him. I've waited for this day since the
last time I felt his lips on mine. Telling myself I was done with
my obsession with Hunter Hansen, no longer in need of his
blistering touch. But I'm an addict when it comes to him, never
being able to resist anything he's willing to give me, and I now
know he feels the same. The urgency in his soft kisses, the
tenderness in his touches, all tell me what I knew a long time
ago—Hunter Hansen needs me as much as I need him. I need
him like the air I breathe and the water I drink.

With big strides, he walks us to my bedroom before throwing
me on the bed, erupting a squeal out of my body.

The craving in his eyes tells me he's starving to get his new
shot of utter bliss we seem to only be able to find with each

other, and I eagerly take off my shirt, settling on my knees on the bed, my hands reaching out to take off his jeans.

He cups my face, looking down at me with a yearning sparkle in his eyes as he wipes away the leftover tears from my cheeks.

"I'm sorry it took me so long, babe."

"Ssh, you're here now." Without giving him time to reply, I pull his boxers down, wrapping my lips around his hard shaft.

"*Fuck!*" he cries out, as my gaze locks with his from underneath my lashes.

His lips part with hooded eyes, staring at me in awe, while his hand caresses my cheek.

Moving my lips up and down his cock, I massage his balls, getting more excited by every moan that leaves his lips. I've been dying to taste him, to make him come undone with my lips like he did when we were still a couple of kids in high school. I can feel my eyes water when he hits the back of my throat, doing my best to keep going while his face turns more concentrated with every thrust. My lips suck on his head like it's my favorite lollipop, a popping sound echoing through the room every time I let it escape my lips.

"Na-ah," he groans, running his hand through my sweaty hair. "I don't want to come in your mouth."

Pushing me off of him, I look up at him with a pout, a grin appearing on his face. Taking off the rest of his clothes, I bite my lip, admiring his strong body. The tattoos on his arm show off his big muscles and his Adonis belt makes me wetter just from staring at it. The boy I've known since high school is completely replaced by a man who exceeds my wildest desires.

"Take everything off, babe," he orders with that boyish grin on his face that instantly makes butterflies flutter through my stomach. I do what he says, teasingly throwing my panties at his chest. He catches them with ease, before bringing them to his nose, breathing in like a madman, stealing the air from my lungs.

"I've missed this." He saunters toward me, his eyes hungry like he's ready to devour me. A finger runs along my cheek as he walks past me, then gets on the bed, settling against the headboard. His hard dick is throbbing against his belly, and I stare at it in awe, eager to feel him inside of me.

"Come here, babe."

Biting my lip, I crawl toward him, placing a leg on each side so I'm straddling him. He grabs his head, gently rubbing it through my slit in long strokes, and I throw my head back at the soft touch on my core.

With my lips pressed together, I let out a muffled moan, enjoying every second of his warm head gliding through my wetness.

"You're so wet."

Without warning, he grabs my hips, yanking me over his cock like his life depends on it, and I suck in a deep breath when he harshly fills me up.

"*Fuck.* Hunter. Condom." I huff, resting my forehead against his.

"No way, babe. I'm done taking things slow. I want you, Charls. I want it all. My last name on your passport. A bunch of kids. *A dog*, yeah?"

His words bring a smile to my face, feeling them in my core, and I nod, pressing a kiss against his lips.

"Promise me." A slight fear etches through his voice, and I now realize how hard this is for him. To open up to the person he loves, knowing one day they might leave him. But if there is one thing life taught me so far, it's that you can't walk away when it's real. When love is real, when love is true, it will consume you until the day you die, making it impossible to truly be happy without it. Not everyone is lucky to find it, not everyone is lucky enough to keep it, but once it reaches your heart, there is no going back.

You can run from love, trying to cross the finish line before it catches up with you, but you can never hide.

I tried.

He tried.

But even though we both agreed to friends from the get-go, it was useless.

Love caught up with us quicker than we were ready. But I understand now.

We were never friends.

We have always been more than that.

We have always been in love.

"I promise," I say, as I start to ride him, his chest tight against mine with our arms wrapped around each other. We hold on for dear life until we explode together, completely melted as one.

EPILOGUE

ALL I EVER WANTED WAS THIS.
YOU.

I have something for you.'

HUNTER

SIX MONTHS LATER

EVEN THOUGH I FEEL fine, I take the ice pack from Charlotte's hand, placing it beside me while tugging her onto my lap.

"This isn't going to help anymore, you know?" I smile.

"Maybe not." She settles into my chest, resting her head on my shoulder. "But I feel better when you do it, anyway."

My hand brushes up and down her spine, comforting her while I feel her warm breath against my neck.

"I hate seeing you like this, you know?"

"I know, babe. But I did win?" I joke, trying to lighten her mood.

"Thank God, you did." I can hear the discomfort in her voice, but being the supportive girlfriend that she is, she will never tell me to stop fighting. She never has, even though she's been hating it since I dragged her to that warehouse when we were still kids.

"You know..." I start, "I've been thinking."

"Yeah?" She lifts her head to look at me, and my hand reaches up to cup her cheek, rubbing my thumb over her soft skin. She's looking at me with anticipation, and I still feel like the luckiest man alive, having her here in my arms. When I finally pulled my head out of my ass and won her back, it only took me a week before I sent Jason back to LA to get my stuff and moved in with Charlotte. I expected it to feel strange to start living in her parental home with her mama's memories all over the place, but it felt more like home than ever before. Giving me the place where I want to start a family.

One day.

"I think I'm gonna quit."

"Quit what?" She tilts her head in confusion.

"Fighting."

Her eyes widen, and I can see her filling with excitement, even though she's doing her best to keep a straight face, looking like a teapot ready to boil over.

"Really?" she says, as casually as possible.

"Really." I chuckle.

"Why?"

"Why not? All I ever wanted was this. *You.* I chose to fight as an escape from my reality, but I don't need to escape anymore. I don't *want* to escape anymore." I press a trail of kisses against her jaw. "I don't want to train four hours a day. I don't want to go back to LA. I don't want to be part of that jet-set life. I don't see any reason to keep going. Hell, I don't have to do it for the money either. I have more money than I can spend in a lifetime. We're set for life. It was fun, but no more. I want to spend my mornings waking up with you on the porch, drinking coffee."

The corner of her mouth curls.

"What are you going to do all day? You're not the type of guy who sits on his ass. You need something to do."

"I was thinking about taking a job at the ice rink. See if they can use a trainer or a coach in the minor leagues. But I could also work at the Bowling Alley. I do own it after all."

She shakes her head, the sunlight dancing in her eyes. "You're crazy."

Her gorgeous eyes light up before her lips crash against mine in a bruising kiss. It's something I've been thinking about for months now, asking myself what it is I really want to do, and every single time, my dad flashes in front of my eyes. The vision of him training and coaching Logan and I, harsh and strict, but a big-ass smile on his face whenever he saw our improvements.

That's what I want.

"You think it's a good idea?"

"That sounds perfect, Hunt. I think that's the best idea," she murmurs against my lips.

"Yeah?"

"Definitely. So, when is your last fight?"

"Yesterday."

"Are you shitting me?"

"Nope." I smirk, shooting her a wink.

"Really?"

"Yesterday was the last fight before my contract needed to be extended. I told Gina after the fight, I wasn't going to renew it."

"EEEK!" Her arms wrap tightly around me, and I bury my nose in her neck, breathing her in.

The moment I left LA and moved back to North Carolina, I knew the life I had for the last couple of years was over. And I couldn't be happier about it. When I left North Carolina, it felt like I gained my freedom, giving me the opportunity to make something out of myself. Opening doors that weren't going to open back in Braedon. But when I finally got my girl ... moving back home was the last thing I needed to feel complete.

I didn't decide that I was going to stop fighting just yesterday. I decided it the day she and I finally worked through our shit, and she gave me another chance.

There was nothing in LA for me.

Everything I need is right here in the form of a sassy dirty blonde with blue-green eyes you can drown in.

"I love you, babe," I hum against her hair.

"I love you," she whispers, then jumps up, making me groan at the loss of her touch.

"We should celebrate! Let's invite Jason and Julie? Have a dinner party? I'll cook."

I rub my hand over my face, looking at my girl clapping like my own personal cheerleader.

"How about we just order in, and you can make us some cocktails?"

"Even better!"

"Just keep the girls outside," I hiss to Jason, who's rolling his eyes at me.

"I can't believe you seriously bought a dog." He takes a sip of his mojito, shooting me a dull look. "Who's going to take care of that thing?"

"I am, duh."

"You're seriously going to leave me all alone in LA?"

"I already did, didn't I?"

"I kinda thought you'd come back, eventually. Maybe with Charlotte." He pouts.

I shove him aside, not buying his theatrics.

"No, you didn't."

"Nah, I didn't. But I'm not ready to move out. I'm keeping the house. It's only fair now that you're divorcing me."

"I've paid for the lease until the end of the year. After that, you're on your own."

"You dumbass," he snickers. "I'm only joking."

"I'm not," I say with a straight face, resulting in him looking at me in shock.

"You didn't seriously pay for the rest of the year?"

"I did. I owe you a lot, Jay. Without you, I wouldn't be where I am right now. Hell, I might even be married to the wrong girl." I pull a face, horrified by the thought.

"No, you wouldn't, because I would've sabotaged that damn wedding. Thank fuck you saw the light. Can't wait for the two of you to finally tie the knot. It's about fucking time. Even though I don't know why Charlotte is giving an asshole like you another shot," he jokes, sticking out his tongue.

"Shut up, and just keep them there or there will be no knot to tie." I walk upstairs to the guest bedroom. Quietly, I open the door, grabbing the big red bow off the dresser before approaching the puppy sleeping on the bed. When he notices me entering the room, his tail starts to wiggle, then he gets up, stretches himself, and slowly approaches me.

"Hey, little buddy. How are you? Are you ready to meet your new mommy?" I pet the head of the little Leonberger, ruffling his fluffy fur with my nails.

"Come on," I say, placing the bow on his collar, then scooping him up in my arms. When I walk downstairs, my heart starts to race in my ribcage, suddenly feeling nervous as fuck. Heat flushes my neck, and I take a few deep breaths before I enter the kitchen, trying to calm down.

Walking toward the screened porch where everyone is seated, I call out to Charlotte.

"Babe?"

"Yeah?" she replies, glancing at the porch door.

"Can you close your eyes? I got you something."

"What?" I hear her screech, and I try to peek through the screen. "A surprise?"

"Just close your eyes." I look at her, with my back toward the door, waiting until she holds her hands in front of my face.

"You ready?"

"Yes! Show me!"

A smile splits my face when I push the door open with my back, taking a few steps until I'm right in front of her.

"Can I open it?"

"Not yet!" I blurt, squatting down and placing the puppy right in front of her face.

"Okay, you can open it."

Her hands move down, then her eyes grow as big as saucers right before she gives me an incredulous look.

"You bought me a puppy?"

I nod, my heart jumping as I watch the priceless look on her beautiful face.

Tears stream down her features when she presses a hard kiss against my lips, then takes the puppy out of my hands, burying her face into the soft fur as she starts to sob.

"You got me a puppy," she cries.

I cup her cheek, glancing at a beaming Jason and Julie, enjoying this just as much as I am, and I push a lingering kiss to her forehead.

"That's not all I got you," I mumble, pressing my forehead against hers.

"It's not?"

"Nope." My hand moves to the collar of the puppy, pulling the ring off the bow that was sitting in the middle. I hold it out in front of her as calmness washes over my body. My heart beats steadily, my nervousness completely gone until all that's left is excitement.

"Charlotte Roux, I know I'm an asshole, and I'll probably screw up more than once, but I will never stop loving you, so will you marry me anyway?"

She folds her hand in front of her mouth, holding the puppy with the other while she frantically nods.

"Yes! Yes! Of course, I'll marry you."

I push out a relieved breath, then give her a longing kiss, feeling happier than I've ever been.

Jason and Julie start to clap, and I wrap Charlotte up in a tight hug with our puppy in between as we smile at them.

"Took you long enough, Hansen," Julie jokes.

"You're stuck with him now, Charlotte," Jason chimes in.

"Well, about that," Charlotte starts, wiping the tears away with the back of her hand, then gives me a mysterious grin. "I have something for you."

"You do? What is it?"

"Well, remember two months ago when we were drunk out here on the porch?"

I narrow my eyes, knowing exactly what she's talking about. We got wasted, had sex outside in the yard, and it was sexy as fuck, having her ride me under the clear sky as I watched the stars around her head.

"How can I forget?" I reply huskily, instantly turned on.

"Yeah, not *that* part." She chuckles, handing our new puppy over to Julie with a knowing look. I raise my brows at Julie in question, who just keeps grinning. "The part after that, when I decided a few more shots would be a great idea?"

"Oh, you mean the part where you were heaving your lungs out? *Such a rookie mistake.*" I laugh, mockingly rolling my eyes.

"Yeah," she admits, pinching the bridge of her nose in embarrassment before looking back up at me. I bring my hand up, resting it on her neck, feeding the need to touch her as she continues her story.

"Well, did you know that birth control is no longer effective if you throw up a few hours after taking the pill?"

"No?" I look at her with confusion, having no clue where this is going.

"It isn't. It's another *rookie* mistake."

"Okay," I drawl. "What's your point?"

"My point is... You gave me something else that night."

I shake my head, completely missing the point while she keeps staring at me in anticipation, waiting for it to click inside my head. Whatever *it* may be.

We keep staring at each other while I try to connect the dots in my head.

"Jesus Christ, Hansen," Julie mutters when it finally hits me.

I gasp for air, my heart jumping out of my chest.

"Are you... Are you... Are we? Fucking hell, are you pregnant?"

She nods, biting her lip, resting her hands on my chest.

"But that's a mojito?" I point at her drink on the table, incredulous.

"It's a virgin mojito."

My eyes move back and forth over her blushing face, wondering if this is really happening.

"We're having a baby?"

"Is that okay?" she asks quietly.

I tilt my head back, closing my eyes for a few seconds, holding Charls tight against my body.

My eyes well up, overwhelmed by the amount of luck that seems to run through my veins, before I dip my chin again, looking at the love of my life.

"It's the icing on the cake, babe."

BONUS SCENE

SCAN THE CODE FOR A LITTLE PEAK INTO THE FUTURE

'This is the last one.'

ACKNOWLEDGEMENTS

To my reader, if I made you cry, pissed you off or made your heart ache?

Good. Because that's how I felt writing it, and I like to share my misery.

I'm a little sadistic like that.

This book was painful to write, in every single way, and to be honest, my heart still hurts when I see the name Hunter Hansen. Most of my books are plotted, based on a little gist or scene that one day appeared in my crazy mind. But this was a story that's written from my heart, with feelings I couldn't control. It was hard, it was messy, it was personal but it's also my favorite book, and I'm thanking you for picking it up!

Hunter Hansen, thank you for sharing your story with me. You're an asshole, I have no clue where you came from, and why you picked me. But I'm glad you did.

Els & Shell, you two crazy bishes we're practically holding up your pompom's in the air for the entire ride, and it was so needed! Thank you for always being hungry for my words, but mostly thank you for the friendship you've given me.

Katie, my go-to when my maverick mind is on a roll, LOL. Thank you for always playing devil's advocate, keeping me sharp and a little less impulsive than I can be. It's a blessing to have someone to spar with that's like-minded.

Thank you to my Fourway. I love the love we have for each other. I love the friendship we share. I love the bluntness we give each other, always pushing each other to do better while also respecting the fact that we're all different. We're all four completely different, yet totally the same, and I hope we get to keep that forever.

Mac, my sweet, loving, caring and way-more-flexible-than-she-should-be-editor. Thank you for being you. My plans change all the time, but you're always here for it. My mental health fluctuates, and you never give me the feeling I can't share it with you. I admire you as a person, because even with a fucking ocean between us, I can see the kindness of your heart.

Steph, I totally threw this book at you at the last minute, but you devoured it and made my day like always. Thank you so much for your kindness and the love you have for this couple!

My dear Boston Lauren, you're a superfan, eating up whatever words I'll feed you. You make me feel special, when really I'm just an author. Please never stop reading my books.

Also, special thanks to Jessica Jones from Forget You Not Designs for giving me the PERFECT cover! Again. The first cover she did for 8 was already my favorite, but this one tops my expectations. It's everything I've ever wanted.

If by this time you're still around, you might need to hear this:

Love is not always fun.

It's messy and it hurts.

But if it's real, love is always enough.

ABOUT BILLIE

Billie Lustig is a blunt, dutch, storytelling mom/wife with a big mouth and an even bigger imagination.

She writes the shit that has your heart palpitating with a happy ending, but when she's not writing she likes to read (obviously), eat (she may or may not have a food addiction), needs a yearly quota of snow (no joke), and listen to country music (someone give me a cowboy hat, please). She mostly runs around in jeans and a sweater, because well, why the hell not?

When she's not running around after her rebel child or preventing her choco lab from chewing up her books, she spends her time writing about alpha-holes and sassy badass heroines.

Being able to speak both English and Dutch at an early age made her read books in two languages with a big preference for English. She tried writing in both languages, but there is basically nothing sexy about describing human genitals in Dutch, so it was an easy choice.

ALSO BY B. LUSTIG

I created B. Lustig to publish books that give you a heavy dose of angst, big-mouthed, heroes, and women that like to challenge them. These are the stories without the guns, criminals, and dark worlds they come from. However, they bring you the same amount of sass and spice as any other Billie book.

Numbers:
8
9
5
7 (TBA)

On The Grid:
Oversteer
Splitstream (TBA)

Made in the USA
Thornton, CO
09/23/23 17:28:51

822427f0-0ae4-4ee9-9021-f2821ee58186R01